I0831728

The Old Witch

J.R. Carlson

DEDICATION

This book is dedicated to young readers who enjoy fantasy and adventure. The older ones can read it too if they wish. ;)

CONTENTS

The Old Witch

ACKNOWLEDGMENTS

Thank you to all of my readers, fans, family and friends for all your love and support. You're all enchanting, fascinating, riveting and encouraging in your own special ways. Keep the magic alive.

1. TWO OLD FRIENDS

Gazing into the scorching flames of her fireplace, the old witch found herself deep in thought. Nightfall had finally arrived and her anticipation was soaring higher than her broomstick ever could. The night she had been planning for years was finally at her doorstep and it felt far too good to be true! An ugly smile crossed her wrinkled old face. Walking across her living room floor, she stood next to a rather tall object covered by an old dusty leather blanket. She was about to face the one thing that had haunted her for centuries! Taking a deep breath, she clutched onto the blanket and threw it aside with a quick sweep of her hand. Beneath the dusty old covering stood a tall body sized mirror.

Even though it hurt the old witch deeply to stare into its depths she knew her deepest of fears must finally be faced. It was also her reason and motivation for the dangerous journey ahead. Staring into the mirror, she shuttered at her own reflection glaring back at her. Wrinkled green skin hung from every part of her 450 year old body. Her nose was extra-long, pointy and a bit curved at the end. Bushy gray eyebrows hung above both eyes along with knotted gray hair covered by a pointy black hat sitting atop her forehead. Extra-large warts dotted her face along with barely visible facial hairs. She sighed at her own reflection. It was quite enough motivation to face her deepest of fears even though the task ahead seemed far too daunting to bear. It made her sad to think that she couldn't make herself young and beautiful again even with all the magic she possessed. She knew there were only a few things in life that magic couldn't accomplish but depression would quickly set in if she dwelled on them for too long.

A pair of green glowing eyes watched her from the corner of the room. "I really think you should take me with you Misty," said a high pitched crackly voice from the shadows. Misty glanced up at her caged raven and responded with her usual slippery and mysterious tone of voice. "I can't afford to lose you Blackbeak. If anything should happen to me tonight I would need you to finish what I've started." Blackbeak flapped his wings agitatedly. "Let me out of this confounded cage Misty," he squawked! Misty frowned. "I've placed a spell on it to open the moment I leave. I don't want you following me Blackbeak," she replied delicately. Blackbeak's gaze met hers directly. "Dragons are dangerous creatures Misty. It would be wise to take me with you. I could at least be a distraction while you take the lamp from that savage beast." Misty stared back at him as if contemplating the matter before shaking her head disapprovingly. "No Blackbeak, there is too much at risk already to let you come with me. I'm sorry. I know we've been through a lot together but this mission is far too dangerous for both of us to go on and if I never see you again…just know I will miss you immensely my friend."

Grabbing her long pointed wand from her deep inner robe pocket, she flicked it in the air casually while muttering the words "BROOMA KA DOOMA!" (It was a silly sounding spell but it got the job done.) Her old straw broom flew from the attic into her outstretched hand. Her summoning spells usually worked quite quickly and she was proud of that fact. Turning towards the glass living room windows she flicked her wand towards them muttering the spell "OPANNO COPRANNO!" The windows jolted open as Misty shoved her old broomstick between her legs and pushed off from the dusty wooden floorboards beneath her. She began flying towards the open windows when a tragic thought suddenly brought her to a quick halt in mid-air. "Blast it all! I can't leave now. This place looks like a pig sty," she complained as her feet slowly floated back to down to land on the dusty floorboards beneath her. A confounded expression crossed Blackbeak's face. "There's no time for house cleaning Misty! You've waited ten long years for this night to arrive and now you can't even leave the house without cleaning it. What kind of spell are you under?"

"Oh Blackbeak, you worry too much. Besides, this won't take long at all," she replied. Misty latched onto her broomstick with her left hand and pointed her wand at it with the other. "CLENSARRO GERMONNO," she shouted. The old straw broom began dancing around the room sweeping up piles of dust as it moved along. A dustpan flew up from the basement as if it knew exactly what was happening upstairs. Working together, they quickly removed multiple layers of dust caked all over the ancient wooden floorboards inside Misty's home. The dustpan flew through the open living room window quickly emptying itself every time the broom filled it with dust. Instantly it returned back for more as the cycle continued.

During the cleaning process, Misty began contemplating something highly important. "Silly me, I almost left the house without my fire amulet. I would have been toast without it! A wand can only do so much you know," she said glancing up at Blackbeak. The raven jumped inside his cage. "I was about to tell you that very thing Misty but you never listen to me anymore." Misty was already at the base of her winding staircase leading up to the attic before Blackbeak had even finished his sentence. Unfortunately, the fire amulet couldn't be summoned in the same way she had summoned her broomstick. Misty knew the only way to control an amulet was by wearing it. She also knew the fire amulet could protect her from the dragon's fire far better than any spell cast from her wand. She often wished her wand magic could be as strong as amulet magic but knew it would most likely never happen. Even though amulets could only produce a single spell, their powers far outweighed anything a wand could ever conjure up.

The winding staircase up to the attic was incredibly steep. Misty huffed and puffed as she made her way up it. "Blast these stairs," she exclaimed under her breath. "I really need to get a one-story house one of these days!" "Either that or get out more often," Blackbeak mocked from downstairs and across the room. "Oh, hush up ya old bird," Misty snapped back! After finally reaching the attic entrance at the top of the staircase she stepped up onto the creaky wooden floorboards and glanced around the dark room. Retrieving her wand again, she muttered the spell "FORSHELLO LIGHTELLO." Immediately, a shield of light surrounded her body; giving her just enough light to see the attic room around her. Several treasure chests lined the attic walls along with various other objects she never tinkered with anymore. Among other things sat ancient rolled-up maps of lands long forgotten, tall staffs filled with mystical powers Misty no longer needed and ancient crystal balls that had long since lost their powers to predict anything accurately anymore. Naturally, everything was covered in the usual ten layers of dust. "Why don't I ever clean anymore," she wondered bitterly? "I've really been slacking in that department! Let's see now….which treasure chest did I put my fire amulet in," she wondered curiously?

Pointing her wand at one of the treasure chests in the far right corner of the room, she muttered the same spell previously used to open the windows. "OPANNO COPRANNO!" The lid quickly popped open as a golden ray of light burst from within; lighting the wooden planks on the ceiling and walls around them. The old witch focused intensely on the objects inside the chest. A solid gold chain attached to a large sparkling ruby red stone encased within a triangular shaped formation of black obsidian sparkled back at her. Misty knew the deep red glow from the fire amulet wouldn't stop until she placed it around her neck. It was as if it wanted to be found and worn. She basked in its mesmerizing glow for a moment; simply enjoying its illuminating quality. Slipping the golden chain around her neck, she smiled as she felt an intense rush of power flow throughout her entire body. A feeling of ice cold water coursed through her veins before her body temperature slowly returned back to normal. She felt as though an invisible heat shield had been placed around her entire body. "It has been a while since I've worn this fire amulet. I almost forgot what it felt like," she said out loud to no one in particular.

A horrific idea suddenly came to her. "What if I can't escape the dragon's fury even with my fire amulet? I'll need a back-up plan," she thought cautiously. Walking over to another old treasure chest, she kneeled down on the creaky wooden floorboards next to it and opened it manually with her own two hands. "I don't need magic for everything," she thought simply as she rummaged through a few ancient spell books and scrolls. Taking off the fire amulet, she laid it on the dusty wooden floorboards next to her. It began glowing again. Its light combined with her aura light was enough to see the objects in front of her quite clearly. She continued rummaging through the chest before moving on to a few others found around the room's perimeter. Still not finding what she was looking for; her temper began to flare! "Where in blazes did it go," she shouted angrily!

Slipping the amulet back over her head, its glow slowly faded away into nothing. Coincidently, the light spell surrounding her aura slowly faded away as well; leaving her in complete darkness! This didn't bother her much. She was comfortable with the dark and knew exactly where her own attic entrance was located. Walking back down the spiraled staircase and into the living room, she bellowed at her pet raven. "Confound it Blackbeak! Where did I put my Map of Midas?" Blackbeak looked tired and angry from being locked inside his cage. Normally Misty would leave his cage door open so he could come and go freely as he pleased. "How should I know Misty? You don't tell me everything you know. Have you tried searching behind the fireplace? I don't think you've stored anything there in years but it might be worth a look." A bewildered expression crossed Misty's face. "Of course, why didn't I think of that?" She walked towards the roaring fireplace. The closer she came to the flames, the cooler she felt; which meant that her fire amulet was working exactly the way it was supposed to. She grinned joyfully as a feeling of power surged through her veins. Reaching her right hand through the flames, she touched the bricks at the back of the fireplace. Feeling around for a bit, she eventually found her target as she latched onto a small metal lever and pulled it downwards. The entire fireplace, including the brick wall behind it, slowly began rotating in a clockwise direction. She jumped back to avoid being hit by the rotating brick wall spinning towards her. A tall granite bookshelf located directly behind the fireplace came into view as the roaring fire disappeared from sight. The only item on the bookshelf was an ancient rolled-up scroll about the length of Misty's arm. An ugly grin crossed her haggard old face as she reached out to grab the treasure map. "This will have to be my bargaining chip if the dragon doesn't give up his precious lamp. After all, dragons are suckers for gold," she thought slyly.

Walking back over to Blackbeak's cage, she summoned her broomstick towards her as she gazed deeply into the raven's green eyes. "Goodbye old friend. I shall miss you. We've had many wonderful adventures together and I hope to see you again soon. But if not, just know this is something I've always wanted to accomplish and I think it's well worth the risk." A tear trickled down her left cheek. She decided to leave before Blackbeak could change her mind. As Blackbeak began to object, she pointed her wand towards the door, spoke the magic words to open it and flew straight outside on her broomstick before anything more could be said. Blackbeak's cage popped open immediately after her departure just like she had promised. He sighed deeply within himself. "Oh Misty, you really stress me out sometimes," the old raven thought miserably to himself.

2. MISTY'S MIRAGE

Misty flew straight towards the Cave of Jewels located at the top of a high snow covered mountain. It was commonly referred to as Claw Mountain because everyone in the little town below, commonly known as Shovelton, was keenly aware of the dragon Claw living at its peak. Many tales had been told of brave little dwarves attempting to tunnel into the Cave of Jewels before being viciously attacked and maimed by the dagger clawed dragon! Very few ever lived to tell the tale.

The rumors didn't bother Misty though. She had been hatching, planning and contemplating her current plan of action for the past ten years. "Nothing could ruin this night for me even if it tried," she thought confidently. The moon was full but barely visible through the dense fog covering the night sky. The old witch pointed her wand at herself muttering the spell "BLANKATTO SURRENDO." Instantly, she felt as though someone had just wrapped an incredibly warm blanket around her entire body! "Wish I had an ice amulet," she thought with a shiver. Soaring high through the air, she glanced down at the cave's snowy entrance. It was easy to spot, especially with the vast amount of swords and shields scattered across the snow covered ground from where dwarves had previously abandoned them while attempting to escape the dragon's fury!

Misty gently landed her broomstick near the cave's entrance. Her feet slowly touched the snow packed earth as she drew her wand again. Pointing it at herself, she muttered the phrase "MIRRAGGO DUBELLO." Instantly, an exact duplicate of herself quickly emerged from her own body and turned to face her. "Ah yes, the old mirage trick," Misty said with a grin. Staring at her replica now facing her; she spoke to it. "I know you're not really me but I need you to go inside and find out where Claw is hiding. This way, if he decides to bite your head off then it will only destroy my spell instead of me. I shall call you Abbey," Misty said with a mischievous grin. Picking up a handful of snow, she pointed her wand at it and muttered a few more magic words. "RAGELLO CONTRERTO," she exclaimed as she watched it transform into a small black piece of cloth. "In order for me to see what you're doing, I'm going to wrap this magical blindfold around my eyes. I'll be sitting here outside the cave and focusing on what you're seeing Abbey." Misty wrapped the blindfold around her own eyes and instantly began seeing the world through Abbey's eyes. "Perfect! Now, go find that dragon Abbey!"

Without saying a word, Misty's twin mirage walked through the icy entrance into the Cave of Jewels. Misty pointed her wand at a nearby snow bank muttering the spell "FORTELLO APPELLO." It quickly transformed into a small wooden fort which sat just outside the cave's entrance. She stepped inside and decided to patiently wait within its new snow covered walls while Abbey explored the cave. Sitting on the floor of the warm one-roomed fort, she patiently waited, watched and controlled the world through Abbey's eyes.

Misty casted a giant orb of light around Abbey to help see her way through the dark cave. Abbey began making her way through the cave; walking through dark tunnels and over giant mounds of earth as she moved along. The cave was rocky and filled with sharp pointed stalactites overhead that seemed as though they might fall on her head at any moment. Misty continued to control Abbey as she moved her body safely through the dark cave. Eventually she came to a large cavern that divided into three separate tunnels. "Which one is the correct path," Misty wondered helplessly? An idea quickly came to her. "Just wait there Abbey. I'll come inside and we'll each take a separate tunnel to help figure out which path leads to Claw. It will help speed things up a bit since we'll both be searching for him. Also, I don't want to wait around out here in the cold much longer. Frostbite is a real thing you know," she said seriously. Misty's mirage stood lifeless inside the cavern simply waiting for Misty to come and find her. Abbey obviously didn't mind waiting since she wasn't a real person and couldn't think for herself anyways.

Eventually Misty caught up with her double ganger inside the large cavern. Misty had cast an orb of light around herself as well to help see her way through the darkness. "Thanks for waiting," Misty told her mirage jokingly! "You know, this mirage trick is something I learned back when Blackbeak went on vacation for a while. I had to have someone to talk to. Of course, getting you to respond is the tricky part," she said jokingly. "Anyways, you take the tunnel on the right and I'll take the middle one. It'll be difficult for me to control both of us at the same time but I'll give it a try." Without her magic blindfold, Misty had to focus deep within herself to see where Abbey was going and what she was doing. She tried controlling her own movements and Abbey's simultaneously. It was an incredibly difficult task. She didn't think most witches were capable of doing what she was attempting to do at the moment. It took every ounce of focus and magic she possessed to keep both of them moving in different directions at the same time! She even stopped moving her own body a few times in order to get Abbey turned around in the right direction. "That dragon better not be down that third tunnel we're not exploring," she thought anxiously!

After traveling through the darkness for what seemed like an eternity, Abbey finally caught a glimpse of a dimly glowing light at the end of her tunnel. Misty immediately stopped what she was doing and put her blindfold back on so she could more clearly focus on controlling

Abbey's movements. Abbey's narrow tunnel finally opened up into another giant cavern which was lit by flaming torches surrounding the entire perimeter. At the center of the cavern stood a giant mountain of glimmering gold! Abbey glanced upward only to find a sleeping dragon lying on top of the massive gold heap. Misty began sweating and so did Abbey. Misty carefully controlled Abbey's slow movements towards the sleeping dragon.

Abbey looked carefully at the mountain of gold and saw a golden lamp lying next to the dragon's head near the top of the heap. Misty gasped! "There it is…the lamp I've so desperately sought after all these years," Misty thought yearningly! Abbey gently lowered herself to all fours and slowly began crawling towards the mountain of gold in front of her. Misty dashed through the cave; quickly retracing her steps and running frantically towards Abbey's location in a desperate attempt to catch up with her. Abbey slowly and quietly crawled up the mountain of gold on all fours. Gold coins and challises trickled down the mountain as the sleeping dragon gently moved a foot on top of the gold heap. Misty desperately hoped the dragon wouldn't wake up anytime soon. Abbey had crawled about halfway up the large gold pile when the dragon suddenly began to snore. Flames shot from his nostrils as Abbey continued her climb.

After a great deal of highly concentrated running and jumping over potential pitfalls, Misty finally reached Claw's Cavern. Pointing her wand at herself, she gently whispered the spell "CHAMELLIOSO" as a stream of blue light wrapped itself around her body before quickly evaporating into thin air. Stealthily sliding up against the cavern wall, her body instantly matched colors with the dark brown rock next to her. She quietly made her way towards the backside of the sleeping dragon desperately hoping he wouldn't wake up anytime soon.

Abbey was just an arm's length away from reaching the lamp. As she reached out to grab it, the dragon's eyes snapped open as he glared directly into hers. Before Claw could move a muscle Abbey snatched up the lamp and hurled it high over his head towards Misty. Misty jumped high into the air to catch it. Having moved away from the cave wall, her camouflage spell vanished completely. Despite her best effort to catch the airborne lamp it landed a couple of feet behind her. She rushed over to pick it up. Just before grabbing it, she stared up at the dragon. Their eyes locked and somehow she knew it would be a really bad idea to make a grab for it. Instead, she continued staring into his deep green eyes. Slowly, she reached one hand into her robe pocket and retrieved the Map of Midas. Slowly and carefully she unrolled it in front of the fierce beast staring back at her. She didn't want him memorizing the entire map so she unrolled it just enough for him to see its authenticity. She also knew that Claw could easily set the map on fire with a simple blow and neither of them wanted that to happen.

The dragon moaned deeply as he reached a clawed foot forward to snatch the lamp from where it lay on the gold heap. One of his sharp curved claws hooked around the lamp's curved handle. Extending his clawed foot over to Misty, he dangled the lamp in front of her. Misty slowly moved the map towards him with her right hand while her left hand gently reached out to take the lamp from the dragon's sharply hooked claw. Laying the map down in front of her with one hand, she gently grabbed the lamp with the other. "It's the perfect trade," she thought cautiously. "Claw wants gold and I want something far more valuable."

Misty respectfully bowed before the great dragon and slowly stepped backwards towards the cavern entrance. She knew it would not be wise to turn her back on him. The dragon suddenly remembered the other girl he had been facing not too long ago. He turned around to face Abbey. Abbey was holding a large golden elephant statue with a glowing red ruby inlayed between its eyes. She began running towards the exit with her treasure in hand! The dragon let out an intimidating low pitched sound and began flying towards her with the Map of Midas now hooked onto one of his claws. In a desperate attempt to lose the extra weight holding her down, Abbey threw the golden elephant backwards through the air towards the pursuing dragon. Instead of hitting him as intended, it hit the Map of Midas just hard enough to rip it from the dragon's claw!

The map fell to the cave floor landing at the base of the giant gold heap. Neither Abbey nor the dragon stopped to acknowledge the fallen map. Abbey continued running towards the exit and was just about there when Claw blew a gigantic ball of flame straight towards her! The scorching fireball slammed into her backside quickly turning her into a small pile of ash!

While the dragon had been distracted chasing Abbey around the cavern; Misty had summoned her broomstick and was now flying towards the Map of Midas now lying at the bottom of the gold heap. Reaching down from the air, she snatched it up and continued flying in a circular direction around the dragon's massive head. She smiled mischievously. "Burn my mirage will you dragon," she cackled! "Let's see how you handle this!" Pointing her wand towards different areas around the dragon's head, she muttered the phrase "MIRRAGGO DUBELLO" multiple times out loud. Multiple replicas of herself quickly appeared with every spell cast. Claw suddenly found himself surrounded by five Misty mirages all zapping him with lightening and fire bolt spells! His thick dragon skin took the heat as though they were nothing but annoying flies landing on him. Taking careful aim, he blew a giant ball of flame at each attacking replica surrounding him! Each mirage quickly turned into ash with every fireball that hit them.

With all the mirages now up in smoke, the dragon began chasing the real Misty through the air! Sweat dripped from her face and arms as she glanced down at her neck to make sure her fire amulet was still attached to her body. Thankfully, it was glowing red and ready to take the heat. As if anticipating the dragon's fire, the glowing amulet shot a red aura shield around her body and broomstick just before a giant fireball came flying towards her from the dragon's gaping mouth. The fireball slammed against the red aura shield surrounding her body and was redirected into the glowing red amulet around her neck. The amulet had completely absorbed the dragon's fire! Misty smiled in relief as she continued flying towards the exit tunnel. The dragon was far too big to fit through the exit tunnel which forced him to land at the entrance. It also forced Misty to jump off her broomstick due to the lack of flight space but she wasn't ready to complain just yet. She had the lamp and the map and was incredibly glad to have survived Claw's wrath. She heard one last roar from the dragon as she turned around to see another giant ball of flame heading straight towards her! The fire amulet absorbed the scorching flames into itself again. Misty let out another sigh of relief! "Good thing I came prepared," she thought gratefully.

3. FACING THE MIRROR

Misty thought the worst was finally behind her until she reached the cave entrance leading into the outside world. Looking past the arched opening, she spotted clouds covering a barely rising sun in the distance. "Morning already," she wondered curiously? Attempting to step past the cave's entrance, she immediately slammed into an invisible barrier causing her to fall backwards and onto the ground. Before getting up, she noticed a faint glow above the arched entrance. Looking upwards, she found an ancient form of writing glowing above her head. Pointing her wand at it, she mumbled the spell "REWORDO." The ancient writing quickly vanished and then reappeared in her ancient witch language of Covawnish. After translating it into her current language, she found the phrase to mean; "ALL ITEMS MUST BE PAID FOR." She looked down at the lamp she had tied to her sash which hung from her robe like a belt. "Somehow I must pay for this lamp before the cave will let me leave with it. But how," she wondered curiously? She immediately regretted taking the Map of Midas back from the dragon after showing it to him. "Perhaps that would have been payment enough," she thought regrettably.

Mulling it over in her mind for a moment, she came to the conclusion that the genie would probably know more about it than her. She gave the lamp a gentle rub. Immediately, a thick blue trail of fog streamed from its narrow opening creating a large thick cloud directly in front of her. The cloud slowly cleared away only to reveal a body sized mirror. Misty felt confused and then angry! She didn't want to look at another mirror as long as she lived! The thought of her own reflection made her cringe with loathing and self-contempt. A deep commanding voice spoke from inside the mirror. "You have summoned the all-powerful genie of the lamp! In order to activate your three wishes you must first face your deepest of fears! Gaze into the mirror Misty," the voice commanded sternly. "Misty turned away from it. "I have no desire to see myself genie. I am a hideous looking witch as you can plainly see. All I've ever wanted for years is to become a beautiful woman again. Is that such a difficult wish to grant?" The deep voice responded; "of course not Misty. You could be the most beautiful woman in all the land but first you must look into this mirror and accept yourself for who you truly are at this very moment."

Misty grudgingly looked into the mirror in front of her. She saw her sagging green skin covered in warts, her long pointy nose and her scraggly gray hair that would never straighten out no matter how much magic she used on it. She absolutely loathed herself! "All you have to do is gaze into your own reflection for a full 20 seconds before making the wish that you want so badly," said the genie. "And yes, I will be counting," he said with a laugh. "Oh you're a barrel of laughs," Misty replied sarcastically. The genie chuckled. "I think I'm hilarious but I'm also quite powerful! By the way, your time starts now!" The number "20" quickly appeared on the mirror just above Misty's reflection. "This is going to feel like an eternity," she thought horribly. The numbers on the mirror began counting downwards from 20 to 19 and so on. A full 10 seconds passed before Misty started having doubts. "What if he's lying? What if it's a horrible game he's playing with me? This is absolute torcher," she thought anxiously. A mere 8 seconds were left on the mirror. She couldn't ignore her self-doubt and hatred any longer. She turned away from the torturous contraption as the numbers on the mirror vanished away completely.

"I can't do it," she sobbed with tears in her eyes. The mirror suddenly vanished as the genie appeared in its place. Floating in the air in front of her was an Arabian looking man with dark skin, jet black hair, a large turbine covering his head and golden wrist cuffs. Only the top half of him was visible while his bottom half was simply a mystical cloud hovering about three feet above the ground. His open vest easily exposed his flat chest and tight abdominal area.

Misty almost forgot about her desperate situation upon seeing the sleek appearance of the genie. Suddenly she thought about how unfair life really was for him to be so incredibly handsome and powerful while she felt so ugly and hideous. On the other hand, it somehow motivated her enough to try the test again. "What's your name," she asked gently? "My name is Mojo," he replied indifferently. "Well Mojo, I must ask…out of all the wishes you've ever granted, have you ever gotten one for eternal beauty?" Mojo rubbed two fingers against his black go-tee. "Actually yes, I did receive a request for that once. The girl wished to become the prettiest woman in all the land. Although I must say it wasn't actually THIS land; so I can still make you the prettiest woman around here if that is your desire?" Misty smiled encouragingly. "Alright, I'll try that mirror test one more time. Perhaps I can get through it this time," she replied hopefully.

Mojo chuckled deeply and quickly transformed himself back into the tall body sized mirror he had previously been. Misty gazed into it and inhaled deeply. "Alright, let's begin," she said with a long exhale. Immediately the big red number 20 appeared at the top of the mirror and began counting downward just as it had before. Once again, Misty stared at her own reflection with complete disgust. However, this time she tried imagining what she would look like if she were the prettiest woman in all the land. The mental image gave her enough hope and motivation to face the dreaded mirror glaring back at her. "Living with this hideous body has been a complete nightmare! Hopefully this will change everything," she thought anxiously.

The numbers finally made their way down from 20 to 0 after what felt like an eternity of waiting on Misty's part. A bright white light suddenly emanated from the mirror quickly encircling Misty within its radiance. The light swirled around her body lifting her high up off the ground and into the air. It quickly transformed into a thick gray cloud as she heard a deep voice inside her head begin to speak. "What is it you wish for Misty?" Misty replied confidently. "You know what I want genie. I wish to become the most beautiful woman in all the land!" Instantly, the gray cloud grew thicker around her; quickly making significant changes to her body until it gently floated her back down to earth. She was out like a light and slept deeply on the cave floor for an entire day before finally waking.

4. THE TWO GENIES

Upon waking she immediately felt like an entirely new woman! Misty looked down at her legs. They were much slimmer and tanner than before. Looking at her arms and hands, she was happy to find her ugly sagging green skin had been replaced with a beautifully tanned and toned complexion. Looking around, she called out for the genie. He quickly appeared in front of her. “Misty, you’re awake! You slept for quite a while.” She glanced around at her surroundings trying to remember where she was at. “Genie, I would like to see the mirror again please. I’m interested to see what my face looks like.” The genie shook his head disapprovingly. “Unfortunately, that will cost you another wish,” he replied regrettably.

Getting caught up in the excitement of seeing her new face and body for the first time, she used her second wish to make the mirror reappear in front of her. Gazing into it, she was absolutely mesmerized by her own reflection! She saw a gorgeous slender young woman who looked to be in her mid-20’s standing at a height of 5 feet 8 inches tall with smooth skin and curves in all the right places. Misty also couldn’t help but notice herself to be completely naked! She glanced over at Mojo.

"Where did my robe go," she inquired inquisitively? "Unfortunately, the transformation process caused it to vanish completely," he responded respectfully. "No worries though Misty; I'll make a new and better one for you to wear immediately." Misty covered herself with her arms. "Is that going to cost me another wish," she asked discouragingly? Mojo laughed as he conjured up a brand new silk robe for her to put on. "No, this one is on the house Misty. Ancient magic functions quite strangely sometimes so I try and make up for it with a few freebies every now and then." Quickly transforming a nearby boulder into a silky smooth robe, he handed it to her to try on. "Hope you enjoy it Misty. By the way, your new body looks incredible! I must say it's quite an improvement from the old, green, saggy skin witch body you had previously. I'm sure you would agree with me since you're the one who wished for it," he said confidently. Misty draped the silky smooth robe around her body carefully tying the sash around her waist. "Absolutely, thank you genie! You've done a fantastic job fulfilling my wish and I'm more than happy to have it," she replied joyfully!

Misty turned to face the mirror again. She noticed her face to be the biggest change of all! She had long black hair, high cheek bones, hazel eyes and a perfectly white smile with every tooth now intact. She was thrilled not to have a long curved nose anymore but instead had a perfectly normal sized nose with no more warts! For the first time in centuries Misty stared into the mirror and loved her own reflection! Of course, she had tried loving herself many times in the past without having a beautiful body but always knew she could do better. She was also aware that outer beauty wasn't necessary in order to love herself inwardly but knew it was something she had always desired. Despite the ridiculous amount of power held in her wand the laws of magic only allowed those with ancient magic to perform specific tasks such as making a person young and beautiful again. This is why she had sought after the genie. Deep down she knew his ancient magic could accomplish things far greater than hers ever could.

She slipped her right hand into the deep pocket of her new silk robe. It felt amazing against her skin and she absolutely loved it! It actually felt a little big on her but she didn't want to return the generous gift Mojo had so freely given her especially since it didn't even cost her a wish. Misty turned towards him. "Thanks again genie! I have magic myself but I never could have done this without you." Mojo smiled back at her. You look absolutely ravishing young lady!" Without warning Misty lunged forward with both arms held wide open intending to hug him. Unexpectedly, her arms fell straight through his ghostlike body! She nearly toppled over and barely caught her balance just in time. Mojo smiled. "I don't have a physical body like you young lady. That is why I can change into just about anything and everything you can imagine. Not to mention I will live forever." A happy expression crossed her face. "I'm just glad you had the power to make me young and beautiful again," she replied joyfully. "I truly am a whole new and wonderful woman now! Even with all of my power there are certain things only ancient magic such as yours can accomplish and I'm truly grateful for you genie."

The cave suddenly began to shake violently beneath her feet! "Let's get out of here Mojo!" She ran towards the cave entrance attempting to leave as quickly as possible. The invisible barrier quickly knocked her backwards just as it had before. "Oh, I totally forgot about that sign above the entrance," Misty exclaimed hurriedly. "It says I need to pay for whatever I take from this cave but I'm really not sure how to do that; any ideas genie?"

Mojo looked at her thoughtfully. "Well, if you're trying to take the lamp with you then you should pay whoever you got it from in the first place. Who did you get if from anyways," he asked inquisitively? "I took it from Claw's layer," she replied simply. Mojo looked a bit worried for her. "If you took the lamp from the dragon's layer then you must pay him for it Misty. It's that simple." It was Misty's turn to feel worried. "But how," she asked? "You must give him something of equal or greater value in return," he replied simply. "Well, I did give him the Map of Midas in exchange for the lamp but….." "But what," inquired the genie? "But, I kind of stole it back from him after he burned my mirage to the ground," she confessed.

The genie shook his head disapprovingly. "I hate to break it to you young lady but this dragon probably won't like you much if you attempt to go back and pay for it now." Misty glanced downward shamefully. "Probably not..." A smile suddenly crossed her face. "You know what…now that I've got my wishes I really don't need the lamp anymore. I could probably just leave it here in the cave now that I've got what I came for," she said thoughtfully.

Mojo looked at her with surprise. "You still have another wish left Misty. If you wish me free from this retched lamp then I will gladly be your travelling companion during any future quests you decide to embark upon." The cave floor continued to shake violently as Misty struggled to keep her balance. She thought it sounded like a pretty good deal. "Alright genie, I'll wish you free on one condition." Mojo frowned. "Oh no, I don't like where this is headed already." "Relax," she replied lightheartedly. "I know it probably defies the ancient laws of magic for me to wish for more wishes so…Instead, I want you to transform a dragon into a genie for me to use anytime I wish. Instead of paying the dragon for this lamp, I'll simply take him with me wherever I go! Since the lamp will be close to Claw at all times, it'll be like I never stole it in the first place," she said thoughtfully. Mojo frowned. "Unfortunately, the ancient laws of magic also state that all genies must have their own lamp to occupy at all times. This means I could transform your dragon into a genie but unfortunately there's not an empty magic lamp lying around to put him in," he replied seriously. Misty placed a hand on her chin thoughtfully. "What if we gave him your lamp," she asked curiously? "I mean, I'm going to free you from it anyways. That would leave an empty lamp for Claw to use right," she asked inquisitively?

The ground suddenly stopped shaking as if by a miracle. Misty steadied herself again on the cavern floor. Mojo placed a hand to his chin contemplating the matter as well. "I like your thinking Misty but we must be extremely careful during this process. This kind of thing has destroyed genies in the past unfortunately!"

Misty's curiosity got the better of her. "Really, how in the world could this kind of thing destroy a genie? I thought genies were immortal?" Mojo shook his head. "Even genies must follow the ancient laws of magic. Otherwise, our immortal souls could be destroyed as well. For example, suppose I transformed your dragon into a genie and assigned my lamp as his own. That would leave me without a lamp. This would break the ancient laws of magic. So, if you rubbed my lamp after that; my genie body would literally have nowhere to go. I would simply turn into a cloud of smoke and float away into the air. The ancient laws of magic give us genies form and substance Misty. Without them we'd simply be little clouds of smoke floating around in the wind. That being said, you must wish me free FIRST before I transform your dragon into a genie. Wishing me free will sever ties between me and my lamp. This will create an empty lamp for your new dragon genie to use. Does that make sense," he asked hopefully? Misty nodded. "I understand Mojo. Every new genie needs a lamp to live in and empty lamps are hard to come by. Although, couldn't you just make a new one appear with your magic," she asked curiously?

Mojo inhaled deeply. "Unfortunately, another ancient law of magic clearly states that a genie lamp cannot be created or destroyed by a genie or any other magical creature other than dwarves and gnomes." Misty's intrigue grew rapidly. "Oh really; so dwarves and gnomes are the makers of genie lamps," she asked inquisitively? Mojo folded his arms across his chest. "If you really must know, they were originally made by ancient gnomes in an effort to take over the world." This peeked Misty's curiosity even further. "Please go on Mojo. I'm curious, couldn't gnomes take over the world faster with genies helping them," she asked curiously? Mojo smiled. "Gnomes are the most prideful race in the world Misty. They do things their way and their way only. All the power in the world couldn't help them if they made up their minds not to use it. No, originally ancient gnomes carefully crafted the genie lamps and figured out how to trap ancient spirits inside them. They convinced the spirits that if they followed the rules given to them for a thousand years then they would be set free. Of course, this was a complete lie."

Misty looked quite confused. "I still don't get it Mojo. How does this help the gnomes take over the world? It only seems to give others more power in my opinion," she stated obviously. Mojo continued. "That's the secret Misty. Ancient gnomes counted on others to use the genies for their own personal greed. They figured they could simply hide away in the woods and let others kill each-other off with their overabundance of greed and power found inside the genie lamps. The only thing they overlooked was that not everyone who finds a genie lamp wants to take over the world or even destroy their enemies. Nope, most people simply want riches or even healthier looking bodies. I've only had a few wishes for world domination within the countless centuries of being a genie. This was the unexpected twist to the gnome's plan of having everyone kill each-other off with an overabundance of power and control. Ironically, the majority of people who find genie lamps don't even care about world domination. The gnomes are starting to realize their big mistake in letting others find the genie lamps in the first place. Now they're out to collect them all back again; not because they want to use them but because they realize they're not accomplishing their original goals by having them floating around in the world." Misty's thoughts quickly turned towards Nick the gnome back at the Forbidden Forest. "So that's why he wanted my lamp so badly," she thought quietly to herself.

Misty looked amazed by Mojo's story. "Wow! An entire race who would rather watch others kill each-other off rather than doing it themselves. You would think they would simply use the genie lamps and wish for world domination themselves. That seems like a more logical thing to do," Misty replied astonishingly. Mojo smiled. "The ancient gnomes created a series of genie rules to accompany their lamps. This helped insure their plans for world domination would not backfire on themselves. Surprisingly, there are more genie rules we genies must live by than most people even know about. As hard as it is to believe, the first one is that we can never serve a gnome. Gnomes made this rule first and foremost to insure their plans for world domination wouldn't backfire on themselves," Mojo replied with a chuckle before continuing. "The other rules are fairly simple. We can't kill anyone. We can't grant others more than three wishes. We can't cause others to fall in love with each-other.

We can't transform others into genies without having an empty lamp to place them in. We can't bring anyone back from the dead. We can't set ourselves free. We can't serve more than one master. Our master is the one who possesses our lamp. We can't transform ancient artifacts into other ancient artifacts. There's also a whole set of rules dedicated to various types of portals and what we can and can't do with them but that's a whole other story."

Misty stretched her arms out refreshingly. "That's quite interesting Mojo but I was hoping we could get a move on with everything; assuming we have a deal of course," she asked hopefully? Mojo nodded reassuringly. "Your wish is my command Misty. Just say the word and it'll be done," he said enthusiastically. Misty stepped backward inhaling deeply. "Mojo, I wish you free," she said with as much gusto as she could muster. Quickly scanning the area, Mojo spotted his lamp lying on the cavern floor only a few yards off to his right. Inhaling deeply, he snapped his fingers and pointed towards it. Instantly, a bright white light emanated from the lamp's opening. The light shot back and forth between the lamp and the genie several times until the lamp slowly began to transform colors from bright gold to charred black. It was as if it had been caught in a long burning fire hot enough to scorch the gold color right off it. Mojo screamed. "It's burning," he exclaimed as if he could feel the intense heat inside himself as well! He felt the invisible ties between himself and his lamp slowly being scorched away! It began to feel overwhelmingly unbearable for him. He suddenly stopped hovering in the air and fell to the cavern floor. Misty was shocked to see the genie out like a light and lying on the dirt floor! Pulling her wand from her robe, she cast a few healing spells on his unmoving body. Unfortunately, none of them brought him back to consciousness no matter how hard she tried.

Misty sat on the cave floor next to Mojo's head carefully attempting to revive him in some way. She reached out to touch him. Surprisingly, her hand did not pass through his body as it had before. For some reason she was actually able to touch and feel his body this time. "Is he mortal now," she wondered curiously? Holding his head in her arms, she removed the large turban covering it. A full head of short black hair laid beneath it. She ran her fingers through it gently. It was incredibly soft and smooth to the touch. She had never felt this kind of closeness with anyone before. Perhaps it was because she didn't enjoy being close to others in the first place…up until now. It suddenly occurred to her that she had never had a lover her entire life! The tides of destiny seemed to be shifting in her favor and she quite enjoyed the feeling.

Cradling Mojo's head in her arms, she observed him to still be breathing but not fully alert yet. For a brief moment she wondered what it would be like to actually have a lover in her life. "I bet an all-powerful genie would make a fantastic lover," she thought gently. A mischievous thought suddenly entered her mind. "I bet I could steal a kiss while he's unconscious like this. He would never even know." She bent over to kiss him on the lips. Mojo's eyes suddenly burst open! She was already committed to her decision as her lips continued moving forward despite his awakening. He quickly became aware of her actions and gently pulled her in closer to help complete them.

Misty gazed into his radiant blue eyes. "I must admit Mojo, I've never actually had a lover before. Although, much of that had to do with the way I've felt about my hideous witch body up until now. I mean, you saw how ugly I was before now." Mojo's right hand trailed down Misty's long black hair. "I should probably tell you that I made you beautiful in a way that even I would find attractive," he replied softly. "Thanks for setting me free Misty. I can't even begin to tell you how horrible it feels to serve evil and self-serving masters. It's just part of the job of being a genie but now I don't have to worry about that anymore thanks to you," he said gratefully. "Also, you're not the only one with a new body Misty. I can feel and touch things that I never could before." Misty was happy for him. "I hope this doesn't mean you've lost your ancient powers," she replied worriedly. Mojo smiled. "Of course not young lady; it simply means I now have a physical body that will live on forever without having to be trapped inside that confounded lamp all the time. I'm finally free to do whatever I desire and am no longer bound to the fate of whoever rubs the lamp. In fact, anytime you see a black genie lamp like this one, it means that its genie ties have been severed and it's now available for another genie to use. It's a rare thing indeed."

Misty was still lying next to him on the cavern floor. She rolled to one side and stood up. "Sorry Mojo, I probably took things a little too far. I know we only just met today but since you've offered to be my new traveling companion I suppose I'll have plenty of time to get to know you better during our travels." Blushing a little, she reached out to help the genie stand up on his new found feet. Mojo smiled as he accepted her help getting up. Having legs was a whole new experience for him since he was so used to flying everywhere. He was also happy to see a pair of poly-blend pants come with them! Looking up at Misty sheepishly, he felt a bit embarrassed. "I have a confession to make. I've never actually walked anywhere before…but now that I have legs; perhaps you could help me out a bit?" Misty smiled. "Of course Mojo; I'm happy to help you learn how to walk but can't you fly still if you wanted to?" Still holding onto Misty's hand for support, Mojo tried hovering a bit above her head. A sigh of relief came to him upon discovering he could still fly! "Well thank goodness for that! Alright, I'm coming down now. Get ready to help balance me out please." Misty gripped Mojo's left hand tighter as he slowly hovered back down to earth. Sliding her right arm around his shoulders and under his arm, she helped steady him as he took a few steps forward. Mojo draped his left arm around Misty's neck and over her shoulder to help steady himself as he began limping and staggering his way across the cave floor.

"I must admit, walking is much harder than it looks. I should really give humans more credit for doing it so well," he said lightheartedly. Misty chuckled. She was really enjoying this situation. Up until now, she had never felt so needed by another individual for such an incredibly long time. She also felt the experience was helping them grow closer together in a strange sort of way.

Mojo decided it was about time he kept his end of the bargain. Turning towards the charred lamp lying on the cavern floor, he snapped his fingers as it instantly flew into his outstretched hand. Holding it outwards, he began speaking again. "A deal's a deal Misty. Don't worry, I didn't forget about my end of the bargain. Let's find out what this dragon looks like in genie form shall we," he said lightheartedly. Mojo whispered a few magic words into the lamp's narrow opening at the top. A long stream of sparkling white light burst from the lamp's tip quickly streaming its way back through the tunnel opening where they had previously escaped Claw's wrath. Even though they couldn't see what was happening on the other end of the tunnel, they assumed the magic to be transforming Claw into a genie at that very moment. As soon as the long white ribbon of magic disappeared from sight, Misty snatched the lamp from Mojo's outstretched hands and rubbed it furiously. If the magic turned Claw into a genie as expected then it wouldn't take long for him to make his way back into the empty charred lamp she now held. To her utter disappointment, nothing came. Misty and Mojo stared at each other puzzlingly. "That's strange. Try one more time," Mojo said enthusiastically! Misty rubbed again; more vigorously this time. Still nothing happened. Without warning, the cave rumbled again. Sharp pointed stalactites fell from the cave ceiling nearly missing their heads.

Mojo scowled. "That's strange! Most dragons aren't powerful enough to resist my magic. This one must truly be a rare exception." Misty walked over to where Mojo was standing and put an arm around him to keep him from falling over on his new found feet. "I have an idea. How about you enchant the Map of Midas for me so that if the dragon touches it he will be transformed into a genie and be forced into your old lamp? Misty retrieved the rolled up parchment from her deep robe pocket and thrust it towards Mojo. She continued to steady his balance to keep him from falling over. It was much like helping a child learn to walk. Mojo nodded. "That's a fantastic idea Misty!" He pointed a finger at the map as the entire parchment began to glow a mystical light blue color. He then pointed towards one of the cavern entrances from where Misty had recently escaped Claw's wrath. The map flew towards it and through the previously traveled tunnel back towards the dragon's layer. "Now, all we have to do is wait," Mojo said confidently.

Suddenly they heard a loud shriek followed by a bright red streak of light flying from the tunnel entrance directly into the charred lamp. The lamp glowed red as if it were on fire and might cause a severe burn if touched! The red glow slowly faded away into its previous black color as the cave began to shake again! The shaking grew worse than before as a giant crack in the cave floor began to open up! It quickly grew wider and wider! Mojo wrapped an arm around Misty's shoulders as they hobbled through the exit just before it collapsed behind them!

5. THE WOUNDED GENIE

Stepping outside the Cave of Jewels, they turned around to assess the damage. The entire entrance had collapsed behind them and was now covered up by boulders and smaller sized rocks. Thankfully, Misty had picked up the lamp and her broomstick just before the earthquake could swallow either of them up. "You've been a great help Mojo," she said coolly. Mojo smiled. "It's nice our individual powers can help each-other out." Wrapping both arms around Misty he attempted to hug her. She pushed him away; "one step at a time mister! We only just met today remember." They both chuckled a bit in an attempt to brush off the slight awkwardness. Mojo pointed at the lamp in her hand. "You really don't need another genie when you've got me around Misty." Misty smiled. "Jealous already are you," she said with a laugh. "On a slightly different note, I happen to know that neither one of us are capable of teleporting. We'll need something faster than my broomstick or your flying speed if we're going to get anywhere fast. No worries though; I've already figured it out! This is where my handy dandy genie dragon will help us out!" She rubbed the black lamp as Claw quickly emerged surrounded in blue flames. Appearing in the air before them, he still looked like the same fierce dragon Misty had encountered back in the cave. The only exception was that the bottom half of him was now a long misty wave of smoke floating high above the ground. He no longer had a visible pair of legs in the same way that Mojo now had a new pair of legs now that he had been set free. Claw had quickly become her own personal genie to command and control at will. "This is absolutely incredible," she thought to herself excitedly!

Even though Claw still possessed large dragon wings, he no longer needed to use them since he was a genie now and managed to hover high above the ground without flapping them at all. A low pitched rumble came from the dragon's massive brown scaled stomach. Throwing back his long lizard-like head he inhaled a giant gulp of air. Misty instinctively knew what was about to happen. "Duck," she shouted! Mojo and Misty dove towards the ground just as a long trail of burning fire shot towards them. Mojo had jumped in front of Misty to help shield her from the blazing fire trail headed their way. The scorching flames burned into his backside as he felt the incredible pain rush through his body! Normally, the dragon's fire wouldn't have affected him in any way but with Claw being a genie now, it hurt Mojo immensely! Claw's normal dragon's fire was now an intensely heated genie fire that could easily harm other genies such as himself.

Misty grabbed her wand from within her robe and muttered the spell "FORSHELLO!" Just as predicted, another burning stream of fire came hurling towards them! Only this time it was deflected by the green energy shield Misty had cast between them. Misty knew she had better act quickly before anything else happened. She grabbed the lamp and held it in the air for Claw to see. With a voice of thunder she screamed at him. "I wish you to never harm me or Mojo ever again!" Instantly the dragon stopped blowing fire. Claw's countenance quickly changed from a rough and furious creature to a gentle and tame pet.

"That's better Claw," said Misty gently. She turned towards Mojo. "That must hurt horribly! Sorry he burned you Mojo." Mojo was casting healing spells on his own wounded backside in an attempt to make the intense burning sensation go away. "Turns out that my healing magic isn't working very well on these burns," he said agonizingly. Misty frowned. "I'm sorry Mojo. I know a few herbal remedies that might help if you'll let me." Mojo smiled. "Well, I don't want to hold up my traveling companion with any unnecessary stops." Misty smiled back at him sympathetically. "It's not a problem. In fact, we can probably get back to the Forbidden Forest pretty quickly once I take care of a few things." She held the lamp up towards Claw again. "Dragon, my second wish is that you will take us wherever we wish to go without complaint!" Instantly a large brown blanket appeared saddled to the dragon's neck. A long fabric harness strung through the bottom of the blanket and around Claw's neck to keep it from falling off during flight.

Misty looked at Mojo. "You can ride in front of me and I will attempt to heal your back on the way there," she said with concern. "That's awfully kind of you," replied Mojo. "Perhaps I can help you mount." Mojo walked behind Misty and wrapped a hand around each of her hips before lifting her and himself up off the ground and onto the dragon's neck. After placing her at the base of Claw's giant sized neck, he proceeded to sit in front of her just like she had requested. "Grab hold of my waist," he said. "I wouldn't want you to fall off during flight." Sitting behind him, Misty gently wrapped her slender arms around his waist as Claw began to lift up off the ground. The brown blanket beneath them seemed to glue them in place as if preparing them for whatever amount of speed and turbulence they might encounter on their journey ahead. Misty placed her broomstick directly behind where she was sitting and tried tipping it over unsuccessfully. "Yep, it's stuck there pretty good," she thought to herself reassuringly.

Misty yelled out to the dragon. "Take us to the Forbidden Forest!" Even though Claw could fly without his wings now that he was a genie, he flapped them out of habit anyways. They quickly began to gain altitude as they lifted up off the ground. They made a direct bee-line towards a thick layer of fluffy white clouds above them. Misty wasn't used to flying so high; even on her broomstick. She remembered a story of Blackbeack chasing a butterfly high above the clouds and then getting attacked by a swarm of them. He called it, "getting the butterflies!" She laughed inside just thinking about it. She wasn't sure if a butterfly could fly as high as they were now though. They soared high above the thick layer of clouds and began flying in a horizontal direction. She imagined the dragon was used to flying at such a high altitudes in order to stay hidden from any animals it might wish to attack later. "No need to spook the prey before chasing them," she thought to herself as if she were Claw.

Misty still had her arms wrapped around Mojo and was enjoying his presence immensely. She hadn't felt this close to another person since….well, since she was a teenager. Memories came flooding back to her mind. She remembered her first and only love as if it were yesterday. She had fallen in love with a young wizard named Merlin oh so long ago….back before a conniving witch named Morgana had stolen him away from her. Even though Merlin was never truly her lover, she often fantasized about what it would have been like to live with him and enjoy his company on a daily basis. Her emotions suddenly became frantic and bitter as she refocused herself on the present moment. She gave Mojo a tight squeeze around the waist that he most definitely noticed. Even though he was still in pain from the dragon burns on his back, he smiled cheerfully at her loving gesture. "Everything okay back there Misty?" She continued hugging him from behind and leaned her head up against the back of his right shoulder. "We're flying much faster than I thought we would. Hopefully we'll reach the Forbidden Forest by nightfall. Then I can find the herbs I need to help heal your burn wounds," she replied optimistically.

Misty looked closer at the burn wounds Mojo had taken on her behalf. The dragon's fire had burned straight through the backside of his open vest which made his burn marks easier to spot through the giant holes found there. "Hey Mojo, if you don't mind, I'm going to rip this vest off you so I can better see and heal your burn wounds okay?" Mojo blushed a little. "That's fine Misty. If you think you got what it takes then please give it a try." Misty made a clean tear up the middle of his vest from the backside and stopped at the collar. The collar was stronger than it looked and wouldn't tear at all. Putting a little more muscle into it, she finally tore it off; leaving a straight rip line down the middle. This exposed all of his burn marks along with the rest of his back. The wounds looked much worse than she had anticipated.

Even though Misty had complete access from the back to start treating Mojo's wounds, she also wanted to make sure his front side was okay as well. "Hey Mojo, do you mind if we get rid of your vest completely so it's not in the way of me checking you out? Um, checking your burn marks out I mean." Mojo blushed again! "This is truly the best magic I've ever experienced," he thought to himself. "Sure, if you think it's best," Mojo replied joyfully.

Mojo grabbed the front of his vest and removed both arms. "You may have the honor of throwing it away if you'd like," he said enthusiastically. "I'd be delighted," Misty replied delightfully. Grabbing the remainder of Mojo's torn vest, she threw it into the clouds below. Her concentration was so focused on Mojo that she had briefly forgotten that they were both still soaring high above the clouds towards the Forbidden Forest while riding on a dragon's neck. For a moment Misty felt a flood of excitement rush through her body. "This is truly an adventure," she thought to herself. Squeezing her arms around Mojo again, she felt his tight muscled abs and bare chest within the palms of her hands. She melted a little inside as strong waves of desire shot throughout her body. Mojo was having some pretty intense feelings for her as well. "Perhaps my newly freed genie body is experiencing some unexpected changes. Or maybe Misty's newly acquired beauty is causing me to feel this way," he wondered? His silent curiosity continued. "When Misty wished for a beautiful new body I was more than happy to make her into someone that even I would find attractive. So, in a way, I must have brought this on myself," he thought subtly.

Misty began casting spells on Mojo's burn marks. Even her most powerful healing spells didn't make them go away. Mojo turned his head to one side. "Even my powers don't work on those dragon burns; so don't feel bad if you can't make them disappear Misty." Misty suddenly had a brilliant idea. She pointed her wand at her own tongue and attempted to say the word SPITTAIRO. Unfortunately, the word didn't come out the way she had intended since she had to hold her tongue out while saying it. She tried it a few more times before Mojo began laughing hysterically! "Nothing like trying to enchant your own tongue," he chuckled. "Tell you what…how about I enchant my own tongue with healing powers and then I'll transfer them to yours. After all, I don't need to actually say spell words out loud in order for them to work like you witches do." Misty nodded. "Sounds like a plan Mojo. But how are you going to transfer the spell from your tongue to mine?" Mojo turned his head just enough to see her out of the corner of his right eye and gently leaned back into her. "How do you think Misty?" Misty leaned forward and delicately kissed him on the lips. Instantly, she felt a transfer of power from his mouth to hers.

The spell was originally meant to enchant her saliva with healing powers. Now that Mojo had made it happen, she gently leaned forward and began licking the burn marks on his injured back. Mojo chuckled at the tickling sensation caused from her tongue licking his back. His dark red burn wounds slowly turned lighter until they became a pinkish color. Unfortunately, they didn't disappear completely. The healing process continued to tickle him. "Stop, that tickles," he said playfully! "Oh, you're so sensitive," Misty laughed playfully. She tickled him under the arms a little as he continued to laugh hysterically. His whole body leaned all the way to the right and didn't even fall off the dragon's neck. "This magical mounting blanket is truly a life saver," he thought with relief.

Mojo felt a sudden wave of tiredness wash over him. He yawned a little too loudly as Misty was quick to notice. "I thought genies didn't get tired," she teased. Mojo laughed. "I guess us free ones do. Some of these feelings are new to me. Perhaps you wouldn't mind if I laid back on you for a while," he asked tiredly? Mojo leaned back into Misty's open arms and let his tired head rest on her chest. She smiled as she wrapped her left arm over his shoulder and down his chest. Her right hand moved upwards to caress his face. With her head directly over his, they made eye contact as she leaned in to kiss him on the forehead. She pulled away before he began speaking. "Perhaps we should try the real thing," said Mojo lovingly. Misty smiled and leaned in once again for another kiss. This time her target hit its mark. A sudden surge of power flooded through both of them as their lips touched! It must have been too overwhelming for Mojo because his eyes closed immediately as he fell into a deep and satisfying sleep. Misty was shocked at how easily he could fall asleep after such a breathtaking experience! Although, it had been a long day for both of them and neither one of them had slept since…well, she wasn't sure when Mojo had last slept because it was still her first day getting to know him. "Wait a second….what is happening," she wondered curiously? "I've literally only known Mojo for barely a day and I'm already kissing him! What is wrong with me? Am I that desperate for love," she asked herself curiously?

With both arms wrapped around Mojo's sleeping body, she squeezed him tighter into her loving embrace before drifting off to sleep herself. The dragon touched ground before she could get as much sleep as she would have liked. The sound of Claw landing jolted her awake. Opening one eye, she spotted the dark forest floor below. "That was a quick trip," she thought. She was about to wake Mojo when she came up with a better idea. Slowly reaching behind her; she grabbed her broomstick. The magical mounting blanket had managed to keep it from falling off the entire trip. Jumping off the dragon's neck and onto her broomstick; she glanced back at Claw. "Follow me," she commanded. She rose into the air on her broomstick and let the dragon follow her back home with the sleeping Mojo still attached to the glue-like mounting blanket atop Claw's neck.

Misty and Claw landed in front of her quaint little cottage on the damp forest floor. Looking up at Mojo, she found him still snoozing on top of the dragon's neck. "Wow, that guy could probably sleep through an earthquake," she thought surprisingly! Dismounting from her broomstick, she opened the front door of her cottage and pointed her wand at the sleeping Mojo. Whispering the spell word "FLOATELLO," he began floating through the air and through the open doorway. Landing gently on her living room couch, Misty quickly covered him with the warm blanket draped over the back of it. Her next plan of action was to get Claw out of sight before any of the other woodland creatures spotted him. Reaching for the lamp attached to the sash around her waist, she rubbed it thoroughly. Instantly, Claw turned into a cloud of smoke as the lamp sucked him back into its depths. Misty smiled. She was glad not to worry about him trying to kill her anymore. Before going inside, she looked around to make sure no mischievous creatures had been watching. Some of the forest creatures were definitely not to be trusted. She knew this from many past experiences she had with them. Some of the plants and trees were even capable of communicating with the animals of the forest. The lack of privacy in the Forbidden Forest disturbed her deeply.

Brushing aside her concerns, she walked back inside her cottage. Instantly, a screeching voice came from the top left corner of her kitchen. "Is that you Misty?!" Blackbeak was perched on top of an old wooden china cabinet. Misty looked upwards and smiled. "Blackbeak! You crazy bird; I've missed you so much!" Blackbeak flew down from the tall china cabinet landing on Misty's outstretched arm. "Looks like you finally got that beautiful human body you've been dreaming about all these years," he squawked. "You look absolutely stunning Misty," he said flatteringly. "Thank you Blackbeak." It wasn't easy getting past the dragon but you know how carefully I planned that little adventure. Also, I managed to turn that fearsome beast into a genie and he's mine now," she said triumphantly!

Blackbeak turned his head and pointed his beak towards the living room. "Who is that muscular young man sleeping on our couch Misty," he asked curiously? Misty smiled. "That handsome devil happens to be the fabulous genie who gave me this fantastic new body," she replied seductively. "He doesn't look like a genie," said Blackbeak. "I set him free," Misty replied. "He's no longer bound to the lamp or anyone else. However, he volunteered to be my traveling companion without me even asking him too," said Misty in a very complimentary sort of way. Blackbeak looked down. "I thought I was going to be your travelling companion," he replied downheartedly. "Oh, cheer up Blackbeak. I haven't forgotten about you. In fact, remember the Map of Midas I took with me to exchange for the lamp?" Blackbeak nodded. "Of course I remember," he squawked. "Well, since I managed to get it back from Claw; we are going to use it to find the Hand of Midas," she said excitedly! Blackbeak squawked. "That will be quite the adventure I'm sure! Would you like me to accompany you both on this quest Misty?" "I would be honored," replied Misty.

Just then a loud snoring noise came from the living room couch. Mojo was out like a light! It was getting late into the night and the sun had long since sunk below the horizon. "Perhaps we had better get some shut eye as well Blackbeak," said Misty with a yawn. Blackbeak squawked. "I actually slept quite a lot today Misty. I think I'm going to fly around for a bit. If you are going to start this quest of yours tomorrow then I would be more than happy to fly ahead and scout out the area if you wish?" Misty nodded. "I would greatly appreciate that Blackbeak." Let me show you the Map of Midas before you go so you can get an idea of which way we will be traveling." Pulling the map from inside her long robe, she unrolled it on top of the kitchen table for him to see. "I have an incredibly long and complicated plan to find the Hand of Midas Blackbeak. It might not all make sense at first but I'm showing you this just in case we happen to get separated during our travels and need to regroup somewhere. Then you'll know where to go." Blackbeak nodded his skinny black feathered head. Misty pointed at the Forbidden Forest located on the southern part of the map. "We'll be traveling in a northeast direction towards the Dessert of Time. Once there, we'll head for the Sand Trap of Destiny and eventually enter the Tunnel of Terror. Assuming we make it out alive, we'll end up in the Dungeon of Death and with any luck we'll be able to find the Bat King. Legend has it that we'll need an anti-gravity amulet to keep us safe inside his layer so I'm going to need you to fly ahead to the Lake of Lost Souls and talk to the Fairy Queen about acquiring one. She can provide you with one I'm sure!" Of course, she'll probably ask for something in return. I'll send the lamp with you to exchange for it."

The raven looked downwards. It was a lot of information to take in. "How am I going to carry it Misty? It's far too big and heavy for me to hold onto for such a long distance." Misty untied the lamp from the sash around her waist and pulled her slender wand from the inside of her robe. Pointing it at the lamp, she muttered the spell "SHRIVELLO" and watched as it quickly shrunk down to the size of a tiny gold coin. Holding it in her right hand, she unhooked a small silver chain bracelet from her left wrist which was hiding under the long sleeve running down her arm. She looped the chain through the lamp's black arched handle. "Carry this with you and try your best to trade it for a couple of anti-gravity amulets if you can. We will need them to defeat the Bat King on our way to find the Hand of Midas. Do you understand Blackbeak?" Blackbeak nodded. "I understand Misty. I will carry it to the fairy Queen. Hopefully she will accept the exchange." Misty nodded. "Thank you Blackbeak. You're more help than you imagine sometimes." Wrapping the small chain around his feathered neck, she clipped it together at the back. The miniature lamp dangled from the center of his black raven chest. "Please don't let anything happen to it Blackbeak," said Misty cautiously. Blackbeak nodded. "Don't worry Misty. Everything will be fine," he replied confidently. "Although, I'm still not sure exactly how the anti-gravity amulet will help us face the Bat King?" Misty looked upwards as if contemplating a memory from long ago. "Well, the Bat King has an army of bats that can lift us off the ground and hold us in mid-air for as long as they wish! This could be a real problem for us to be suspended in the air for long periods of time. The anti-gravity amulets can defy the laws of gravity in multiple ways. They can add gravity or take it away based on how you use them. In this case, they will add gravity to our bodies to keep the bats from suspending us in the air until…well, I think you know where that would lead to," said Misty cutting herself short. "Basically, they can cause heavy amounts of gravity or they can lift you up as well. My broomstick can help me fly around but the amulets allow a greater portion of weight to be moved around without any problems. For example, a group of bats could easily move me and my broomstick around in the air but the amulet would allow me to move the whole group around just as easily without any trouble from them. I hope that makes sense Blackbeak," she finished thoughtfully.

Blackbeak nodded. "I understand. We must still be cautious Misty. The Bat King's army could still be a bigger problem than you might think," he squawked. Misty frowned. "Don't worry Blackbeak. Between my power and my beautiful sleeping genie over there, everything will be alright. Speaking of sleep…it's getting rather late Blackbeak and I'm tired. We should both get some shuteye for the long journey ahead tomorrow." Misty yawned and walked over into the living room to take another look at her sleeping genie before going to bed. To her surprise, he was gone!

6. MORGANNA'S CURSE

Misty was in shock! Where had her handsome lover gone too? She thought he had been sleeping on her couch the entire time. She looked around for any open windows he may have flown through. Nothing was knocked over and there wasn't any sign of a break in. "Do genies normally fly off at night," she wondered? He was fast asleep just moments ago.

Even though she worried about him wondering around the dangerous woods alone; she also knew he had enough power to take care of himself out there in the wild. She was also getting incredibly tired. "Looks like we'll have to go looking for Mojo in the morning Blackbeak; I'm far too exhausted to do anything right now," she said as she walked up the stairs towards her bedroom in the attic. Within minutes of laying her head on the pillow, she was out like a light.

"Rise and shine sleeping beauty," said a deep familiar voice! Misty opened her eyes to see a smiling Mojo staring back at her, holding a plate of pancakes in one hand and a cup of orange juice in the other. "I don't know if you're a breakfast person but I thought I'd give it a try," he said cheerfully. It took a few seconds for Misty to fully register what was happening. "Mojo! Where the heck were you last night? We were worried sick!" Mojo frowned. "I don't know if you know this but sometimes genies do a little sleep flying when we're in a deep state of rest. That being said, even I don't know where I went last night," he said with a chuckle. "It's similar to what humans call sleep walking except for genies it's sleep flying!" Misty laughed. "That's interesting!" Mojo smiled back at her. "While I was sleep flying, I had a dream about this tiny little man who wore a small red hat. He asked me where my lamp was at. I told him you had it Misty. For some reason he seemed to know who you were but I guess it really doesn't matter since it was all just a dream anyways."

Misty frowned. "Oh no, you were probably sleep talking to Nick the gnome. Did he have a long white beard, pointy shoes and innocent looking emerald eyes?" Mojo nodded. "That's the guy." Misty's brow furrowed. "Everybody in this forest knows not to trust Nick the gnome," she said agitatedly. Mojo chuckled. "Oh, what harm could that little man possibly do anyways?" Just then, a sharp knock came from the back door. Misty gasped in horror! "We've got to get out of here!" Mojo wrapped an arm around her shoulder securely. "It'll be fine Misty, I can protect you." The mysterious man behind the door started shouting. "I know you're in there Misty! Misty looked around the room in search of Blackbeak. He was sitting on top of the dusty china cabinet observing everything from his perch above. "Get out of here Blackbeak," she said anxiously. Blackbeak flew up to the attic and out the upstairs window where he could more easily shield himself from the view of any prying eyes surrounding the backdoor area.

Mojo moved towards the backdoor to open it. Misty walked slowly behind him. Upon opening it, he saw nothing but the dense forest trees and plant life surrounding the cottage. Looking downward, his gaze fell upon Nick the gnome. His long white beard gave the impression that he was an elderly man. However, since all gnomes began growing beards at the age of eight it was hard to tell their exact age most of the time. Guessing a gnome's life span was difficult since they would normally stop keeping track of their own age after the first few hundred years or so.

Nick looked up at them. "I knew I'd find you here genie." Mojo glanced over at Misty then back down at Nick. "Alright, you got me," he said superficially. "What is it that you want little man?" Nick's face turned red with rage! "Little man? Little man? How dare you call me that sir! I am offended and outraged by your complete lack of mannerisms and I would bid you good day if I didn't have business to discuss with Misty here." Mojo frowned. "Look, whatever you say in front of her, you can say in front of me. Consider me her new business consultant." Nick laughed. "Unfortunately, the business between me and Misty started long before you ever showed up genie. What's your name anyways?" Mojo frowned. "I am Mojo and I already know who you are….Nick the gnome," he said in a slightly mocking tone of voice. Nick smiled. "Once again, my reputation precedes me. Now, please leave us to our business genie." Mojo was starting to get upset. Misty looked at him and put an arm around his shoulder. "It'll be okay Mojo." Mojo looked at Nick suspiciously. "Alright, I'll be sitting on the living room couch if you need me." Nick laughed. "Don't count on it. This matter requires much more discretion than you could possibly comprehend genie. Perhaps you should go fly around in the woods for a bit. It would put all of our minds at ease," he said seriously. Mojo's temper continued to rise. "I don't think you realize the extent of my powers little man!" The genie began to grow taller and far more muscular in size! Misty grabbed hold of Mojo's right elbow. "It'll be fine Mojo. Just come back soon." Mojo shrunk back down to his normal size and pointed at Nick. "I've got my eye on you little man. Yep, you heard me correctly short stuff," he exclaimed mockingly! Nick's face turned a raging red again. "So help me…say little man one more time and you'll wish you'd never been born genie!" Mojo waved his hand dismissively. The back door flew open simultaneously. "Oh please don't hurt me little guy," he replied mockingly on his way out. Nick slammed the door shut behind him and wished it would have hit him on the way out. "Your friend is a real pain," Nick said furiously. "He's just a very protective person," Misty replied defensively.

Nick looked up at her. "I'll get right to the point Misty. We both know I gave you the fire amulet many years ago to help aid you on your quest for the lamp. We also made a deal that when you were finished using your three wishes that you would hand the lamp over to me in exchange for letting you keep the fire amulet. To be honest, I didn't think you'd actually make it past the dragon but you never cease to amaze me Misty. By the way, your new witch body looks quite dazzling! I can only imagine that was the work of the genie no doubt?" Misty smiled. "Why yes it was and thanks for noticing. I am becoming rather fond of it. It's far better than that old shriveled up body I used to have that's for sure. However, I must tell you that I used my last wish to set the genie free. He is as free as a bird now." Misty suddenly realized the impact this statement would have on Nick. Just as predicted, fumes practically flared from his nostrils. His face flashed red with rage again. "Misty, we had a deal and you broke it!" "You can still have the lamp as promised Nick. It just won't be any good now that the genie is free." Nick scowled. "Mark my words young lady, there will be consequences!" Nick turned around to storm out the way he had come in. "Good thing he's tall enough to reach the doorknob or this whole situation might be really embarrassing," Misty thought hysterically to herself as he slammed the door behind him. She breathed a sigh of relief now that he had finally removed himself from her presence. Although, the thought of Nick returning for revenge was truly a haunting one! She felt the need to leave the premises before anything worse should happen to her.

Pulling her wand from the inside of her robe, she summoned her broomstick from where she had previously left it the night before. It came soaring down the staircase and into her outstretched hand. Not wanting to wait for Mojo to get back, she hopped on it, threw open the backdoor with another spell and soared high into the bright blue sky. Flying through the air and over the trees, she noticed a fairly large beehive dangling from one of the branches nearby. Lowering her flight path, she hovered up next to it. Retrieving her wand again, she casted a Scouting Spell on the giant swarm of bees surrounding the beehive and told them to go locate her friend Mojo. She transferred a quick mental image to them of what he looked like just so they knew who to look for exactly. Immediately the swarm of bees scattered in multiple directions looking for the lost Mojo. Misty landed her broomstick underneath the tree with the beehive dangling far above her head. She knew she must be at that particular location in order for her little bee scouts to lead Mojo back to her once they found him. "After all, bees always come back to their hive," she told herself cleverly. "Although, this could be quite a long wait;" she thought with a sigh.

Misty glanced around at her surroundings. Spruce, maple and ash trees grew abundantly all round her. It was a bright sunny day filled with blue skies and damp humid weather. It was definitely summertime and there was an abundant amount of plant and animal life scattered throughout the woods around her. A cute little gray bunny hopped from behind a bush nearby and stared at her. "Aww…your big blue eyes are adorable," she said admiringly.

Misty knew her newly enchanted scouting bees might take a while to find Mojo so she sat underneath the tall leafy maple tree on the long green grass beneath it and patiently waited for them to return with her genie friend. Glancing upwards, she spotted the empty beehive dangling from the long-reaching branch high above her head. Her gaze fell upon a single lone bee lagging behind the rest for some unknown reason. Upon closer inspection, she noticed that it wasn't a bee at all. It was a fairy! The little fairy was about to fly into the empty beehive when it paused in mid-flight and began flying directly towards Misty instead. Even though the fairy was small, Misty could tell that she had long blond hair and was covered in a sparkling emerald dress with a slit down the side which showed off her slender left leg more than the other. "You look gorgeous," Misty exclaimed flatteringly. "Thank you my dear," replied the fairy gently. "My name is Pixie. I am here gathering honeycomb to take back to my people. You look pretty yourself. What may I call you?" Misty smiled. "I am Misty. I am here waiting for my genie friend Mojo to return. Also, what do you need the honeycomb for? I didn't think fairies ate honeycomb?" Pixie chuckled. "Oh, we don't eat it. It's for a job I have to do. If you promise to keep it a secret I'll tell you exactly what it's for," she replied cautiously. Misty glanced around to make sure no one was eavesdropping in on their conversation. "I promise I won't tell a soul Pixie," Misty replied seriously. Misty knew this is how fairy's made friends. They would tell you a secret and if you ever told anyone then they would never trust you again. She knew that even though they were complete strangers who had just met, it was serious business indeed. "I give you my word as a witch. May I grow a thousand warts if I ever tell a soul," replied Misty with one hand held over her heart. Pixie snickered. "Alright, I'll take a chance on you Misty. My secret is that I am Pixie, the maker of Pixie Dust! Basically the reason every fairy in the World can fly is because of me," she exclaimed proudly! Misty smiled. "That's truly amazing Pixie but what does that have to do with gathering honeycomb?" Pixie looked back at her. "Well, honeycomb is part of the magical mixture I use to make Pixie Dust Misty." "Oh, I see," responded Misty thoughtfully.

Misty suddenly remembered that Blackbeak was on his way to meet with the Fairy Queen. "You don't happen to be from the Lake of Lost Souls," she asked curiously? Pixie shook her head. "I'm not from there but that's where I'm heading now," she replied cheerfully. Misty quickly reformulated her entire travel plan. "What a coincidence! Me and Mojo are actually headed that way as well. Perhaps we could all travel there together. You would be great company Pixie," said Misty joyfully! "I would be happy to join you in your quest," Pixie replied happily. "Although, I should probably ask; what is your quest anyways?" "Well, our ultimate goal is to find the Hand of Midas," Misty replied cautiously. She was beginning to share her secrets with Pixie and wanted to choose her words carefully. Pixie looked at her seriously. "Oh, that is quite the quest to embark on but why would you need to go to the Lake of Lost Souls to find the Hand of Midas? I guarantee it's definitely not there." Misty hesitated before replying. "We need a few things to get through our journey. One of those things is an anti-gravity amulet that the fairy Queen could provide," replied Misty cautiously. Pixie shook her head disagreeably. "What makes you think she would just give you one of those? Also, why would you even need one?"

Pixie's curiosity was starting to annoy Misty; mainly because they had only just met and she didn't know if Pixie could be trusted. "Well Pixie, I know you told me one of your secrets and I'm incredibly grateful. One of my secrets is that I have something quite valuable to offer the

Fairy Queen in exchange for an anti-gravity amulet. I may have said too much already but it would be used to escape a certain someone who may try and capture us on our quest to find the Hand of Midas." Pixie's curiosity suddenly peeked. "Ok, I know you're probably getting tired of all my prying questions, especially since we've only just met but I have to ask…is it to help escape the Bat King's army?" Misty was shocked that Pixie actually knew what it would be used for. "Why yes it is. How did you know?" Pixie looked at her solemnly. "The Bat King has attacked my people for centuries. We've had to use anti-gravity amulets to help keep his army from flying away with our army and doing who knows what with them!"

A look of sadness crossed Misty's face. "I'm sorry Pixie. I bet his army has caused the fairies far more problems than you want to think about." A tear slid down Pixie's smooth cheek as she wiped it away. "The Bat King killed my parents Misty," she said sadly. "That is why I became an inventor and created Pixie Dust. It was to help my people escape from his horrible army! Even though fairies are born with wings, they still need my Pixie Dust to help them fly." Misty looked confused. "Why can't they fly without out it? Being born with wings should be enough right?" Pixie looked downhearted again. "Unfortunately, my people were cursed by a despicably evil witch many ages ago. The witch put a curse on my people to never fly again." Misty gasped! "Was that witch named Morganna by chance?" Pixie looked shocked by Misty's perceptive response. "Why yes it was. How did you know?" Misty glanced downward at the forest floor. "I've heard stories about how Morganna came to the fairies for help. Apparently, she was trying to fight off a relentless dragon that kept attacking her but the fairies wouldn't help her so she cursed them." Pixie looked dumbfounded. "Is that what you were told because the truth is much different!" Misty looked astonished. "Really, what's the real story then?" Pixie glanced back at her. "My people did help Morganna chase the dragon away into a cave somewhere. The fairies called it Claw's Cave because that was the name of the dragon. The dwarves living in the town below called it the Cave of Jewels because that's where they mined the majority of their treasure from. Sufficed to say, it almost caused an act of war between the fairies and dwarves. You can imagine their anger at having a dragon living in their most precious of mines and blaming the fairies for driving him there! It took much negotiating by our great Fairy Queen to keep the dwarves from going to war with us! We already had the bat army attacking us. We didn't need an army of dwarves attacking us as well! To make a long story short, the fairies asked Morganna for her pet raven in exchange for helping her keep the dragon off her back. Apparently, her little raven held some highly unique protective powers that would have shielded us from the Bat King's army. Unfortunately, Morganna wouldn't give up her pet raven and a fight broke out over it. She cursed all the fairies and their ancestors with the inability to fly for the rest of eternity!"

Misty could tell Pixie was upset. "I would be upset too if I were a fairy," she replied delicately. "What kind of protecting power did this raven have anyways," she asked thoughtfully? Pixie glanced off into the distance as she wiped another tear from her eye. "Supposedly, her raven held the power to shield an entire town from intruders somehow," she replied mystically. "That would definitely come in handy," Misty agreed solemnly.

Although Pixie had never actually said the name of Morganna's raven, Misty knew exactly who she was referring too. However, something else was on her mind entirely. "I probably shouldn't tell you this Pixie but Morganna is actually my Great, Great Grandma," she said disappointedly. Pixie stared at her with amazement. "This could actually be a good thing Misty," she replied hopefully. "How so," Misty asked? "Well, many fairies believe it to be what we call a Bloodline Curse. In other words, it can only be broken by an ancestor of Morganna's. Misty looked slightly confused. "I wouldn't have the slightest idea how to break it," she replied with bewilderment. Pixie hesitated. "None of us are really sure how to break the curse Misty. Otherwise, we probably would have done it by now. Also, we could be wrong about it being a bloodline curse. It's just a theory but perhaps others could break it as well but we'll never really know for sure until it happens."

Misty suddenly had a genius idea. "Alright Pixie, I would be more than happy to help break this curse on one condition." "What's that," Pixie asked curiously? "When we get to the Lake of Lost Souls, I need you to help me acquire an anti-gravity amulet from the Queen. Also, my friend Blackbeak might be there. I would appreciate your help in locating him as well when we get there." Pixie nodded, "I would be more than happy to assist you Misty. Also, what does Blackbeak look like just so I know what to look for when we get there?" Misty was a little hesitant to tell her because she could already calculate what her reaction would be. "Well, he's a black feathered raven who…." Pixie gasped! "Oh, tell me it's not the same raven the fairies wanted to take from Morganna," she said fearfully. Misty nodded. "Actually, yes it is." Pixie placed both hands over her mouth in absolute terror. "Let's hope we get to the lake before he does," she said horrified. Misty looked at her with concern. "Why? They wouldn't hurt him if they wanted to use his powers in the first place right?" Pixie flew next to Misty's face and landed on her left shoulder. "The problem is that many fairies have already formed various ideas and theories about how to break the curse. Many believe it could be broken by sacrificing something Morganna holds dear…such as a former pet or magical object she once carried. Thankfully no one knew she had a blood relative or they probably would have been searching for you this entire time Misty!" Misty sighed with concern. "Don't worry Pixie. I'll keep it a secret if you will." Pixie wrapped an arm around Misty's neck while standing on top of her left shoulder. "You have my word as a fairy Misty. I won't tell a soul. Besides, we're friends now. We have to keep each-others secrets." Misty glanced around to make sure no one was listening in on their conversation. "Well, let's get headed to the Lake of Lost Souls then," she said worriedly. "I thought you were waiting for your friend to show up," Pixie asked curiously? Misty looked off into the distance. "I'm waiting for Mojo to return but it sounds like saving Blackbeak might be the most pressing concern of ours at the moment!"

Misty was trying to think of a way to let Mojo know where they were headed. Pulling her wand from her inner robe pocket, she pointed it at the beehive dangling from the tree branch above their heads. "What are you doing," Pixie asked curiously? Misty muttered the spell "WRITELLO" as a long stream of blue light jetted from her wand and into the empty beehive. Instantly, large white letters appeared at the top of the beehive entrance reading; "Go to Lake of Lost Souls Mojo." Pixie chuckled. "Well, you couldn't have made it any more obvious for him," she said with a laugh. Muttering the phrase "BROOMA KA DOOMA," Misty's broomstick quickly flew into her outstretched hand. Even though it was only an arm's distance away, she thought it fun to show off for her new friend. Pixie smiled, "quite impressive Misty." Misty smiled back at her new friend with satisfaction. "Thank you my friend. We better get going. I would hate for anything bad to happen to my friend Blackbeak." Throwing a leg over her broomstick, she pushed off from the ground and into the air. Pixie flew next to her for a while before landing on her left shoulder to rest for a bit. "Well, it's off to Never Never Land," she said with a laugh. Misty didn't understand the reference. "What do you mean," she asked? Pixie laughed again. "I really don't even know. It's just something a lot of fairies say before flying anywhere. I'm sure there's a story in it somewhere."

7. FOLLOWING THE BEES

Mojo was still incredibly upset with Nick the gnome! He had been flying around the Forbidden Forest trying to blow off steam when suddenly he spotted a massive swarm of bees in the distance. They were flying towards him with an alarming amount of speed and agility! He didn't know why they would be after him especially since he had never seen them before his entire life. The closer they came, the more convinced he became that they were about to gain up on him for a major stinging session! He quickly made a 180 degree turn around in mid-flight and veered off towards the left in hopes of having them pass by. Instead, they changed course during mid-flight. "What kind of monstrous bees are these," he thought frantically! "Alright, if you guys want to play tough, you better get ready," he shouted confidently!

Mojo quickly came up with a strategy to avoid getting stung by the entire swarm of bees darting directly towards him! He transformed himself into an extra-large boulder. The bees weren't fooled by his new appearance and quickly rearranged themselves to form the shape of an arrow. The arrow pointed at the boulder and then pointed back the way they had just come. "Very clever," Mojo thought to himself. "They obviously want me to follow them." Transforming back into his normal genie self, he pointed at the bees. "Lead the way fellers." The bees began flying back the way they had come. Mojo didn't know why they wanted him to follow them but he knew it must be important so he flew closely behind them. "What a weird bunch of bees," he thought curiously.

After flying through a large number of trees and over a river, they finally arrived at an empty beehive. Mojo saw the writing Misty had inscribed on it which read; "Go to the Lake of Lost Souls Mojo." For a brief moment he wondered if perhaps someone else in the woods might be named Mojo. After deciding that he was probably the only Mojo in the woods, he took to the air and began making his way towards the Lake of Lost Souls. Using his genie powers, he caused a map to appear in his hands. Taking a quick look at it, he knew exactly where to go! Transforming himself into a black feathered raven, he decided it best that no one recognize him in his true form. After all, he knew there were creatures in the world who possessed ancient artifacts powerful enough to capture genies; free or not.

Flapping his raven wings northward, he glanced back at the swarm of bees behind him. "Thank you my friends," he squawked back at them. Although they probably didn't understand him; he felt good saying it anyways. The sun was setting and his daylight quickly faded into the night sky. Flapping his wings with superhuman speed, he desperately hoped to reach the Lake of Lost Souls before Misty did!

8. FIGHTING THE EAGLE

Time drug on as the sun rose in the distance. Hovering high in the air, Blackbeak spotted the lake a few miles ahead of him. His raven wings were exhausted and he was desperately ready for a much needed rest. He had been thinking about what he would say to the Fairy Queen upon arriving. Perhaps he could convince her to just let him borrow the anti-gravity amulet. Without warning, a giant net flew over his entire body and began pulling him backwards! Blackbeak turned his head to look behind him. Two winged fairies hovered in the air just behind him. One was holding the net gun which had just been used to capture him while the other carried a gun with a much larger barrel attached to it. This made Blackbeak sweat a little. The net gun sucked the net tighter around him as it pulled him backwards towards the fairy holding it in his hands. Blackbeak flapped harder and faster in an attempt to break free. Unfortunately, his claws couldn't break the tightly woven net strands despite his best efforts.

"Stop struggling," commanded a deep sounding male voice. "By order of the Queen, we are hereby ordered to capture and bring you in!" Blackbeak suddenly had a brilliant idea. He stopped flapping and began to fall. Hoping the weight of his body would overpower the strength of the guard holding onto the net, he let gravity push him and the net downwards. To his disappointment, his capturer held Blackbeak's entire body weight without falling himself. Blackbeak took a closer look at the bold little fairy holding onto the net gun. The little guy only wore a few items of clothing. He wore a tan leather loin cloth, a pair of brown leather shoes and a glowing amber amulet! He was shirtless and clearly a muscular fellow with a full head of jet black hair. Instantly, Blackbeak recognized the amulet to be an anti-gravity amulet. "So, that's how he's able to keep me up in the air without my weight pulling him down," he thought intriguingly as he continued staring at the glowing amber colored amulet dangling around his neck.

The other fairy hovered up next to the one with the net gun and held up his bigger gun for Blackbeak to see. "I could put you to sleep right now bird! This gun will be much worse than the net gun if you decide to fight us. I promise you that!" This fairy was built very much like the first. He had chiseled abs, light brown hair, leather shoes and a brown loin cloth as well. He held a deep commanding voice much like the first. Blackbeak noticed him to have light brown hair while the other one holding the net gun had dark black hair. "At least I can tell them apart by their hair color," he thought cleverly to himself.

Blackbeak stopped struggling and let the young man holding the net gun carry him through the air without fuss. "I was actually on my way to see your Queen," said Blackbeak simply. "If that really is true then we must set you free immediately and help aid you on your quest," the black haired fairy said sarcastically. "It is true," replied Blackbeak. "May I at least know who you are and what the Queen wants with me," he inquired inquisitively? The black haired fairy responded authoritatively. "The Queen will share what she wants after we take you in. Don't worry about our names. You won't be seeing much more of us after we throw you into the dungeon!" The brown haired fairy flew alongside Blackbeak's net; his gun at the ready in case any desperate attempts to escape were made.

Blackbeak knew there was no way out of the net so he decided to just close his eyes and catch a few winks before arriving at their destination. His only consolation was that he didn't have to spend all of his energy flying anymore. He'd leave that to the two robotic fairies that did whatever the Queen told them to do. "They probably don't even know why they were sent to capture me," he thought miserably to himself. "These guys are nothing more than puppets on a…" His thoughts was interrupted by a high pitched screeching sound that sent shivers through his black feathered body! Turning his head, he quickly spotted a giant bald eagle jetting towards them at an incredibly swift pace! Its long talons shimmered in the morning sunlight as it flew directly towards them! Judging by its outstretched claws and quick flight towards them; the group braced themselves for a brutal attack.

The eagle made a giant swoop towards the black haired fairy holding the net gun. Lunging backwards, he narrowly dodged the razor sharp talons headed for his face. During the process, he accidently let go of the net. Blackbeak quickly plummeted towards the ocean below; his body still entangled in the net. Adrenalin rushed through his system at the thought of possibly dying! Desperately flapping his wings, he still couldn't free himself from the thick net surrounding him. Thankfully, the brown haired fairy swooped down to save him and caught the net opening with both hands! He shouted at Blackbeak. "Grab the gun from my holster and shoot that blasted eagle!" The fairy turned around to reveal a long gun holster attached to his back. He held onto the net with his backside facing it. Blackbeak hadn't noticed the gun holster there up until now. He was surprised at how much trust this young guard was placing in him. Reaching his tiny raven claws through the holes in the net, he latched onto the handle of the small gun sticking out of the holster attached to the young fairy's back. "If only I had longer human arms it would be much easier," he thought wishfully. "Good thing these fairy guns are small enough to grip onto," he thought gratefully.

Carefully balancing the gun with his raven feet, he took aim and shot towards the attacking eagle. Something went terribly wrong because the brown haired fairy holding the net suddenly let out a scream of agony! "You idiot! You were supposed to shoot the eagle!" His eyes closed as his body fell backwards through the air. His hands let go of the net holding onto Blackbeak as he fell towards the ocean below. With the top of the net now open, Blackbeak quickly made his escape through it. Seeing the brown haired fairy falling towards the ocean below, Blackbeak made a beeline in his direction. Catching up with the unconscious falling fairy, Blackbeak hooked his claws through the free flowing part of his leather loin cloth. Surprisingly, it didn't tear off completely like he had anticipated. Instead, he managed to save the undeserving fairy from what most certainly would have been his unforeseen death. Blackbeak sensed the young fairy to be a little more exposed then he would probably feel comfortable with if he were awake at the moment; assuming he was still alive of course. Blood seeped from the guard's upper chest where the bullet had pierced through him. Even though shooting him had been a complete accident, Blackbeak resented the young guard for having captured him in the first place. On the other hand, he also knew that saving this pesky fairy might very well help his cause while addressing the Queen.

Blackbeak continued carrying the brown haired fairy towards the Lake of Lost Souls. The two guards were planning on taking him there anyways. "They would've just saved me a trip," he thought to himself ironically. He glanced backwards to see if the eagle was still fighting with the black haired fairy. Sure enough, they were attacking and dodging each-others blows as if the fight would go on forever. Neither one of them gained an advantage over the other. The fairy was too quick and the eagle too strong! "Hopefully I can get away without either of them noticing," he hoped desperately.

The brown haired fairy that Blackbeak was now holding onto felt extremely heavy beneath his talons and he felt as if he were about to drop him. "Anti-gravity amulets must not work on the unconscious," he thought discouragingly. He wished desperately that he could somehow snatch the amulet from the unconscious fairy and put it around his own neck. "If only I had longer arms," he thought again wishfully. "They would sure come in handy right now!" Just then, a brilliant idea came to him and he felt stupid for not thinking about it earlier. He moved a wing up next to his black feathered chest to rub the miniature lamp still hanging from the small chain around his neck. Without hesitation, the almighty dragon genie flew from the lamp's opening as he quickly expanded in size! Claw flapped his massive wings alongside Blackbeak as he continued making his way towards the Lake of Lost souls. Blackbeak felt a little intimidated flying next to the dragon. His only comfort was that Claw was now a genie and would do whatever he commanded. He glanced over at the fierce looking dragon flying next to him. Claw glared back at him. "Well, if you're not going to say anything then I'll make my first wish! I wish to have a long pair of magic arms to use whenever I want!" Claw blew a puff of mystical blue smoke around Blackbeak as two giant arms made of blue smoke attached themselves to his back and draped over his wings like a cape. Although, they didn't stop him from using his wings either. His claws were still hooked onto the brown-haired fairy's loin cloth dangling below him. Blackbeak moved his long magic blue arms below the fairy and let him drop into them. Blackbeak was incredibly happy with the length of his new magic arms as he continued carrying the unconscious fairy beneath him.

Suddenly a loud shriek of pain came screaming from behind him! Turning his head, he watched the black-haired fairy get slashed across the chest by the bald headed eagle! The guard fell backwards as the eagle rushed forward to take a stab at his throat. The black-haired fairy dodged the razor sharp talons headed for his neck. A single claw hooked onto his anti-gravity amulet on the way down; tearing it from his neck. The eagle took another side swipe at his head barely missing his skull. Taking its newly found treasure, the eagle flew away from the injured fairy as he continued falling towards the ocean below.

Blackbeak didn't really feel like being the hero today but decided to show some mercy towards his captors. Extending one of his magic arms towards the falling fairy, he managed to snatch him away from certain doom. He was clearly unconscious and was losing copious amounts of blood from the giant slash across his chest. Blackbeak felt relieved to have his two magical arms to assist him because he now carried two unconscious fairies in each of them. He continued flying towards the Lake of Lost Souls with each of them carefully tucked away inside the palms of his hands. "What a crazy day," he thought to himself!

The bald eagle had flown away with the stolen anti-gravity amulet from the black haired fairy. Blackbeak was happy to see it go. He couldn't possibly even consider battling the eagle with his hands as full as they were. Although, he was tempted to let the two fairies fall to their doom. However, he also considered what his heroic rescue might mean to the Fairy Queen; especially when trying to acquire the anti-gravity amulets Misty had sent him to get.

Suddenly, a giant beam of amber colored light engulfed the three of them and instantly began pulling them inward towards the lake at a much quicker pace than they were travelling! Blackbeak decided to just relax and let the mysterious vacuum beam pull them inwards. After all, he was headed in that direction anyways and he was exhausted from flying around all day.

9. MISTY THE TRAVELER

Misty flew towards the Lake of Lost Souls as quick as her broomstick would carry her. Pixie held onto her shoulder for dear life the entire flight. In the distance, Misty could see the lake as it sparkled and shimmered in the sunlight with a deep blue tint giving it a uniquely beautiful quality. At the center of the lake stood an entire city built on the water! It was surrounded by a tall cement wall with guards stationed on top and giant machines scattered around its perimeter. She wasn't sure what the machines were used for but knew they must be important enough to keep around the city's perimeter. Somehow, all of the little homes and shops within the city walls were floating in place on top of the lake as if they had been built on solid ground. All of the buildings were interconnected by multiple bridges spanning from one side to the other. "This is quite a magical little city," Misty thought silently. Since fairies were incredibly small creatures the city wasn't very large by human or even witch standards but Misty still found it quite enchanting. Her gaze shifted towards the southeast portion of the city where something oddly peculiar caught her attention. She noticed a well-lit gravity beam pulling a black bird and two fairies inward towards the top of the city walls out skirting the city's perimeter. "Could it be," she wondered curiously? Suddenly it dawned on her what the machines on top of the city walls were used for. She could see what they were being used for right at that very moment.

Pixie saw what was happening as well. "Misty, I know what you're thinking and you're definitely right. Your raven friend could be caught inside that gravity beam. However, we need to think this through carefully. Chances are the guards will take him to the Queen's palace at the city's center. It would be best for us to go straight to the palace and request an audience with the Queen instead of breaking the law in order to rescue your friend." Misty nodded agreeably. "You're right Pixie. A peaceful approach is always better."

They headed towards the palace in hopes of gaining audience with the Queen. Misty couldn't help but wonder where Mojo was at the moment. "Did he find the message I left for him back in the forest? Is he following the swarm of bees I enchanted to help him find me," she wondered curiously? "Perhaps he's close behind me now," she hoped silently to herself.

10. THE GRAVITY BEAM MACHINE

A little blond fairy named Alvin had been assigned to work on the Gravity Beam Machine that day. It was his lucky day to actually pull something in from the skies above. Having gone quite a few months without spotting anything worth latching onto, he was beginning to grow rather bored with his job. Peeking through the small lens attached to the top of the Gravity Beam Machine, he spotted two guards who looked to be in some sort of trouble. He also spotted a black raven holding onto one of the wounded soldiers below his talons. "That's no ordinary raven," he said to himself as he looked closer at the long magical arms and hands now holding onto the wounded guard below his raven body. Alvin had watched the eagle attack and decided it was time to provide some assistance for the two guards who had been beaten up pretty badly. Since the gravity beam covered such a wide diameter, he managed to encircle the two guards and the raven within its scope before firing. Instantly, the wide beam shot towards them and began pulling the three of them inwards towards the top of the city wall where Alvin was located.

Watching the three of them ride the gravity beam towards him,

Alvin brought the Jargon Band strapped around his wrist up to his mouth and spoke the passcode into it. All Jargon Bands looked the same and his was no different. It was simply a wristband made of small obsidian arrowheads all strung together by a stretchy fabric that could easily adapt to the size of a user's wrist. Each arrowhead held a tiny green stone at its center. Each emerald stone would light up once the passcode was spoken into it. It was a fairy invention used for communication and Alvin felt the need to use it at the moment. He spoke the passcode into his Jargon Band and it quickly began glowing green indicating that it had been activated. "BACKUP BACKUP 119…COME IN GUARD LEADER! We're going to need a backup patrol. I repeat, a backup patrol is currently needed." Strangely, the guard leader didn't respond to him at all. However, a small guard patrol armed with spears and anti-gravity amulets quickly showed up to aid him. They seemed to come out of nowhere which is exactly what they were trained to do. They arrived just in time to watch the three outliers finish being pulled in from the gravity beam. All three of them made a gentle landing onto a giant padded mat lying around the Gravity Beam Machine. Immediately, the backup patrol tried releasing the two injured fairies from the raven's vice-like grip on them. Blackbeak was happy with his new set of magical hands and wasn't about to release his two captives just yet. Since the guard patrol had not seen the eagle attack, they could only assume that the raven had hurt the two injured guards in some way. Judging by the long bleeding slash across the black haired fairy's chest and the gunshot wound in the others; they began making some quick assumptions!

Blackbeak held onto the two fairies intensely with his new magical hands. "I must speak with your queen immediately," he commanded. The backup patrol continued prying and squeezing at his magical hands in a desperate attempt to release the two fairies held tightly within his grasp. The head guard ordered his patrol to cease and desist and began speaking to the raven in his most deeply authoritative voice. "The Queen won't speak to just anyone. What makes you think she'll take time out of her busy schedule to meet with you raven?" Blackbeak looked serious. "Because she might want her two injured guards back. I will exchange them for two anti-gravity amulets," he replied diplomatically.

The guards looked at each-other with surprise. No one had ever blackmailed them for anti-gravity amulets before. They also knew that only the Queen had the power to give such precious objects away; especially to this random raven nobody seemed to know anything about. "I'll speak with her personally," replied the patrol captain solemnly. "Now please, release my men so we can treat their wounds." Blackbeak shook his head. "How do I know you won't just throw a net over me once I let them go," he asked cautiously? The captain returned his gaze solemnly. "I give you my word as captain. No harm will come to you raven."

Blackbeak didn't want to give up his bargaining chip so easily but he also knew that both fairies had been severely injured during their battle with the eagle. "Alright Captain, I'll give you the most wounded one. The other one will stay in my custody until you deliver the anti-gravity amulets to me." Blackbeak willed one of his magical arms to disappear. Immediately the wounded brown haired guard fell from the sky as the Captain flew up to catch him. He handed him to another guard standing next to him. "Rush this young man to the Circle of Healing as fast as possible," he commanded authoritatively.

The Captain sighed. "I'm not trying to tell you what to do raven but I honestly think the best way to get what you want is to let us bring you into the Queen. She is not someone who enjoys traveling far. I would recommend letting us bring you in just to guarantee an audience with her. Are you okay with that?" Blackbeak thought about it for a moment. "Do what you must Captain but I'm not letting go of this young warrior until I get what I came for," he replied seriously. The Captain nodded agreeably. "Alright, well don't be offended by what we're about to do next then." He made a gesture towards one of the guards holding a net gun. The guard fired it directly at Blackbeak! The net shot from the gun and instantly covered him and the young warrior. Blackbeak continued clutching onto his captive despite being trapped once again inside a net.

The guards proceeded to fly their capture towards the center of the city where the palace was located. They all wore anti-gravity amulets, which made pulling heavy objects through the air much easier for them. Blackbeak didn't understand why the guards didn't just give him one of their amulets and be on their way. He supposed there might be some sort of negative consequence for doing such a thing or perhaps they were harder to obtain then he had imagined. Of course these were all assumptions he kept them to himself while the guards continued to fly him and his captive through the giant open palace doors.

11. MOJO'S FLIGHT

Mojo was flying towards the Lake of Lost Souls as fast as his disguised raven body would carry him. He didn't want to be seen in his true form. He knew there were too many selfish individuals in the world who would try their absolute best to capture a genie if they ever had the chance! Why he chose a raven form of all things was beyond him and he really didn't see a reason to transform himself into any other bird. After all, he could have just as easily disguised himself as a pigeon, a robin or practically any other creature imaginable but he really didn't think much of it as he continued flying towards the Lake of Lost Souls. His thoughts were focused on Misty. Even though they had only known each-other for such a short time, he was starting to have some pretty deep feelings for her. He didn't used to have these types of feelings for anyone back before she had set him free. Perhaps there was something about being a freed genie that gave him more human like qualities? He noticed his emotional nature becoming deeper than it had ever been previously; not only towards people but towards the whole world around him as well. Even the trees, air and setting sun all seemed to provide a sense of inner peace and harmony that he had never experienced before. He was starting to understand how humans felt on a different level of being and was taking it all in with the greatest degree of satisfaction.

After flying for what seemed like an eternity, Mojo finally spotted the Lake of Lost Souls in the distance. The sun was setting; leaving a beautiful array of orange and purple clouds reflecting from the shimmering lake below. Mojo became slightly entranced by its beauty as he spotted the city of fairies standing majestically at the lake's center. He hovered in midair for a moment, taking in the dazzling view of all the little homes and shops sitting on top of the water at the center of the lake. The entire lake was surrounded by trees and would have been a hard place to find without any kind of guidance. "Good thing I have a map or I would have been completely lost trying to get here," he thought gratefully.

Mojo spotted the palace at the center of the city. Hoping to find Misty there, he continued flapping his way towards it. "I hope Misty isn't in any kind of trouble already," he thought anxiously.

12. BLACKBEAK'S CAPTURE

Seeing the long procession of guards dragging a captured raven through the air was quite a site for the palace onlookers. Many of the palace servants flying from point A to point B paused in mid-air just to watch the proceedings. A few of the servants accidently bumped into each-other in midair while being distracted by the long procession of guards. Many were extremely curious about the raven's presence and why the guards had captured it. Their thoughts connected with tales of Morganna's pet raven as they began to spread rumors amongst themselves.

The guard patrol wasted no time escorting the raven to the Throne Room entrance. Before entering, the Captain announced their presence to the two guards standing just outside large double-door entrance. One of them told the Captain to wait while he announced their arrival to the Queen.

Upon hearing of the raven's presence, the Queen quickly dismissed her audience standing around her inside the Throne Room.

She apologized for the interruption in their daily proceedings and explained that she had an urgent private matter to attend to. The courtiers hastily cleared out of the large elaborate room in an orderly fashion. The guard patrol proceeded to fly the captured raven inside the Throne Room for questioning.

The Queen flew over to where the guards had sat the net down with Blackbeak and the captured guard inside it. She glanced down at the raven and guard both trapped inside the net on the hard marble floor. Crossing her arms sternly, she began to speak. "I know why you're here raven. I've been tracking your whereabouts for quite some time." Blackbeak looked shocked. "Why such interest your majesty," he asked curiously? "That's a great question Blackbeak. Yes, I even know your name! That might surprise you but I don't expect you to remember much after what that horrible witch put you through." Blackbeak seemed surprised. "What witch? I hope you're not referring to Misty. She has been awfully good to me your Highness." The Queen glanced at him pitifully. "Before I go on, let's make your situation a little more comfortable." She looked towards the guards. "Take this net off him and bring a wooden perch for him to stand on," she commanded. Immediately the guards left the room to fulfill her request.

"I hope you don't mind having a little conversation with me Blackbeak. We have much to discuss," she said gently. "It would be an honor your grace," he replied politely. Blackbeak observed the Queen to have radiant white teeth, long blond hair draping neatly down her back, deep sapphire eyes and a slender body build. Her facial expressions were easy to read due to her prominent facial features. A long white and yellow dress covered her body down to her ankles. A golden crown studded with brightly colored jewels sat atop her head and sparkled from the sunlight shining through the tall arched windows surrounding the entire Throne Room. "You look absolutely radiant my lady," Blackbeak said flatteringly. "Thank you raven; that's very kind of you to say," replied the Queen with a smile.

A guard came groveling through the doorway carrying a heavy

wooden perch in both hands. "Where shall I put this your majesty," he asked gasping for breath? "That perch must be a lot heavier than it looks," thought Blackbeak as he watched the struggling guard attempt to move it closer to him. "Set it next to my throne so that we may both be comfortable during our conversation," the Queen commanded promptly. "With pleasure your grace," replied the guard as he picked up the heavy perch to move it again. The Queen motioned the raven to follow her up a few steps towards her throne. Just like her crown, her throne was made of pure gold and inlayed with many brightly colored jewels as well. A lavishly bright purple cushion sat on the seat of it for the obvious reason of making the simple act of sitting a much more pleasant one. The Queen noticed Blackbeak eyeing her golden throne as she sat on it. "Gold is nice to look at but sitting on it all day can get a bit tiresome," she said with a smile. The two guards smiled as well out of pure politeness.

The guard managed to place the heavy wooden perch next to the Queen's golden throne. Blackbeak flew over to land on the "T" shaped piece of wood. He stood just a little lower than the Queen's head. He knew it must have been designed that way on purpose just so she could continually stare down at him during their conversation. It didn't bother him to much though because he didn't plan on being there for any long period of time anyways.

"I know you don't remember a whole lot about who you truly are Blackbeak," said the Queen gently. "In order to have a real and meaningful conversation with you, I must help revive your memory." She glanced over at the Captain of the Guard standing between her throne and the double-door entrance. "Fetch me my court wizard Captain," she commanded sharply. "And take all of your guards with you. I want my wizard here as quickly as possible." The Captain nodded agreeably. "It will be done your majesty." He commanded all of his soldiers to follow him towards the exit to help him search for the court wizard.

With the Throne Room doors now closed, Blackbeak observed himself and the Queen to be quite alone. The Queen was quite aware of this fact as well. "I need you to keep anything that is said between us a private matter," she commanded urgently. "Do you understand?" "Don't worry your Highness. I'm good at keeping secrets," he replied confidently. The Queen smiled. "That's good because what I'm about to tell you may come as a complete surprise to you!" Blackbeak continued staring at her seriously. "I'm quite calm under pressure your grace. I'm sure I can handle whatever it is you have to tell me," he replied reassuringly.

Just as the Queen was about to tell Blackbeak the shocking news, a loud shattering sound pierced the air followed by a hot ball of flame jetting through the tall arched window directly behind her golden throne from where she was sitting. Shattered glass flew across the room as Misty zoomed through the open window riding her broomstick hurriedly though the air! Blackbeak spotted her instantly. "MISTY," he squawked with surprise and excitement! Before the Queen could react to the intrusion, Misty shot a freezing spell from her pointed wand directly at her. The Queen instantly froze in place; a look of shock permanently etched on her face. Misty landed on the shiny marble floor next to Blackbeak. "Are you okay my friend," she asked with concern? Blackbeak nodded. "I'm fine Misty. In fact, me and the Queen were actually having a really great conversation before you came barging in here." He noticed a little fairy hovering above her shoulder. "Who is your new friend," he asked curiously? "Oh, this is…." Pixie tried interrupting Misty before she could finish introducing her but it was too late. Misty had already said her name out loud. Despite the fairy Queen being frozen into place, she still heard the name quite clearly. Pixie turned towards the frozen Queen only to watch her face turn a raging red! Pixie knew she had crossed a line the second she came barging into the Queen's Throne Room. Misty quickly made the connection between the two of them. "Oh Pixie, I'm sorry. I may have said too much. I hope I haven't gotten you in too much trouble." Pixie was sitting on top of Misty's left shoulder. "Well, I could be banished from this land forever but I was never really fond of this place anyways," she said in a lightly disappointed sort of way.

"Looks like we've got a lot of catching up to do Misty,"

Blackbeack squawked. "Unfortunately, we don't have much time. The guards will return soon. They went to find the court wizard. Apparently, he's going to help restore some highly important memories I've long since forgotten." Misty frowned. She knew exactly what memories he would be getting back because Pixie had so diligently filled her in on the details during their flight to the palace. Quickly forming a plan, Misty walked over to the frozen Queen and stood next to her stunned body. "Alright your majesty, I'll make you a deal. If you agree to pardon all of us for what we've done here today, I'll unfreeze you and let your court wizard restore Blackbeak's long forgotten memories. Do we have a deal? Blink twice if you agree." The Queen managed to blink twice and Misty unfroze the rest of her body as promised.

Before saying anything, the Queen began rubbing her arms as if trying to thaw ice out of her frozen veins. Finally, she glanced up at Misty and then over at Pixie. She glared at Pixie furiously! "We've got a lot to talk about little missy! Yes, I will pardon you for barging in here and aiding this witch but we both know you've got a lot of explaining to do!" The Queen noticed herself becoming emotionally explosive. Taking a deep breath inward, she turned her focus towards Blackbeak and the rude witch who had just shattered her delicate stain glass window. "What is your name my dear," she asked Misty politely? "My name is Misty. Blackbeak and I came from the Forbidden Forest. We have traveled far to see you my lady. I sent him ahead to discuss a possible trade deal with you your eminence." A look of curiosity crossed the Queen's face. "A trade deal," she asked curiously? Misty continued. "We are on a quest and need a couple of anti-gravity amulets to help aid us along our journey," she replied seriously. The Queen glanced down at the floor and then back up at Misty. "I'm sure we can arrange a trade of some sort," she replied confidently. Two guards suddenly opened the Throne Room doors and stepped inside. The court wizard followed behind them mumbling something about how he is was never given enough notice for meetings like this. He was dressed in a long purple robe embroidered with randomly disbursed golden stars throughout. A long white beard drooped past his chest and he carried a tall brown walking staff made of wood. Even though his long beard gave the impression of being old, the sheer amount of energy in his step gave the impression that he might be much younger than anyone would suspect.

"Your Highness; I must protest being summoned so suddenly," the wizard bellowed in his deep gravelly voice. "A wizard is not a mere commoner and should not be treated as such. However, since I am here I might as well ask…what seems to be the problem," he asked with a grunt? "I'm sorry for the short notice Morpheus but this is a matter of emergency," replied the Queen calmly. "Sorry to interrupt," said one of the guards standing next to him. "I couldn't help but notice the broken window and shattered glass lying all over the floor. Is everything okay your Highness? Shall I remove this witch from your presence," he asked; pointing a finger at Misty. "Thank you Phil but I shall be fine," replied the Queen. "My unexpected guests decided to drop in unannounced while you were away fetching Morpheus for me. Thank you both for your loyal and dedicated service but I currently require privacy. Please leave us and the wizard to continue our business in private," she commanded. "As you wish your Majesty," Phil replied gesturing the other guard to follow him outside the Throne Room.

After leaving, they shut the giant double-doors behind them. The Queen turned towards her court wizard. "Thank you for coming Morpheus. I know it was unexpected but it will all make sense soon. Morpheus, meet Blackbeak. Blackbeak, meet Morpheus." Morpheus took a good look at the jet black raven standing on the wooden perch in front of him. As if a light suddenly switched on in his brain, he gasped in awe! "You're not suggesting this to be the same raven who…" The Queen interrupted his train of thought. "Yes Morpheus, that is exactly what I am suggesting but there is only one way to know for sure." Morpheus knew exactly what needed to be done. He reached into the inside of his purple robe and pulled out a small vile filled with a green glowing substance. "This is Memory Serum," he said to Blackbeak. "A drop of this will help you remember everything from your past; the way it truly happened. Will you allow me to administer a drop of it to your tongue Blackbeak?" Blackbeak nodded. "I'm not afraid of my past," he replied while opening his beak. The wizard tipped the small vile just enough to let a single drop fall into his open mouth and onto his small raven tongue.

Instantly, Blackbeak fell asleep as if someone had just knocked him out cold! Losing consciousness, he fell off the wooden perch and onto the hard marble floor below. Long forgotten memories quickly began to resurface. He pictured himself arguing with a young witch named Morganna. He was telling her that he wouldn't mind going with the fairy Queen to help protect her city. However, Morganna insisted that he stay with her because she didn't want to lose him forever. He kept saying that protecting an entire people was far more important than being with her. Tears fell from Morganna's eyes as she reached for her long black wand inside her robe. Pointing it at a nearby window, she spoke the spell "OPANNO COPRANNO" as it opened instantly. Between her tears, she managed to speak. "Fine Rueland, if you want to leave then go ahead. Get out of here!" The raven flew from the top of the old dusty bookshelf and onto Morganna's shoulder. He squawked in her ear. "I don't want to leave you Morganna but I have the power to protect the whole Fairy Kingdom and they need my help." Morganna turned her head to look into his emerald green eyes. "The fairy Queen will keep you in her service forever Rueland. She won't allow you to leave her kingdom ever again for fear of being attacked by the bat army while you are away. We'll most likely never see each-other again Rueland but if you really must go then I understand," she said sadly. A single tear dripped from her right cheek as she looked away from him. "I'll miss you as well Morganna," he replied with an equal amount of sadness in his voice. He hated leaving Morganna in such a sad condition but knew that a greater cause beckoned him onward. He began flying towards the open window nearby. A trail of sparkling silver light hit his backside almost immediately after exiting through the open window. The blast of silver light trailed back to Morganna's outstretched wand. Instantly, Blackbeak forgot who he was and where he was heading. He kept flapping his wings desperately hoping he was only experiencing a temporary laps of memory. Flying towards the Forbidden Forest, he eventually landed on the window ledge of a small cottage in the middle of the forest. He didn't know whose cottage it belonged to but it seemed like a safe place to land.

Misty was doing some manual cleaning with her broom when she noticed the lone raven perched just outside her kitchen window. She opened it and let him inside. Being completely exhausted from his long flight, Blackbeak fell fast asleep.

The truth serum gently began to wear off as Blackbeak slowly regained his consciousness. He found himself standing on the wooden perch inside the Queen's Throne Room once again. He immediately began connecting the dots in his mind in an attempt to remember who he was and where he had come from before meeting Misty inside the Forbidden Forest. Glancing upward, he quickly spotted a group of familiar faces staring down at him. "Blackbeak, you're awake," Misty shouted excitedly! "Do you remember who you are now," the Fairy Queen asked inquisitively? "I do," replied Blackbeak seriously. "I also remember that you're the one who gave me the name Blackbeak," he said looking at Misty. "I gave you that name because you couldn't remember anything about yourself when I first found you," replied Misty. "His real name is Rueland," the Queen replied before continuing. "He is called that because his one magic power is enough to rule any land that he so chooses. However, he has never used his powers to their full capacity. This is why I have gone to such great lengths to restore your memory Rueland. I want you to do me the honor of protecting the Lake of Lost Souls from any possible intruders that may attack us. I will reward you handsomely for such valiant efforts of course," she said diplomatically. Rueland's gaze drifted off into a random corner of the room as he considered the possibilities. "Your Majesty, I don't know how to use my power and even if I did, it sounds like it would be a lifetime of service like Morganna was saying," replied Blackbeak seriously. The Queen glanced at her court wizard worriedly. The wizard stared down at Blackbeak thoughtfully. "I can help you remember your powers so you can use them to their fullest extent," he said enthusiastically.

"May I have some time to consider your offer," Blackbeak asked seriously? "Of course," replied the Queen. "But until then, I insist that you stay here in the palace with me. My wizard will escort you to your chambers Rueland. I hope you don't mind if I call you by your true name," she said politely. "Not at all," replied Blackbeak even though it wasn't really a question. He was still getting used to hearing his real name. "What about my friend Misty? Can she stay here too," he asked hopefully? "Of course she can," replied the Queen generously. "We have plenty of rooms in the palace. I'm sure we can spare another one for her as well," she replied with a smile. The Queen's gaze turned towards Pixie who was now sitting on Misty's shoulder. "Don't think I've forgotten about you little missy. We are going to have a serious talk Pixie. Morpheus, please escort Rueland and Misty to their chambers. I'm going to speak with Pixie alone," she commanded agitatedly.

"Follow me Misty and Rueland," Morpheus said calmly. "You'll enjoy your new quarters I'm sure," he said stroking his long white beard. Pixie reached into the little purse she carried around her shoulders and grabbed a handful of sparkling Pixie Dust from it. She threw it over her left shoulder and onto her fairy wings attached to her back. Flapping her wings, she hovered over to where the Queen was standing and landed on the marble floor next to her. "Your majesty, I did not mean any harm by helping the witch get here," she said humbly. "I know that Pixie. I am more concerned about the quality of your Pixie Dust. Many fairies have fallen from the skies lately due to your non-potent mixture of Pixie Dust! Many have fallen into water or have been caught by other concerned fairies who saw it happen. Unfortunately, not all of your Pixie Dust users have been so fortunate. Many have even fallen to their deaths Pixie! I should sentence you to a lifetime in prison young lady! However, seeing as the entire fairy people must continue to rely on your Pixie Dust in order to fly; I am willing to try and remedy this entire situation." The Queen took a second to regain her well-mannered composure before continuing. "Have you been using quality ingredients in your mixtures lately," she asked inquisitively? Pixie glanced downwards towards the floor. "I'm ashamed to say I may have cut a few corners lately but that's because some ingredients have been extremely hard to find! For example, the Elderberry's are not as abundantly available as they once were and when I do find them, they are much too ripe to use effectively. But since it's all I have available, their lack of potency ends up creating a much shorter lifespan for the Pixie Dust as a whole," Pixie admitted carefully.

The Queen frowned. "I am deeply concerned about this Pixie. I'm not only concerned for the safety of my people but also because my spies have informed me of a dark fairy now living among us. He's a thief of the worst kind Pixie! We both know that honey and honeycomb are key ingredients for making Pixie Dust. Without them, we might as well sprinkle good old fashioned dirt on our wings and be done with it," she said sarcastically. "Who is this dark fairy you speak of your majesty," Pixie asked curiously? "He goes by the name of Drake," answered the Queen. "I've sent multiple guard patrols out to capture him and they haven't returned yet. That was many months ago and I can't spare any more. The remainder of them are needed here to defend the city against the Bat King and his army. The Bat King's army is ruthless and we never know when he will attack again. This is why we need Rueland's memory to return. He has the power to defend our fragile city against the bat army but can't do so until he remembers how to use his powers again. Our army will be completely useless if they can't fly Pixie. That is why we need the Pixie Dust to work like it should."

The Queen continued seriously. "Of course, we can always use the anti-gravity amulets to fly but unfortunately the emerald gem found inside them is far too rare to find enough for our entire army to wear. I've traveled to the Dwarf Kingdom in search of obtaining more emeralds for our anti-gravity amulets and they simply haven't mined enough for our entire army to use. Rumor has it that there is an entire city made from emeralds somewhere nearby but no one has ever found it twice in a row. Apparently, a dark wizard managed to turn the entire city completely invisible before anyone could trail back to it the second time. Anyways, the point is that we're stuck using Pixie Dust to fly around for now and we need every ingredient possible to make it happen! This is why we must find the honeycomb thief before our people are rendered completely helpless! Without the proper ingredients to make Pixie Dust, the Bat King's army will destroy our entire city Pixie!" Pixie shook with fear. She understood what the Queen was telling her and it troubled her deeply. "Do you know where Drake is hiding now," she asked? "None of my spies have found him yet unfortunately," replied the Queen. "However, many crop growers and tavern keepers have all confirmed the same rumor…They tell me Drake is currently trapping bees and stealing honeycomb in the outlying fields of Nectarville. I'm sure you can imagine the large number of bees who pollinate the countless rows of fruit trees in that town." Pixie nodded agreeably. "So, if we find Drake, how are we supposed to convince him to stop capturing bees and give up his large stash of stolen honeycomb," she asked with concern in her voice? The Queen stared at Pixie solemnly. "Capturing Drake could be incredibly dangerous Pixie. I'm more concerned with finding his large stash of stolen honey and honeycomb in order to help recover them. Remember, the whole point of this mission is to recover enough ingredients to make enough Pixie Dust for an entire army! The army must fly Pixie! So here's my plan…If you ever find Drake, tell him you're a bee and honeycomb seller on the black-market and that you are interested in buying his entire stash at the lowest price possible. Try setting up a time and place to meet with him; preferably at his place of residence. From there, our forces can stealthily move in to recapture the millions of bees and large amounts of honeycomb he has stolen from hundreds of merchants and bee keepers throughout the outlying villages."

Pixie thought over the plan for a moment. "What if he sets up a meeting at a place other than where he has stashed all of his stolen goods? Also, if I am going to buy bees from him to sell on the black-market then I'll need a large amount of money your Highness," she replied worriedly. The Queen looked back at her confidently. "If the first meeting is not at his secret layer then continue to set up meetings with him to buy more and more of his bees and honeycomb until he trusts you enough to invite you back to wherever he is keeping them. I will provide you with a small fortune of rubies to buy whatever you need," the Queen replied encouragingly. "What if Drake asks me where I got all of my rubies from," Pixie asked timidly? "Tell him that you've sold enough bees on the black-market to become quite wealthy. Tell him your main buyers are filthy rich dwarves who enjoy honey harvesting and orchard trolls who need bees to pollinate their fruit trees." Pixie smiled. "I like your plan your majesty. Would you mind if I took my new friend Misty with me," she asked politely? The Queen smiled back at her. "By all means, take Misty with you. I'm sure you two could protect each-other fairly well. I'm tempted to send Rueland with you as well for protection. He's not entirely aware of how to use his protective powers to their fullest extent just yet but I'm sure with a little more training he'll soon come around. I'm hoping Morpheus will teach him quickly so the kingdom will be safe again from the Bat King's army," said the Queen seriously. "That sounds like a great plan," Pixie agreed. The Queen continued. "Well, let's get some rubies for you to take on your journey then," she said joyfully. She called out for her two guards standing just outside the Throne Room. One of them stepped inside immediately. "Yes, my Queen. How may I serve you," he asked with a bow? "Fetch me my Royal Treasurer immediately," she commanded. "Yes, your grace," he replied before marching back towards the exit. The Queen turned to face Pixie again. "My royal accountant will retrieve the small fortune of rubies for your journey ahead. After all, I don't want Drake thinking you're a charlatan," she said with a laugh. Pixie gave a nervous chuckle. "I shall have to dress the part I'm sure." "Not to worry," replied the Queen. Just go buy yourself some outdated clothes from the farmers market after I give you your rubies. Also, I'm sure you'll have no trouble acting the part of a shady salesman my dear," she stated confidently. Pixie wasn't sure whether or not to take that as a compliment so she kept quiet.

The Queen continued speaking with Pixie for a good half hour before the guard finally returned with the palace treasurer. He was a slender looking fellow with dark brown hair neatly combed and parted on the left side. He looked slightly taller than the average fairy and was equipped with the standard set of wings every fairy had been given at birth. He was young and full of energy. He wore dark brown colored pants that tucked into his tall leather boots, a white V-neck shirt that tucked into his pants and a three point brown hat with a tall red feather standing tall from its top. He smiled at Pixie. His teeth were white as pearls and Pixie couldn't help but blush a little as he held out his hand to shake hers. "Hi, I'm Andrew," he said confidently. "And you are?" Pixie began to stutter. "I'm p-p-p-pixie," she said. She reached out to accept his handshake as she stared into his gorgeous hazel eyes. His confident smile combined with everything else absolutely captivated her. It suddenly became difficult for her to say anything at all.

"The Queen tells me I am to provide you with a substantial amount of rubies from the treasury," said Andrew coolly. Pixie was far too stunned by Andrew's sheer attractiveness to respond coherently. Somehow she managed to nod as he continued speaking. "Considering the incredible sum of rubies the Queen wants me to give you, I would like to make absolutely sure they don't fall into the wrong hands. That is why I have brought this special case along with me." A long brown leather strap crossed Andrew's chest which Pixie hadn't even noticed up until then. Pulling it over his head, Andrew revealed a large black briefcase that had been hiding behind his back the entire time. The briefcase had two golden hinged locks holding it together on both ends and a six digit spin dial combination lock at its center. "To open the hinged locks, you will need the six digit combination," said Andrew. "This black box cannot be opened by magic of any kind. It's also important to remember that magic alone can never transform anything into a genuine ruby; which is why they are so valuable!" Andrew turned his back briefly on Pixie and the Queen while he turned each of the six combination dials to their correct numbers. Turning back around, he addressed the Queen directly. "My Queen, would you provide a table for us to sit this case on please," he asked politely? "Of course Andrew," she replied graciously.

The Queen retrieved her wand from a deep pocket located on the side of her long white and yellow dress. The pocket was built into the dress in such a way that even Pixie hadn't noticed its presence until now. Pointing her wand at the shattered glass still lying on the floor from where Misty had barged through; the Queen spoke the spell "TABELLO FORMELLO." Almost instantaneously a thousand bits of shattered glass rose into the air, came together and quickly formed a solid glass table right in front of them. "Thank you your grace," said Andrew politely. Sitting the black briefcase on top of the glass table, he opened it in front of Pixie and the Queen without letting them see the secret combination now showing on the spin dials. After opening it, he quickly mixed up the combination numbers so that no one in the room could see what they weren't supposed too. The shimmering deep red rubies caught their eyes immediately! Their warm red glow filled the case with a magnificence that could make a poor man drool. Andrew smiled and shut the case quickly. "They're magnificent I know! However, our main objective is to keep them safe so that no one steals them from you Pixie. How many people do you plan on taking with you on your journey?" Pixie began thinking. "Well, I was hoping to take my new friend Misty with me." Andrew nodded. "Considering the fact that this case holds three and a half million credits worth of rubies, we will need to maintain the highest level of security possible throughout your journey. In order to do this, I am going to break the six digit combination up into three parts. I will give the first two digits to you Pixie. The next two digits will go to your friend Misty and the last two I will keep here with me." Pixie interjected. "But how will I communicate with you when I need the last two digits," she asked curiously? Andrew smiled. "I'm glad you asked." He reached down to where the closed black briefcase was sitting on the table and moved the rotating handle back and forth three times while whispering the phrase; "JEWELS ARE FOR FOOLS." A tiny secret compartment suddenly opened up on top of the closed case. Andrew reached inside and pulled a pair of identical looking wrist bands from within. Pixie looked at them closely. The bands were made from small black obsidian arrowheads all strung together with a stretchy kind of fabric allowing them to expand and retract comfortably based on the wearer's wrist size. Each tiny arrowhead held a small emerald stone at its center. "We will be able to communicate with these," said Andrew seriously. "We call them Jargon Bands." Slipping one of the bands onto his left wrist, he gave the matching one to Pixie. She slipped hers over her left wrist as well. He continued. "If you need to communicate with me for any reason, simply touch your Jargon Band and say the words; "Andrew my darling, I would love to have dinner with you tonight" and that should work out perfectly," he said with a laugh. "Go ahead and give it a try if you'd like," he said with a grin.

Pixie smiled back at him as she held the Jargon Band up to her mouth and spoke into it. "Andrew my darling, I would love to have dinner with you tonight." Andrew cracked up laughing. "Why that's awfully sweet of you Pixie. Would this evening at sunset work for you?" Pixie chuckled. "Sounds like fun. But I should probably ask….what's the real password? Andrew continued laughing. "Alright, you got me Pixie. The real password is JIBBER JABBER CHITTER CHATTER," he said seriously. Instantly, each emerald inside each arrowhead began glowing a bright green color! Andrew leaned in and spoke into his Jargon Band. "Testing, testing, one, two, three….," he said lightheartedly. Pixie could hear his voice coming from her Jargon Band even though he was standing in the same room with her. She smiled and spoke into her Jargon Band as well. "Wow, that's amazing Andrew. I assume this is how I'll get the last two digits to the briefcase when I need them," she asked? Andrew nodded. "Yep, so just to recap; you'll take the first two digits of the combination, Misty will take the middle two and I will have the last two. When it comes time to actually open the case to retrieve the rubies, contact me through your Jargon Band and I will give you the last two digits to open the briefcase. Also, you'll need to give this other Jargon Band to Misty when you get the chance so she can communicate with me as well." Handing Pixie a second Jargon Band to give to Misty, he smiled charmingly at her. Are we clear on everything," he asked confidently? Pixie nodded. "Everything except where we'll be going out tonight," she replied with a blush.

13. TWO SCHEEMING GUARDS

The two guards standing just outside the Throne Room had heard everything that had been said. They spoke amongst themselves about how dull and boring their lives really were when compared with the grand adventures Misty and Pixie would soon be going on. The amount of rubies Pixie would be carrying with her didn't escape their attention either. They couldn't help but become jealous of the little "non-deserving fairy" who would be carrying more rubies with her than they made in a year! Fantasies flooded their minds with images of what they would do with three and a half million credits of rubies. Eventually, greed and jealously got the better of them as they began to brainstorm possible ways of taking the little briefcase away from Pixie without anyone ever catching them. However, they also knew it would require all six digits to open the combination lock as well. Various schemes continued to hatch between them until they eventually came to the conclusion that they would have to get Blackbeak to do their dirty work for them. They figured that since the Queen already trusted him she would never suspect him of any kind of shady activity. The guards snuck away from their posts just long enough to go find the bird. They figured that no one would notice their absence for a while anyways.

Blackbeak was snoozing on his wooden perch enjoying a deep nap when his chamber doors gently cracked open. Quickly and quietly the guards entered his room and threw a net over him before he could wake from his slumber. One of the guards lit a few candles located in various places around the room so everyone could see each-other better. "What is the meaning of this highly rude intrusion," squawked Blackbeak as he quickly woke from his slumber? The guard holding the net gun wasted no time launching the large net over the raven and quickly closed it shut so he wouldn't have a chance to escape. "Look raven, I don't like this anymore than you but the Queen has sent us here to do her bidding and we want to make sure you comply with her demands," he lied confidently. "She wants you to know she doesn't completely trust your friends Misty and Pixie. She wants to make sure they accomplish her bidding of recapturing the stolen bees and honeycomb from the dark fairy Drake. She is giving them a large amount of rubies held inside a six digit combination briefcase to trade with him in exchange for the stolen goods. The first two numbers will be given to Misty. The middle two numbers will be given to Pixie and the last two will be held by Andrew the Treasurer. The Queen demands that you discreetly retrieve the first four digits of the combination from Misty and Pixie before they leave on their adventure. You must then give them to us for safe keeping. Pixie will get the last two digits from Andrew when the time comes. Apparently, Andrew won't give Pixie the entire combination for fear of someone trying to steal the briefcase from her. Once you have obtained the first four digits of the combination from Misty and Pixie, you are required to report them to us for safe keeping. The Queen feels this is a necessary precaution to help ensure the safety of the large number of rubies that Pixie will be carrying. Do you understand Blackbeak," the guard asked confidently? Blackbeak nodded. "I understand sir but I don't understand why the Queen wouldn't tell me this herself considering the dire importance of the situation." "She's a busy person," replied one of the guards persuasively. "She has many matters to deal with so she occasionally sends us to do her bidding for her," lied the guard. Blackbeak nodded again. "I understand gentlemen. Thank you for passing the message on to me. I will be sure to give you the four digits as soon as I find out what they are," he replied reassuringly. "Thank you raven; your service and cooperation is much appreciated. We're sorry to have used the net gun on you but it was an extra precaution we had to take. You understand I hope." The guard holding the net gun released Blackbeak from the net surrounding his body. "Once again, I'm sorry for the inconvenience," he said apologetically. Both guards turned to leave. "Um, excuse me. What are your names," Blackbeak asked inquisitively? The guards turned back around to face him as one of them responded. "I am Phil and this is Bill," said Phil. Blackbeak nodded his black feathered head. "Aw, rhyming names….that should be easy to remember," he replied lightly. Both guards nodded and turned back around to exit the premises without delay.

14. THE DUPLICATE RAVEN

Night had fallen as Mojo finally arrived outside the palace walls. He couldn't believe how tired his transformed raven body was feeling. "I'm a genie," he thought to himself. "I shouldn't be feeling this tired. Perhaps something about being free is causing me to have more human-like qualities," he wondered curiously? In the distance, he spotted a dim light flickering from an open window in the upper west wing of the palace. Landing on the window ledge, he peered inside. He spotted two small fairies speaking with each-other; a lady and a man whom he had never seen before. A long pair of flowing red drapes stood near the tall arched window. He quickly concealed himself behind them in an attempt to determine whether the two unknown fairies in front of him were friend or foe.

"Alright Pixie, the two middle digits you will need to open the briefcase are 2 and 4 in that order. Can you remember that?" "Of course," replied Pixie. "And thank you for the lovely date Andrew. It was absolutely delightful. Perhaps we could do it again sometime," she asked hopefully? "Of course," Andrew replied cheerfully. "But I hope next time you won't be so mean to me," he said jokingly. "Mean?" Pixie laughed. "I was only swatting a nasty fly off your face," she said teasingly. "Those invisible flies sure know how to get around," he replied jokingly. "Oh you…" Pixie was suddenly interrupted by a sudden gust of wind blowing the nearby curtains high into the air. The motion of the curtains moving drew their attention towards the nearby open window. Mojo's cover was literally blown away! He decided to make like a tree and leave before the palace guards were called in after him. Turning around, he quickly flew back out the window from where he had come in. Andrew spotted him immediately. "Hey you, get back here!" Throwing a handful of Pixie Dust over his shoulder and onto his wings, he chased the escaping raven out into the cold midnight air.

Mojo was shocked at just how fast the little fairy behind him could fly! Andrew stretched his right hand forward to grab Mojo's raven foot dangling in front of his face and barely missed his target as it swerved to the left. "I'll get you raven," Andrew screamed! "You won't get away with what you know." Mojo saw a nearby clock tower just in front of him and began flying loops around it. After winding around it for the fourth time, Andrew felt quite dizzy but was absolutely determined to catch the spy raven flying in front of him. Suddenly Mojo took a nosedive straight towards the ground! Andrew was right on his tail! The cobblestone street continued to get closer and closer as they plummeted towards it. Mojo pulled out of the dive a mere second before smashing into it! Andrew wasn't so lucky. He couldn't pull out of the dive fast enough and smashed directly into the hard packed cobblestone street below! He went out like a light.

Andrew woke up inside the Circle of Healing and instantly knew where he was because of the glowing green orbs circling around his head. They were emitting rays of green light that spurted into his injured head. "Just lye still sir," said a gentle female voice from behind him. "You are being healed. It will take some time but your head sustained a nasty injury from smashing into the cobblestones. My name is Luna." Andrew glanced up to see a beautiful fairy standing above him. She had long brown hair that draped down past her waist. She was slender with a white complexion. Her eyes were a deep blue color like the ocean and he felt himself gazing into them far longer than he had intended too. Luna smiled at him. "And you are?" Somehow he managed to break the trance she had cast on him. "Um, I'm Andrew," he replied sheepishly. "I'm the treasurer for the Queen's Accounting House." Luna sat down on the same soft mat Andrew was now lying on and gently slid her right arm around his shoulders. "Do you think you can stand up Andrew," she asked gently? Andrew began lifting his legs and draped his left arm around her shoulders for support as he slowly stood up. Using Luna as a crutch, he managed to balance himself alongside her with both feet planted firmly on the soft mat beneath him. "Thank you Luna," he said gratefully. "I'm glad you're here to help me." Luna smiled. "It's my job to help the injured fairies. I do the best I can." Andrew couldn't help but notice how incredible her pearly white teeth were.

Andrew came to the conclusion that he had become a little too love struck with women lately; first with Pixie and now with Luna. "I can't understand why the Queen's accountant would be out smashing himself into cobblestone streets," she said teasingly. Andrew smiled. "Well, I have a deep fascination with cobblestones and really just wanted to kiss one but perhaps I was moving too fast for it to handle," he replied jokingly. Luna laughed with him before becoming serious again. "No really Andrew; what happened out there? You got me curious now."

Andrew continued. "Alright, the truth is that I was chasing someone who discovered a secret of mine." Luna suddenly became even more fascinated. "Oh, now I'm even more curious. You can tell me. I'm really good at keeping secrets,' she replied reassuringly. "Well, I will tell you that it has to do with huge amounts of rubies and someone overhearing certain information to which he was not privy to," Andrew replied thoughtfully. "Ohh…this person is a HE," Luna teased. Andrew laughed. "I've said too much already," he replied jokingly. A sudden burst of pain shot through his head again. "Oh, my head is hurting again," he said weakly. "You should lay back down," replied Luna delicately. Gently grabbing him around the shoulders, she slowly helped him lie back down on the pillow lying beneath his head. The green orbs around him continued to shoot green healing light into his injured head.

"Just take a little nap here," Luna said softly. "You'll recover soon, I promise." Before Andrew could drift off any further, Luna reached into her pocket to retrieve a Jargon Band. She held it out for him to see. "I know you're tired Andrew but the muscular guard who found and brought you here also found this torn band lying next to you. Is it yours by chance?" Andrew was too hazy and tired to think clearly. All he managed to say before drifting off to sleep was; "no I don't think so."

Luna thought to herself. "Well, if he can think clearly enough to remember he was an accountant for the Queen then he was probably telling the truth about this not being his Jargon Band." She rolled up her right loose hanging sleeve with her left hand and spoke a passcode into one of the Jargon Bands strapped across her wrist; "LOST AND FOUND." Hey Morpheus, I know you said to let you know if I found any lost magical objects here at the Circle of Healing. Apparently, this guy named Andrew says this isn't his Jargon Band so just thought I'd let you know in case you ever want to come and pick it up sometime." Morpheus's scratchy voice responded almost immediately. "Thank you Luna. I'll swing by and pick it up as soon as possible. I appreciate you letting me know." Luna nodded; "just happy to help Morpheus." She spoke the shutdown passcode before anything else could be said. "LOST AND FOUND, SHUT ER' DOWN." Immediately her Jargon Band stopped glowing green as the connection between them was instantly terminated.

Mojo continued flying around the city still trying to figure out what to do with the information he had just overheard. He wasn't sure what it all meant but knew it must have been important enough for a fairy to chase him around the city for it. He wasn't sure what significance the digits 2 and 4 had or what they should be used for. Circling back towards the castle he decided to make another attempt at locating Misty. He knew she must have reached the palace long before he had and he was absolutely determined to find out where she had gone to.

Flying towards the upper east wing of the palace, Mojo hoped to find something or someone there that might lead him to Misty. He spotted a glowing light glimmering from an arched window above him. Landing on the window's ledge, he peered inside. Two candles sat burning on a nearby nightstand as he made out the figure of a woman lying on a bed inside. She was much too tall to be a fairy and looked to be about the same height as Misty. Mojo suddenly became overly excited! "Could it be," he wondered anxiously? Using his genie powers to open the glass window, he quickly flew inside. Landing next to her bedside, he stared down at the sleeping girl below him. It was Misty alright! "She is just as beautiful as the day I gave her that ravishing new body," he thought to himself proudly. He took a moment to simply take in her exquisite beauty. Her delicate soft skin, long black hair and lushes red lips practically beckoned him to kiss her! He instantly transformed himself back into his genie form and ever so quietly leaned over her sleeping body.

Misty woke up instantly! Not knowing what was happening, she screamed at creepy intruder standing above her bed! "Shhhh…it's okay," said Mojo in a soft and reassuring voice. She looked up at him. "Mojo!" He put a finger to his lips. "Shhh...it's me darling," Mojo replied gently. Without much thought, she wrapped her arms around his outstretched neck and pulled him in towards her. "I thought I lost you," she said worriedly. "The bees gave me your message back at the Forbidden Forest," replied Mojo. Misty pulled him in for another kiss. One kiss led to another and then three. It wasn't long before they were making sweet passionate love together all night long.

15. PIXIE'S FURY

Pixie wasn't sure what happened to Andrew. She remembered him chasing that nosy eavesdropping raven outside her window. She would have flown after them but thought it best to leave the chasing to Andrew. She fell asleep shortly after the chase had begun and decided to piece things together in the morning when her energy would be higher.

Morning finally arrived as Pixie woke with the hope of finding Andrew somewhere in the castle. Flying down to the dining hall, she hoped to find him there eating breakfast. He wasn't there but just so it wasn't a total loss she decided to have the palace cook make her a bite to eat while she was there. A lovely looking fairy brought Pixie some freshly made biscuits and honey along with some freshly squeezed orange juice. "You're lucky to get honey. We've been running short lately and it's quickly becoming a rarity at the local market," she told Pixie after bringing her another glass of orange juice. Pixie thanked her for her kind service as her thoughts turned towards all the traveling she would soon be doing in order to find the dreaded Drake somewhere in Nectarville. She wanted to say goodbye to Andrew before leaving. Her date with him last night was truly a night to remember and she was having second thoughts about leaving him so soon.

Hustling through breakfast, she continued searching the palace grounds for Andrew. Her next stop was at the Accounting House located on the east side of the palace. It was a giant building held up by large granite pillars. Inscribed on top was the phrase; "House of Rubies." Pulling open one of the heavy double-doors, she rushed inside. Directly in front of her stood a wide and well-crafted marble desk. A young fairy woman with long brunet hair sat behind it. "Excuse me," said Pixie politely. "Do you know if Andrew is in today," she asked inquisitively? The beautiful brunet glanced up from the handful of parchment lying on her desk. "I'm sorry but Andrew hasn't checked in today. I'm not sure why. He was supposed verify a pressing matter regarding a recent exchange of rubies. I'm not sure where he is now," she said. "Well, if he comes in, could you please tell him that Pixie dropped by to ask about him," she asked hopefully? "Of course," replied the brunet cheerfully.

Pixie left the House of Rubies flying back outside onto the cobblestone streets. Not sure where else Andrew would have gone, she began contemplating various other places he might have ventured off too. "Let's see…the last time I saw him, he was flying after that pesky raven. Perhaps the raven flew back to his castle chambers for some rest." She quickly began flying back towards the palace to find Blackbeak's chambers in hopes of possibly finding Andrew there. Considering the large number of rooms inside the palace, she wasn't exactly sure which one Blackbeak was staying in. "Perhaps one of the guards on duty yesterday knows where his chambers is at," she thought hopefully. "After all, they did escort him and Misty to their sleeping quarters last night."

Since the palace entrance was always open, Pixie quickly made her way through the entrance and towards the Throne Room. She stopped to speak with the two guards standing just outside the doorway. She recognized them as the same two guards who had been on duty yesterday. She figured they would know where Blackbeak's chambers could be found. Bill and Phil looked surprised to see her. "What can we do for you," Phil asked curiously? Pixie glanced up at the much taller guard towering over her. He had short black hair and a slender body build. "I would like to speak with Blackbeak and was hoping you could tell me where his chambers are located," she said simply. Bill stepped forward. "I'm sure we could help you out young lady." Phil elbowed him in the side. "Absolutely, we'd love to help you mam but the thing is…we've actually been running low on Pixie Dust lately and would really hate to run out of it completely if ya know what I mean?" Pixie sighed. "Look fellers, just because I invented Pixie Dust doesn't mean I have an unlimited supply of it just lying around. In fact, I'm actually running low on it myself." Phil frowned. "Well that's a shame. It would really help us help you but we probably shouldn't share such confidential information with you anyways." Bill turned towards Phil. "Yea, you're right Phil. We should continue being the loyal and trustworthy guards we've always been. Giving out such confidential information would be a complete breach of trust and privacy." Pixie reached into her small purple purse dangling from around her left shoulder. Quickly opening it, she reached inside to retrieve a small handful of sparkling gold Pixie Dust. It glittered and shimmered as the light bounced off it. She held a handful out in front of her. "Oh alright; you may each have a small bit of it but don't think that I'm just loaded with this stuff!" Phil held both palms together in a cup-like motion as he reached out to accept the small handful from Pixie. Giving another small handful to Bill, she looked into her small purse only to find it almost empty. She held her purse out for the two guards to see the inside of it. "See what you've done! I'm almost out myself!" Her temper began to flare. "Alright, I gave you what you wanted…Now please take me to Blackbeak's chambers!" Both guards took off their metal helmets and carefully slid open a secret compartment inside the top of them. Slipping their Pixie Dust inside them, they quickly closed the small compartments and replaced their helmets on top of their heads. "A deal is a deal," Phil replied seriously. "Follow me young lady. Bill, stay here and guard the Throne Room if you please." He proceeded to escort Pixie towards Blackbeak's chambers while Bill continued to stand guard outside the Throne Room. Pixie followed Phil cautiously through a number of narrow hallways and up a long flight of stone steps towards Blackbeak's chambers.

Arriving at an arched wooden doorway, Phil knocked politely on the raven's chamber door. Since it was still early in the morning Pixie thought their chances of catching him there were pretty good before he decided to go anywhere. A few seconds passed before the raven squawked from inside. "Come in." Phil opened the door as they stepped inside. Blackbeak stood on a wooden perch next to the bed which he obviously wasn't going to use. A couple of lit candles stood next to him on top of a nightstand. An arched glass window embedded into the wall behind the bed allowed more light to seep into the dusty old room. "I just woke up," Blackbeak squawked tiredly. "What can I do for the two of you," he asked curiously? Pixie looked up at Phil towering over her. "Thank you for escorting me here good sir but I'd like to speak with Blackbeak privately now if you don't mind," she said politely. Phil nodded agreeably. Before turning to leave he shot Blackbeak a look that clearly said; "If you say anything about last night you will pay dearly raven!" "It's amazing how much can be said with a simple glance," Blackbeak thought considerately. "It was a pleasure assisting you madam," Phil said to Pixie on his way out. "Yea I'm sure it was," Pixie replied sarcastically. Phil closed the chamber doors behind him on his way out.

"Alright Blackbeak, fess up! What happened last night," Pixie asked accusingly?! Blackbeak thought she had somehow found out about the blackmailing incident with Phil and Will the night before. So he responded carefully. "I'm sorry Pixie I can't tell you. I'm sworn to secrecy." Pixie felt a boiling rage rise within her. "I don't like what happened any more than you do birdbrain! The combination is supposed to be a very big secret and you were spying on us the entire time raven!" Blackbeak fluttered his wings surprisingly. "I'm really not sure what you're talking about Pixie," he replied innocently? "Oh don't play dumb with me birdbrain," Pixie yelled! "Don't act like you didn't hide behind my curtains last night and discover the secret numbers of 2 and 4. Also, what the heck happened to Andrew? I've been searching all over for him," she demanded angrily! "I'm sorry Pixie, I still don't know what you're talking about," replied Blackbeak unknowingly. "Don't lie to me Blackbeak! You were snooping around my chambers last night, spying on me and Andrew!" Blackbeak didn't get flustered easily but was now becoming quite agitated. "Now see here young lady; I was here in my chambers last night and had a highly unpleasant visit from the guards during that time as well." Pixie looked at him sternly. "Okay bird, I'll ask the guards if you were here last night. I should have just asked Phil about it on our way up here," replied Pixie furiously. "Oh don't do that Pixie," said Blackbeak worriedly. "I'll get in more trouble than I already am." Pixie felt like strangling him but continued to keep her temper in check. "You better hope they verify your stupid story Blackbeak or I'll be back and you'll discover I'm being quite pleasant right now," she yelled furiously! Pixie made her way back towards the exit and stormed out with more vigor than two cats fighting over the last scrap of food!

Blackbeak didn't want Bill and Phil thinking he had snitched their blackmail story to Pixie or he really would be in a world of trouble. He also knew he had better leave the palace soon before the two scheming guards decided to pay him another visit. Flying through the open window nearby he began searching for Misty. "We need to leave this city as fast as possible," he thought seriously.

16. BLACKMAILING GUARDS

Misty was in the middle of catching Mojo up on all the latest events when suddenly a loud pecking noise came from her chamber window. Turning around to locate the source of the commotion, they found Blackbeak attempting to get their attention from outside the window. Pulling her wand from her robe, Misty muttered the phrase "OPANNO COPRANNO" as the window popped open to let him inside. Flying through the opening Blackbeak landed on top of a nearby nightstand. Misty was overjoyed to see her old friend again. "Blackbeak, I'm so happy to see you," she said excitedly! Mojo was currently in his normal genie form and decided to chime in as well. "I don't believe we've had the pleasure of meeting. My name is Mojo," he said enthusiastically. Blackbeak looked at him curiously. "You must be the genie Misty found in Claw's Cave. I'm sure glad she made it out alive!"

Mojo was about to respond but Blackbeak cut him short. "We need to get out of here Misty," he said frantically. "The guards will be looking for me soon!" "What why," Misty asked worriedly? "Because they want me to find the full combination to the briefcase and I'm sure they'll hunt me down if I don't get it for them. Also, Pixie is upset with me because she thinks I overheard the two digits Andrew gave her." Mojo suddenly realized the mixed-up mess he had gotten himself into. "I must confess something to both of you," he said seriously. "I'm the one who overheard Pixie's two secret numbers given to her while disguised as a raven. I eavesdropped on Pixie and Andrew's conversation last night and heard more than I should have." Misty looked at him seriously. "Oh, this isn't good Mojo." "You need to go find Pixie and Andrew and tell them that it wasn't Blackbeak who overheard them. It was you!" Mojo nodded. "I'll go tell them right away Misty." Mojo transformed back into his raven form and flew out the open window. Misty smacked the palm of her hand against her forehead. "So he transforms back into a raven…what an idiot!" Blackbeak nodded agreeably. "You think he would have learned a lesson by now," he replied dumbfounded.

Mojo remembered the nasty cobblestone crash Andrew had experienced and decided to fly towards the Circle of Healing in an attempt find him there. Upon landing, a beautiful brown-haired woman greeted him. "Is Andrew still here," he asked? "He went to visit the Queen," she responded gently. Mojo took flight again and headed back towards the palace Throne Room in hopes of finding him before his situation got any worse than it already was!

Flying through the open palace doors and straight to the Throne Room entrance, Phil and Bill watched Mojo land in front of them. Phil smirked. "Glad to see you again Blackbeak! We recently talked to Pixie. Good job covering up for last night but you're a horrible storyteller my friend. I mean, if you're going to tell a good cover story you should at least get your facts straight. For example, if you were hiding behind Pixie's drapes last night and she saw you then there's really no point in telling her why we came to visit you last night is there? See what I mean? Of course, we didn't want to give her a reason to suspect you of spying on her last night so we verified your stupid cover story. But come on, telling her it was probably another raven hiding behind her drapes….you can do better than that my friend. I hope you at least got Pixie's two digit code like we told you to get. You did get the code right?" Mojo nodded. This obvious mix-up between him and Blackbeak was becoming much more apparent. "I was actually wondering if either of you have seen Andrew lately," he asked hopefully? Bill looked at Phil. "Going straight to the source I see. Way to think ahead Blackbeak! Andrew requested an audience with the Queen this morning but we told him that her schedule was all booked up. After all, we wouldn't want him ratting you out for spying on him now would we? See, we really are on your side my friend. You just keep focusing on getting that briefcase combination for us!" Mojo glanced over their shoulders. "Where would Andrew be now," he asked curiously? "He would probably be at the House of Rubies or possibly visiting his new lady friend Pixie," replied Phil. "Thanks," Mojo responded gratefully. I shall try both of those places. "Good luck Blackbeak," said Phil encouragingly. "And make sure to keep us informed as soon as you get the full combo. Trust me, you don't want us to come looking for you!" Without another word, Mojo flew back towards the front entrance and out into the open air.

He flew towards the Accounting House or the House of Rubies as it was commonly called. Since it was only a short flight east of the palace Mojo arrived quicker than anticipated. Hovering in the air, he glanced over the large building made of well-polished marble and granite. Four tall pillars held up the wide triangular shaped roof with the phrase "House of Rubies" carefully etched into it. "What a magnificent looking building! I bet someone poured a lot of money into this business," he thought to himself as he flew through the open door at the front entrance. Landing on the wide front desk near the entrance, he transformed back into his natural genie form. The fairy sitting at the front desk jolted with surprise to see this happen but quickly resumed her composer. "What can I do for you," she asked inquisitively? Mojo jumped off her desk and onto the floor. "I'm looking for Andrew. Is he around?" Pretending as if this kind of thing happened to her every day she responded casually. "Why yes, he just came in actually. Just head down the hallway; his office is door number 228. Go ahead and fly right in. I'll let him know you're coming. What is your name sir," she asked curiously? Mojo flashed his pearly whites at her charmingly. "My name is Mojo and you are?" She smiled back at him. "Just call me Rita." "Your hair looks fantastic Rita," replied Mojo flatteringly. "Thank you Mojo," she responded joyfully.

Rita was wearing an obsidian arrowhead Jargon Band around her wrist. Bringing it up next to her mouth, she spoke the passcode into it. "Andrew is the greatest accountant in the whole wide world and no one will ever surpass him." Instantly, each of the emerald stones inside each black arrowhead lit up with a green glow. Rita sighed as she spoke into the glowing green band again. "Andrew, could we please change the passcode? You know you've got an ego the size of a…" Andrew interrupted her. "Whoa there Rita; don't speak like that in front of potential customers. Who needs my superb accounting skills today," he asked with a laugh? Rita sighed again. "A genie named Mojo is here to see you Andrew." Andrew's smooth baritone voice continued emanating from her Jargon Band. "Sounds good Rita; send him in please." Rita responded with as much enthusiasm as she could muster. "You got it chief." Andrew laughed. "Don't forget I installed an off switch to shut down your Jargon Band," he said with a chuckle. Rita palmed her forehead while trying not to think about it. "Please don't remind me Andrew." Andrew continued. "You know if you don't say it then your band won't turn off and if it doesn't turn off then I'll be able to hear everything your boyfriend Chuck says when he comes to visit and if that happens…" Rita interrupted him. "Alright already! Andrew is my favorite boss in the whole wide world and I would do anything for him." Andrew's laughter quickly faded away as her Jargon Band quickly stopped glowing green.

Rita looked up at Mojo. "Sorry about that. My boss can be a little weird sometimes. You'll find him at door 228 down the hallway. "Sounds like he's in a cheerful mood," said Mojo playfully. Rita snickered. "Yea, it's all fun and games until you end up working here," she said with a laugh. Mojo laughed too as he made his way past her desk and down the smooth granite hallway towards Andrew's office.

Finding door 228 he reached out to knock on it when suddenly it opened up unexpectedly. "Well, well…if it isn't…oh, never-mind…I thought you were someone else," said Andrew in a confused tone of voice. "Who did you think I was," Mojo asked curiously? "For some reason I thought you might be that blasted Blackbeak coming to apologize for what happened the other night," responded Andrew coldly. "What happened the other night," Mojo asked curiously? "Well, that's a private matter between me and him but I really don't even know you good sir. Let me introduce myself. My name is Andrew," he said enthusiastically extending a hand out for a polite handshake. Mojo shook his hand firmly. "Pleased to meet you good sir. I'm Mojo," he responded confidently.

"So, what brings you to my office today Mojo," asked Andrew courteously? "Perhaps you need a loan or would like to start an account with us," he asked assumingly? Mojo shook his head. "On the contrary, I'm actually friends with Misty and just want to sort a few things out regarding Blackbeak," he replied sincerely. "Oh, what kind of things," Andrew inquired curiously? Mojo continued. "The raven you saw the other night was actually…." Two guards suddenly burst through the office door interrupting Mojo's confession. "What's the meaning of this," Andrew inquired furiously?! Bill and Phil flashed their sharp pointy spears at Andrew and Mojo. "We need to speak with Mojo immediately," said Bill commandingly! It's an important matter that can't wait a second longer," Phil added urgently. "Alright, don't be long. I've got business with him as well," replied Andrew carefully. "Oh, we'll be quick," Phil replied tactfully. Both guards grabbed each of Mojo's arms and forcefully escorted him out through the entrance doors and onto the front cement steps of the Accounting House.

"We caught up with Blackbeak and he told us everything," said Phil dramatically! "He told us that you were the one who was disguised as a raven last night and that you were the one who spied on Andrew and Pixie. Let me tell you something Mojo. If you tell Andrew what we're up too, you'll wish you had never been born!" Mojo laughed. "You boys are funny! Let me tell you something…never mess with an all-powerful genie who can play with you the way a dog plays with its chew toy!" Mojo's entire body lit up like a lightning bolt! Waves of energy surged through him and quickly jolted into the two guards. The shock was so powerful it knocked them off their feet as they soared backwards through the air! Both bodies eventually came crashing back down onto the cobblestone street several feet away from Mojo. "I would advise taking an extra-long vacation," Mojo yelled after them before hovering back into the Accounting House.

Flying straight back into Andrew's office Mojo acted as if nothing out of the ordinary had just happened. "Is everything okay," Andrew asked coolly? "Yea, just taking care of business," Mojo replied casually. "It must have been pretty serious for the palace guards to show up like that," Andrew observed non-dismissively. Mojo looked around at nothing in particular. "Yea, I'll be honest with you Andrew. Those guards were trying to stop me from telling you the truth." "What do you mean," Andrew asked curiously? Suddenly a panting and exhausted Phil came crawling through the open office doorway. "Wait Mojo, we'll get you and your friend's anti-gravity amulets if you just cooperate with us." Mojo glanced down at the exhausted Phil lying on the floor in front of him before looking back towards Andrew. "Excuse me for a moment." Mojo reached down and grabbed Phil by the collar and ever so easily hovered him through the air back out to the front entrance of the Accounting House. Holding him high in the air he pressed Phil's body against the cold hard granite building. "Get them for us now Phil and I'm going to tell Andrew about your dirty little secret right now!" Still panting; Phil gasped. "Yes, I'll get them right away!" Mojo dropped him to the ground as Phil took off running towards the palace as fast as his little legs would carry him. Mojo assumed Bill to have taken off in that direction as well since he was nowhere in sight.

Turning around Mojo walked back into the House of Rubies. Andrew was already at the entrance waiting for him. "What was that all about," he asked curiously? "Oh, let's just say a couple dim witted guards thought they could blackmail an all-powerful genie," Mojo replied lightheartedly. Andrew continued. "So, what was it you wanted to tell me Mojo?" Mojo looked off into the distance as if carefully contemplating what he was about to say next. "Oh, I just wanted to say thank you for helping my friends out the other day. I know you were under the Queen's orders but I still think you did an excellent job with everything," he replied enthusiastically. Andrew sensed Mojo wasn't telling him everything but accepted the compliment anyways. "Thanks Mojo. I do what I can to help those in need. Unfortunately, I have other accounting business that needs attending too unless there's anything else you need?" Mojo continued. "No, you've been quite helpful Andrew. I appreciate all you've done and bid you farewell my good man."

Mojo turned around to leave. Before getting very far, Andrew caught his attention again. "Oh by the way, the Queen recently called a meeting in which all of your friends will be attending. It's being held in the Throne Room. Your friends should be gathering right about now if you'd like to join them." Mojo was astonished. Such vital information seemed to be an after-thought for Andrew. However, he was grateful for the important information. "Thanks for letting me know," Mojo replied gratefully. "I'll be heading that way now."

17. THE ANTI-GRAVITY AMULETS

Mojo flew directly to the palace and into the Queen's Throne Room where he found Misty, Pixie, Blackbeak and the Queen all talking amongst themselves. The Queen watched as Mojo flew through the open entrance door and landed on the shiny marble floor next to them. Misty had previously mentioned his possible attendance to the Queen. In response, the Queen told Bill and Phil to keep the Throne Room doors open just so they wouldn't have to announce Mojo's presence upon arrival. Now that Mojo had arrived, the Queen decided it was time to address the entire group as a whole. Clearing her throat, she spoke up loud enough for everyone to hear her. "Ladies and gentlemen, thank you all for coming. I'm glad you could all be in attendance this fine day. You all look well rested and ready for your adventure to begin. However, before sending you out into the dark and cruel world, I feel it necessary to mention a few important points of your journey. Remember, your goal is to travel to Nectarville, locate the dark fairy Drake and convince him that you are black market bee sellers who want to buy his entire supply from him. Find out where the captured bees are located and retrieve them. It's important to recapture the stolen honeycomb as well.

Remember, this is a necessary ingredient to make Pixie Dust with which keeps us fairies flying! Please bear in mind that without Pixie Dust our entire army will be rendered completely helpless against the Bat King and his army. A fairy army who can't fly is nothing but bat food! I know that sounds gruesome but it's absolutely true! In the unfortunate event that my plan fails I want you to capture Drake and bring him to me for questioning. I desperately hope such risks won't be necessary. However, please use every precaution necessary if you must capture him. He is a dark fairy filled with conniving and mischievous magic."

The Queen turned to address Pixie and Misty. "Did Andrew give you both the two digit codes to open the briefcase?" "Yes your Majesty," they responded in unison. The Queen reached deep into her dress pocket to retrieve two Jargon Bands. She handed one to Pixie and one to Misty before continuing. "Please wear these ladies. They will help you communicate with Andrew to get the last two digits when you need to open the case of rubies. This is a security measure we are taking just in case something happens to the briefcase. In the unfortunate event that it gets stolen and both of you captured, the thief wouldn't have enough information to open the last two digits of the combination lock. Please keep it as safe as possible. I know Pixie is fully aware of how to use a Jargon Band. Have you ever used one before Misty?" Misty shook her head. "Witches don't use such things your highness. Perhaps it's a fairy thing?" The Queen nodded agreeably. "It actually is a fairy thing Misty. Basically, all you have to remember in order to communicate with someone is to simply speak the passcode into your Jargon Band and it will instantly connect you with all other bands holding the same passcode. I will demonstrate. Pixie, may I see the band I just gave you please?" Pixie handed the obsidian arrowhead band back to the Queen. She accepted it and quickly slid it around her wrist. Holding it up next to her mouth, she spoke the passcode into it. "If riches were fishes we'd all have a fry!" Instantly, each emerald gemstone located at the center of each small arrowhead began glowing a bright green color. "And that's how you know it has been activated," said the Queen instructionally. She spoke into her Jargon Band with her mouth held next to it. "Hello Misty, can you hear me?" Misty heard the Queen's voice coming from her own glowing band around her wrist and began speaking into it as well. "That's interesting. You need the passcode to initiate communication but not if someone has already started the process. Is there a passcode to turn off communication between the bands," she asked curiously? The Queen spoke into her Jargon Band again. "Enough sound; shut er' down." Misty chuckled a bit as both Jargon Bands quickly stopped glowing their bright green color. Suddenly she started laughing again hysterically! "I'm sorry your majesty. Those passcodes are just so funny!" The Queen smiled back at her. "They're designed that way on purpose. A funny passcode is a memorable passcode. After all, you wouldn't want to be stuck in the middle of a sticky situation and not remember your passcode would you?" Misty finally stopped laughing as she covered her mouth with her right hand. "Of course not your highness; I'm glad they're memorable phrases for sure." The Queen continued. "Just remember to contact Andrew for your last two digits when the time comes," she said in a concerned voice. "Andrew has a Jargon Band too and should have heard our conversation before I used the shutdown passcode. Perhaps he was busy and just didn't want to say anything at the moment." Slipping the Jargon Band off her wrist, the Queen handed it back to Pixie who gently slipped it onto hers.

"Do you have any questions before your journey begins," the Queen asked? Pixie chimed in. "Um, would you mind if we took a few anti-gravity amulets with us on our journey your highness? There are a number of situations where they could prove quite useful to us," said Pixie assuredly. "I'm sure they would be quite helpful," replied the Queen agreeably. "I will provide each of you with an anti-gravity amulet as well as a map of the entire kingdom so you may journey to Nectarville without getting lost." She called for her two guards to enter the Throne Room. Bill and Phil entered immediately. "How may we serve you your grace," Bill asked respectfully? "Please fetch me a map of my kingdom and four anti-gravity amulets," replied the Queen commandingly. "Yes your Majesty," they replied in unison again. Before leaving the room, Phil shot Blackbeak a look that clearly said; "you're a dead bird!" Blackbeak felt safe in the Queen's presence so he shot Phil a look back that clearly said; "you couldn't hurt me even if you tried."

While waiting for the guards to return with the map and anti-gravity amulets, they discussed the journey ahead in much greater detail. The Queen observed the group with great concern. "Just remember that Drake has incredibly dark magic so it would be in your best interest to stay on his good side or simply steer clear of him altogether." "Don't worry your Highness. I'm sure he's no match for my powers," Mojo and Misty replied simultaneously. The Queen laughed at their over-cockiness. After giving the group a few more words of advice, Bill and Phil finally arrived; carrying four precious anti-gravity amulets along with a map of the kingdom. Two of the amulets were a smaller size for Pixie and Blackbeak to use. The other two were witch and genie sized amulets that could easily fit around Misty and Mojo's necks. The Queen did the honor of placing the amulets around each of their necks individually. Each anti-gravity amulet consisted of a large amber colored stone encased inside an obsidian black triangle pointing downward and attached to a black cord which could easily be worn around one's neck.

"I have specific instructions you will need to remember in order for your anti-gravity amulets to work," said the Queen mysteriously. "I will try and simplify them for you. Just know that you can either go up, down or simply hover in place while using them. To go upwards, simply rub the amulet clockwise. A counter-clockwise rub will stabilize you in mid-air and just one more counter-clockwise rub will cause you to descend slowly towards the ground. Basically, counter-clockwise motions will cause heavier gravity to descend upon you while clockwise motions will cause you to be lifted higher into the air. Any questions," she asked curiously? Since the process sounded simple enough to understand no one responded.

"Before moving on to looking at the map, I want each of you to try using your anti-gravity amulets just to make sure you've got the hang of it," said the Queen with concern in her voice. "I know many of you are already used to flying but there's much more to these amulets than simply flying." Everyone began rubbing their amber stoned amulets in a clockwise direction. Like a balloon, they began rising towards the ceiling. Since they were all used to flying, this was really no big deal for them.

With all four of them now up in the air, the Queen continued her instruction. "Excellent! Now that you've all got the hang of flying let's try moving some heavy objects around." Pointing her wand at her golden throne nearby, she spoke the spell "BOULDAIRO FORMAIRO." Her golden throne instantly transformed into a large heavy boulder. "Alright, I want you all to practice moving this heavy boulder through the air one at a time," she commanded pointedly. They each took turns lifting and maneuvering the heavy boulder through the air. The level of difficulty was harder than any of them had imagined. Using their anti-gravity amulets in conjunction with the heavy boulder required a certain amount of skill, dexterity and balance. Since strength was not a factor in lifting or maneuvering the heavy boulder they quickly learned to rely and improve upon a different set of skills entirely. Misty accidently dropped the boulder a couple of times on top of the hard marble floor below. "Don't worry," said the Queen. "We can repair that in a jiffy. Just try and stay focused." Pixie and Blackbeak dropped the boulder a few times as well and quickly discovered themselves to be more affective when all four of them lifted the boulder together. "And that's the power of teamwork," said the Queen instructively. However, it's important you learn how to lift it on your own in case a situation ever arises where you must do so. Your friends may not always be there to support you unfortunately and that is why we must learn to support ourselves."

The Queen made each of them practice a variety of movements with the large boulder and coached them through each one individually. They learned from each other as they each took turns practicing and watching each other attempt to move and maneuver the large boulder through the air. "Excellent Mojo," said the Queen admiringly! "You can get it off the ground. Now try hovering with it." Mojo rubbed his amulet in a counter-clockwise direction and quickly began hovering in mid-air while carrying the heavy boulder. "That's perfect," said the Queen delightfully. "Changing direction in mid-air simply requires you to shift your body weight towards the direction of your choosing." With both hands held firmly beneath the boulder, Mojo shifted his body weight to the left. As instructed, the entire boulder along with himself moved to the left. He leaned to the right. As expected, everything shifted to the right. "Perfect! Now come back down here with it," prompted the Queen. Mojo rubbed his amulet in a counter-clockwise direction as he slowly descended back down towards the palace floor. After safely landing back on solid ground, the light emanating from his anti-gravity amulet quickly faded away as if to show that its power wasn't currently being used.

"Well done everyone," said the Queen enthusiastically. "Now, let's take a look at this map and I will tell you the quickest way to travel to Nectarville. Misty, if you could provide a small table for us please," said the Queen commandingly. Misty pulled her wand out and transformed the large boulder they were using into a small table. Laying the map on it, everyone circled around it as the Queen began to speak again. "Here is the Lake of Lost Souls," she said pointing towards the center of the map. "Nectarville is a two and a half day journey and is located here." She pointed in a northeastern direction. "However, you can obviously see there are a few obstacles between here and there. Your first stop will be the Dessert of Doom. Assuming you make it out alive, your next stop will be the Forest of Fire followed by Mudslide Mountain. Nectarville is located just on the other side of it. Any questions," she asked casually? "Um, could you give us a few more details about these places," Misty asked hopefully; trying to hide the fear in her voice. "Of course," replied the Queen.

"The first thing you should know is that most of these places would be incredibly hard to pass without your anti-gravity amulets. So please use them as often as necessary. The Dessert of Doom is filled with large circles of quicksand. Avoid stepping into them by using your anti-gravity amulets to safely glide over them. Ferocious underground monsters live there as well. They like to surprise their victims by popping out of the sand when they least expect it." Mojo frowned. "Oh goodie," he said sarcastically.

The Queen continued. "The Forest of Fire is no place to fool around either. It's filled with tree elves who like to shoot fire arrows at just about anything and everything that moves. Last but not least,

Mudslide Mountain is exactly what it sounds like. The slightest noise can trigger an avalanche which could easily bury even the most enormous of monsters! It's absolutely crucial that you take note of every little sound that is made while crossing this mountain. Even snapping a twig or kicking a rock could trigger your impending deaths! This particular mountain was cursed by Morganna many ages ago so that any attempt to fly over it will be futile. A heavy force-field surrounds its top making it impossible to fly over and no one has ever removed it no matter how hard they've tried. Morganna cursed this mountain because she knew it would be used often by Pixie Dust merchants who would fly over it in attempt to sell their goods to the good people of Nectarville. Morganna really wanted to slow down the buying and selling of Pixie Dust and she did just that by cursing Mudslide Mountain with a thick force-field located right at the top!"

A look of complete discouragement crept onto the faces of everyone in the room. The Queen sensed the silent fear in the room and attempted to lighten the mood. "On the bright side, think of all those bees and honeycomb you will be rescuing! Think of the countless number of fairies who will continue to fly because there will be enough raw ingredients to make the Pixie Dust needed to keep our army flying and defending the city from the Bat King and his ruthless army!" The thought of risking life and limb to save a group of bees and some honeycomb sounded a bit more than they had bargained for. So everyone gave a half-hearted smile in an effort to humor the Queen.

The Queen rolled the map up into a scroll formation and handed it to Misty. "My last request is that you all stop by the House of Rubies on your way out just to let Andrew know you're leaving. After all, he still holds the last two digits of the combination to the briefcase. You still have the briefcase I assume," she asked Pixie urgently? Pixie's gaze shifted towards Misty. "I actually gave it to Misty for safe keeping. I figured her witch powers could protect it better than I could." Misty reached deep inside her inner robe pocket and retrieved a tiny black box which she held neatly in the palm of her hand. Clutching her wand with her other hand, she aimed it directly at the small black box and spoke the spell "BENLARGO." Blue waves of energy shot from her wand into the tiny black box. It quickly grew back into its original size as she placed it on top of the glass table nearby. "Well done," said the Queen. "I hope you each remember your two digit codes to open it." Misty and Pixie nodded with affirmation. The Queen turned towards Blackbeak and Mojo. "I know neither of you were given codes to the briefcase and that is for a good reason. Mojo, you didn't even arrive here until after I ordered Andrew to give Misty and Pixie their two digit codes. Additionally, I was planning to keep Blackbeak here with me to help protect the city from the Bat King and his army. On the other hand, you all might be better protected if he came along with you."

Blackbeak and Misty exchanged glances in a way that held an entire conversation between them. They had been friends long enough to read each-other's expressions quite well. In a single glance Misty told Blackbeak that she would easily abandon the Queen to save him if necessary. His return glance revealed that perhaps he should stay behind to help protect the city. Misty scowled with disappointment. Blackbeak quickly rearranged his composure to say that he would be happy to come along and help protect her if needed. Her facial expression quickly changed to reveal a much happier one. They each smiled back at each-other and took comfort in knowing they were willing to look after each-other no matter what the circumstances might be.

The Queen continued speaking. "I believe we have covered everything there is to discuss unless any of you have anything else you'd like to say," she asked sincerely? Mojo was bursting at the seams to say something. "Your Majesty, with all due respect, I am a freed genie now and I have just about every power you can imagine. I'm fairly certain I won't need your anti-gravity amulet to survive this journey." The Queen chuckled. "Yes Mojo, you may have many powers I am sure but even genies have limits. Shall I prove this to you now or would you prefer to learn the hard way on your quest?" Mojo laughed in retort. "No need to prove it your highness but my powers do go farther than you could possibly imagine," he said braggingly. "However, I will take your anti-gravity amulet on this journey if it pleases your majesty," he replied respectfully. "Oh Mojo, that hot headedness of yours is going to get you into a lot of trouble someday if you're not careful," responded the Queen sincerely. "We fairies have magic as well but there are some powers even we don't possess. Thus, we must rely on things like Pixie Dust and amulets to survive. There's nothing wrong with admitting you're not the most powerful person in the world Mojo. Even with all of my powers as Queen of the fairies, I'm willing to admit this as well." Mojo turned his head in attempts to hide the comical smile now crossing his genie face.

The Queen decided to drop the subject and let Mojo find out on his own just how wrong he was about not needing an anti-gravity amulet. "Alright everyone, just remember to stop by the Accounting House on your way out. Is there anything else we need to discuss before your journey begins," she asked curiously? Blackbeak chimed in. "How will we know this Drake fellow when we see him?" The Queen stared at him thoughtfully. "Well, I don't mean to over-simplify this but he'll be the only dark fairy in Nectarville who is capturing bees and stealing honeycomb. I promise you'll know him when you find him. There's just something about his dark aura you can't help but notice." Blackbeak nodded. "Wish we had a little more to go on my lady but I suppose we'll make do with what we have," he replied respectfully. "Sorry I don't have more of a description for you Blackbeak. Unfortunately, every spy I've sent out to find him has never returned. Thus, I can't tell you what he looks like simply because I really have no idea. Any other questions," she asked the group? Not hearing a reply, she continued. "Very well, I will take your silence as an indication that you are all ready for the journey ahead. The last thing I should mention is that your anti-gravity amulets are an incredibly slow way of traveling anywhere so I would suggest using your normal methods of flying to get where you are going. What I'm suggesting is that Misty should keep using her broomstick. Mojo is a genie and can fly naturally. Blackbeak obviously has wings and Pixie has wings and more importantly…Pixie Dust to help her fly as well! Pixie, you should hang onto Misty during her flight to help conserve as much Pixie Dust as you possibly can. Remember, it's getting much harder to make now days due to our lack of ingredients. Also, Misty's broom-speed can easily outmatch your flight speed so it would be best to hang onto her the whole way there." Pixie tried not to look offended by the Queen's jabbing comment.

The Queen reached into her tall dress pocket to retrieve her wand. Pointing it at the large stain glass window behind her throne, she spoke the spell "VANNISCO IMPENDICO" as it vanished completely from sight! A bright blue sky quickly revealed itself behind where the window had previously been. A gentle breeze blew through the new opening into the Throne Room. Misty used her wand to summon her broomstick which was leaning up against a nearby wall. Pixie grabbed onto Misty's robe as she propped the broom between her legs in preparation for takeoff. Mojo and Blackbeak were ready to go as well. "Be careful out there," exclaimed the Queen. Everyone nodded reassuringly as Misty led the group forward in flight through the extra-large hole in the wall where the stain glass window had previously been located. Pixie held onto Misty's shoulder for support as they took flight. Since her supply of Pixie Dust was running low, she decided to take the Queen's advice and save as much as possible for the times when she really needed it. All four traveling companions flew out into the warm summer's air. The Queen quickly caused the tall stain glass window to reappear with a simple word and wave of her wand. Instantly reappearing, it was as if the window had never been missing in the first place. "Hopefully that's the last time I have to repair that window," she thought to herself silently. "It has been broken far too many times to count now."

18. THE VOICE OF MORPHEUS

The group landed in front of the House of Rubies only to find Morpheus standing next to a large marble pillar near the entrance. "Andrew told me to give this to you," he said holding out a Jargon Band for Pixie to take. "Thanks Morpheus," she said accepting the wrist band from his outstretched hand. "My pleasure; Andrew knew you'd probably be missing him but didn't want you to waste any more time than necessary before setting out on your quest," replied Morpheus with a smile. "I know the Queen gave you and Misty Jargon Bands to communicate with him but this is a personal one just for you Pixie. After all, you probably wouldn't want Misty listening in on all of your personal conversations between you and Andrew right?" Pixie slid the Jargon Band over her left wrist. It rested up against the other Jargon Band the Queen had given her to communicate with Misty and Andrew simultaneously. "Tell Andrew I'm grateful and happy he wants to speak with me privately." Morpheus stared at her confidently. "I'm sure you can tell him yourself Pixie. He said the passcode for this Jargon Band is I WANT TO DATE ANDREW AGAIN and the shutdown passcode is GOODBYE MY LOVE." Pixie laughed. "That's hilarious! Thanks again for giving me the message Morpheus. I'll be sure to get in touch with him soon."

Morpheus glanced over at Pixie. "Andrew also said to remember to get in touch with him when you need the last two digits of the combination and he'll be ready to give it to you. Do you still remember the passcode," he asked hopefully? "Of course," she replied confidently. Putting her wrist next to her mouth, she spoke the passcode into her obsidian arrowhead Jargon Band. "If riches were fishes we'd all have a fry!" Morpheus nodded reassuringly as Pixie's band activated and began glowing green. "Well done," replied Morpheus delightfully. "You remember the passcode to turn them off I hope," he asked hopefully? Misty nodded. "Enough sound; shut er' down," she replied as the emerald stones inside both arrowhead bands quickly dimmed their glowing green light into nothing. Mojo couldn't help but snicker a bit at the silliness of the passcodes. Morpheus smiled joyfully. "Looks like you're all ready to go then. I wish you all a safe journey and remember that we're all counting on you to help recover the ingredients necessary to make Pixie Dust. Our army will be completely helpless against the Bat King's army without it. Oh, there's one more thing I must tell you." Blackbeak looked away. He had a bad feeling it had something to do with him. Morpheus continued. "The Queen has requested for you to stay Blackbeak. She would prefer that you stay and go through Wizard's Training with me as your mentor. It would help you remember your powers and you could better help protect the city in case the bat army shows up again."

Blackbeak glanced downward with disappointment before turning back towards Morpheus. "I would be happy to help protect the fairy city with my new found powers but I also think my friends need protecting as well." Morpheus nodded. "I absolutely agree Blackbeak. However, since you're not fully capable of using your powers to their fullest extent yet without my training; I would strongly suggest staying behind with me so I can help your memory return to its formal self. It would be helpful for everyone involved if you did." Blackbeak shook his head. "As much as I desire to help the fairies defend themselves; my first loyalty is to my dearest and oldest friend Misty. After all, if our mission fails then we won't have the ingredients needed to make the Pixie Dust anyways." Morpheus continued. "That's exactly right; which is why we need a backup plan in case this mission does fail. You are the backup plan Blackbeak. If our army can't protect us due to the lack of Pixie Dust then we'll absolutely need your protective powers to help save us from the Bat King and his army when they arrive!"

Blackbeak carefully observed the small group he was about to leave with. "I do see the logic in it," he said downheartedly. He turned towards Mojo. "I really don't know you or Pixie very well," he said glancing over at Pixie. "But I do know you quite well Misty," he said shifting his gaze towards her. "And I'll miss you immensely," he exclaimed sadly. Misty bent down to wrap her arms around her raven friend. "I'll miss you as well Blackbeak but we'll see each-other again; I'm sure of it!" Blackbeak took a moment to use his new magical arms to return Misty's hug. "Stay out of trouble my friend. I'll be here when you get back," he said reassuringly.

Letting go of Blackbeak, she wiped a tear from her eye. "Please take good care of my friend," she said to Morpheus as her broomstick lifted off the ground and into the air. "Oh, don't worry Misty. He's in good hands," Morpheus replied reassuringly. Waving goodbye; Mojo, Misty and Pixie took to the air and began flying in a northeastern direction towards the Forest of Quicksand.

It wasn't long before Andrew was seen walking out of the House of Rubies. "Oh hello Morpheus," he said. "I've been waiting for Pixie and her friends to show up. The Queen told me they were going to start their journey soon. I was really hoping to give Pixie this Jargon Band before she left so we could have more private conversations during her travels. Unfortunately, I must have misplaced the other Jargon Band connecting her and Misty. I can't find that blasted band anywhere! Anyways, you haven't seen the little group around here lately have you?" Morpheus responded before Blackbeak could say anything. "Actually yes, they just passed by. I can hurry and catch up with them if you'd like me to give it to her," he asked confidently? Andrew shoved the Jargon Band into Morpheus's outstretched hand. "Yes, please hurry!" Morpheus glanced over at Blackbeak who was flapping his wings in the air next to him with a look of suspicion etched on his face. "Follow me Blackbeak and I'll explain everything on our way there." Throwing a handful of Pixie Dust over his shoulder and onto his fairy wings, Morpheus launched himself into the blue sky above.

Morpheus and Blackbeak took off in the direction they last saw the group heading. After putting enough distance between themselves and Andrew; Morpheus rolled up his right sleeve and spoke into one of many Jargon Bands strapped across his wrist. "Backup, backup 119. Come in mother bird. I repeat, come in mother bird." Blackbeak glanced up at him curiously. "What are you doing? I thought you already gave Pixie the Jargon Band from Andrew. Why would he give you another one unless…" His thoughts were interrupted by Phil and Bill flying up next to him. Phil aimed his net gun directly at him. "Follow us birdbrain or we'll drag you behind us!" Morpheus turned towards the two guards. "Well done boys. You know what to do with him. I've got other business to attend to so carry on without me. I'll be along later to question him." Without another word, Morpheus began flying in the opposite direction. Bill and Phil flew alongside Blackbeak with him sandwiched between them. Phil flew in front while Bill guarded the raven from behind.

"What's the meaning this," Blackbeak asked frantically? Phil turned his head backward to look at Blackbeak. "The Queen wants to ensure the city's safety along with a large number of rubies she has just sent away with your friends Pixie and Misty. They will eventually return for you and you might as well learn how to defend the city from the bat army while you're here. We don't want to imprison you Blackbeak but we will if you don't cooperate with us!" Bill chimed in from behind. "I hope you found that six digit combo like we requested! It's important because even the Queen doesn't know what it is and we must have it in case the mission fails and the rubies need to be returned to her." Blackbeak continued to follow Phil through the air. "I still don't know what the combination is but I hope that won't be a problem with me assisting the Queen in defending the city." Phil veered to the left. "Actually, it might be a bit of an issue Blackbeak but don't worry about it. It's nothing we can't handle at the moment." Blackbeak noticed an exceptionally tall looking waterfall just below them as they began descending towards it. "Well that's good to hear," he replied unreassuringly. "They're probably leading me into a trap," he thought to himself worriedly.

Phil spoke up again. "See that waterfall down there. That's Turban Waterfall. We don't want the Bat King knowing you're here or it might cause trouble for all of us. The Queen has asked us to hide you there while you relearn your powers." Blackbeak looked confused. "Hide me in a waterfall? Do you plan on drowning me there or what?" Bill laughed. "You're a funny bird! No, we're going to hide you behind the waterfall so word doesn't get back to the Bat King that you're here." They were extremely close to the waterfall now. Phil hovered in front of the falling water without letting it touch him and began speaking loudly enough for Blackbeak to hear him over the sound of the rushing water. "Bill, we could really use your giant umbrella right about now! Bill flew up next to Phil and pointed his net gun up in the air. He flicked a switch forward next to the trigger on the net gun before pulling the trigger itself. Instantly a giant umbrella popped out of the nozzle! It was large enough to cover all three of them easily. "Quickly, fly under this raven," Phil commanded eagerly. Blackbeak realized he had a chance to escape but knew Phil was holding onto a real gun that could easily shoot more than just umbrellas or nets at him. "Alright," replied Blackbeak as he flew underneath the giant umbrella. Holding the giant umbrella over the three of them, they slowly flew behind the waterfall as heavy amounts of water bounced off the top of it. Blackbeak made a mental note of the waterfall's location at the northern most point of the Lake of Lost Souls. He also assumed it to be responsible for the majority of water found inside the lake surrounding the floating city of fairies held at its center.

The three of them landed on a rocky ledge at the edge of a cavern just behind the waterfall. Blackbeak observed it to be a deep and dark looking cave. Shreds of light shimmered between the falling water but not enough to see into the cavern depths in front of them. Phil reached for what looked like a torch standing on a holster up against the stone wall. He holstered his large gun back into its holster slung across his back. Flicking a small switch at the torch's base with his thumb, flames quickly erupted from its top. Bill continued pointing his net gun at Blackbeak's backside. "We must take every precaution to keep you from being seen Blackbeak. You understand I hope?" Blackbeak didn't believe a word either of the guards had breathed from the moment they had threatened him to get the six digit passcode from Pixie, Misty and Andrew. Despite his doubts, he continued to play their little game. "Absolutely, I understand Bill. I only want to help the Queen and the kingdom. You know that." Bill and Phil smiled reassuringly at each-other.

They continued walking through a dark tunnel with Phil's torch lighting their way. Eventually the tunnel opened up into a much larger cavern. Using the little light they had, Blackbeak made out a large number of shelves lining the cavern walls. Each shelf held a number of mysterious objects. Among them, he found a great number of Jargon Bands, rolled up scrolls, unlit candles and even a few skulls! Blackbeak shuttered inside and couldn't help but wonder if he was being led into a trap. He was almost certain of it but couldn't see any possible means of escaping with Bill and Phil constantly watching his every move. He also noticed a small round table sitting in the middle of the room with a lone wooden chair beneath it. He couldn't help but wonder if someone used this particular room as a study area for some unknown reason.

Moving past the mysterious room, they came to an old wooden door built into the side of the cavern. Blackbeak found it odd that anyone would take the time to build a door into the side of a dark cavern like the one standing in front of him. Phil reached into his pocket and retrieved a small golden key which fit the door's lock perfectly. Twisting the key and pulling the handle, the door opened easily as he motioned for Blackbeak to come inside. "This is where you will stay until Morpheus returns from his other duties. Don't think of yourself as a prisoner. Think of yourself as a highly coveted individual who can't be seen until precisely the right moment." Blackbeak flew inside as Phil held the door open for him. He found himself inside a much smaller room with a soft dirt floor and hard stone walls surrounding him. Everything was natural except for the wooden door that Phil instantly closed behind him. Blackbeak heard the lock click into place as Phil dropped the metal key back into his pocket. "Don't worry bird, Morpheus will be along shortly. I'm sorry to lock you up like this but the Queen has ordered us to keep you hidden away from the townsfolk. We don't want any rumors flying around and getting back to the Bat King and his army. Think of yourself as the Queen's secret weapon. Once Morpheus gets through with you, you'll be able to take on the entire bat army my friend!" Bill took a moment to add his two cents as well. "Once you've come to grips with your new found powers, we don't want you thinking of us as your enemies either. Remember, we're just following orders Blackbeak."

That being said, both guards proceeded to leave Blackbeak alone as they made haste back to the palace and to their posts just outside the Queen's Throne Room. With both of them now in position just outside the entrance; Bill glanced at Phil with concern etched on his face. "Do you think we're doing the right thing Phil? I mean, some might say we're overstepping our bounds to do what we're doing." Phil glanced back at him confidently. "It's for the good of our people Bill. You heard it yourself; even the Queen considered having Blackbeak stay here in order for this to happen. Of course, she didn't actually order us to do this but I think we both know Morpheus is doing the right thing by taking matters into his own hands. Once the Queen realizes Morpheus ordered this to happen to save our kingdom from the bat army; she'll forgive and forget this whole thing ever happened. I guarantee it!" Bill nodded agreeably. "I think so too Phil. Let's just hope she doesn't find out about it before Blackbeak performs his heroic duties or we're both in for a world of trouble!" Phil glanced around the perimeter to make sure no one else was eavesdropping in on their conversation. "Why do you think we stashed the raven up in Turban Waterfall? That was for our safety you nitwit! We can't have the Queen finding out about our brilliant plan until he actually saves the city from the bat army. When that happens, the Queen will thank us for doing what we did. I guarantee it! Also, it's important that he doesn't feel like a prisoner because we don't want him thinking we are his enemies. Trust me, once Morpheus teaches Rueland how to use his forgotten powers we don't want him as an enemy. That is for certain!"

Bill scanned the perimeter for possible eavesdroppers as well. "Well, I hate to be a downer but what if he's still upset about us blackmailing him to get the ruby case combination? That would be reason enough for revenge." Phil sighed deeply. "You really don't think very far ahead do you Bill? Just stick with our story. It was the Queen who sent us to get the combination just like it was the Queen who sent us to keep him away from any gossipers or bat spies. It's okay to blame the Queen for now because when Rueland actually does save our city from the bat army then this whole charade will be worth the effort we've put into it! At that point, the Queen will forgive us and Rueland will forgive us too because it will all be for the greater good of saving the city! See what I mean Bill?" Bill nodded agreeably. "I'm starting to see the big picture now. I'm also really glad you explained it to me again. Sometimes I just don't get it after the first three or four times you know." Phil laughed thinking it was a joke. Bill laughed as well not realizing what was so funny.

After making a quick stop at the Circle of Healing to pick up Andrew's Jargon Band from Luna; Morpheus found himself in front of Turban Waterfall. Reaching into his inner robe pocket, he retrieved his long black wand found within. Pointing it at the waterfall, he shouted the phrase "PARTELLO MORPHELLO!" The water instantly parted into two separate streams as he flew between them and into the small cave entrance behind the waterfall. The two streams quickly reconnected after flying past them. On the wall to his right hung an unlit torch. Aiming his wand at it, he spoke the word "ILLUMINOTTO" as it instantly caught fire and burned with an unnatural amount of light. He could have flicked the switch on the bottom of the torch in the same way Phil had previously done but he always enjoyed opportunities to use his magic. "I am the court wizard after all," he thought to himself over-zealously. Grabbing the bottom end of the torch, he continued making his way further into the cave's depths. The dark sanctuary ahead had served as his hideout for a great many years and he was happy no one else had discovered it as of yet. He wasn't happy about having to share its location with Bill and Phil but knew sacrifices had to be made in order for his plan to work properly.

The cave entrance opened up into a much larger cavern. A large number of shelves sat inside the walls themselves and were filled with various magical objects. Spell books, scrolls, maps, potions and a variety of other odd looking items had been carefully sorted and shelved with each shelf having a golden plated label at its base. A wooden table and chair stood at the center of the cavern where Morpheus had spent many long years studying the various objects lining the shelves and forming various plans for his future. "This kind of thing should be expected from a court wizard," he thought dismissively to himself.

Rolling up his right sleeve, Morpheus carefully eyed the row of Jargon Bands strapped across his wrist. "I really should invent a new kind of Jargon Band that can accept more than one passcode at a time. This form of magic is so old it's pathetic," he said out loud to no one in particular. Since all the bands looked exactly alike, the only way to tell them apart was to speak the passcode into all of them simultaneously to see which one would light up. One of them was given to him by Andrew to give to Pixie….which he obviously didn't do. Another one connected him to Pixie. She thought this was legitimately from Andrew. He had also just added another one to his collection which he had just picked up from Luna at the Circle of Healing. This one was supposed to be Andrew's band that connected him with Misty and Pixie. "Well, he obviously knows this one is missing now. Luckily it happened to break off his wrist during his fall or Luna never would have come by it and I never would have got it. The knock on the head must have really made him forget about it," he thought gratefully to himself. A few other Jargon Bands were strapped around his wrist connecting him to other people as well. At the moment he couldn't remember which one was which simply because they all looked exactly the same. Each Jargon Band was made from black obsidian arrowheads with tiny emerald stones embedded into the center of each one. "Oh well, I'll just have to remember the passcodes to each of them. That's all that really matters anyways," he thought dismissively.

Before speaking the passcode into any of the Jargon Bands, he quickly remembered his orders to Bill and Phil to bring Blackbeak back to Turban Waterfall. Walking over to the locked wooden door nearby, he produced a silver key from his pocket which he quickly used to unlock the door and walk inside. Blackbeak stood in the far left corner of the dark room; desperately trying not to think about his dismal situation. Morpheus closed the door behind himself. "Sorry for taking so long Blackbeak. I got held up with other pressing matters. Oh, it's so dark in here. Let me light the room for you. Oh dear, there's nothing to transform in here. Mind if I borrow a couple of feathers?" Blackbeak's mood suddenly shifted from depression to an explosive angry rage in a matter of seconds. "Excuse me! Who do you think you are old man?! Your goons drag me into this cold dark place and you act like everything is okay! Well I've got news for you buster! Everything is not okay so don't even pretend like it is!" Morpheus inhaled deeply. "My sincerest apologies Blackbeak; you're absolutely right. Everything is not okay and I'll be completely honest with you. The Queen was considering the possibility of you staying at the palace so you could go through Wizard's Training with me. Unfortunately, she changed her mind at the last moment so you could go with your friends and help protect them on their journey. However, I took it upon myself to get you back here. I think it's best for this entire city if you stay and help defend us against the bat army. They could be here any day now and we can't afford another attack like the one we had previously. Believe me, we lost about half of our entire army last time we were attacked and I honestly don't think we could survive another one without your help! It's that serious Blackbeak. I know the Queen is counting on your friends to bring back the ingredients necessary to make enough Pixie Dust for the rest of our army but that's not going to be enough to shield us from their extreme forces. We need your protective powers Rueland!"

Blackbeak's mood quickly changed again from extreme anger to a more sympathetic nature. "Oh, well in that case…I didn't realize how desperately my services were actually needed here. Otherwise, I might have reconsidered the possibility of staying at the palace with you." Morpheus cleared his throat. "The Queen has a way of understating desperate situations sometimes and that can be quite an issue for all of us. Believe me, this is the best thing for all of us; I can assure you. That being said, I don't want the Queen knowing you are here. She'll find out soon enough but I prefer that time be when you become the hero in her eyes as well as everyone else's. I hope you understand what I'm saying Blackbeak." Blackbeak nodded. "I understand wizard. However, I don't want to feel like a prisoner here either. I must be able to come and go as I please." Morpheus glanced down and then leftward as if contemplating what to say next. "I'm not sure how to tell you this Blackbeak. I don't want you thinking of me as your enemy but I also don't want anyone else seeing you either. All it takes is one blabbermouth to ruin it for the rest of us. If word gets back to the bat king that you are here then he could easily send his forces back here to capture or even kill you! No Blackbeak. We mustn't take any chances. I truly am sorry for locking you in here but I hope you can that I'm really trying to protect you. However, I want your stay here to be as comfortable as possible so I am more than happy to provide any furnishings necessary to make that happen." Blackbeak sighed deeply. "Well, perhaps we could start with a little more light in here and a place to sleep would be nice." Morpheus nodded. "Absolutely! Since I will be your magical mentor for the time being, let me begin by explaining a few things to you Rueland. The first thing you must remember is that magic cannot simply create something out of nothing. This is why I asked for a few of your feathers earlier on. We can transform things with our magic but can never create something out of nothing." Blackbeak nodded understandingly before Morpheus continued. "The second thing you must remember is that we can never transform ordinary objects into rubies. This is why they are so rare and valuable because if anyone could create them with magic then they wouldn't have any value at all. The last thing you should remember is that we can never extend our own lifespan with the magic we possess. It simply can't be done. Rumor has it that an ancient form of magic far older than anything you or I possess has this ability but very few people have ever discovered how to do it exactly. Chances are anyone who has discovered such a valuable secret has probably never shared it with anyone else. So if you ever figure out how to magically enhance your own lifespan please don't hesitate to share such valuable knowledge with me Rueland. I'm here for you; remember that."

Blackbeak shook his head. "That's all well and good wizard but it's still dark as night in here and I don't want to pluck out my own feathers just so you can transform them. Any other ideas?" Morpheus placed a hand to his chin as if contemplating something. "Let me go back to my study area for a moment. Perhaps I can scrounge up a few objects that can be transformed into comfortable furnishings for you. I'm sorry to lock the door again but I'll be back soon my friend so don't worry about a thing."

Leaving Blackbeak in the dark room all by himself, he shut and locked the door behind him as he ventured out into the adjoining study area. Looking through a bunch of old scrolls; he tried to figure out which ones would be of no use to him anymore. Before getting very far into his search, his thoughts were quickly interrupted by the sound of Andrew's voice coming from one of the Jargon Bands strapped around his wrist. Andrew's smooth baritone voice came through one of the now glowing Jargon Bands. "Pixie, are you there? Come in Pixie…"

Quickly grabbing his wand, Morpheus pointed it directly at his own throat before speaking the spell "IMMAUTO REPETTO." Leaning over, he spoke directly into the talking band. "Hello Andrew. Is that you?" His voice now sounded much higher pitched and matched Pixie's voice perfectly. The reply came. "Why yes it is. I'm so glad Morpheus caught up with you on your way out of town to give you the Jargon Band. I wanted to give it to you so we could speak privately Pixie. After all, we did have an incredible date the other night and I'll never forget it." Morpheus shuttered at the thought of it. He didn't want to play this little game with Andrew but felt it necessary to achieve his desired results. He continued to reply in Pixie's cute high pitched and pleasant sounding voice. "We had a pretty good time; didn't we? I'm glad we were able to spend some quality time together Andrew. I really got to see a side of you I never even knew existed." For a brief moment Morpheus became amazed at his own cleverness before hearing Andrew's reply on the other end. "Aw yes, it's a shame the Queen had you go off and join your friends in this quest. I was truly hoping you could have stayed here with me. There are so many more fun adventurous things we can do together." Morpheus did everything he could to keep from gagging on his own saliva before continuing. "I'm sure there's a bright future ahead of us Andrew. Um, I have to ask though…Morpheus was in such a rush to give me the Jargon Band from you that he forgot to mention the passcode. Lucky you called me. Otherwise, I wouldn't have been able to call you without it." Andrew continued. "That's okay Pixie. I think I was in such a rush to have Morpheus deliver the band to you that I forgot to give him the passcode. I can give it to you now though. Are you ready for it?" "Ready when you are cute stuff," replied Morpheus trying not to choke over his own words. "Okay, it's ANDREW, ANDREW, ANDREW….I WILL LOVE YOU TIL THE END OF TIME!" Chills surged down Morpheus's spine! "I hate you so much right now you little dweeb," he thought silently. He forced himself to chuckle in Pixie's cute little voice as Andrew shared a good laugh with him. "And how do I turn it off," he asked curiously? "The off code is I'LL BE HOME SOON." Morpheus glanced off into the distance. "You are a clever one Andrew. I hate to cut you short but I've got to go now." Andrew continued speaking. "Just curious, have you reached the Dessert of Doom yet," he asked curiously? "Um, not yet," replied Morpheus. "Um, how did you know that's where we're heading," he asked? "The Queen told me all about your travel plans," replied Andrew coolly. "That's interesting," said Morpheus rubbing his chin thoughtfully. "Did she happen to mention where we are going after that?" "Well, she said you would then be heading towards Avalanche Mountain and finally over to Nectarville where you'd eventually find Drake and somehow convince him to give you the stolen bees and honeycomb one way or another." Morpheus grabbed a nearby piece of parchment and quickly scribbled the plans onto it as Andrew continued speaking. After a brief pause in the conversation, he replied. "Yes, that is exactly what she told us," he replied affirmatively. "Your listening skills are quite top notch Andrew," he continued flatteringly. I really do appreciate your kindness. It means a lot to me." "No problem," replied Andrew coolly. "Although, I should mention that even though I enjoy communicating with you privately there's another reason I wanted to give you that Jargon Band Pixie." Morpheus knew what Andrew was about to say but decided to let the silence speak for itself. Andrew continued. "I kind of lost the Jargon Band the three of us were meant to use. I'm not really sure where it went so we'll just have to use this one in the future. Although, I do have a sneaky suspicion I might have lost it while chasing that blasted raven who was spying on us that one night. I remember waking up inside the Circle of Healing and later realized my Jargon Band had somehow gone missing. I don't want to accuse anyone of stealing it but perhaps the raven I was chasing may have come back to claim it for himself. I'm not really sure. Unfortunately, it's practically impossible to duplicate a Jargon Band. It takes a special skill set just to make one of those things but at least we can use this one for now."

Morpheus decided to give a little playful pushback on the matter. "Oh Morpheus, it would have been so great having our own secret Jargon Bands to chat on but now I'm going to have to tell Misty about it. I wouldn't want her trying to connect with the three of us and have you not be there. I'll tell her and Mojo that if they ever need to contact you to just go ahead and borrow my band since that's really the only way for them to communicate with you now. The Jargon Band's the Queen gave us are practically worthless now since you don't have yours to connect with. So we'll just go ahead and throw ours away." Andrew interjected sharply. "No! Don't do that. Jargon Bands are worth quite a bit of money. You can always trade them in at a Jargon Band shop if you need the rubies. I'm an accountant. Trust me; they're quite valuable for sure." Morpheus nodded agreeably and continued speaking in Pixie's high pitched girly voice. "Well thanks again Andrew. You've been incredibly helpful. Let's chat again soon."

Morpheus suddenly remembered how Blackbeak had been waiting for his return the entire time he had been speaking with Andrew. "I'll talk to you soon sweet girl," replied Andrew. "I'm truly delighted to hear your beautiful voice again Pixie. Hopefully we can chat much more often in the future." Morpheus felt sick inside from pretending to be in love with him but continued the charade anyways. "Absolutely my sweet; take good care of yourself, bye for now darling." He quickly closed the communication line between them with the passcode: "I'LL BE HOME

SOON." Morpheus breathed a sigh of relief from finally having the conversation over with. He made a point to write down the passcodes in case he ever forgot them in the future.

He was happy to note that all communication lines had been set up according to plan. Andrew now had absolutely no connection with Misty, Pixie or Mojo even though he thought otherwise. "This will work perfectly," Morpheus thought mischievously. Then he reminded himself that he wasn't actually a bad person but that his plan needed to be executed for the good of the people. Remembering Blackbeak again, he decided to check up on him before doing anything else. Rolling his right sleeve down over the Jargon Bands strapped across his wrist, he grabbed a couple of ancient rolled up scrolls and walked back over to the old wooden door currently housing Blackbeak. Quickly unlocking it, he stepped inside. Blackbeak had grown quite annoyed by now and his voice clearly reflected his agitation. "Good riddance! What took you so long wizard? I told you before; I don't want to be treated like a prisoner here!" Morpheus sat the scrolls down up against the stone wall across the room from Blackbeak. "I'm sorry Rueland. The time really slipped away from me. Anyways, since I will be your magical instructor for the time being, I will start by teaching you a simple lesson in transformation. You said you wanted a more comfortable living space and I don't blame you. That being the case, I've brought a couple of old scrolls we can use to transform into whatever furniture or necessity you wish to enjoy. Remember, we cannot simply make something out of nothing. We always need an object to make the transformation process possible. Also, always bare in mind that we cannot transform objects into…." Blackbeak cut him short. "Rubies…and that's why they are so valuable. Yes, yes, I get it wizard. Can we move on with the lesson please?" Morpheus nodded. "Patience is also a valuable asset but we can talk about that at a later time. Why? Because I have the patience to wait for that particular lesson and so should you." Blackbeak sighed with frustration as if waiting for Morpheus to finish his rambling.

Morpheus continued. "Lesson number one: since you do not own or possess a wand, it's important to remember that your magic comes from deep within yourself. This is good because no one can steal it away from you in the way that someone might confiscate or break a wand. On the other hand, it's also bad. It's bad because your particular type of magic will be drawn from your own inner energies. This means that the more magic you use the more tired and drained you will feel from using it. The process starts simply by imagining what you want to achieve by using your magic. You must clearly see something happening in your mind that you want to have happen. You must then channel all of your inner energies from the center of your body through the tips of your wings. Simply imagine a flowing stream of light traveling through your body and into the object you wish to transform with your magic. Let's start by transforming one of these scrolls into a small bed for you to lie in. You think you can handle that Rueland?" Blackbeak glanced at the rolled up scrolls leaning up against the wall across the room from him. "Let's put one of the scrolls right about here," he stated pointing his wing close to the center of the room. Morpheus quickly moved one of the scrolls towards the center of the small cavern and dropped it on the dirt floor where Blackbeak was pointing. "Is this where you imagine your new bed to be," he asked hopefully? Blackbeak motioned his wing to the left a little; "a bit to the left if you please." Morpheus sighed and gently kicked the scroll to the left. "How about there," he asked with a bit of frustration in his voice? "That should do nicely. Thank you," replied Blackbeak calmly.

Morpheus continued. "Okay, now just remember everything I've taught you so far. See if you can implement it." Blackbeak spread his wings and pointed them together in front of his black raven body. He pointed them directly at the ancient rolled up scroll lying on the dusty cavern floor. Carefully channeling all of his energies, he imagined what he wanted to achieve as a surge of bright light came flowing through his body. It channeled from his inner core and into the rolled up scroll lying on the ground in front of him. To his dismay, nothing happened at all. The scroll didn't even budge. Morpheus sighed. "I forgot to mention, you also need to imagine what it would feel like to reach your desired outcome as well. For example, what would it feel like to have a nice soft bed to lie in?" Blackbeak responded. "I imagine it would feel soft, warm and cozy. Morpheus interjected. "Well done. Now, along with imagining the bed in front of you; try thinking about what that particular feeling would feel like as well." Blackbeak centered his energies once again and channeled them towards the rolled up scroll lying on the floor. A bright stream of white light jetted from his inner body through the tips of his wings and into the rolled up scroll. Instantly it began transforming into a small bed with plenty of soft blankets and more pillows than Morpheus had ever seen in his life! "Why all the pillows," asked Morpheus? Blackbeak laughed. "I'm a bird. The real question is…why the bed?" Morpheus chuckled. "Good point. Well done my friend. You're getting the hang of this so far. As you can see, I brought a few more worthless scrolls for you to practice on as well. Feel free to lay them wherever you wish and transform them into whatever your heart desires. I have some other business to attend to at the moment but I'll return shortly to check up on your progress. Rest assured, you're doing astonishingly well Rueland. Don't worry about a thing. Just keep at it."

Morpheus quickly made his way back out into the study area of the cavern. Closing the door behind him, he locked it promptly. He knew Blackbeak was expecting him to return shortly but he still had one more person he wanted to speak with. Bringing his wrist full of Jargon Bands up to his mouth, he spoke a passcode into them. "I'LL BE RICH ONE DAY!" One of the arrowhead bands instantly activated a glowing green color as Morpheus continued speaking. "Duncan…come in Duncan. Are you there?" A brief silence followed before a rough and twangy sounding voice came in loud and clear. "Blast it all Morpheus! I told you to always use my code name! It's DRIZZLE! You're lucky I wasn't surrounded by anyone who might be out to get me!" Morpheus chuckled. "Oh, I'm sorry DRIZZLE. You know, you and Drake wouldn't have to be on the run like you are if you'd just accept my offer. Have you decided to take it yet?" Another brief silence filled the air before Duncan's twangy voice was heard again. "I haven't caught up with Drake yet but I'll mention it to him when I do. He's the boss not me." Morpheus continued. "Well, you better hurry up Drizzle. My patience is wearing thin. Also, since I'm the honeycomb buyer for the entire palace, you must know that I have access to funds you couldn't even begin to imagine. You would be wise to accept my offer quickly before someone else does. Let's set up a meeting at Drake's place and we'll discuss this matter in person. Sound good?" Duncan laughed. "You can't fool me into giving away our hiding place old man. I'm fully aware that you work for the palace and could easily send the guards out to arrest us. Yes, I know your offer is generous but for all we know you might just be trying to get us arrested. No, I'll have a talk with Drake about it when I catch up with him. Goodbye for now old man." Duncan quickly spoke the shutdown passcode to cut off communication between them. "GET YOUR OWN STUFF."

Morpheus began thinking to himself. "I really hope Duncan accepts my generous offer. It would save Misty, Pixie and Mojo from having to continue on with their journey. It would also free up that case full of rubies which might just happen to get lost before it gets back to the Accounting House if Pixie's not careful. Wouldn't that be a shame," he thought mischievously.

19. DRAKE THE THIEF

A group of bees gathered around a giant beehive dripping with honey. They hadn't built it but decided to make it their new home after finding it. They didn't seem to care how it had gotten there or which group of bees it had previously belonged to. All they knew is that it was much bigger than the one they had built for themselves and they were going to make it their home now. One by one, each bee flew away from their newly discovered home to collect pollen from the nearby flowers. Oddly enough, the flowers around that particular beehive were much bigger than anything they had ever seen before. That didn't matter to them either. Pollen was pollen and they were going to collect it one way or another to make as much honey as possible. Fortunately for Drake, each bee did not seem to notice the other bees that were being eaten and swallowed alive by the giant plants surrounding the enormous beehive! Of course, this was all part of his plan. These plants were specifically grown and enchanted by Drake himself in order to fulfill a specific purpose. That purpose was to lure the precious bees in one at a time until the trap snapped shut on all of them. Once shut, the plant would suck the bee down through its long hollow stem and into a large glass jug which Drake would collect and bring back to his secret layer for a safe deposit. These magical plants could only live for so long without being attached to the soil so Drake made sure not to keep them out of the sun for too long before returning them to a safe pot of soil to keep them alive. He called these specially designed plants Snap Trappers. He thought it was a clever name for them and rather snappy at that. He was still trying to come up with a clever name for his extra-large beehives that he used to lure the bees into their new home while getting trapped by his Snap Trappers below. He thought about calling them Honey Homes but the name just didn't stick well with him and he knew a sweeter name would eventually come to mind.

Drake found himself surrounded by peach blossom trees and was staring upwards at one of the giant beehives hanging high above his head. Pointing his long black wand upwards at it, he muttered the phrase "LONGELLO EXTENDO" under his breath as his wand began to grow longer and longer as it extended higher and higher towards his extra-large beehive. Within seconds his wand had grown tall enough to reach the beehive high above his head. He rocked it back and forth with his extra tall wand in an effort to knock it down from the tree branch it was attached too. It didn't take long before the beehive came crashing down to the grassy earth beneath. The bees became extremely angry with their new found attacker and began attacking him! Drake had expected this and quickly muttered two more spells right in a row. The first one was "RETRACTONDO" to get his wand back to its normal size and the second one was "FORSHELLO" which caused a magical body shield to appear around himself. Each angry bee flying towards him simply bounced off his invisible body shield and away from him. He moved closer towards the giant beehive lying on the grass in front of him and attempted to pick it up but found that his body shield continued to knock it away from him every time he got close enough to grab it. "This is frustrating," he thought angrily. He knew that in order to actually pick up the beehive he would have to lower his body shield just long enough to grab it. "This is going to be tricky," he thought to himself cautiously.

The giant swarm of bees continued attacking him and bouncing off his body shield. "I must distract them somehow," he thought tactfully. "Any spell I cast at them will bounce off the inside of my body shield and hit me." He contemplated the situation a moment longer before deciding on his next plan of attack. He made a mad dash directly into the giant swarm of bees as hard as he could in an attempt to knock the majority of them through the air and off of his body shield. Pointing his wand at the inside of his body shield, he inhaled nervously and muttered the spell "DESHELLUPELLO" as it disappeared completely from around him! Grabbing the extra-large beehive and snap trap lying at his feet, he began running as fast as his legs would carry him desperately hoping the stinging bees behind him wouldn't catch up with him.

He ran to the nearby dirt road found on the outlying edge of the orchard. Tied to one of the large cherry trees stood his two horses attached to a cloth covered wagon. Quickly making his way to the back of the wagon, he hurled the beehive and snap trap into the back. Just then, he felt a couple of bee stings sink into the back of his neck. "Ouch! Dumb bees! I'll make ya'all pay for that," he shouted angrily! Retrieving his wand from his inner robe pocket, he shouted "FORSHELLO" again as his body shield reappeared around himself. Unfortunately, he managed to trap a single bee inside his body shield with him! Screaming frantically, he began swatting his wand around at it desperately trying to kill the little varmint! "So help me little bee, you'll be sorry you ever messed with me!" Without thinking properly, Drake shot a small lightning bolt from his wand at the attacking bee. Missing it completely, the lightning bolt slammed up against his body shield and bounced back directly into his stomach! Clenching his stomach with one hand, he accidently smacked the flying bee with the other. It slammed against the inside of his body shield and bounced back like a rubber ball hitting a wall. Not missing his opportunity, Drake quickly bounced the bee back and forth between the inside of his body shield and his hand several times until the bee finally passed out and fell to the ground from over-exertion. Drake glanced down at the dying bee as he continued to clench onto his painful stomach with both hands. "That'll teach ya; ya worthless stinger," he shouted angrily!

By now, the majority of bees that had bounced off Drake's body shield had returned with a vengeance. "I'll teach ya'all a lesson you'll never forget," he shouted frantically! He bent his head downward like a bull getting ready to charge and ran head-first into the thick swarm of bees! His body shield bounced them left and right through the air with a force to be reckoned with! They skyrocketed across the grassy fields for miles!

Suddenly Drake heard a gravelly voice yelling through the dense fruit trees at him. "Stop thief! I hear you out here! Don't think I don't know what you're doing. When I catch you….so help me….I'll bury you deeper then farmer Joe's well on the south end of town!" Drake knew he had better get out of there quickly! Lowering his body shield again, he untied his two horses and jumped onto the wooden plank driver's seat sitting at the front end of the covered wagon. "Giddee up," he shouted snapping the reins into action. The horses began trotting at an incredibly slow pace. "Come on Glue and Molasses…pick up the pace," he shouted! He quickly realized that Glue and Molasses were probably not the best get-away horses to take on this journey but knew they were the only horses he owned.

Glue and Molasses picked up the pace just enough to outrun the angry farmer chasing after them with his pitchfork raised in the air. Drake glanced back at him. "You best quit eating your wife's apple pies farmer Brown! Looks like they're catching up with you," he shouted back hysterically! In response, Farmer Brown hurled his sharp pointed pitchfork towards the back of Drake's covered wagon. It flew straight through the back opening and through the front covering next to Drake's head at the front of the wagon. Drake turned his head just enough to see the sharp three pointed prongs sitting within an inch of his face! "Wheew…that was close," he thought with relief! He hadn't been prepared for that kind of an attack on any level. "I really must be more careful about who I steal from in the future," he thought to himself cautiously.

Glue and Molasses continued trotting his covered wagon down

the dirt road towards the bustling city of Nectarville. Drake had business to attend to and was counting on the merchants being far more friendly to him than farmer Brown had been. Grabbing his long black wand from his inner robe pocket, he cast another body shield over himself. It came in handy as he backhanded the sharp prongs of the pitchfork sticking through the wagon cover on his right. The sharp prongs slid through the thick wagon covering and fell onto the inside floorboards of his wagon. Carefully inspecting the newly made prong holes in his wagon covering, he became disgusted that he didn't know a spell to repair them with. "Drat! I'll have to have it repaired manually," he thought frantically. I can't have my buyers thinking I have enemies," he thought tactfully.

It didn't take long before he had arrived on Merchant Street in Nectarville. The whole street ran straight through the center of town which made it an easy access point for all who lived there. The entire street was lined with merchant tents all selling a variety of wares as numerous as the variety of fruit trees filling the orchards of Nectarville. Drake could already hear the large amounts of haggling commonly found between merchants and buyers. The price of an item was usually set at a higher price in anticipation of a buyer trying to haggle his way downward. Unlike most of the fairies on the road ahead of him, his business was with selling to the sellers. He knew the honeycomb shops enjoyed buying their goods from him at wholesale prices. He often made up stories about where his honey and honeycomb had actually come from. Sometimes he would raise the selling price if he could convince a buying merchant that his goods came from the Frosty Bees of the Northland. Everyone knew the Frosty Bee was the only type of bee that could survive in freezing temperatures as if it were nothing. Many fairies even believed that Frosty Bee honey could make them impervious to the cold. Since it was just a myth however; he got away with selling many such items for much higher prices and never failed to miss an opportunity when presented with one. Despite Drake's many lies about where his honey and honeycomb actually came from, he knew his merchant friend Yachmed was fully aware of his thieving ways. Yachmed had once been a honeycomb thief himself and had told Drake that he had left that life many years ago. He decided that honest work was the best way to go and continually tried convincing Drake to give up his thieving ways and go into the retail business with him. Drake always turned him down though because he enjoyed the thrill of being chased by angry bee farmers and furious bees. He said it made him feel more alive in a twisted sort of way.

Eventually Drake reached a merchant tent with a giant wooden sign attached to the top which read, "Honey for Money." Drake grinned. "What a clever shop name," he thought sarcastically. Steering his wagon around to the backside of the tent, he jumped from the driver's seat and onto the soft dirt below. Tying his horses to the hitching post, he quickly made his way through the back entrance of the tent. Upon entering, he found two long wooden benches sitting on opposite sides of each-other. This portion of the tent had been sectioned off as a waiting area for all wholesalers wanting to make deals with the shop owner. In between both benches hung a small golden bell dangling from a long silver string attached to the roof of the tent. Drake rang it and sat down to wait.

It wasn't long before he heard a deep masculine voice coming from the front of the tent. "Hold your horses, I'm coming." A tall muscular man dressed in tight fitting pants and an open vest shirt stepped into the waiting room. He had short black hair and a wide face by most standards. He carried a wide bladed sword attached to his waist which was hard for anyone to ignore. He often used his sword to scare off potential thieves from stealing his precious merchandise. His gaze fell upon Drake sitting there in the waiting room. "Aw, Drake my friend! What brings you in today? Got more honeycomb for me to buy I suppose? You wouldn't believe how much I'm selling it for now days and it's still a bargain for most people who can't seem to find it anywhere else! Drake glanced downward as if contemplating some bad news. "Yachmed my friend, I'm afraid I must drive the price up this time. I almost got stabbed by a flying pitchfork on my way here! It's not easy getting honey or honeycomb for you anymore. That being said, I barely managed to get 14 jars of fresh honey and 8 blocks of honeycomb. They're all sitting outside in my wagon just waiting for you my friend. Obviously, the honeycomb is much harder to come by these days so I'm asking 100 rubies per block for it and 20 rubies per jar of honey as well.

All together; we're looking at a 1,080 ruby price tag. Can you handle that?" Yachmed crossed his big muscular arms across his chest. "Make it an even 1,000 rubies and you've got yourself a deal Drake!" Drake placed a hand on his chin and glanced upward as if contemplating the deal further. "Alright Yachmed, you drive a hard bargain but I'm willing to give it all to you for 1,000 rubies." The two men shook hands on their new found deal. "Help me get it out of the wagon will you," Drake asked confidently? "Of course," replied Yachmed.

They quickly made their way out towards Drake's covered wagon which had been parked near the back entrance of the shop. Stepping outside at just the right moment, they quickly spotted Molasses and Glue being led away by an unknown stranger wearing a mask. "Stop thief," Drake yelled furiously! Yachmed pulled his wide bladed sword from the sash around his waist and began chasing after the covered wagon vigorously. Drake quickly retrieved his wand from his deep robe pocket and sent a freezing spell hurling towards the hastily retreating wagon. To his astonishment, the bright blue ball of light bellowing from his benign wand bounced off the blatantly bolting wagon and came flying directly back towards him! He jumped out of the way just in time for it to hit the ground behind him. Yachmed came running back and stood next to Drake. "Sorry my friend, I couldn't catch the thief. You're horses are much too fast!" Drake laughed. "The thief must have cast a spell on them to make them run faster. Believe me, there's a reason I call them Glue and Molasses." Yachmed laughed between breaths of exhaustion. "What are you going to do now Drake?" Drake shook his head disappointingly. "I'll track down that good for nothing horse thief and when I get my hands on…Hey, you didn't happen to get a good look the scoundrel did you?" Yachmed put a hand to his chin thoughtfully. "Didn't catch much; the thief wore a mask, a turban and looked quite slim. The turban prevented me from seeing a hair color so there's not much I can really tell you Drake. Sorry about that." Drake sighed. "It just isn't my day Yachmed."

Drake slowly walked away with his head drooped downwards. Yachmed felt bad for him. "Hey Drake, I think I already know why but I just have to ask…why do you use horses? Why don't you just fly everywhere like all the other fairies around here," he asked curiously? Drake turned back to face him. "I think we both know there's a shortage of Pixie Dust here in Nectarville. Without it, we can't fly anywhere. So I'm saving as much a possible for a rainy day." Yachmed nodded. "You're not the only one who does that. Believe me; I'm starting to see more horses on these old dirt roads than there ever used to be. Back in the day, Pixie Dust used to be given out freely to any fairy who asked for it but now the ingredients are much harder to get a hold of and merchants are selling them for incredibly high prices! I really hate that stupid witch for cursing the fairies to never fly again but I also enjoy the profits that come from the unfortunate situation." Drake nodded. "Perhaps things will be different one day my friend. Until then, we must do what we can to make ends meet." Drake turned away from Yachmed with his head hung low. "Alright Drake, take one of my horses! I can't stand to see you walk away without any form of transportation," said Yachmed sympathetically. Drake turned back around to face the muscular man. "You mean it Yachmed? Really?" Yachmed nodded. "I guess I have a soft spot for my favorite honeycomb dealer," he said lightheartedly. "Wait here a moment and I'll grab my stable stamp for you to use."

Yachmed walked back through the back entrance of his tent shop. He soon returned with a small metal square which had his merchant logo stamped into it. His logo was a beehive wrapped in a long pointed ribbon which read, "Honey for Money" on it. "Take this to the town stable and they will give you my horse Drake," Yachmed said confidently as he held the metal square out for Drake to accept. Drake pushed the offer away delicately. "That's very kind of you my friend but I don't need your charity." Yachmid shoved the stable stamp back towards Drake. "I insist! Take my horse so you will have a way to get around town. That two-timing thief obviously stole your mode of transportation along with your inventory. It's the least I can do." Drake held out his own hands to accept the gift gracefully. "Thank you my friend. You are very kind." Yachmed gently punched Drake on the shoulder. "Hey, I can't have my best honeycomb vender quit on me just because of a little setback," he replied playfully. Drake smiled. "You're too good to me Yachmed. If I ever recover my wagon, you can be sure I'll continue doing business with you."

Shaking hands on their agreement, Drake began walking back towards the long line of merchant tents sitting on both sides of the main dirt road leading through the middle of town. Many merchants tried drawing him in to buy their various items but he ignored them and continued walking towards the town stable. One particular shop caught his attention on the way there. A bright red banner sown high over the tent entrance read: "The Magic Box" in sparkling gold letters across the top. "This must be new. Perhaps I'll drop in to take a peak," he thought curiously.

Stepping inside the shop, he glanced around curiously. Surprisingly, he found himself alone and couldn't see any goods for sale anywhere. All he saw was a long glass case cabinet separating him from the merchant who was supposed to be standing behind it. A strange feeling of loneliness and mystery washed over him. "What kind of a shop is this," he wondered creepily? "Hello; is anybody here," he called out. "Shopkeeper, are you back there?"

Just then an old man's voice shouted from the back of the shop which was separated by a pair of long brown curtains. "I'll be there in a moment good sir. If you would like to inspect my wares then please press the small button located on the bottom side of the glass cabinet. Drake gazed through the top of the transparent cabinet and didn't see anything inside it. "Sorry, but I'm not seeing a button here," he said hesitantly. The mystical voice replied from behind the curtain again. "Oh, the button is made of glass too so you wouldn't be able to see it. You'll need to feel around on the bottom side of the cabinet to find it," he replied reassuringly.

Drake leaned down on one knee and placed his right hand up against the bottom side of the glass case in front of him. Running his hand along the smooth glass surface at the bottom, he felt the slight curvature of the button beneath. "Oh, this must be it," he thought joyfully. He pressed inward as multiple small glass stained boxes began to appear inside the larger glass cabinet. All the boxes were only about a foot in length and height but the variety of colors they came in were quite eye catching. The one that caught Drake's attention the most sat right in the center of the rest of them. It continually changed colors from red to green to blue to purple and so on. He continued staring at it until he felt quite entranced by its presence.

"Aw, I see the Transformation Box has caught your eye," said the old man from behind the counter. Drake shook his head and forced himself to look away from the colorful box. "It's quite intriguing," he replied. "What does it do exactly?" The old man's eyes were quite wrinkled around the edges and his white hair suggested him to be quite old indeed. "This multicolor Transformation Box has the power to change any object into any other object that you desire. However, you must be willing to pay the price for it as well," he said cautiously. Drake stared at him thoughtfully. "What price would that be exactly," he asked curiously? Without hesitation the old shopkeeper replied. "It will take a bit of youth from you every time you use it," he said with obvious regret in his voice.

Drake noticed the old man's regretful tone and asked the obvious question. "I'm guessing you've used it quite a bit then?" The old man nodded. "You'd be right about that young man. In fact, I bet you couldn't guess how old I really am even if you tried." Drake looked at the old man a little closer. Judging by his wrinkled skin and white hair, he looked to be in his 80's but he didn't want to insult the old man so he ventured on a lower number. "I bet you're about 75 now. Am I right?" The old man laughed. "Well, if you cut about 40 years off that then you'd be correct young man," he replied with a grin. Drake's smile turned upside down. "You're 35 years old? No way! Wow, that Transformation Box really did a number on you good sir! You must have got some good things out of it though I would imagine?" The old man sighed. "Well, let's put it this way…I had a wife and family once. I was a simple merchant just trying to provide for his family when I came across another merchant selling this Transformation Box. He was an old man much like I am now. He promised this little box would change my life forever. He said I could change rocks into gold with it. Sure, he told me about the curse that accompanied it but I didn't care. I just wanted to make some money and provide for my family. I was a honeycomb merchant at the time so I traded every bit of inventory I owned in exchange for the little box you see in front of you. Long story short, I put rocks in the box and they came out as rubies just as predicted. By the time I had returned home to my wife and kids to tell them the good news, they didn't even recognize me anymore! The only part of my story they actually heard was that I had traded all of my merchandize for this little box. After hearing that, they didn't want to listen to anything else I had to say unfortunately."

A tear trickled down Floyd's left eye. Drake placed a hand on his shoulder comfortingly. "I'm sorry for your loss Floyd. My name is Drake by the way. Judging from your heart wrenching story, I can tell this box has brought you nothing but pain and misery my friend. So how about letting me take it off your hands," he asked empathetically? Floyd straightened up and wiped a trailing tear from his eye. "Believe me Drake, I know the power of this box can be tempting beyond all measure but you must trust me. It's not worth your youth. Life is far too precious to put a price tag on and yet this Transformation Box does exactly that. You look like you're in your early 20's. Am I right?" Drake nodded agreeably. "That's right. I must say though Floyd; I don't have a wife or kids to go home to. Basically, I live for myself and don't have anyone else to impress so a little aging doesn't bother me none."

Floyd was taller than Drake and stared down at him during their conversation. "What do you do for a living young man," he asked curiously? Drake continued staring up at him. "I'm a honeycomb wholesaler," he replied confidently. Floyd sighed. "You really do remind me of myself at your age Drake. Although, I was probably a bit more of a ladies man than you," he said jokingly. Drake laughed. "That's okay Floyd. I'm probably richer than you were at my age," he replied in retort. Floyd glanced down at the Transformation Box sitting inside the glass case. "I seriously doubt you have enough rubies to pay for this incredibly rare and dangerous item," he said seriously. Drake looked at him seriously. "Name your price old man!" Floyd cleared his throat. "Well for starters, calling me old man won't help you get a cheaper deal ya little whippersnapper! That being said, I'm asking for three million rubies for it!" It was Drake's turn to clear his throat. "Are you insane old man?! I've got plenty of inventory to sell but even that would be a stretch! How about this…I will give you my entire inventory of honey, honeycomb, beehives and bees plus a half a million rubies on top of that in exchange for this Transformation Box." Floyd laughed. "Ha! You really expect me to believe that you have a half a million rubies just lying around? You think I was born yesterday?" Drake looked at him seriously. "You're right. I don't have that much with me YET but I can get it for you soon though. Hold onto this Transformation Box for me and I'll be back within the week; you can count on it. They quickly shook hands on their new found deal. Before Drake could exit the shop, Floyd said; "it's really not worth it Drake. Believe me; I'm only making the price so high in an attempt to discourage you from buying it." Drake turned around. "Then why would you have it in your display case if you didn't want to sell it Floyd?" Before Floyd could answer, Drake stormed out of the shop determined to sell enough of inventory to get enough rubies necessary to buy the rare Transformation Box! Under his breath Floyd muttered; "because it's killing me Drake."

20. FIGHTING THE DRAGON

A bright orange and purple sunset filled the sky as the sun began sinking below the horizon. Mojo flew in front with Misty trailing behind him on her broomstick. She let out a gigantic yawn! "Hey Mojo, I know you're probably not tired since you're a genie but I think it's time we stop for a rest. We've been flying all day and I'll probably fall off my broom if we go any longer!" She knew Pixie wasn't tired since she had simply attached herself to her shoulder the entire flight there. Mojo agreed and they quickly made their decent towards the forest floor.

They had just enough light to see past the trees and branches below them as they slowly came to a landing feet first on the soft forest dirt below. Misty dismounted from her broomstick as Pixie detached herself from her shoulder and began hovering in the air next to her. Throwing a handful of Pixie Dust over her shoulder, she managed to keep herself above ground for the time being. She knew her small stash of Pixie Dust wouldn't last much longer and the thought of being stranded alone without it frightened her immensely. "Misty, I don't want to frighten you or anything but I'm getting a bad feeling about being in this forest. Call me crazy but it feels like someone or something is watching us right now!" Mojo was only a few feet away and happened to overhear her. "Oh, stop being such a worry wart Pixie. I'll protect us if something happens," he said reassuringly. "Perhaps we should set up camp," he suggested confidently.

Mojo pointed towards a small nearby tree as a stream of blue light shot from his pointer finger into the base of its trunk. The tree creaked a bit before toppling over right in front of them! Misty and Pixie jumped back in fear of being smashed by the falling tree but knew Mojo wouldn't let that happen. Mojo continued shooting magical beams of light into the fallen tree until it began hovering in the air. He made a few chopping motions with his hands as the tree began getting sliced into perfectly sized portions of wood as if a group of invisible wood cutters were there chopping it up into perfectly sized pieces for them! He quickly moved the wood pile through the air into a centralized position directly in front of them. Snapping his fingers, a roaring fire instantly blazed to life in front of them! "Show off," Misty said with a grin! Mojo knew he had impressed her and returned the smile along with a slight blush. "I can make chairs for us too if you'd like," he replied confidently. "Oh, let me do that," responded Misty. Pulling her wand from her inner robe pocket, she pointed it at a few small rocks sitting around the campfire. After chanting a few incantations, they instantly enlarged themselves to form a couple of perfectly shaped stone benches. Mojo glanced at Misty joyfully. "Impressive my lady!" Misty couldn't help but blush. Pixie watched the interaction between them. "Oh you two disgust me," she said playfully. Sharing a laugh, they continued chatting late into the night.

The common need for survival brought them closer than they had ever been. "Where are we all going to sleep tonight," Pixie asked curiously? Mojo and Misty were now sitting on the same stone bench facing the campfire with Pixie sitting on an adjacent bench next to theirs. "Oh, how silly of me," replied Mojo. "Give me a second." Standing up from his bench, he pointed a finger towards a patch of dirt near the campfire. Streaks of blue light shot from his hand into the dirt where he was pointing. The dirt began swirling faster and faster into the air until it became incredibly thick and almost impossible to see through. As the dust settled, they observed three canopy tents ready and waiting for them to use. Misty smiled glancing over at Mojo. "You're quite the show off Mojo," she said flatteringly again. He leaned in and draped his arm gently around her shoulders. She responded by leaning in to rest her head up against his left shoulder. "A show off and a charmer," she replied lovingly.

Before Misty and Mojo could get any more intimate with each-other, a loud howling sound came bellowing from behind them! The surprise jolted them into a standing position immediately. Suddenly, one growl quickly turned into two, then three and so on. "Oh no, we're surrounded," Pixie shouted! Staring out into the darkness, they spotted a large number of red glowing eyes gazing back at them hungrily. "No worries," replied Mojo confidently. He circled his right hand high above his head as if about to lasso something. Streams of bright blue light quickly encircled them and expanded in size to form a massive bubble shield around them. The bright red eyes surrounding them slowly emerged from behind the trees and into the light of the campfire. The group could now make out the large number of werewolves now encircling them. They were closing in fast; their sharp teeth gleaming from the light of the fire!

The lead werewolf jumped towards Misty smacking directly into the magic shield surrounding them! He bounced off the transparent shield and onto the dirt forest floor. Five more werewolves jumped out at them from behind the dense forest trees only to meet the same fate as the first. "The shield won't hold much longer," Mojo shouted! "We must escape quickly!" Misty summoned her broom towards her which was currently leaning up against a nearby boulder. The broom came flying towards her outstretched hand only to smack up against the invisible shield surrounding them. "Oh, that's not good," she exclaimed with a frown. One of the werewolves noticed what had happened and quickly made his way over to where her broomstick was now lying on the dirt and picked it up with his teeth. Misty became furious as she watched the wolf walk away with her broomstick! Pixie formulated a quick plan. She rubbed the miniature lamp dangling from the silver chain around her neck. Instantly the dragon genie emerged from the lamp's opening. Claw's extra-large scaled body was far too massive for the invisible shield surrounding them as he shattered it completely! It fell apart and disappeared with the audible sound of glass window smashing against a stone floor. Claw glanced around at the large number of werewolves surrounding them. Before he could do anything else, one of the werewolves jumped high into the air towards him. The werewolf's sharp claws dug into their target as they penetrated the dragon's thick skin and stuck into the dragon's upper front leg! A scream of agony escaped the dragon's throat as he furiously twisted his body back and forth in an effort to knock the clingy werewolf from his leg. Swinging his long fat tail towards the small group of werewolves nearby, he knocked four of them off their feet and through the air! The one sticking to Claw's front leg finally lost its grip and soared high through the air as well. Before any more werewolves could attack him, Claw inhaled deeply into his large dragon belly and forcefully blew outwards. A long stream of scorching red flame shot from his mouth towards the pack of werewolves. Many of them turned to ash instantly while the rest of them retreated back into the woods from where they had come.

Mojo, Misty and Pixie were all standing behind Claw the entire time the battle had taken place between him and the werewolves. A look of shock crossed their faces at what they had just witnessed. They all felt highly privileged to have the dragon on their side! "Thank you so much Claw," said Misty gratefully. "We owe you our lives," Pixie agreed. Mojo expressed his sincere gratitude as well for what Claw had just done to help save their lives.

Misty was still upset that one of the werewolves had managed to steal her broomstick away from her. She turned towards Claw. "We hate to be a burden Claw but would you mind giving us a lift to the Dessert of Doom? Those blasted werewolves ran off with my broomstick and we are still quite exhausted from the day's journey. Claw nodded his long neck agreeably. Misty turned towards Mojo. "Would you mind helping me mount Mojo," she asked eagerly? "I'd be happy to," he responded gladly. Walking up behind her, he gently wrapped his muscular genie arms around her waist before lifting her up off the ground and onto Claw's neck. Pixie quickly joined them. Claw lifted them up off the ground with his massive wings and began flying in a northward direction towards the Dessert of Doom. It was a cool breezy night lit by a full moon and plenty of twinkling stars in the distance. All three of them quickly fell asleep while letting Claw take them safely to their destination.

21. ROBBING THE THIEF

Drake finally arrived at the Nectarville stable. Two guards holding spears and wearing metal plated armor stood on opposite sides of the over-sized stable entrance. This was meant to be a town stable where anyone could park their horses while walking through the Nectarville marketplace. It was a convenient service conveniently paid for by the loyal tax payers of Nectarville. Thus, a person didn't need to pay to park his or her horse inside the Nectarville stable. However, the horse owner did need identification to help protect against any possible thievery that may occur.

Drake approached one of the stable guards standing at the entrance and flashed the metal logo Achmed had given him. "Please release my horse," Drake commanded. He handed the small metal plate to the guard standing on his right. The guard reached out and accepted the trinket from Drake's hand. Inspecting it carefully, a look of curiosity crossed his face. "One moment please." The guard walked back into the stable while the other one continued to stand guard at the entrance. He soon reemerged holding the reigns of a beautiful black stallion. "She's a beauty," he said admiringly. "Yes she is," replied Drake agreeably as he began to mount the stallion. He was no stranger to riding horses but still preferred his covered wagon more than anything. He gave the reins a good flick to get the horse moving again. "Thank you good sir," he shouted to the guard as he began riding westward.

After passing by a few more merchant shops, he travelled up the dirt road for about half a mile before arriving at the designated spot for Nectarville's inns and taverns. The dirt road transitioned into a cobblestone pathway leading straight between the old buildings. The first tavern he saw was on his right. It had a large wooden sign hanging from a tall metal pole near its entrance. In old style lettering, the words: "The Grinning Gator" was printed just below a picture of a smiling alligator. Drake brought his stallion to a slow trot and made his way towards the back of the tavern. It wasn't long before he spotted his covered wagon along with Molasses and Glue standing right in front of it. Raising his voice, he shouted. "Duncan are you there?" A skinny middle aged man with short brown hair and a large belt buckle jumped out from the back of the wagon upon hearing his voice. Duncan spotted him. "Ya old scoundrel," he exclaimed with a grin! "You got me the horse just like you promised!" Drake continued walking towards him while simultaneously leading his black stallion alongside him as well. "I told ya I'd pay you back for your troubles in Old Man Baker's Orchard," he replied with a smirk. Duncan scowled. "It's a pity Old Man Baker shot my old one." Drake glanced at him sympathetically. "No worries Duncan; I take good care of my employees. Harvesting honey and honeycomb from other people's orchards can be a tricky business." Duncan nodded. "Especially when they're chasing after you with sharp pointy objects; I've had javelins thrown at me, arrows shot at me and even came close to getting caught in a tree trap." Drake shook his head. "No worries Duncan. I've got a plan that will make us richer than kings!"

Duncan looked intrigued as Drake continued. "As you well know, we've collected honeycomb for quite some time now and we now have quite the stash saved up. Lately I've been scouting around trying to find the best buyer for our inventory and I've finally found something that can make us wealthier than dwarf miners!" Duncan was on the edge. "Don't make me guess Drake! What is it?" Drake glanced around cautiously to make sure no one else was eavesdropping in on their conversation. "I found a special item for sale called the Transformation Box. It can literally transform any object into anything you desire!" Duncan looked amazed. "How much does it cost? Also, would it be possible for us to snatch it without the merchant noticing?" Drake stared off into the distance as if contemplating the possibilities. "The merchant, Floyd, has seen my face already and knows I want it so the element of surprise is already gone. It took some doing but I managed to convince the old man to sell it to me in exchange for my entire inventory along with an additional 500,000 Rubies." Duncan slapped a hand over his own forehead! "Are you kidding me Drake?! We've spent years collecting our inventory. Are you seriously willing to risk years of hard work in hopes that this little magic box will do what you're saying?! Did you at least see a demonstration of its powers I hope?" Drake stared off into the distance again. "Of course I did," he lied. "I wouldn't put our entire fortunes at risk for nothing. You've just got to trust me Duncan." Duncan scowled. "Obviously magic is everywhere Drake. I've seen hornets transform into toads. I've seen rocks turn into bread. Heck, I've even seen flying arrows turn into a delicate ruby red roses but every magical creature on this planet knows that nothing in the world can transform into a ruby! That's why they're so valuable. Believe me Drake, I've looked into this matter extensively and it just can't be done. It has been said that even the great court wizard Morpheus can't transform objects into rubies….and if he can't do it…well…" Duncan's voice trailed off knowing full well he didn't need to finish that sentence. Drake looked at him seriously. "I knew you'd say that Duncan. So how about we both go back to the merchant who first showed me the Transformation Box and I'll get him to give us a demonstration of what I'm talking about. Assuming you're convinced on the matter then we'll split the cost of it and unload our inventory onto the old man. I know it sounds risky but trust me; this could be the chance of a lifetime Duncan!" Duncan exhaled heavily and lowered his gaze. "Alright Drake, take me to this old man merchant of yours and I'll tell you what I think." Drake smiled. "You won't regret it Duncan; I promise."

Drake was about to walk back to his covered wagon when

Duncan chimed in again. "Um, you should probably be careful about taking that covered wagon back into town so soon. Achmed might see you and start asking questions. In fact, I should be careful taking this new stallion of mine around his shop. He might get a little suspicious of what we're up too." Drake nodded agreeably. "Good point Duncan. Perhaps we should head back to my place first. We'll take the long way back just so Achmed doesn't see us. It's getting dark already so perhaps we should stay the night at Black Hawk Inn and head out first thing in the morning. What do you think?" Duncan glanced upwards at the darkening sky. The sun was sinking below the horizon and it wouldn't be long before nightfall would soon be upon them. "Oh alright, let's stay at Black Hawk Inn tonight and we'll make our way back to your place first thing in the morning. I suppose the inn is as good a place as any to park our horses for the night," he said thoughtfully. "How about we stop at the tavern to celebrate my new horse," he suggested stepping closer to his new black stallion standing next to him. Drake shook his head disappointedly. "What have I told you about drinking on the job Duncan?" Duncan rolled his eyes with annoying familiarity. "I know, I know…it's a waste of hard earned money and it clouds my better judgment when trying to steal from others." Drake nodded with satisfaction. "And don't forget it my good man," he said confidently. "Alright, let's head on over to Black Hawk Inn and get some shuteye then." Drake handed Duncan the reins to the slender stallion. "Treat her well and she won't let you down my friend. I can already tell she'll be much faster than old Glue and Molasses over there," he said pointing towards his two disappointments standing behind Duncan. Duncan smiled. "That's a sure fire bet. I honestly think Achmed could run faster than those two snails," he replied with a laugh. Drake laughed along with him. "It's sad we've resorted to stealing from our loyal merchants. Back in the day it was all fun and games; taking from the local orchards and farmers but look at where we've ended up now Duncan." Duncan shook his head. "I know. It's a shame really. Perhaps one day we'll confess our misdeeds and give everything back." They enjoyed the awkward pause for a moment before laughing at how stupid that sounded. "See, this is why you're my number one co-worker," Drake teased jokingly. "It's because you can spot a slow poke a mile away before he even realizes you're wearing his shoes!" The two of them continued laughing and joking all the way back to Black Hawk Inn where they parked their horses at the inn's stable and settled in for the night.

22. THE SAND TRAPPER

Heading towards the Dessert of Doom, the little group had been traveling on Claw's neck for about a half a day now. Sleep had overtaken them when suddenly a high pitched shriek awoke them from their deep slumber. Misty was the first to pier downwards through the clouds at the hot dessert sand below. Gasping at the horrifying sight below her; she spotted many large circles of quicksand. They all funneled inward and downward as the sand continued to be sucked down towards the center of each individual circle.

Misty's gaze followed the high pitched shrieking sound that continued with annoying repetition. She spotted a giant red flowering plant emerging from the center of a large quicksand pit below her. At first glance, the frightening massive plant looked like a giant closed pedaled rose that continued to rise higher and higher into the sky. It looked totally harmless to Misty until the five pedals opened wide to reveal a large black and yellow circled center lined with incredibly sharp thorns! The center circle was hollow and led downward into a thick green hollow stem which led directly into the quicksand itself. The plant looked large enough to eat small animals if it so desired. Six long leaves detached from its thick green stem. Each leaf was surprisingly thick and was covered in sharp pointed needles. "This must be the dessert Sand Trappers the Queen warned us about," Misty exclaimed cautiously.

The Sand Trapper flung a handful of pointy needles at them as they flew past it. The long pointy needles barely missed their heads as they ducked just in time to avoid them. The Sand Trapper was quick to fling a second round of needles at them again! Claw soared higher in an attempt to dodge incoming needles. The higher elevation was enough to keep the little group safe riding on his neck but not quite enough to avoid getting hit himself! The second round of needles sunk deep into the Claw's stomach! He groaned loudly and quickly lost control of his situation. His body tipped sideways; almost far enough to knock everyone off his neck. Somehow he managed to stabilize himself again without anyone falling off completely. The magic blanket on his neck helped stabilize the group as well but would only work for so long if he somehow managed to get turned upside down completely. Suddenly, Mojo's commanding voice filled the air. "Everyone take flight before Claw keels over on us!" Misty replied. "I don't have a broom Mojo. What am I going to do?" Mojo wrapped an arm around her back and another underneath her legs before lifting off into the skies with her held securely in place. Pixie took to the skies as well. In an effort to save Claw from acquiring any further damage, she quickly rubbed the miniature lamp dangling from the small chain around her neck. Claw instantly turned into a stream of black smoke before being sucked back into the lamp's opening.

The little group attempted to fly past the Sand Trapper in an effort to get to safety but the giant plant had other plans for them. Its six spiky leaves wrapped around its stem as its five massive pedals closed together. Suddenly, its head began spinning a full 360 degrees in a counter-clockwise direction. It was similar to watching a basketball spin on top of someone's finger. The group felt mesmerized watching the plant's head spin faster and faster in front of them. Suddenly, they felt themselves being sucked inward towards it as if a force stronger than gravity was pulling them towards it. Trying desperately to escape the

Sand Trapper's inward pull, their efforts came to no avail.

Mojo turned to face the Sand Trapper and began shooting large bolts of fire at it in an attempt to destroy it once and for all. The bolts of flame were simply absorbed by the Sand Trapper in a way that seemed to make it come alive even more. It was as if it were feeding on Mojo's magic in a horrible sort of way. Misty was slung over the genie's shoulder and couldn't see what was happening in front of him. "Oh, I wish those stupid werewolves hadn't took off with my broomstick," she screamed out desperately! She suddenly remembered the anti-gravity amulets they all had around their necks. "Oh duh," she thought stupidly to herself. Grabbing the amulet dangling around her neck, she rubbed it in a clockwise circular motion just as the Queen had instructed. The pulling force sucking her inward instantly lightened up. "Mojo, hurry and rub your anti-gravity amulet!" He did as he was told. Instantly, he felt the pulling force around him die as well. His ability to escape was immediately realized as he quickly turned away from the large plant to fly away with Misty still flung over his shoulder.

Pixie was currently being sucked in by the plant's inward pull and was now within its grasp. Mojo screamed out to her. "Use your anti-gravity amulet Pixie; hurry!" Just as Pixie began to rub her anti-gravity amulet, the Sand Trapper's pedals opened up again. It lunged towards her! The pedals were far stickier than they appeared as they latched onto her right leg! "Let go of me," she screamed! "Help me Mojo," she pleaded desperately! Mojo knew he had to get Misty to safety but didn't want to leave Pixie behind either. He flew back over to where Pixie was about to be swallowed alive by the massive plant. Misty was still slung over his shoulder as he reached out to Pixie in an effort to save her. Pixie grabbed onto his hand and held on tight! The glue like substance holding onto her leg began sliding down the plant's pedal and slowly drug her along with it! Mojo desperately tried pulling her free from the sticky substance as it continued pulling her closer and closer towards its hollow center. Pixie began crying. "Oh Mojo, it's over for me. Save yourself!" Mojo attempted to shoot fire bolts and lightening spells at the horrifying plant in an effort to free Pixie from its vice-like grasp but nothing worked. It was as if all of his spells were being absorbed into the plant and giving it even more energy than it had before! Misty was still slung over Mojo's right shoulder like a gunny sack and couldn't do anything to help save Pixie at the moment even though she desperately wanted to! "I promise to kill this plant if it's the last thing I do," Mojo shouted to Pixie just before her entire body slid down into the depths of its long hollow stem. Mojo broke free from the plant's pulling force and flew Misty towards a tall sand dune nearby.

He carried Misty a safe distance away from the monstrous plant before setting her down on the hot dessert sand. "Wait here Misty. I've got some killing to do!" His anger had boiled past its limits as he prepared himself for some serious revenge! Scorching bolts of lightning shot from his body as he flew headfirst towards the monstrous plant with his fist outstretched towards it. The giant plant opened its mouth in an attempt to swallow him whole. Surprisingly, Mojo flew directly into the belly of the beast with the speed of a torpedo headed inward to annihilate its worst enemy.

The Sand Trapper was ready for him though. Detaching its six long leaves from their stem, it reached up just in time to snatch Mojo out of the air. Its sharp needle leaves jabbed through him with the force of a thousand javelins! Mojo's pain didn't last long before the Sand Trapper had swallowed him whole and alive!

Watching from a distance, Misty didn't know whether to cry or seek revenge immediately. A tear streaked down her cheek as a burning rage sizzled through her veins. She desperately wanted to kill that horrible monster and avenge her fallen friends. On the other hand, she didn't want to die along with them either. Her thoughts and emotions were a jumbled up mess of sadness, confusion and rage. Torn between the actions of fighting and fleeing, an idea suddenly came to her. Holding her Jargon Band up to her mouth, she spoke the passcode into it in hopes of speaking with Andrew. "IF WISHES WERE FISHES WE'D ALL HAVE A FRY. He'll know what to do," she thought desperately.

Her Jargon Band glowed green showing it had been activated

correctly. "Hello Andrew, are you there?" She shouted into the hat. "Can anyone hear me? Hello, Andrew…are you there? I desperately need your help right now! Please answer," she pleaded! The sadness in her voice was hard to mask and she felt another tear about to surface in her right eye. Just when she was about to give up on getting a response, she heard the calming and reassuring sound of Andrew's voice on the other end. "Hello Misty, is everything okay," he asked with concern in his voice? Misty did everything she could to hold back the constant weeping she wanted to express at the moment. "No Andrew, all of my friends just got swallowed by a giant Sand Trapper here in the Dessert of Doom and all the magic in the world couldn't destroy the stupid thing!" Misty somehow managed to speak between her sad spurts of crying. "I…just…don't know….what…to do Andrew," she sobbed with tears in her eyes.

Morpheus glanced up into the air for a moment. He hated to hear anyone cry. It tugged at his heart strings and he actually did feel bad for her. He continued speaking in Andrew's cool and calming tone of voice. "There, there Misty….I'm truly sorry to hear about your friends. It makes me sad to hear such horrible news. If I were there right now I'd wrap my arms around you and not let you go until we both felt even a tiny bit better." Hearing those words actually did help her feel a tiny bit better and she was glad he was there to help provide some sort of comfort. "Thank you Andrew, I know we don't really know each-other that well but I appreciate the sympathy for sure," she replied gratefully.

Since Morpheus actually did feel bad for the sobbing Misty he decided to offer a helping hand. "Um, Misty, I don't actually know much about Sand Trappers but I think the court wizard Morpheus once told me that they keep their victims tied up underground using their incredibly strong root system. From what he told me, Sand Trappers continually suck the life out of their victims with their roots. That's how they stay alive for so long in such dry and deserted places. It's a long drawn out process that could take years to devour an entire body. I know that sounds disturbing but it also means your friends are most likely still alive and trapped in the underground catacombs of the dessert. Tell you what, let me talk to Morpheus more about it and maybe he'll know what to do to help get them out of there. Sound good," he asked reassuringly?

Just the possibility of her friends still being alive gave Misty enough hope to stop crying. Gently wiping a tear away from her already soaked cheek bone, she managed to speak again. "Oh thank you Andrew. You've given me the greatest hope anyone could ask for. Please talk to Morpheus for me as soon as possible and see what he can do to help my friends escape from these underground catacombs. I'm just happy to know that they could still be alive! Thanks again for the encouragement Andrew," she replied with heartfelt admiration in her voice.

The conversation between them was starting to melt Morpheus's cold heart just enough to where he even felt a touch of empathy for her. "Alright Misty, I'll do that. But in the meantime, I want you to stay away from that monstrous Sand Trapper. I don't want it swallowing you too. Do you understand?" Misty agreed with his request. "Don't worry. I'll stay away from it Andrew but what am I supposed to until you arrive…twittle my thumbs and count sand particles," she asked jokingly? Morpheus laughed. "I can tell you're feeling better already," he replied reassuringly. "Just try to stay cool until I talk to Morpheus and find out how to rescue your friends out there. Alright?" Misty agreed. "Alright, I wish I could give you an exact location of where to find me but you'll just have to look for a small green tent that I'm about to conjure up while I wait for you to get here." Morpheus laughed. "Just stay close to your Jargon Band. You might be hearing from Morpheus soon. I'm sure he can give you some better instructions on what to do next. But in the meantime, try to get some rest Misty. Talk to you soon. Morpheus closed the communication line between them with the shutdown passcode. "ENOUGH SOUND; SHUT ER' DOWN."

Misty's Jargon Band quickly stopped glowing green the moment the shutdown passcode was spoken thus indicating the closed communication line between them. With her other hand, she reached down into the hot sand and grabbed a handful of it. Hurling it forward with an energetic heave, the sand misted out in front of her. Pointing her wand at it, she spoke the words "MORPHICO TENTELLO." Instantly, her handful of airborne sand quickly transformed into a small one-man tent right in front of her. "Well, at least it's shady," she thought to herself gratefully as she laid her body inside the open ended tent. Grabbing another handful of sand from the other open end of the tent where her head faced, she conjured up a large fluffy white pillow to rest her head on. She decided it would be best to try and get some sleep while she had the chance. "Sleeping opportunities seem to be getting fewer and further between," she thought tiredly before dozing off to sleep.

23. THE MIDNIGHT VISIT

Drake and Duncan were fast asleep in their separate beds when a loud knock came thudding on their bedroom door! Duncan jumped out of bed faster than you could say Jack Robinson! Drake was up just as quick. The two conniving thieves were vigilant during all hours of the night for fear of getting caught.

With the quickest of pace, Drake rushed over to the side of the door that swung inward. "Who's there," he shouted. A faint voice came from the other side of the doorway. "Sorry to disturb you gentlemen but I have some important news from old man Floyd." Drake looked over at Duncan. "What kind of news can't wait until morning," he shouted through the closed door? "Open up and I'll tell you," the voice replied firmly. Duncan gestured for Drake to switch spots with him. He wanted some backup just in case their mysterious visitor decided to try anything stupid. Drake moved forward into Duncan's former position behind the closed door while Duncan moved in front of him to answer it. He gently cracked the door open and peaked outside into the red carpeted hallway. He didn't see anybody standing there so he backed his head away from the opening and shouted. "Don't play games with me sir…show yourself!" "I'm down here," replied the faint voice. Duncan's gaze fell downwards as he scanned around for the mysterious speaker. His eyes fell upon a smaller sized gentleman with a pointy hat and a thick gray beard. His beard gave him the appearance of being old but the life in his green sparkly eyes told another story entirely. "My name is Nick the gnome," he said politely. "I work as a messenger for people who don't like to travel long distances." Drake moved towards the open door so that Nick could see him as well. "What's important enough to wake us in the middle of the night for? Also, who told you we were staying here? Was it that desk boy because so help me he will pay for his insolence if that's who it was," he exclaimed furiously! Nick glanced downward shamefully. "I may have tipped off the desk boy to tell me your room number good sirs…but believe me, it was all for a good cause I can assure you." Duncan felt like he wanted to slap the little gnome across the face. "Be quick with your news little man! I'm tired and desperately want to go back to sleep!"

Nick turned his head to the right and then to the left. The hallway was empty and it was the middle of the night so he felt safe telling the two men his closely guarded secret. "Like I was saying, old man Floyd sent me with important news for Drake. Which one of you is Drake?" Duncan pointed towards Drake. "He's Drake and I'm Duncan. Speed it up little man; you're bothering me!" Nick kept his voice low and began speaking much faster to accommodate for Duncan's foul mood. "Floyd says he is willing to meet with Drake at his place tomorrow evening. He says he will lower the price of the Transformation Box simply because he is getting to old to use it much longer. Apparently, he wants to pass it along to a much younger person. He wants to meet you at your place of inventory so it will be easy to make the exchange. He sent me to get your residential location and to confirm the meeting for tomorrow evening. Is that acceptable to you Drake," Nick asked politely? Drake nodded. "Sounds like a good deal to me. I'm just wondering why old man Floyd wouldn't come find me himself?" Nick continued staring upwards at Drake. "He said he had other business meetings to attend tonight and tomorrow morning so he simply didn't have the time to travel here but that is why I have a job," Nick replied gratefully.

Drake nodded. "I understand. Tell Floyd to meet me at the base of Boulder Mountain on the south side. That is where I live and that is where our inventory is stashed at as well. Tell him we'll make a deal for the Transformation Box tomorrow evening at sunset. Also, let him know he can spend the night at my place if he needs a place to stay." Nick nodded understandably. "I'll let him know for sure. Once again, I'm sorry to wake both of you but I get the feeling that whatever this deal is about, it must have been worth the trip if old man Floyd wanted me to disturb you at this late hour," he said confidently. Duncan placed his left hand on top of the wooden door and slowly began closing it. "Thanks for the message Nick. Please don't let the door hit you on the way out cause it's closing now." Nick turned around to leave and felt a gentle nudge from the door behind him. Before it could close completely, Drake grabbed the door handle and opened it again. "Sorry about that Nick," he said with a chuckle. "My friend here is a bit tired and so am I at the moment. Have a good night my friend." Before Nick could reply Drake had shut the door behind him.

Before retiring to their individual beds, Drake decided to give Duncan a bit of valuable advice. "Remember Duncan, a good con artist must be kind at all times. We shouldn't make enemies no matter how small or insignificant they are." Duncan was already lying in bed and had turned out the lantern he was using for light. "That's a good point Drake. You're right as usual. Someday I'll be smarter than you; I just know it." Drake laughed. "Sorry, ya can't con a con my friend. Pleasant dreams," he replied as he tucked himself into his own bed across the room from Duncan. It wasn't long before both conniving thieves had fallen fast asleep and were counting mountains of rubies within their dreams.

24. CON THE COBRA

Mojo's eyes opened wide. Something wrapped itself tighter around his chest and legs. Glancing downwards, he discovered the thickest root he had ever seen curled tightly around his body! It was about a foot thick and was pinning him against a flat dirt wall directly behind him. Not only was he being held hostage by the constricting root but he also felt like it was somehow draining his life away in the slowest way possible. Turning his head to the left, he found Pixie pinned up against the same flat dirt wall next to him. They were each being held hostage by similar thick roots jutting out from a thick dirt ceiling just above their heads. Mojo observed them to be trapped underground inside a narrow tunnel of some sort. Pixie was within touching distance of him and looked to be sleeping at the moment. "Pixie, wake up," Mojo yelled. Pixie quickly came back to consciousness. "What's going on," she asked? "Why am I all tied up like this?" Mojo stared at her with concern. "I think the Sand Trapper must have swallowed us whole and we are now being held hostage by its roots down here in this underground catacomb…but I'm no genius. Perhaps this is all just a bad dream and we'll wake up soon," he said hopefully. "I wish," she replied desperately.

Mojo tried using his genie powers to set himself free from the twisted root encircling him. The root must have held some sort of protective shield around it because it didn't budge at all in response to his magic. Pixie managed to toss a bit of pixie dust at the root encircling her. With her arms wrapped tightly against her sides, it took some serious effort to reach into her purse and grab a pinch of pixie dust found there. With a hard flick of her wrist she managed to toss a bit onto the root surrounding her. Unfortunately the root didn't respond to the pixie dust powder at all. "What are we going to do," she cried out loud?! "Our magic isn't saving us and we're tied up tighter than a sail to a mast!

Suddenly Pixie remembered the miniature lamp dangling from the small chain around her neck. She thought about summoning Claw to help rescue them but then remembered the injuries he had sustained from the Sand Trapper during their battle with it. "Maybe he wouldn't help us right now," she thought discouragingly. "Perhaps Claw is still too injured from our recent battle with that monstrous plant to give us any kind of assistance," she thought silently. Pixie's arms were tied so tightly against her own body that she couldn't reach the lamp dangling around her neck even if she tried. She started to realize just how trapped they were and began to panic. "Mojo, we could die down here! What are we going to do," she asked desperately?

Mojo exhaled despairingly. "Perhaps you could try rubbing the…" Pixie cut him short. "My arms are tied way to tightly to reach it! I can't break free from this blasted root! It's like it has a…" Mojo finished her sentence. "…protective shield around it. That seems to be the case Pixie. I'm really not sure how we're going to…" A loud hissing sound cut Mojo short this time as his gaze quickly darted leftward. Pixie heard it as well and began to panic even more! She had identified the monstrous sound long before either of them even saw what it was.

About 20 feet down the dimly lit tunnel, they managed to spot an elongated pair of glowing red eyes. The narrow slit eyes slowly moved towards them at a steady pace. The deep hissing sound continued growing louder as it came closer. They tried frantically to break their bonds in a desperate attempt to escape the monster now moving towards them. The Sand Trapper's roots were too strong to break but they continued struggling until the giant head of an incredibly over-sized cobra came into view and rose high above their heads!

"Give me one good reason to let you live," the cobra hissed darkly. "Choose your words carefully for they may be your last." The snake spoke slowly and with an airy tone that filled their souls with a great amount of fear. Mojo decided to make a brave attempt at communicating with the monster towering high above his head. He averted his gaze away from the giant cobra's glowing red eyes just in case they might curse him with some sort of irreversible spell. Staring directly at the dirt below him, he slowly responded to the giant snake glaring back at him. Somehow he managed to get the words out despite the shakiness of his voice and trembling of his body. "If…if it's food you seek, we can give it to you master snake." The snake spoke again. "I live on the fear of these roots genie. They fear I will eat the little food they have and that sustains me." Mojo decided to try again. "Is there any way I could convince you to let us go? What may I call you master snake?" The giant cobra opened its gaping narrow jaw to reveal the sharpest and deadliest pair of fangs Mojo had ever seen! "We'll do anything you ask master snake! Please don't kill us!" The venomous cobra extended his long double-ended tongue towards Mojo's neck. Both ends of his split tongue wrapped around Mojo's neck and slowly began to squeeze. "I could bight your head off right now genie but I think your powers may be of use to me." Between choking and gasping for breath, Mojo managed to form a reply. "Anything snake. Please let me go." The giant cobra released his split tongue from around his neck. "My name is Con. There is a water hole nearby being blocked by a wall of Sand Trapper roots. Clear a path for me genie and I will let you live." Mojo responded quickly. "Of course Master Con, I will gladly do this for you. Please spare my friend Pixie here too and we can both help you." Con's cobra head twisted just enough to observe the small fairy girl trapped within the strangling roots. "You must help the genie clear a path to the watering hole," he said commandingly. Pixie nodded agreeably.

Con's sharp fangs lunged at the large root wrapped around Mojo's chest. Mojo watched his life flash before his eyes as the cobra's fangs came within inches of piercing his heart! A sigh of relief escaped his lips as he felt the large root slowly loosen its grip from around his chest. It loosened just enough to allow the rest of his body to slip through onto the tunnel floor beneath. Taking in a massive gulp of air, he felt completely relieved from finally escaping his constraining root prison. Con shifted towards Pixie and quickly released her from her bonds as well. The roots Con had bitten into fell to the dirt floor and quickly withered away into the earth as if seeking refuge from the poisonous venom he had injected into them.

"Follow me," Con hissed sharply. Since they could barely see anything inside the dark tunnel, Mojo thought up a way to light their way forward. However, he was more than a little hesitant to use any kind of magic Con might not agree with. "Um, Con…" The giant cobra head turned to face him. "What now little man?" Mojo was still trying not to stare into Con's glowing red eyes so he continued averting his gaze elsewhere. "It's blacker than soot down here Master Con. Would you mind if I used a bit of magic to give us a flicker of light? I thought I'd check with you first just in case," he said trying to hide the fear in his voice. A fearful pause followed before Con responded. "Perhaps you'd rather see in the dark," he replied mystically. Mojo was about to say that he could simply conjure up a couple of lanterns when all of the sudden a flash of green light shot between Con's red eyes and his own! Before Pixie could say anything, Con had shot green spurts of light into her eyes as well. Pixie and Mojo could instantly see quite well through the darkness! "Wow, this is incredible," Pixie said with awe in her voice! Turning her head towards Con, she caught his bright red eyes gazing into hers. Her body grew cold just looking at him. "What's the matter little girl; afraid? You should be! I won't hesitate to kill either of you should you decide to escape!" Pixie was too struck with fear to respond and was happy when Mojo responded for both of them. "Yes Master Con. We will obey your every command. Please, lead the way." Con turned his gaze away from them and continued slithering down the long narrow tunnel in front of them. Waiting patiently for his long serpent body to finish turning around, they began following him through the tunnel. Con looked to be over ten feet long and five feet wide! They'd never seen a snake that large their entire lives and a strong sense of fear continued to linger with them as they walked.

Even though Pixie was enjoying her new found night vision, she couldn't help but wonder what her eyes actually looked like in a mirror. She figured they probably looked similar to Con's but her curiosity got the better of her. Glancing over at Mojo, her suspicions were confirmed. His eyes were glowing red just like Con's! "Well, they don't look that bad," she thought to herself dismissively. She would have asked Mojo to tell her if her eyes looked similar to Con's but didn't want to disturb the delicate silence at the moment. "Survival is the most important thing," she told herself as they continued following Con through the ever narrowing tunnel.

25. A DARING RESCUE

Dawn arrived as the sun rose high in the clear blue sky. Misty's eyes opened wide. She glanced around at the thin walls of her tent as they swayed back and forth in the slow moving breeze hitting them from the outside. The soft dessert sand gently cradled her body beneath the thin layer of tent covering separating her from the ground beneath. "This must be the softest bed I've ever slept on," she thought joyfully." She wondered when Andrew would show up and worried that he might not find her for a very long time since the Dessert of Doom was such a large place to search for someone.

Misty reached outside of her open tent flap located just above her head and grabbed a handful of warm dessert sand. Pulling it back into the shade of the tent where she was lying, she retrieved her wand with her other hand. Tapping the handful of sand with her wand, she spoke the phrase "BAKETRANSMELLOW" as it instantly transformed into a nice little chocolate chip muffin for her to eat. Sitting up inside her tent, she took a nice big bight from her newly made muffin. "Oh, this is delightful," she thought gratefully. "Good thing I visited that little baker's shop just outside the Forbidden Forest or I wouldn't even know these little treats exist," she thought happily.

She stepped outside her tent to stretch her body when all of the sudden her entire tent vanished into thin air! "What in blazes," she shouted! She glanced around to find her new intruder. Without warning, a finger tapped her left shoulder from behind. Turning to catch the mischievous person responsible for all the commotion, she found no one there. Suddenly, another finger tapped her on the right shoulder this time. Turning again to catch the mysterious prankster invading her space, she still found nobody there. Suddenly, a loud and unexpected voice boomed directly from behind her. "Boo!" Losing her balance, she about toppled over from fright. The mysterious prankster reached out to steady her fall. Catching her wrist and back, the mysterious intruder pulled her back into balance. Desperate to discover who the mysterious stranger actually was; she finally found it to be the one and only court wizard Morpheus! Even though he was grinning from ear to ear, he looked a bit awkward for a man with his type of facial expressions. He began laughing. "Oh, I'm sorry Misty. I just couldn't help but have a bit of fun with you," he said with a chuckle. Misty smiled back. "Morpheus…I was expecting…" "I know…" he said, interrupting her. "Andrew couldn't make it unfortunately. No, I take that back. He could have made it but decided to send me in his place to help deal with any foul creatures we might encounter in this horrible place. You see, Andrew is an accountant. Simply put, he is used to dealing with rubies; not creatures who might try tearing him limb from limb," he said seriously. "I see," Misty replied understandingly.

Misty couldn't help but wonder about her long lost friend. "How is my good friend Blackbeak holding up," she asked thoughtfully? Morpheus folded his arms across his chest. "His former powers are slowly returning Misty. I've been teaching and training him the best I can. It's a slow process but it should be worth the effort if the bat army ever decides to attack our little city again. At least we'll have our secret weapon to back us up this time around. I am currently trying to keep his presence a secret from the rest of the citizens at the Lake of Lost Souls. If word gets around that he's there then there's no telling what the Bat

King might do to capture or kill him unfortunately." A look of worry crossed Misty's face. "Please protect him Morpheus. He's my best friend in the whole world and we've known each-other for a great number of years. Unfortunately, I never got to know much of his past before I met him. Morganna cursed him to forget everything before he found me in the Forbidden Forest. Please take care of him the best you can Morpheus. Promise me," she pleaded urgently! Morpheus gently rested a hand on her shoulder reassuringly. "I promise Misty, I'll do my absolute best to take care of Rueland. After all, he could be the saving grace our little city needs to survive and I don't want to take any unnecessary risks with him either. He's in good hands though. I assure you." Misty smiled thankfully. "That means a great deal to me Morpheus. I appreciate it more than you know."

Misty observed Morpheus bit closer than before. For some reason he seemed much younger than she had remembered while speaking with him in the Queen's Throne Room. She almost didn't recognize him with his long gray beard trimmed off completely. His clean cut look seemed to have taken about 20 years off his appearance. Even though he still had the same wise sounding voice, he looked to be about the same age as Misty along with short black hair, a prominent long chin and hazel colored eyes that continually seemed to draw her into his world. She couldn't help but wonder if he had changed his appearance in an effort to impress her. "Morpheus, you look much younger than I remember. What did you do to yourself?" Morpheus rubbed his chin thoughtfully. "Well, I thought I'd try going for a younger look. I was starting to feel like an old man." Misty laughed. "I know the feeling. You probably wouldn't believe how old I actually am even if I told you. A look of curiosity crossed his face. "Alright, I'll bight. How old are you then?" Misty observed the perimeter carefully as if about to reveal a big secret. "It's kind of a big secret but I'm actually 972 years old in witch years." Morpheus motioned a hand forward. "Stop right there little missy. I know how you witches calculate your so called years. You do it based on the number of cycles a full moon makes in an actual year. So I'd have to divide by….oh never-mind. I'm not in the mood for all that math right now."

Misty was still thinking about her friends. "I'm assuming Andrew must have told you what happened to Mojo and Pixie," she asked hopefully? Morpheus nodded. "Of course he did and I'm here to help the best I can. You'll just have to trust me. I've been practicing magic for the majority of my life. Being a court wizard has its perks. Having access to many of the Queen's resources has greatly increased my experience and knowledge on matters such as this."

Reaching into his robe, he produced a small glass vile filled with a bright red liquid that sparkled when the light hit it just right. "What's that for," Misty asked curiously? "This is my Alpha Elixir Misty. It's what we'll use to satisfy the Sand Trapper's roots who are currently holding your friends hostage in the catacombs below this sand infested death trap!" Misty looked at him curiously. "Satisfy the roots? What do you mean?" Morpheus held the vile up towards the sun and focused on it with one eye open. "The Sand Trappers in this dessert have incredibly deep roots that connect inside a deep underground catacomb of intricately connected tunnels. A single root from each Sand Trapper tunnels down and connects into a very large underground pool of water known as the Well of Life. This is where their water source is located. Since this dessert can go many months without getting a single drop of rain, it is necessary for these Sand Trappers draw water from the Well of Life in order to keep them alive."

Misty was still confused. "So what does this Alpha Elixir have to do with the Well of Life," she asked curiously? Morpheus put the small vile back inside his robe pocket. "That's a great question Misty. This elixir will keep the Sand Trapper's thirst satisfied for a good five years if we mix it into their Well of Life." Misty suddenly became enraged. "Why in the world would we want to satisfy their thirst for five years Morpheus? They just ate my friends! Do you not remember that little detail," she screamed furiously! Morpheus held both hands out in front of him. "Calm down Misty. Let me finish. Your friends are most likely being trapped by the Sand Trapper's roots inside the underground catacomb right now. The roots are feeding on their fear. They literally eat fear for breakfast! However, once this elixir is mixed in with their water supply they will be completely satisfied and their roots will relax enough for your friends to escape their awful clutches! I hope you understand what I'm saying." Misty nodded. "I think I'm getting it so far. So, I guess my next question is how are we going to find the Well of Life if it's located somewhere underground and how are we going to get down into it?" Morpheus smiled. "You really are a sharp one! No wonder the Queen liked you so much," he said flatteringly. Misty smiled. "Really, what did she say about me?" Morpheus pulled a rolled up piece of parchment from his inner robe pocket and unrolled it in front of her. "Oh, she just thought you were quite an intelligent woman. Anyways, take a look at this map. This shows us where all the Sand Trapper quicksand pits are located and which ones will lead us into the Well of Life." Misty scanned the map carefully. "This is really great Morpheus but where are we on this map?" Morpheus blinked a few times before responding. "I'm not really sure Misty. Keep this to yourself but I'm a portal traveler so I couldn't really get a good aerial view of our current location." Misty gasped! "You're a portal traveler?! I thought all portal objects were done away with clear back in ancient times. Portals are something that witches and wizards tell fantasy stories about to their children. How in the world did you manage to get your hands on one?"

Morpheus glanced upward at the clear blue sky. "I'm the Queen's court wizard Misty. I have access to a great number of magical objects that most people wouldn't even dream of owning. Anyways, the point is that I can't actually fly anywhere simply by using a portal. I will need something to fly with if I'm going to come with you. Misty's expression turned to dismay. "I'm sorry to say my broomstick was smashed into pieces by a recent battle with a pack of werewolves," she exclaimed sadly. "Otherwise, we could easily use that to fly around on. So, why can't you just portal into the Well of Life," she asked curiously? "Unfortunately, I can only portal into places I've been too before," Morpheus replied half-heartedly. "Portal travel is an ancient form of magic and has its own set of rules sadly. Anyways, we can do this one of two ways. We can either locate the correct quicksand pit by walking around this dessert for days or we can combine our magic and conjure up a new broomstick for you to use. While we're at it, we might as well conjure up something for me to fly with as well." "I like that idea," Misty replied enthusiastically. "Great," said Mojo happily. "Well, let's not waste any more time. Grab your wand and I'll grab mine." They both retrieved their wands from their robe pockets. "Okay, let's start with getting a new broomstick for you Misty. I'm going to throw a handful of sand up into the air and together we'll make it transform. The spell is BROOMAIRO FORMAIRO. We must speak the words in complete unison or the spell simply won't work. Are you ready?" Misty held her wand out in front of her. "Anytime you are," she responded confidently. "All right, here it goes," replied Morpheus.

Grabbing a palm full of hot dessert sand, he threw it high into the air in front of them. Pointing their wands at the airborne sand, they spoke the words "BROOMAIRO FORMAIRO" but not in complete unison. Flashes of colored light shot from their wands and hit the swirling sand in the air above them. Morpheus shook his head disappointedly while exhaling anxiously. "Let's try speaking the words together before I throw the sand in the air that way we can get it right next time. Agreed?" Misty nodded. "Alright, let's give it a try." Misty and Morpheus tried practicing the spell in better unison. A couple tries later they finally got it right. Eventually they each felt confident enough to cast the spell correctly in complete unison. Morpheus threw another handful of sand up into the air as they each casted the spell with perfect unison! The handful of sand instantly transformed into a perfectly crafted broomstick. Misty was delighted to see her new form of transportation floating in the air next to her. Reaching out to grab the smooth wooden broomstick, she pulled it in towards her. Feeling its power surge through the wooden handle, a smile crept up on her face. "This is incredible Morpheus! Thanks for the help! Although, I was under the impression that all flying objects had to be handcrafted before they could be enchanted. At least that's what the Witches Guild taught me back when I was a part of their little group." Morpheus smiled. "Being a court wizard, I have access to knowledge and information that most magical creatures are not privy too. There are probably many things I could teach you Misty. Now, let's make me a flying surfboard shall we," he exclaimed joyfully! A funny look crossed her face. "Well aren't you Mister

Hotshot," she replied jokingly. "What do you mean," he asked? "I just mean that we witches use broomsticks because they're much easier to balance on during flight. You're probably going to fall off a surfboard my friend! Even if you used magic to keep your feet on the board, your uneven balance might be a problem." Morpheus looked at her seriously. "What if I told you I've found an ancient spell that allows me to keep my balance perfectly at all times." She chuckled hysterically. "I'd say you're either lying or have gone completely insane. But then again, we did just make a brand new broomstick appear so…perhaps all things really are possible." Morpheus nodded agreeably. "Well, let's try making my surfboard shall we? The spell we'll use is SURFAIRO FORMAIRO WAVAIRO. On three let's say it together. Morpheus counted to three as they casted the spell in complete unison. "Alright, let's give it a go with the sand this time." He threw another handful of sand up into the air as they casted the spell in perfect unison. Colorful flashes of light bolted from their wands hitting the falling dirt as it came misting back down to earth. Nothing happened. They repeated the enchantment in hopes of getting it right this time. Still nothing happened. A look of disappointment crossed Morpheus's face. "I'm not sure why it's not working," he exclaimed with frustration. Misty crossed her arms defensively. "Well, I hate to say it but we either have the wrong spell or we're not pronouncing it correctly," she replied delicately. Morpheus snapped his fingers. "I knew I shouldn't have bought that phony spell book from that peddling kid," he exclaimed harshly. A look of compassion crossed Misty's face. "Don't let it get you down Morpheus. You can use my anti-gravity amulet if you'd like. The Queen gave it to me and I'm sure you would know how to use it. I'm not sure why I didn't think about it until now but it would definitely help you get around if you'd like to use it?" Morpheus nodded. "Oh alright; I was really hoping to have my own flying surfboard but I suppose an anti-gravity amulet will work just as well. Thanks Misty," he replied gratefully.

Misty pulled the anti-gravity amulet over her head and gave it to Morpheus. "I assume you know how to use it." He nodded as he placed the amulet over his head. "Well, let's go for a little flight and we'll figure out which quicksand trap we need to dive into." Misty wasn't too excited about having to dive into a pit full of quicksand. "Don't worry Misty; I'm here to protect you. Those Sand Trappers won't touch you with me around. I promise!" Misty felt extremely relieved to have Morpheus there to help protect her. "Thank you Morpheus, I greatly appreciate your help." Straddling her broomstick, she took off into the air. Morpheus rubbed his anti-gravity amulet three times in a circular clockwise motion and rose into the air as well. It wasn't long before the two of them were flying around the Dessert of Doom making fun of all the Sand Trappers who couldn't quite reach them as they soared passed their snapping jaws.

After teasing the sand monsters for a bit, Morpheus yelled back at Misty as they soared through the air. "Alright Misty, let's take a gander at that map again and figure out where we're headed exactly." They hovered up next to each-other in the air and gazed at the open map in Morpheus's hands. Comparing the map layout with their aerial view from above, they could see a particular pattern of quicksand pits below them. They spotted eight extremely large quicksand pits forming an octagon shaped pattern below them. At the center of the octagon stood the biggest quicksand pit of them all. "That's the one we need to dive into," said Morpheus pointing directly at it.

Just as he pointed towards the center pit, a massive Sand Trapper emerged from its center as if cued into action by Morpheus's pointing. The giant plant monster seemed aware of their presence as it opened its sharp pointed thorn pedals wide in their direction. Flying above its massive head, they hovered just out of reach. Morpheus pulled the Alpha Elixir from his pocket and cautiously dangled it directly over the Sand Trapper's head. "What are you doing," yelled Misty. "I thought we were supposed to drop the vile into the Well of Life?" Morpheus carefully concentrated on his massive moving target below. "This quicksand pit leads directly into the Well of Life Misty." Aiming carefully, Morpheus dropped the Alpha Elixir into the giant gaping mouth of the Sand Trapper below as it moved upwards to take a swipe at them. They watched the vile fall past the monstrous plant's thorny mouth and down through its large hollowed out stem which connected it with the giant sand pit below it. They watched with anticipation as it slowly began to keel over. It looked as if it was falling asleep right in front of them. Falling backwards, its body slammed into the quicksand surrounding it as its thick stem folded over. Slowly, it began to be sucked inward by the quicksand around it until its monstrous plant body became entirely immersed inside the sandy earth beneath it.

Staring into the continually sinking hole where the Sand Trapper had been just moments ago, Morpheus threw up his hands in victory. "Now's our chance Misty; follow me!" He clasped both hands over his head as if about to take a swan dive into the center of the quicksand pit. Misty placed a hand over her mouth in fear as she watched him dive head-first into the sinking pit of quicksand beneath them. She was extremely hesitant to follow him into the sinking pit but decided to put her fears aside and do it for the good of saving her friends. Taking the broomstick out from between her legs, she flung it over her head so it was now raised vertically above her in the same manner that one would carry an umbrella. Slowly making her decent towards the large pit of quicksand feet first; she took comfort in not diving in head-first. Either way, she knew her face would soon be covered in mud and she closed her eyes on the way down.

26. FIGHTING THE COBRA

Mojo and Pixie finally reached the wall of roots where Con had been leading them to. The wall was about eight feet tall and ten feet wide. It was the thickest wall of roots any of them had ever seen! It was abundantly clear the Sand Trappers did not want anyone passing through their thickly intertwined barricade. If what Con had said was true then it would make sense that the roots wouldn't want anyone touching their one and only source of water no matter who invaded their space.

Con's fiercely large cobra head twisted around to face them. "Let's not waste any more time," he hissed sharply. "If you fail to clear a path soon, your lives will soon be over," he hissed threateningly.

Mojo squeezed past Con in an effort to get closer to the wall of roots. Summoning forth his most powerful magic to help clear the path ahead; sparks, flashes and fire shot from his hands into the thickly layered root wall. To his dismay, even his most ancient form of magic didn't have an effect on it. He couldn't believe how impervious to genie magic the roots actually were. He considered himself to have some of the strongest magic in the world and it didn't even phase the roots not even a little bit! Suddenly he remembered how Con had bit the roots earlier to help set them free. "Con, perhaps you could try biting the roots like you did earlier when you set us free. That would probably work! Con opened his large narrow jaw to reveal his poisonous dripping fangs. "You don't think I've already tried that genie? There are too many for that. They grow stronger with every second that passes. We must reach the water soon or I'll suck the water from your body if you don't hurry," he hissed venomously! Mojo continued shooting lightening and fire bolts at the roots in a desperate attempt to break through them. They still wouldn't budge! Pixie flew over next to Mojo and threw a handful of Pixie Dust at them in an attempt to make them move. The roots didn't respond to that either. Despite their best efforts the roots were impenetrable no matter what they attempted to do to them.

Con continued to let them try everything they could think of to clear a pathway for him. Nothing worked and he quickly grew impatient and thirsty with every second that passed away! His desire to suck the water from Mojo and Pixie's bodies grew worse. His thirst had become unbearable. "I've given you all a chance at living," he hissed threateningly. "You've each failed to clear a path and must now suffer for not doing so!" Without giving them a chance to reply, Con lifted his large cobra head high over Mojo's and flashed his poisonous dripping fangs with the intent of striking him dead! Mojo was about to throw up a body-shield to protect himself when suddenly the earth began to shake violently beneath them! "Wait," Mojo exclaimed! Con stopped his strike in mid-air as he watched the root wall behind Mojo begin to collapse on itself. "What's happening," Pixie screamed out loud?!

Within seconds, the eight foot root wall had completely collapsed to the ground near their feet. The group jumped back just in time to avoid getting smashed by the collapsing wall. A dim light shimmered through the newly revealed opening in the tunnel. Mojo was about to enter the newly made entrance when Con's massive cobra head knocked him out of the way. "My apologies Master Con," he responded respectfully. Letting the long cobra slither past him, Mojo resumed his position behind him.

Pixie followed Mojo and the long bodied cobra into a dimly lit cavern. They observed it to be a large circular room with walls made from hard compact dirt. Many thick roots protruded from the hard dirt walls and ran directly into a small pond located at the center of the cavern. "This must be the Sand Trapper's water supply," Mojo thought silently. No one was really sure why but the water had a deep red tint to it.

Following the cavern's light source upwards, they found it to be emanating from a small opening in the dirt ceiling above them. Quicksand seeped through the opening above them but instead of falling directly downwards, it veered off to the side and ran down the dirt walls surrounding them. Upon further inspection, they found a small two inch wide divot encircling the entire room. The quicksand from the walls flowed into the small deep divot encircling the cavern. It seemed to be a draining system the roots had created in order to not be completely drowned out by the continually flowing quicksand coming in from the gaping hole in the ceiling above them. They weren't really sure where the quicksand drained off into after flowing through the deep divot but were quite happy not to be drowning quicksand at the moment.

Out of the corner of his eye, Mojo noticed a heap of quicksand on the cavern floor begin to move! He didn't say anything though because he was highly sensitive to the fact that Con might turn on them for any reason at all. He continued watching it as if expecting something to happen. The heap of quicksand lying on the floor had a human form to it. It slowly stood up and began wiping the dirt off itself. As the dirt fell away, Mojo quickly recognized the person beneath. It was Misty! It took everything he had not to scream her name out loud! Misty spotted him as well. Mojo placed a finger to his lips in a hushing gesture before pointing towards Con who was slowly slithering his way towards the watering hole at the center of the cavern. Misty turned her head towards the giant cobra and instantly put a hand over her own mouth to keep from screaming at the sight of the giant venomous snake. She glanced around for Morpheus and quickly spotted him lying only a few feet away from her. Bending down to touch him, she gently nudged his shoulder and whispered in his ear. "Shhh…we must be quiet Morpheus. There's a giant sized cobra over there," she whispered pointing to her right. Morpheus sat up and wiped the dirt away from his eyes and face. Following her pointed finger with his eyes, he found the monster she was pointing at. An instant wave of fear washed over him as he laid his head back down on the dirt cavern floor.

Con slithered over to the pond of red colored water and was about to dip his fangs into it when a wave of intense fear came flooding from Morpheus's direction! Con turned towards the fearful wizard lying in the mud close by. "Mmm…water and a meal," he hissed. "What a nice surprise!" He quickly began slithering towards the frightened wizard. Morpheus could see the large cobra coming towards him and tried to stand up. His entire body felt frozen with fear! He pulled his wand from his robe and pointed it at the monstrous snake. "Don't come any closer cobra! I'll send you into a world you'll never return from," he said trying to sound confident. Con paused for a moment to laugh the worst kind of laugh imaginable. "You can't hurt me wizard. I will enjoy watching you squirm as I suck the life out of you!" Another intense wave of fear flooded Morpheus with absolute dread. His hands shook as he continued pointing his wand at Con. "BURNELLO CORPELLO," he screamed! A giant hot fireball shot from the tip of his wand towards the oncoming snake. Unfortunately, his shaking hands caused his aim to be thrown off completely and his fireball hit the dirt next to him. Shooting another fireball at the oncoming snake, he missed again. The intense fear coursing through his veins threw off his aim immensely. The giant cobra lifted his thick skinned body high above the wizard's head and flashed his venomous fangs at him.

Just as Con was about to bite Morpheus's head off; Mojo screamed at him. "Wait Master Con!" Con's open mouth paused in mid-air as he turned to face Mojo. "You've waited years to drink from this refreshing pool that we've helped you get to. Please, spare the foolish wizard for just a moment and have a drink. You deserve it Master Con," Mojo said soothingly. Con moved his jaws away from Morpheus's head. "Perhaps you're right genie," he replied. "I've waited far too long to quench my thirst."

By now, Misty had her wand out and was pointing it directly at Con. He hadn't seen her yet because he was too focused on Morpheus and Mojo to even notice. She could see Mojo's plan to distract the snake but also knew they'd have to face him again at some point. Instead of waiting for the inevitable to happen she decided to sneak up on him. Muttering the same spell Morpheus had used only moments ago, a fireball shot from the tip of her wand slamming into the snake's backside! He hissed painfully. A large black mark left its imprint where her fireball had scorched into him. Turning his head to face her, Con hissed angrily. "You will pay for that witch," he hissed angrily! He decided to attack the menacing wizard first and turned to face him directly. Con launched his venomous fangs towards Morpheus and sunk them deep into his neck! Morpheus screamed out in pain and fell to the ground. Pixie and Mojo screamed as well from seeing the wizard fall. A wave of fear froze them in their tracks despite their intentions to help him.

Picking up her broomstick from the dirt cavern floor, Misty mounted it and flew towards Morpheus in an attempt to save him from another possible attack. Knowing he was too heavy to pick up from the ground she flew up next to him and rubbed his anti-gravity amulet in a clockwise motion. This gave him enough lift-off for her to grab and move him through the air and away from the giant cobra. Con struck out at Misty's leg as she flew past him but barely missed. She managed to guide the poisoned Morpheus through the air with his anti-gravity amulet keeping him weightless as they moved along.

Moving Morhpeus through the air, Misty hovered his body above the Well of Life. She rubbed his anti-gravity amulet counter-clockwise and let him fall into the waters below. Misty desperately hoped the Well of Life would heal his snake wound before he died of poisoning. He dropped into the pool of water with a loud splash! It was deeper than it looked and he now had to force himself to stay afloat even with the poison continually working its way through his body. The massive amount of fear he felt quickly floated through the air in Con's direction.

Picking up on it immediately, Con felt like a buffet of food had been prepared for his easy consumption! Quickly slithering his way to the red pool of water; Con coiled his massive body up as he patiently waited for Morpheus to make his way back to shore before eating him. While waiting on the shoreline, he decided to take his long awaited drink of water from the Well of Life. Reaching his head into the red water, he gulped it down in massive quantities. It felt incredible to finally have a drink after waiting as long as he had. Previously, he had survived by sucking tiny amounts of water from the Sand Trapper's root system in order to stay alive. "No wonder these Sand Trappers guarded this water so well," he thought reasonably as he sucked the water up in massive amounts. Suddenly, it occurred to him why the Sand Trappers had let down their guard at the root wall and why the water was a red tinted color. "Oh no," he thought frantically to himself. "There must be something in this water to make the roots sleep or die! That is why the root wall crumbled so easily!" Just as the thought occurred to him, a sudden wave of tiredness washed over his large cobra body. The Alpha Elixir inside the water had done its job and Con fell asleep instantly. Since his head was directly over the pool when he fell asleep; he sunk straight into it! His deep coma combined with his lack of bodily control caused him to drown in the Well of Life.

The injured Morpheus was still trying to keep himself afloat inside the life giving pool. Misty had just noticed what happened to Con and screamed out to Morpheus. "Don't drink the water Morpheus! You'll drown if you do!" The poison in his system was taking its toll and he wanted to make it back to dry ground before he drowned as well. Misty landed on the shore just in front of him and held out her broomstick for him to grab onto. Reaching out for it, he grabbed onto it as she pulled him into safety.

After reaching dry ground, Morpheus rolled over onto the dirt and closed his eyes. "No Morpheus, don't die," Misty screamed! Mojo and Pixie rushed over to help him. Mojo tried healing his poisoned body with his genie magic but the cobra's venom had spread too far inside him for it to do any good. Misty and Pixie tried their best to save him as well but nothing worked. Suddenly, Pixie had an idea. She flew over to where the quicksand was sliding down the dirt walls and scooped up a handful. With her other hand, she mixed a pinch of Pixie Dust in with her handful of quicksand. Mixing it together with her fingers, she gently poured her homemade concoction onto Morpheus's neck where the bite marks were located. "Let's tip him sideways so the poison can drain out," she suggested confidently. Mojo and Misty rolled Morpheus onto his side so the wound faced into a more downward position. Pixie cupped both hands together and dipped them into the Well of Life. Filling her hands with water, she dumped it on top of the mud concoction she had applied to Morpheus's wound. The life giving water quickly washed away her concoction of quicksand and pixie dust from the wound. "The wound disappeared completely," Mojo exclaimed excitedly! Pixie's carefully chosen mixture had worked its healing magic on Morpheus's venomous wound. They each breathed a sigh of relief after seeing the healing take place.

Morpheus sat up and glanced around at his captivated audience now staring down at him. Rubbing his neck where the snake bite had previously been, he stared up at Pixie. "Thanks for saving me Pixie. I couldn't have done it without you," he exclaimed thankfully. Pixie smiled. "Glad I could help," she replied sincerely. Misty wrapped an arm around his shoulder and grabbed his other hand to gently help him stand up. "We all thought you were a goner Morpheus," she said seriously. Morpheus stood up with Misty's help. "I thought I was too. That snake's venom was quite deadly. Where is he now anyways," he asked curiously? Mojo pointed towards the Well of Life. "I'm not sure why but the water over there knocked him into a deep coma while he was drinking it…then he drowned in it!" Morpheus nodded as he fit the puzzle pieces together in his mind. "The Alpha Elixir is quite potent as well. It should keep these Sand Trapper roots sleeping for months! Misty and I came searching for you two and here you are," he said looking over at Mojo and Pixie. "Here we are," Pixie repeated repetitiously.

Morpheus's expression suddenly became quite serious. "I have to be honest with you three. I didn't just come here to save you." "Oh,"

Pixie replied curiously? Morpheus continued. "I also came because there are many fairies back at the Lake of Lost souls who have forgotten how to make Pixie Dust. The entire Pixie Guild seems to have been affected by some sort of memory loss curse. They must be reminded how to make it again before every fairy runs out of it and completely loses their ability to fly. It's bad enough Morganna cursed us to never fly again but losing our memory of how to make Pixie Dust is even worse! Will you return with me and help the Pixie Guild remember how to make Pixie Dust again Pixie," Morpheus asked passionately?

Pixie looked at Morpheus seriously. "It sounds like Morganna might be floating around the Lake of Lost Souls causing all of this to happen. If I do return with you, we'll need to be extra careful." Morpheus moved closer to her and gently placed a hand around her shoulders. "Don't worry Pixie. You'll be safe with me." Pixie smiled and put a hand on his back in response. "That's comforting. Thanks Morpheus." Morpheus turned his gaze towards Misty. "I know you're probably worried about your friend Blackbeak. He's doing fine. He's learning new skills that will help defend our city against the bat army should they decide to attack again. The Queen has a sneaky suspicion Morganna has returned and is cursing the Pixie Guild to forget how to make Pixie Dust. She hopes Blackbeak will talk some sense into her since they have quite the history together." Morpheus shook his head. "The last thing we need is for our entire army to lose their ability to fly just before the bat army attacks! It's an absolute recipe for disaster. You can be sure of that," he said angrily.

Mojo decided to chime into the conversation as well. "Is the Queen requesting me and Misty to return as well," he asked curiously? Morpheus shook his head. "No, she would like you both to continue your quest to find Drake and the stolen honeycomb. Honeycomb is a key ingredient in making Pixie Dust. It wouldn't surprise me if Drake was working for Morganna and stealing the ingredients needed to make it," he replied suspiciously. Pixie placed a hand over her own mouth as if she had just discovered something extremely important. "Oh no! If she's doing what I think she's doing….she's probably going to try and steal the

Pixie Guild List from the Queen! We must return to the palace before Morganna gets there first!" Misty stared at Pixie curiously. "What do you mean Pixie Guild List? What is that exactly?" Pixie was surprised that Misty had never heard of it before. "Only qualified members of the Pixie Guild are allowed to make Pixie Dust. Only the Queen holds the Pixie Guild List of everyone who is allowed to make it. It's a crime for non-authorized fairies to make Pixie Dust. If it's mixed incorrectly, the concoction could be fatal for all those who use it! Basically, a fairy must first join the Pixie Guild to learn the correct ways of making Pixie Dust. This helps us avoid potential injuries to those who make it incorrectly. All those who learn the skill and make it correctly are then added to the Pixie Guild List. This helps us keep track of which dealers are authorized to make and distribute it. It's not only a legal concern but it's a safety issue as well."

Pixie glanced at Morpheus worriedly. "How are we going to get back to the palace? I should tell you I'm only a pinch away from running out of Pixie Dust myself." "No worries Pixie," replied Morpheus as he moved closer to her. "We'll use my portal to get back." Mojo looked shocked. "Portal? That's ancient magic my friend. How did you manage to come by one of those?" Morpheus turned towards the genie. "Like I was telling Misty earlier; a court wizard, such as myself, has access to a variety of objects that the average person would never even dream of owning." Mojo folded his arms across his chest seriously. "I'm a genie filled with ancient powers and even I can't travel by portal! Not only that but I've been around much longer than you have my friend," he replied seriously. Morpheus folded his arms in an attempt to mirror the genie's posture. "Well, I'm sure you're aware of the differences between object magic and self-magic." Mojo waved his hand in the air dismissively. "Yes, yes I know. Object magic is far more powerful and specific than self-magic. Objects such as talismans are far more specific with their abilities," he said meticulously. Morpheus nodded agreeably as he pulled an object from his robe pocket. Holding up the object for all to see, they observed it to be a small palm sized crystal ball with a flat bottom that could easily be set on a flat surface without rolling away if needed. At the top of the ball was a small hole drilled into its center. "This is my portal device or my Vortex Vacuum as the ancients once called it. It's much like a genie lamp except it's used for portal traveling instead," he said simply. Placing the flat bottom of the Vortex Vacuum into his palm, he gripped onto it tightly. With the hole at the top, he spoke the word "TRANSPINNELLO!" Instantly, a dark black and blue vortex shot from the hole at the top of the Vortex Vacuum. The group gasped as a dark swirling vortex formed in front of them.

Morpheus was happy to have such an fantastic magical object at his disposal. "Ready to go Pixie," he asked gesturing towards the swirling vortex in front of him? Pixie felt hesitant to leave Misty and Mojo behind but continued on anyways. "Alright, let's go." She didn't necessarily have a reason not to trust Morpheus and knew the significance of getting back to the Pixie Guild as soon as possible. She glanced back at Misty. "Before I go, I should return the lamp to you Misty. You'll probably need it more than I will throughout your journey." She took off the small chain holding the miniature lamp from around her neck and dropped it into Misty's outstretched hands. "Take care Misty. I hope you and Mojo find that conniving thief Drake and get back what he has stolen!" Misty pocketed the lamp as she waved goodbye to her. "Thank you Pixie. I hope you find all of the Pixie Guild members and remind them how to make Pixie Dust again before they forget the recipe completely. If all goes well, Mojo and I will have more ingredients for you to use soon. Take care my friend."

Pixie was about to step through the open portal when Morpheus stopped her. "Before you step through, perhaps you should give Misty your two digit combination just in case she needs it. Andrew told me all about the briefcase; that's how I know." Pixie glanced at Misty and Mojo cautiously for a brief moment. "Well, I suppose we're all on the same team so I'll just tell you my two middle digit combo is 2 and 4." Morpheus nodded with satisfaction. "Excellent! Now, just to be on the safe side, perhaps Misty should tell you her two digit code as well. Bad things could happen to either of you unfortunately so it's best that we share this information just in case something goes wrong. Misty nodded agreeably. "You're right Morpheus. You never know what bad things could happen to any of us. Pixie, my two digits are 1 and 8 in case you ever need them. I'm still holding onto the ruby case in hopes of finding Drake," Misty said confidently. Pixie nodded agreeably. "I wish you and Mojo the best of luck in finding him," she replied sincerely. Morpheus pointed towards his open portal swirling next to them. "Alright, let's get a move on Pixie. No time to waste."

Pixie threw her last handful of Pixie Dust onto her fairy wings before flapping her way through the portal. Morpheus waved goodbye to Misty and Mojo before entering the portal as well. "I wish you both the best of luck in catching Drake and remember Andrew is always available if you need to reach him for the last two digits of your code." The portal closed off and vanished into thin air before another word could be said.

27. TWO BAT SPIES

Blackbeak was sick of waiting for Morpheus to return. "That confounded wizard has been gone long enough," he exclaimed spitefully! He continued speaking to himself sarcastically as if he were Morpheus speaking to him. "Don't worry. You're not a prisoner here Blackbeak. We're only hiding you here until the bat army attacks Blackbeak," he chided bitterly! "If that confounded wizard thinks he can keep me here without letting me roam free then he's got another thing coming," he exclaimed angrily! He could feel the rage and tension building inside himself from being trapped inside the little cavern behind Turban Waterfall. "I must get out of here," he muttered desperately.

Blackbeak observed his surroundings carefully. A wooden locked door stood between himself and freedom. He had successfully transformed a few of Morpheus's old scrolls into well lit candles which gave the room just enough light to see everything around him.

Suddenly a brilliant idea occurred to him. "If I can transform random objects into other objects then why not the door itself," he thought brilliantly to himself. It was as if a light switched on inside his brain! He found it disturbing that he hadn't previously considered what he was now thinking about. He laughed at his own stupidity. "Oh, I'm such a klutz," he said with a chuckle. "This whole time I've been feeling completely trapped when in reality I've had the magic needed to transform my way out of here this entire time!"

Reaching deep within himself, he imagined the locked door in front of him quickly turning into a net gun and holster. Channeling his core energy into the tips of his wings, he clasped them together and pointed directly at the locked door in front of him. Instantly, a green ray of light shot from deep within himself and slammed into the locked wooden door in front of him. Just as he had imagined, it quickly transformed into a net gun and holster for him to carry around his back. Using his extra-long magic arms he had previously wished for; he slung the holster and gun over his shoulders and behind his back. He grinned with satisfaction knowing it was no ordinary net gun he had transformed the door into. "Heaven help the fool who stands in my way with this contraption," he told himself reassuringly.

Even though he had not gone through as much Wizard Training as Morpheus was planning on; his previous memories were slowly returning with every second that passed by. His memory of how to use his former powers was slowly returning to him. He flew towards the waterfall entrance. Without even thinking about it, he quickly conjured up a body shield around himself as he soared through the down pouring waterfall in front of him! The falling water bounced off his invisible shield without touching his feathers even a little bit.

He soared high above the down-pouring waterfall to get his bearings straight. He observed his current position in relation to the Lake of Lost Souls. Spotting the lake many miles south of him, he quickly began flying towards it. "Perhaps the Queen will be interested to know what has been happening around here lately," he thought curiously. Turban Waterfall fuelled a river which ran into the Lake of Lost Souls and was its main source of water. Blackbeak followed the river directly towards the city. He saw a great number of trees and wildlife surrounding the river as he continued making his way towards the city.

Out of the corner of his eye, he spotted a couple of bats hanging from a tall tree branch off to his left. They looked to be sleeping upside down until their beady little eyes quickly shot open and spotted him staring back at them. Immediately they took to the air after him! Blackbeak couldn't help but wonder if they were spies from the bat army out to capture him. He picked up the pace; flying faster and faster towards the Lake of Lost Souls. The two bats behind him picked up their pace as well!

Instead of trying to out fly them, he reached his long magical arms out to retrieve his net gun from its holster strapped across his back. Grabbing the net gun, he quickly turned around in mid-flight and aimed it directly at them. "Alright you two; don't make me pull this trigger! You'll be untangling yourself for weeks if I let this net fly!" One of the bats returned a comment in a freaky scratchy pitched voice. "We just want to talk to you raven. Is that too much to ask?" Blackbeak somehow managed to fly backwards through the air during his conversation. "Alright, I'll call a brief truce if you will?" The other bat who hadn't spoken yet replied in a screechy scratchy sounding voice as well. "It's a deal raven. Let's talk on that willow branch down there."

All three birds made a landing on the extra-long willow branch just below them. One of the bats began speaking before Blackbeak could say anything. "Word has reached our glorious leader that the magical raven of old is now residing at the Lake of Lost Souls. Our majesty the king has sent us out to find him. You are the only raven we have seen in days. What is your name good sir?" Blackbeak knew they would be searching for the raven by the name of Rueland so he decided to give them the name he had gone by for years. "My name is Blackbeak. Who are you bats searching for anyways?" One of the bats chimed in. "We are looking for a raven by the name of Rueland. You wouldn't happen to know where we could find him; do you?" Blackbeak laughed. "Even if I did…what makes you think I would just tell you where he is?" One of the bats cleared his throat. "I'm sorry, we're being rude. My name is Matt and this is Rat." Blackbeak smiled. "You're telling me you bats are Matt and Rat?" "That's right," replied Rat. "Our families like rhyming names. It makes it easy to remember our brothers and sisters. We've got siblings named Kat, Tat, Chat and Fat. Other bat families are jealous we've taken all the good names but that's a bat family for ya." Blackbeak couldn't help but feel a little dumbfounded at what he was hearing but quickly recovered his composure. "That's interesting Rat. I'm happy to meet you both but since I'm obviously not the guy you're looking for I'll just be on my way."

Blackbeak was about to take off again when Matt chimed in. "Hold up a second Blackbeak. We need to make absolutely sure you're not the ancient bat of mystery our master has sent us to find." Blackbeak chuckled. "Oh yea; and just how do you plan on doing that boys?" Rat chimed in again. "We must put you through the test." A worried expression came across Blackbeak's face. "What kind of test did you have in mind exactly?" Matt glanced back at him thoughtfully. "Just stay right there for a second Blackbeak. Rat, go get it." Blackbeak turned his head towards Rat as he had already descended towards the ground below. "Get what exactly? What are you talking about?" Matt stared at him seriously. "It's a simple test really and it'll be over before you know it. Don't worry. It should be absolutely painless…assuming you pass of course," he replied with sneer.

Blackbeak quickly became worried again as Rat picked up a small stone inside one of his talons. He flew back up towards the branch they were standing on. Matt continued speaking. "There is an ancient prophecy that says a stone shall never harm the raven of old." Just as Blackbeak began putting two and two together he glanced up just in time to see Rat drop a small stone directly on top of his head. Blackbeak was just as shocked as they were to see the small stone bounce off an invisible force field surrounding him and towards the ground below. He glanced back at Matt with surprise. "Wow, maybe Rat over there is just a bad aim," he exclaimed hopefully. Matt shook his head. "Nope, the test has been done and the truth has been discovered. You are the one and only raven of old we have been searching for Rueland. You must come with us. Our glorious king awaits your presence." Blackbeak shook his head. "And what if I refuse to go with you; then what?" Rat flew down to land on the branch next to them and overheard his question. "Then our army will attack your precious fairy city without delay. Perhaps this would be a more peaceful path for you raven. You might be able to discuss some sort of peace treaty with our beloved king on behalf of the fairy people but you never know. He can be difficult to deal with sometimes." Blackbeak shook his head. "You boys could be leading me into an obvious trap but despite the risk I am willing go with you. If it means keeping peace between the fairies and bats then I will gladly discuss terms with the bat king. Take me to your leader," he finished confidently!

Matt and Rat began flying in a southeast direction as Blackbeak followed close behind them. He began thinking of what he would say to the bat king when they arrived. He wanted to be prepared for any kind of negotiations he might encounter on behalf of the good fairies at the Lake of Lost Souls.

28. A GIFT FROM MORGANNA

Jimbo Jenkins was a proud Pixie Guild member. He was only human but found the trade of selling Pixie Dust to fairies quite beneficial! Even though he didn't have wings and couldn't fly, he could have easily used his own product to fly anywhere he wished. However, he knew that any product used would be unsellable and would not be profitable for him in the long run. He enjoyed travelling on foot like most humans since none of them possessed a pair of wings anyways. His travels had brought him to the Lake of Lost souls on this sunny afternoon. He was a handsome young fellow in his 20's with short brown hair, light brown skin and a delightfully charming smile. He carried a brown leather shoulder pack filled with his own special mixture of Pixie Dust along with his own special ingredients used for making it as well. He had memorized the secret recipe just in case he ever got robbed of his wares. This way the bandits would get his merchandize but never actually know how to make the stuff. Being a member of the Pixie Guild had taught him to make Pixie Dust the correct and proper way. However, in order to sell it for a much higher price he added a secret ingredient to the mix which caused it to last far longer than the traditional method of making it. This is why his customers preferred buying it from him over other dust peddlers because they knew his merchandize would last ten times longer than the normal Pixie Dust that they could buy anywhere else on the market.

Jimbo thought back on a fond memory he had of when he had first told his mom that he was a "dust peddler." She scolded him endlessly; not fully realizing just how valuable such a trade actually was at the time. Since then, he had grown quite wealthy from his many travels and trades. He made his mom proud and she was quite happy with his success wherever his journeys took him. Unfortunately, his dad had passed away when he was a young lad and he had to learn what it meant to be a man early on in life.

Casually strolling down one of the cobblestone streets at the Lake of Lost Souls, Jimbo's plan was to eventually connect up with the main street to go visit some of his favorite merchants. He hoped to unload his inventory on them for a nice profitable sum of rubies. While walking between two brick buildings, he spotted a tall slender woman dressed in a dark hooded cloak sitting on a wooden barrel just across the street from him. Walking over to her, he introduced himself. She was facing away from him and her face was completely covered by the dark hood around her head. The building in front of him provided enough shade for them not to be scorched by the heat of the day. "The shade feels really nice," he said to the woman as he approached the barrel she was sitting on. "Indeed it does," replied the haggard sounding voice from underneath the hood. "My name's Jimbo," he responded with his hand outstretched. He was hoping she would introduce herself and shake his hand in response. An air of disappointment crept over him as she introduced herself but didn't reach out to shake his hand or even turn to face him for that matter. "Just call me Morgan," she replied with an elderly tone in her voice. "What's a nice woman like you doing out here sitting on this randomly tipped over wooden barrel," he asked curiously?

Morgan glanced downward without showing her face to him. "I was on my way to deliver a gift to the Queen but an old woman like myself can barely get around these days," she said with dismay in her voice. "Oh," replied Jimbo curiously? "What gift did you want to bring her? I would be happy to deliver it for you," he responded energetically. "Oh, that's quite kind of you to offer," she replied flatteringly. "I wouldn't want to impose on your generosity though." Jimbo stared down at her. "It's not a problem. Really, I'm happy to help," he exclaimed genuinely. "Well if you insist," she replied thankfully. Reaching into her robe, she produced a small wooden circle with colorful strings that criss-crossed each-other at its center. Three long eagle feathers hung from the perfectly crafted circle. Jimbo recognized the object immediately. "Wow, what a magnificent Dream Catcher," he said admiringly. "Thank you," replied the old woman. "I made it myself. Dream catchers are a hobby of mine." Jimbo smiled. "It's fantastic! I'd be happy to give this to the Queen for you. Also, if you're interested I'm selling my special version of Pixie Dust I've carefully perfected throughout the years." "Is that right," the elderly woman replied curiously? "Yes indeed," Jimbo responded enthusiastically. "In fact, that's why my customers love me so much. I've come up with a creative way of making Pixie Dust last longer than it usually does. It helps my buyers save the few rubies they have to use on other worthless trinkets." The old woman still didn't turn to look at him. "That's truly amazing Jimbo. What's your secret if you don't mind me asking?" Jimbo glanced around to make sure no one else was listening. The street was completely bare besides the two of them. "Well, can you keep a secret," he asked hopefully? The old woman nodded her hooded head. "Even if I couldn't, an old woman like me wouldn't be much competition anyways," she replied with chuckle. Leaning in closer, he responded. "I use ground-up seaweed from the Lake of Lost Souls. Rumor has it that spirits fly around the lake at night and touch the seaweed with their angelic hands. Apparently, this gives it a life extension quality that most seaweed wouldn't normally have."

The elderly woman stood up with her hooded face still pointed away from Jimbo. "That's truly fascinating Jimbo. I hate to run out on such a good conversation but my grandson was planning to visit soon and I must get back to see him. Thanks again for delivering my gift to the Queen. Your good turn has truly helped this old woman out; you can be sure of that," she said in her crackly old voice. Jimbo nodded. "I'm glad I could help Morgan. Take care of yourself. I'm positive the Queen will absolutely love your gift!" The old woman began walking away from Jimbo. "It'll be a nice surprise for her I'm sure," she replied mystically. They parted ways; each walking in opposite directions. After walking a safe distance away from Jimbo, Morganna slipped her slender wand out from her deep pocket, turned around and silently shot a bright stream of red light towards the back of Jimbo's head. He stopped dead in his tracks to massage the back of his scalp. He thought perhaps a giant bug had bitten the back of his head but since he felt nothing there he continued walking towards the Queen's palace. "What a gullible little child," Morganna thought to herself darkly.

29. ESCAPING THE CATACOMBS

After Pixie and Morpheus had vanished through the portal, Mojo and Misty were left wondering how they were going to escape the deep catacombs they currently found themselves trapped in. They contemplated flying through the small entrance hole above them where all the quicksand was leaking in and running down the walls around them. However, they knew it would just lead to the inside of a Sand Trapper's hollow stem and eventually to its sharp thorn mouth. Neither of them had the desire to deal with that monster again at the moment. They considered any other alternative to be far better than that one.

They also contemplated where they would need to travel next in order to finally reach Nectarville. The Queen had told them their first three stops before arriving in Necatarville would be the Forest of Fire, the Dessert of Doom and finally Avalanche Mountain. Even though they were both concerned with how to proceed with the journey ahead, they were simply happy to see each-other safe and sound again.

Misty ran up to Mojo and threw her arms around his neck in a warm embrace. "I'm just happy you're alive Mojo! I was devastated when

I saw you get eaten by that Sand Trapper! I thought you had died for sure," she exclaimed lovingly. She pulled him in closer as he wrapped his arms around her waist. "For a while, I thought we really were going to die," he replied seriously. "Just because I'm a genie doesn't mean other magical creatures can't hurt me." They continued embracing each-other silently. Misty was waiting for Mojo to lean in and kiss her but her patience had reached its end as she leaned in to kiss him instead. A magnificent surge of power filled their bodies as their lips locked. It was as if the magic within them had combined forces to create one of the most magical moments they had ever experienced! Mojo was the first to speak. "In all my years as a genie, I've never felt magic like this," he exclaimed as he leaned into her warm embrace. After kissing him again, she responded. "I'm pretty sure magic like this could never come out of a wand," she replied enchantingly. Mojo responded. "You're absolutely right Misty."

Even though Misty had noticed Mojo's red snakelike eyes, she hadn't mentioned them because of her overwhelming happiness to see him again. Her curiosity suddenly got the better of her as she pulled away for a moment. "Um, Mojo…I am curious. You're eyes look very much like…" Mojo finished her sentence for her. "A snake….I know. Cobra Con gave them to me and Pixie to help us see through the dark tunnels. It helped us make our way through these underground tunnels. What do you think of them," he asked curiously? She shook her head. "I like being with you Mojo. That's all that matters." He smiled. "I think you're avoiding my question," he said playfully. She chuckled a bit. "Alright, I really don't like them. You look kind of creepy with them snake eyes. Perhaps there's a way to get them back to normal somehow," she replied hopefully. Mojo nodded. "They might look a little creepy but I've got excellent night vision now. Perhaps they'll come in handy later on in our journey," he said optimistically. Misty pulled him in for another big juicy kiss on the lips. "I love you Mojo. I'm happy if you're happy," she responded sincerely. He kissed her back. "I love you too Misty. How about we build our home down here in this gorgeous sandpit," he said playfully. Misty pushed him away teasingly. "Oh heck no," she replied with a laugh. Mojo laughed with her. "Of course I'm joking. What I mean is let's get out of here."

Misty stared at him lovingly. "I'm tempted to forget about our quest and just go wherever you go Mojo," she said adoringly. "At the same time, I also can't help but feel how close we are to finding Drake. We must be quite close to Nectarville by now." Mojo nodded agreeably. "The Queen said we'd have to cross through the Forest of Fire, the Dessert of Doom and Avalanche Mountain before finally reaching Nectarville. I'm pretty sure we've already made it through the Forest of Fire and this is the Dessert of Doom. The only place left to cross is Avalanche Mountain. Thankfully we have our trusty dragon to help us with that," he said cheerfully. Misty remembered the miniature lamp in her robe pocket and considered taking it out at the moment but decided to wait until they had finished their planning.

Before anything else could be said, Misty found herself being lifted up off the ground by Mojo. He cradled her body inside his muscular arms. "Hold on Misty. We're getting out of here," he exclaimed confidently. They hovered off the ground as Mojo flew them towards the small opening in the ceiling above. They were about to break through a whole lot of quicksand which was continually sinking in through the opening and running down onto the cavern walls nearby. "Close your eyes," Mojo shouted. "This is going to get messy!"

Bursting through the quicksand barrier above them, Mojo jetted straight through the Sand Trapper's hollow stem and out its thorny mouth! Soaring high into the air, they could see the group of plant monsters below. Mojo landed on a tall sand dune overlooking the group of Sand Trappers. He slowly let Misty out of his arms and onto the dessert sand below. She wiped the quicksand away from her eyes and mouth. Mojo followed suit as they gazed into each-other's eyes. Misty reached out to embrace him. "Oh Mojo, you saved me. You're my hero," she exclaimed lovingly. Mojo hugged her back. "No problem Misty. I'm sure you would have done the same for me if you had your broomstick or anti-gravity amulet with you. Speaking of which…where are…" Misty cut him short. "Oh no! I accidently left my broomstick down there and I forgot to get my anti-gravity amulet back from Morpheus! He borrowed it because he didn't have anything to fly around with. I'm such a klutz," she said stupidly. Mojo hugged her again. "It's okay Misty, we have the dragon to help us out and I can always carry you if needed," he replied with a smile. Grinning back at him, she responded joyfully. "You're the best Mojo! I'm so glad you're my traveling companion!" A group of ravenous vultures flying overhead quickly grew tired of watching them smooch and decided to search elsewhere for dead prey.

During one of their hugs, Misty happened to glance upward and caught a glimpse of a bald eagle soaring high over their heads. "Hey Mojo; look! A bald eagle," she exclaimed excitedly!" "I'm pretty sure that's a sign for good luck," he replied cheerfully.

Even though Misty and Mojo felt madly in love with each-other, they also felt the need to press on with their journey. Pulling the miniature lamp from her robe pocket, Misty rubbed it vigorously. It didn't take long for Claw to appear. "Nice to see you again Claw," she said happily. "Looks like you've recovered from that nasty fight we had with those vicious werewolves," she said tenderly. "We need you to fly us over Avalanche Mountain and straight to Nectarville," she commanded gently. The large dragon nodded understandingly as Mojo carefully hovered Misty and himself onto the dragon's neck in preparation for lift off. The magical brown mounting blanket was still draped around his neck and helped them stay balanced during flight.

Claw was soon flying through the air and heading straight towards Avalanche Mountain. Misty sat in front of Mojo on top of the dragon's neck. Leaning back against his shoulder, she enjoyed his warm embrace as Claw continued flying them through the warm misty air. They were happy Claw had been around long enough to know exactly where he was going. Misty's thoughts drifted back to the time she had fought with him in order to get the lamp out of his cave. She became grateful for that particular struggle because she never would have met Mojo if it wouldn't have happened. It suddenly dawned on her that she had gained much more than expected when first setting out on her journey to become young again. Not only had she become young again but she had found the best boyfriend any witch could ever ask for. She was incredibly grateful to have Mojo around and continued to remind him of that every chance she got.

30. RACE TO BOULDER MOUNTAIN

Drake and Duncan slept late into the morning. They didn't have anywhere to be anytime soon. Their only meeting was set for that evening with Floyd and they both had a pretty good idea how long it would take to travel to the base of Boulder Mountain. Of course, Drake always factored in a little extra time for Glue and Molasses. He kept reminding himself there was a reason why he had given them those particular names and vowed to get faster moving horses someday.

Drake was shaving the peach fuzz off his face and Duncan was packing a few items he had used the night before into his small travel bag. "Hey Drake old buddy; what would you say to a friendly wager," Duncan said challengingly. Drake took another swipe at his face with his single bladed razor. "What exactly did you have in mind?" Duncan shoved his night shirt into his travel bag. "Well, I was thinking it would be fun to race our horses against each-other." Drake frowned. "Oh Duncan, you know that wouldn't even be close to a fair challenge; not with old Glue and Molasses there to back me up," he replied with a laugh. Duncan continued packing. "I thought you might say that. So, just to keep things fair, how about I give you an hours head start to Boulder

Mountain. What would you say to that?" Drake began to shave the other side of his face. "I'd say give me a two hour head start and you've got yourself a deal. What did you want to wager anyways?" Duncan finished packing and threw his travel bag over his shoulder. "Let's say whoever wins gets first crack at the magic box....assuming it's the real deal of course," he said with a chuckle. Drake finished shaving and wiped his face with a small hand towel hanging from a hook next to him. "Alright, it's a deal Duncan!" Both crooks shook hands on their new found wager. "So, what do you plan on doing with your two hours of free time before you head out," Drake asked curiously? Duncan smiled. "Well, I saw a gorgeous young lass walk into the tavern yesterday while I was waiting for you to arrive. Figured she's probably staying in one of the inns around here I imagine. I'll probably hobble down there for a while in hopes of seeing her pretty face," he replied with a grin. Drake punched him on the shoulder playfully. "Duncan you dog! Ditching your partner in crime to go find a life partner; you sly devil," he said jokingly! Duncan grinned. "I'm tellin' ya Drake, this girl had the look of an angel and the body of a temptress," he replied with a laugh.

Drake threw his travelling bag over his shoulder and opened the bedroom door to leave. "Well, last I checked; neither one of us own a watch Duncan. So, we'll obviously need to go somewhere that actually has a clock on the wall so we can agree on your leaving time," he said seriously. Duncan double checked the bedroom for any unpacked items before closing the door behind them. They walked down the narrow carpeted hallway towards the stairs ahead. "There's a clock in the tavern," Duncan suggested blatantly. Drake stopped dead in his tracks. "Remember what I told you about drinking on the job Duncan?" Duncan looked hurt for a moment. "We're technically not on the job yet boss...and I was only suggesting that because that's where I saw that beautiful girl yesterday. She might still be hanging around there somewhere." Drake looked Duncan directly in the eyes. "Two things Duncan...First of all, you need to be sober to make that long ride to Boulder Mountain, especially at racing speed. Second of all, don't let this girl hold you up if you find her. Remember, we've got a job to do back at Boulder Mountain. Floyd is going to meet us there to trade for the magic box. So please don't get distracted. This'll be a big break for us if we can get our hands on that little Transformation Box. It'll mean we can transform rocks into rubies Duncan! That's kind of a big deal! Also, keep your manners up to par. Floyd hasn't met you yet and we want him to be impressed when he does. Understand what I'm saying?" Duncan nodded. "I hear ya loud and clear boss. Remember, we've been in this business for years now and I've never let ya down yet. You can count on me Drake," he replied confidently. Drake nodded and proceeded down the wooden staircase towards the lobby. A pretty blond haired lady stood behind the front desk and smiled at them as they walked up to it. "Will you boys be checking out today?" Drake nodded. "Yes mam. The room was quite comfortable. Give my regards to the cleaning staff if you please," he said kindly. Flashing her pearly whites flatteringly she responded. "Absolutely, thank you sir," she replied nicely. Duncan decided to take a shot in the dark. "Just curious, did a woman with long red hair happen to come by here yesterday?" The pretty blond looked at Duncan. "Sorry, can't say I've seen a redhead around here in quite some time. Gingers are a rare bunch around these parts," she exclaimed mystically. Duncan grinned sheepishly. "All the more reason to find one," he said with a wink. The pretty blond giggled at his response. "Best of luck good sir," she replied before pausing for a moment. "But if ya can't find her; I'll be off from work in a couple of hours if you're interested," she hinted charmingly. Duncan looked at Drake and Drake shot him the look of death! Duncan looked back at the pretty blond. "I'd love to take ya up on that offer if I'm still hangin' around town then," he replied smoothly. "What's your name anyways?" She reached behind the counter to grab a business card with her name on it and handed it to Duncan. "It's right there just in case you forget," she said with a wink. Duncan smiled and looked down at the card. "Your name's Black Hawk Inn," he asked jokingly? She chuckled and gave him a playful slap on the arm. "No silly, it's Coreena Cordell," she replied with a laugh. "Well, it has been a pleasure meeting you Miss Cordell. My name is Duncan and this here is Drake," he said politely. Coreena flashed her pearly whites at them again. "It's a pleasure to meet you both and if either of you are ever back this way, just ask for Rena," she said winking at Duncan. Drake reached around Duncan's neck and grabbed him by the shoulder in a side embrace. "We would love to stay and chat Rena but we really must be getting along. We've got business to attend to up at Boulder Mountain. Ta ta for now," he replied kindly as he moved Duncan away from Rena and towards the exit. Once out of earshot, Drake continued speaking as they walked outside and towards the stables. "I know you're infatuated with women Duncan but I really need you to stay focused on the task at hand. I'm starting to wonder if this race is a good idea after all," he said as they opened the horse stalls in front of them. "Well, there's no going back now," replied Duncan simply. "After all, we shook on it remember?" Drake laughed. "That's an odd thing for a horse thief to say to another," he said jokingly. "But you're right Duncan. After all, if we can't trust each-other than who else is there?" Duncan nodded. "I couldn't agree more," he exclaimed confidently.

They slowly led their three horses outside of the stable and onto the cobblestone street nearby. "I forgot, where did you park the covered wagon," Duncan asked? Drake continued leading Glue and Molasses in a northward direction. "It's just on the other side of the stable here," he responded nonchalantly. Duncan chimed in again. "Perhaps I should leave old Swifty here at the stable. It would probably be safer than some of the other places around here." Drake looked at him suspiciously. "Oh, don't kid yourself Duncan, you just want an excuse to go visit Rena again," he replied with a laugh. "And of course you'd name your new horse Swifty right before our big race," he responded jokingly. Duncan laughed. "Figured it's a good name for a getaway horse," he replied lightheartedly.

Drake found his covered wagon just around the corner and quickly began hitching his horses to it. "If you want to leave your horse here and follow me back to the tavern then we'll agree on a leaving time for you. I'm pretty sure the tavern has a clock on the wall we can check out," Drake said casually. Duncan climbed up onto the long wooden drivers-seat built for two. Drake climbed up next to him. "Scootch over; I'm driving," he said authoritatively. Duncan moved over to allow room for Drake to sit next to him. Drake grabbed the reins and flicked them just hard enough to get old Glue and Molasses moving again.

They made their way onto the main road and veered towards the nearby tavern. It wasn't a long trip but leaving the covered wagon outside the tavern made Drake a bit uncomfortable even for a few minutes. "Oh, come on," said Duncan. "We just need to go inside and see what time it is. Tell you what, I'll go in and check if you're worried about the horses getting stolen." Drake parked the covered wagon next to the metal lamppost just outside the tavern. It wasn't where he was supposed to park his horses but he wanted a good view of them from the tavern window just in case something were to happen.

Drake hopped down from the covered wagon and tied his horses to the lamppost in front of him. "I don't think so Duncan. You're not getting off that easy. I'm pretty sure you'd give me much less of a head start if I didn't check the time with you," he said lightheartedly. "Alright," Duncan replied; "but don't blame me if we come back out here and your horses are gone. That's why I left mine back at the Black Hawk Stable; to avoid this very thing," he replied seriously. Drake shook his head and walked towards the tavern door. "Oh, you worry too much Duncan," he said casually. "After all, we'll only be a minute." Duncan walked next to him towards the tavern door. "A minute is all it takes my friend." There was a big wooden sign above the door which read: "Trickle Down Tavern."

Once inside, they took a look around. Since it was the middle of the day, the tavern was mostly empty. Plenty of tables and chairs were spread throughout the joint. Clear windows surrounded the room lighting it with natural incoming light that bounced off the dust particles emanating from the ceiling and wooden floorboards beneath their feet. A few loners sat at separate tables drinking their poison of choice. A giant grandfather clock stood against the southern wooden planked wall. Observing at the current time; it read 12:24 in the afternoon. "Alright," said Drake. "It appears my two hour head start to Boulder Mountain will put you at a 2:30 leaving time." Duncan looked dumbfounded. "Can't you read a clock Drake? It would put me at 2:24. Nice try though," he retorted with a laugh. Drake decided to try and explain his logic to him. "Well, by my calculations it'll be 12:30 by the time I untie my horses and get back on my wagon. That would be fair wouldn't it?" Duncan shook his head. "Oh, if you wanna be picky about it then go ahead! It won't take much to catch up with you anyways." Drake punched him on the shoulder playfully. "I'll see you at Boulder Mountain my friend and I know you're probably sick of me telling you this but…" Duncan cut him short. "I know, I know….don't drink on the job and don't let the women distract me from my duties." Drake smiled. "See, I am a good teacher," he replied with a laugh as he began heading back towards the exit.

They said their goodbyes and parted ways. Duncan walked up to the bartender behind the counter. "Have you seen a pretty ginger around here by chance? I happened to catch a glimpse of her last night but couldn't talk to her none." The bartender was a big muscular man with a bald head and tattoos running down both arms. "What can I do fer ya," he asked with a deep scratchy voice? Duncan placed a hand on the wooden counter that separated them. "Unfortunately, my boss says I can't drink on the job but I'm just wondering if you might have seen a beautiful redheaded seductress walk through here recently?" The muscular bartender grabbed a wet rag sitting next to him and began wiping down the counter in front of him. "Aw yes, every poor sap in this town has their eye on that one. She goes by Lilly. She doesn't come in very often cause the men around here are generally pretty rude to her. I don't blame her for wanting to stay away from them," he replied sympathetically. "Let me guess…you're another desperate guy looking for love right," he asked with a laugh? Duncan chuckled. "Yea, I'm just another desperate guy looking for companionship. Attractive women seem to be a rare find these days," he replied seriously. The bartender continued wiping down the counter. "I hear ya there. I've heard just about every sob story imaginable from just about everyone living here. They all try drowning their sorrows in ale and then come back the next day with the same old problems. Ya wanna know a secret," he asked in a hushed tone? Duncan leaned over the counter to better hear what he was about to say. The bartender leaned in closer and whispered in his ear. "I don't think the alcohol actually solves their problems like they think it does. It only numbs their emotions for a while so they can't feel the pain. People really need to learn how to deal with their own emotional problems but I'm not going to tell them that. It's bad for business," he said with a laugh! Duncan threw a hand in the air carelessly. "Don't worry, your secret is safe with me," he replied with a chuckle.

Since Duncan had some time to kill before heading out to Boulder Mountain, he sat down on one of the tall stools next to him and continued speaking with the bartender. "Well, it's nice to make your acquaintance good sir. My name is Duncan and you are?" The bald bartender reached out to shake his hand. "The name's Dale. Pleased to make your acquaintance. So, what brings you to the finest tavern in all of Nectarville," he asked in a funny salesman sort of way? Duncan laughed. "Well, since you told me one of your secrets; I'll let you in on one of mine." Dale smiled. "Oh, this ought to be good," he said leaning in closer to hear him better. Duncan continued. "Me and my business partner Drake are heading to his place up at Boulder Mountain. We plan on exchanging our entire life fortunes for a stupid little box called the Transformation Box. Ever heard of it before?" Dale glanced around to make sure no one else was eavesdropping in on their conversation. "Aw yes! Old man Floyd came in here one night and got hammered pretty hard. He was drunk as a skunk and tried selling that little box to me and half the other bastards in here. We laughed him right out the door! None of us believed that stupid box could actually turn normal everyday objects into rubies. I mean, it goes against the laws of magic and nature. Everyone knows that," he said seriously. Duncan looked intrigued and a little worried at the same time. "Well, did he at least give you a demonstration," he asked hopefully? Dale shook his head. "You would think he would have at least tried to convince us it was the real deal. Perhaps he was just too drunk to think clearly but the more likely reason is that it plain doesn't work." Duncan suddenly became even more worried than before. "Oh no, I've got to beat my friend back to Boulder Mountain or he'll trade away our entire life savings for a worthless box that doesn't even work!"

Duncan stood up from the tall stool he was sitting on and began heading towards the exit. "It was nice meeting you," said Dale enthusiastically. Duncan waved his right hand high over his shoulder with his back facing Dale. "Thanks for warning me Dale. I hope business gets better for you tonight," he said walking out through the tavern door and into the fresh air outside. He couldn't wait around for two hours. He had to warn Drake about what Dale had just told him or their entire life savings would be traded away to that conniving con artist Floyd! Duncan made a mad dash towards Black Hawk Inn.

His slender legs finally carried him to the inn's stable where he had left his stallion. Finding Swifty right where he left her, he opened the stall and untied her from the wooden post nearby. Picking up the saddle from the small mound of hay in her stall, he threw it over her back and secured it tightly underneath. Gently leading her by the reins outside the stable, he carefully mounted her. Swifty squirmed and brayed at the new found weight on her body but this didn't bother Duncan any. After riding horses most of his life, he figured he could handle whatever Swifty could throw at him. He began pacing her towards the main road and didn't get very far when a familiar voice shouted out to him. "Duncan! Oh Duncan!" He turned around only to find the pretty blond haired Coreena running after him. She must have seen him pass by the inn from the window on the way to the main road.

Duncan brought Swifty to a halt before turning her around to face Coreena who had finally caught up with him. "I'm glad I caught you Duncan," she said exhaustedly. "The redheaded girl you were asking about just checked into the inn. I happened to see you ride by just now and thought maybe I could catch you and tell you about it!" She paused to catch her breath while Duncan smiled at her. "That's awfully sweet of you Coreena and I would love to come meet her but I really need to catch up with my business partner Drake right now. We're trying to meet with a guy named Floyd this evening and I really need to tell Drake not to make the deal that will probably ruin our financial futures forever!" Coreena frowned. "Oh, that doesn't sound good Duncan. Although, I hate to see you miss out on meeting a pretty girl because of a lousy business deal," she replied gently as she touched one of his legs tangling from the side of his horse. Her gentle touch didn't go unnoticed. He glanced down at her from atop his horse. "Believe me Coreena, this is one of the hardest decisions I've ever had to make but I don't want to lose my entire life's savings either! Drake might invest in something that doesn't even work without me being there to warn him about it," he replied frantically. Coreena moved closer to his horse and sensually moved a hand up the side of his leg. "Well, I hope you'll at least come back to visit me," she replied seductively. Duncan moved his left hand downward to embrace hers. "I will definitely come back to visit you Coreena. You can count on that. You'll just have to give me some time to make this journey first."

As Duncan talked, he happened to catch a glimpse of the long red haired lady out of the corner of his eye. She had just stepped outside Black Hawk Inn and was moving in a southward direction away from him. Her long red hair and slender body was perfectly visible from where he set atop his black stallion as he watched her walk away in the opposite direction. He squeezed Coreena's hand even tighter. "Keep a lookout for me darling. I will return soon. We'll get to know each-other much better when I return; I promise. That is if you're okay with that?" Coreena nodded and kissed his leg gently. "Do what you must Duncan and return to me soon. I'll be here when you get back." Duncan reached down and gently ran his fingers through her long blond hair. "You can count on it my lady," he said lovingly.

Duncan turned his stallion around and began riding northward. Even with his back facing Coreena, he waved a hand up in the air somehow knowing she would wave back at him. After putting enough distance between them, he snapped Swifty into a faster paced gallop towards Boulder Mountain. "Catching up with Drake will be easy as pie; especially with old Glue and Molasses leading his way," he thought with a chuckle. He pushed Swifty to her max speed in an effort to beat Drake to Boulder Mountain.

31. THE PIXIE GUILD LIST

Pixie and Morpheus flew through the portal opening and found themselves behind a large bright red tent. "Where are we," Pixie asked curiously? Morpheus turned his head towards her. "We are back at the Lake of Lost Souls behind a special shop I wanted to show you," he replied mysteriously. "That was the quickest trip I've ever been on. It sure beats flying though that's for sure. Is there any way I could get my own portal device too," she asked curiously? Morpheus scanned the area for eavesdroppers. "It's ancient magic Pixie. No one should even know I have it. It would only cause large amounts of greed and suspicion among the magical community if you understand what I'm saying," he said carefully. Pixie nodded. "I understand Morpheus. What shop is this anyways?" Morpheus continued walking towards the tent entrance. "You'll see. Just follow me," he replied confidently.

The three of them moved around towards the front side of the merchant tent. The bright gold letters above the tent entrance read; "PIXIE'S POCKET." A bright white banner with red letters stretched out beneath which read: "GOING OUT OF BUSINESS!" Pixie frowned as she turned towards Morpheus. "I think I've been here before." Pixie connected the missing puzzle pieces together in her mind as they entered the shop. "Let me guess, you want to show me how the owner of this shop has truly forgotten the recipe for Pixie Dust. Am I right?" Morpheus snapped his fingers. "You got me Pixie! That's exactly why I brought you here. So, you can either humor me and we can speak with the owner of this shop or we can go straight to the Queen's palace. Which would you prefer?" Pixie glanced around the tiny shop in hopes of spotting the owner. Nobody was there at all. "Oh alright, we can talk to the owner if he shows up anytime soon."

Scanning the area inside the shop; they found long white tables filled with neatly organized bags of Pixie Dust sitting on them. They were small pocket sized bags that could easily be carried by anyone looking to buy them. Above each stack of Pixie Dust stood a sign stating the price along with how long each bag would last. Some bag sections were labeled with a "2 Day Expiration" while others were labeled with a "4 Day Expiration" and so on and so forth all the way up to a "14 Day Expiration" period.

The shop owner seemed to have appeared out of nowhere spotted them before they saw him. "Pixie; is that you," he asked curiously? Pixie followed the sound of his voice. An elderly gentleman now standing behind the counter at the front of the shop stared back at them. "He must have been hiding out in the backroom," she thought silently. The owner had a long gray pointy beard and bushy gray eyebrows. Pixie instantly recognized him. "Jawkew! It's good to see you!" She walked up next to him and wrapped her arms around him tightly. He was a fairy just like her and she felt overly excited to see him again! "Last time I saw you, I was teaching you how to make Pixie Dust," she said energetically! Jawkew released his embrace and gently cradled his hands in hers. "I've obviously grown much older since then but I'm extremely glad to see you Pixie!" Pixie glanced at him worriedly. "Why, what's going on Jawkew," she asked with concern in her voice? He looked at her seriously. "I need you to show me how to make Pixie Dust again Pixie! I've completely forgotten how to make it even though I've done this job for over 17 years now!" Pixie touched his arm gently. "Oh my friend, it's not your fault. We have reason to believe Morganna is back and is cursing the entire Pixie Guild to forget how to make Pixie Dust. We can only hope she hasn't gotten a hold of the Pixie Guild List yet. We're all doomed if she finds it," said Pixie worriedly. Jawkew glanced over at Morpheus. "What's he doing with you," he asked curiously? Pixie continued to look into Jawkew's eyes. "He's here to help make sure Morganna doesn't get a hold of the Pixie Guild List. This is the court wizard Morpheus," she replied introducing him politely. "Nice to meet you," Jawkew replied respectfully. His attention turned back to Pixie. "Pixie, would you at least write down the Pixie Dust formula for me to follow. I'm going out of business soon because I can't remember how to make it and it's not just me either. Many other Pixie Guild members are losing their memories of how to make it as well. If we were selling normal merchandise like food or clothing then things would be different but we're talking about the possibility of all fairies not being able to fly again! That's kind of a big deal Pixie," Jawkew exclaimed dramatically!

Pixie put a hand around Jawkew's shoulders in an attempt to comfort him. "I know it's a big deal Jawkew and I'm sorry your business is going under but you know the laws regarding the making of Pixie Dust. Unfortunately, they are extremely specific. Only qualified Pixie Guild members are allowed to make Pixie Dust and one of the qualifications is the ability to memorize the formula so that cheap imitators won't be able to steal it. This is why we've never written it down before." Jawkew nodded. "I've been making Pixie Dust by memory for 17 years now Pixie and all of the sudden I can't remember how anymore! Please help me," he pleaded desperately. Pixie leaned in to hug him. "Don't worry my friend. We'll get to the bottom of whatever is happening and if it's Morganna who's behind this then we'll do our absolute best to stop her! You can count on that," she said confidently. Jawkew hugged her back. "Please be quick Pixie! I don't want to sell other boring merchandise for a living. It's just not as fun and it costs a small fortune to buy inventory from vendors. The whole process of starting a new business is a nightmare Pixie! Please hurry for all of our sakes," he pleaded while letting go of their embrace. "Don't worry Jawkew. I'll do my best. I promise," Pixie replied sympathetically. "Um, before I go…do you mind if I grab a couple bags of Pixie Dust on my way out? I recently ran out and could really use some more at the moment." Jawkew waved a hand in the air carelessly. "Take what you must Pixie. If it will help you along your journey then I insist you take as much as you need. Don't worry about paying for it. If you can sort this whole ordeal out with Morganna then that'll be payment enough." Pixie smiled gratefully. "Thank you Jawkew. We'll get to the bottom of this as soon as possible I assure you. Thanks again."

Pixie grabbed a few bags of Pixie Dust with the highest expiration dates available sitting on the table and placed them in the small purse around her shoulder. She walked towards the exit with Morpheus following close behind. "Nice to see you again Jawkew," she said as they left the shop. "You as well," replied Jawkew. Once outside, Pixie turned towards Morpheus. "I can see why you brought me here," she said simply. Morpheus nodded. "Hopefully you can see how important our mission is now," he replied convincingly. Pixie agreed. "Let's pay the Queen a little visit," she exclaimed confidently. "We'll need to get the updated Pixie Guild List from her so we can go visit each guild member individually and remind them how to make Pixie Dust again. I would have went through a lesson with Jawkew back there but it wouldn't have been appropriate during shop hours. We'll need to visit him during a more private time when he can really focus and enjoy a good long lesson on how to make Pixie Dust again. A shop is no place for that kind of lesson with customers constantly going in and out like they do." Morpheus nodded. "I agree absolutely. However, we mustn't take too long during our visit with the Queen. I promised Blackbeak I would return shortly to continue his training. He has learned much from me already but he still has much to learn as well." Pixie glanced at him curiously. "Where is he now anyways?" Morpheus shook his head. "Unfortunately, I can't reveal that information at the moment but I assure you he is safe and in good health. The Queen wants his location kept confidential for safety reasons of course," he lied smoothly.

They continued making their way towards the palace which was located at the city's center. Pixie paused in mid-flight. "Hey wait a second…why don't we just portal into the palace?" Morpheus looked at her seriously. "Unfortunately, the ancient fairies who built the palace placed a magical barrier around it to protect the Queen and all who live there. The invisible barrier keeps portals from coming in and out of it. It also keeps particular types of curses and hexes from entering that could potentially harm the Queen as well. Thus, we need to enter by foot or by flight. Sadly, I don't have wings so it looks like I'll be walking there while you fly alongside me," he said pointedly.

Pixie spotted the anti-gravity amulet hanging around his neck. "Did you forget about your amulet," she asked curiously? Morpheus glanced down at it. "Oh, I completely forgot. Looks like we can fly to the palace after all," he replied joyfully. Morpheus rubbed the amulet in a clockwise motion as his body slowly lifted up off the ground. Pixie reached into her purse and grabbed a handful of Pixie Dust which she threw over her shoulder and onto her fairy wings. She began flying alongside Morpheus as they slowly made their way towards the palace.

Flying past a number of shops and homes on their way there, they eventually came to a landing alongside the front entrance. Bill and Phil were standing guard outside; each holding a long pointed spear in their hands. "Well, if it isn't our little friend Pixie," said Phil enthusiastically. "Did you bring us some good news," Bill asked? Morpheus interjected. "We must speak with the Queen immediately," he said urgently. A serious expression crossed Phil's face. "Unfortunately, the Queen is currently in a meeting at the moment," he replied politely. "With who," Morpheus asked? Bill replied. "Well, he's a human who introduced himself as Jimbo Jenkins. He wanted to present a gift to the Queen. Morpheus stepped forward. "Could you at least try to get us in after he comes out," he asked hopefully? Phil glanced over at Pixie. "We can sure try but there's no guarantee she'll be able to see you both."

Just then a slender young man with brown hair opened the Throne Room doors and stepped outside. "You must be Jimbo Jenkins," Pixie asked curiously? Jimbo smiled. "That I am. I was just delivering a gift to the Queen from an elderly woman named Morgan. Apparently, she was too old to deliver it herself so she had me do it for her." "Wait a minute," said Morpheus. "An elderly woman named Morgan…that couldn't possibly be…" All three of them shouted the name in complete unison; "MORGANNA!!"

Fearing for the Queen's safety, Morpheus bolted towards the Throne Room doors quickly dashing inside! Pixie followed close behind with the two guards trailing behind her! They found the Queen standing next to her golden throne examining the new gift Jimbo had just left with her. "Isn't it beautiful," she exclaimed holding the dream catcher up towards the light for all to see. Morpheus recognized the magical object she was holding. "No my lady; you mustn't…" Before he could finish his sentence, a black stream of thick mist quickly emanated from the center of the mysterious looking dream catcher. The thick mist swirled around the three eagle feathers hanging from the dream catcher's wooden ring. The dark whirlwind swirled faster and faster around the eagle feathers until they broke off from the small wooden hoop they were attached to. Soaring higher into the air, the feathers quickly came together and transformed themselves into a bald headed eagle! Morpheus couldn't help but wonder if it was the same exact eagle that had attacked Blackbeak when he had first arrived at the Lake of Lost Souls. Blackbeak had mentioned it to him during one of their magic lessons together. "This must be the same eagle that injured the two fairy guards who tried capturing Blackbeak not to long ago," Morpheus thought silently.

The bald eagle gently descended towards the hard marble floor below and instantly transformed itself again! Another stream of thick black mist shot from the center of the dream catcher and swirled around the eagle. The black mist grew taller and wider until it reached a height of about six feet before disappearing completely. As the dark mist cleared, the figure of an elderly woman appeared standing in front of them. They all recognized her immediately. "MORGANNA," they shouted in unison!

The old witch in front of them was the ugliest creature they had ever seen! She was about six feet tall with a long pointy nose, green skin covered in warts and a tall pointy hat that covered her gnarly gray hair. She wore a long black dress and carried a tall bronze staff in her right hand which formed the shape of a cobra's head at the top. Even though no one said anything, they found it to be an eerie resemblance of Con's head. Morganna glared at them with disgust. The two guards rushed for the exit! Pointing her eerie open-mouthed serpent staff towards the open double-doors, a bright red stream of light shot towards them and slammed them shut! "Don't leave yet. The party is just beginning," she said with a smirk. "After all, we've got business to discuss," she said with a crackly sounding voice.

The Queen tossed the dream catcher aside as if it were a poisonous object she wanted nothing to do with. "Morganna, if you've got something to say then say it and let the others go. They don't need to be a part of whatever it is you are planning here," she pleaded authoritatively. Morganna frowned. "Oh but they do…" Glancing over at Pixie and Morpheus she continued. "Aww…I see this little fairy has had a run in with my cobra. Con's eyes glow within you," she said mystically. Pixie and Morpheus stared at each-other observingly. Morganna waved her long bronze cobra staff in the air. "Who do you think this staff was modeled after," she asked rhetorically? An air of fear washed over Pixie as she considered the possibility of Con being in league with Morganna. She wondered if Morganna had somehow found out about Con's death and had come back for revenge.

Morganna pointed at the two frightened guards with her cobra staff. "You two, take them down to the dungeon and lock them up. You will then return to your posts. If anyone inquires about the Queen, tell them she is no longer taking appointments today for any reason. Is that understood?" The guards nodded fearfully. Red light shot from her cobra staff and into the eyes of the two guards. Instantly, their eyes matched Pixie's cobra slit eyes as well. They were red glowing snake eyes similar to Con's before he had passed away. The two guards felt as if they were under some sort of trance as they pointed their spears at Pixie and Morpheus. "Follow us," they commanded authoritatively. Morganna grabbed the Queen firmly by the back of the neck. "You will leave the

Queen with me. We have important matters to discuss," she stated commandingly. The two guards saluted respectfully and began marching Pixie and Morpheus down to the dungeon below. Morpheus seriously considered fighting Morganna in an attempt to save the Queen but knew himself to be outmatched at the moment. He shouted a few words of encouragement to the Queen as the guards escorted him and Pixie out of the Throne Room. "Don't worry your majesty! We'll be back soon! Don't lose hope!"

Phil marched in front of them while Bill guarded from behind. Bill closed the double-doors on their way out of the Throne Room. Upon hearing the doors click shut, the Queen turned towards Morganna. "Aren't you afraid my guards will tell someone what is happening?" Morganna shook her head. "Not at all dearie, everyone with Con's eyes is under my control." Morganna took a step forward. "I had to find another pet after you stole mine away from me," she said contemptuously. The Queen stared downward to avoid Morganna's gaze. "That was ages ago Morganna. Rueland chose to stay with me; you know that. You could easily have him back if you wish," she continued calmly. Morganna spit on the floor next to the Queen's feet. "It wouldn't be the same little lady," she replied distastefully. "No, I am here to get the Pixie Guild List and you're going to get it for me," she said commandingly. The Queen folded her arms defensively. "I most certainly will not," she replied reproachfully. Morganna pointed her snake staff at her threateningly. "Be a good girl and get the list for me or I'll turn you into a toad and feed you to my cobra," she said threateningly. The Queen threw her hands in the air. "It's impossible now! Drake stole the Pixie Guild List a long time ago," she confessed. Morganna stomped her bronze staff heavily on the marble floor beneath her. "Who is this Drake character you speak of and where can I find him?" The Queen glanced downward and inhaled heavily. "Drake is an evil thief who lives somewhere in Nectarville. He has been stealing huge amounts of honeycomb from the beekeepers living there and from other lands around it. I've sent a special team out to find him." Morganna sighed. "You better not be lying to me or you will pay dearly my dear!"

The Queen continued to avoid Morganna's gaze. "I promise it's the truth. The only problem is that one of your new found prisoners was part of the group I sent out to find him. She would know more about Drake's current location than I do." Morganna began to pace back and forth anxiously. "And which prisoner are you referring to exactly," she asked pointedly? The Queen turned her head away from Morganna distraughtly. "The two prisoners you just sent to the dungeon might know where to find him. Their names are Morpheus and Pixie." Morganna placed a hand to her chin thoughtfully. "I suppose I'll have to chat with our new found prisoners," she replied darkly. "In the meantime, I can't have you wondering around the palace announcing to the whole kingdom that I'm here," she said sharply. She pointed her cobra staff at the Queen. "I'm taking you to the dungeon as well little missy. Get moving!" Better yet, I can't be seen marching you down there so I suppose I'll just have to keep you up here in the Throne Room until my faithful guards return." Morganna pointed her tall bronze staff at the Queen's large golden throne. A streak of red light shot from the mouth of her cobra staff into the Queen's golden throne. Instantly the throne transformed into a large iron cage. "Aww….perfect for a Queen," she exclaimed sarcastically. "Now get inside," she ordered forcefully. "So help me Moraganna; you will pay dearly for this" the Queen responded angrily! "Duly noted," Morganna replied carelessly. "Now hurry up! I've got prisoners to interrogate," she shouted commandingly!

The Queen stepped into the open metal cage reluctantly while Morganna slammed the iron barred door shut behind her. She locked it closed with a golden padlock which slid around the bars nicely. Upon hearing the lock snap shut, Morganna produced a single golden key from within her dress pocket and held it up for the Queen to see. "Don't worry your highness. Once I get what I want I'll set you free again," she exclaimed as she pocketed the key in front of her. The Queen grabbed the bars of her cage and shook them violently. "You'll never get that list Morganna! Drake is harder to catch than you can imagine!" Morganna frowned. "You better hope I catch him soon or you might be trapped in there far longer than you wish my dear," she replied threateningly.

Morganna shot another stream of red light from her cobra staff which swirled around her own body until it transformed her back into the bald eagle she had once been. Flying around the iron barred cage that held the Queen hostage, Morganna made her way back towards the magical dream catcher lying on the floor next to it. Her entire eagle body quickly shrunk down in size as she flew closer to it. Flying straight towards the center of the dream catcher, she vanished completely from sight as she soared through its center of colorfully woven fabric.

A streak of panic overcame the Queen as she realized just how alone she truly was at that moment. She was locked inside an impenetrable iron cage inside her own Throne Room without any way of escaping! The two guards on duty had been enchanted by Morganna and the rest of the group had been taken down to the dungeon below. Things were not looking good for her. She tried using a number of spells to escape her iron barred cells but nothing worked. She decided that her only way out would be to cooperate with Morganna the best she could unless a miracle were to somehow present itself. Sitting on the floor inside her cage, she curled up into a fetal position and cried.

Down in the dungeon, a dark swirling vortex quickly appeared in front of the large iron barred prison cell holding Pixie and Morpheus. They had been placed there by the two entranced guards who were now under Morganna's control. Morganna flew her eagle body through the newly opened portal and landed on the hard dirt floor just in front of their cells. Bill and Phil stood on opposite sides of the prison door in front of her. "Both of you, go guard the Throne Room entrance and make sure no one enters or leaves it," she commanded. They both saluted respectfully and walked towards the cement staircase leading upward to the main floor of the palace.

Morganna turned to face her captors through the iron bars in front of her. "The Queen has recently informed me the lot of you have been searching for a troublemaking fairy named Drake. I need to know where he is hiding," she demanded. Pixie and Morpheus remained silent. Morganna raised her serpent staff and pointed it directly at Pixie. "Tell me where Drake is hiding little fairy or I'll erase every memory you've ever had from that tiny head of yours," she said threateningly. Pixie spoke up timidly. "I…was on my way to find Drake but ended up coming back here with Morpheus. He said the Pixie Guild needed me so I returned here with him," she replied as if confessing to a horrible crime she had just committed. Morganna pointed her long bronze staff at Morpheus. "We're going to have a little chat Morpheus." Morganna pointed her serpent staff at the keyhole of the prison cell holding them. A glowing red light shot from the mouth of her cobra staff into the dark keyhole. There was a loud click as the cell door unlocked and Morganna rested her right hand on the door. Slowly pulling it open, she continued speaking. "Only Morpheus is allowed to follow me," she said commandingly. "You will stay here for now little girl."

Morpheus slowly made his way towards the slightly opened cell door. "Thank you madam; I am truly grateful for your kindness." "Oh shut up wizard," she replied slamming the cell door shut behind him. "What about me," Pixie pleased devastatingly? Morganna glared back at her. "You're of no use to me little fairy. You don't have the kind of power I require at the moment. You will stay here until I've either found Drake or you get lucky enough to escape. Better hope I find him fast or you might be here for quite a while my dear!" Locking the cell door again with a quick zap of her cobra staff, her attention quickly turned back towards Morpheus. "I'm sure you're familiar with portal travel. Are you not?" Morpheus nodded. "Good," she replied. "Any court wizard worth his salt would have his own portal device by now. I assume you have one," she asked pointedly? "Morpheus nodded agreeably. "Excellent," replied Morganna. "You must tell me exactly where Drake can be found so we can track him down and get my guild list from him," she commanded authoritatively. A confused expression crossed his face. "Well, he was last seen in Nectarville stealing honeycomb. He is a thief but I should tell you that two others are currently tracking him down as well. If they're close to finding him then they'd probably be near Avalanche Mountain by now."

Morganna rubbed her pointy green chin. "We will split up

Morpheus. You will search for this Drake character in Nectarville and I will transport myself to Avalanche Mountain to search for him as well. Remember, all I want is the Pixie Guild List. I don't really care about your friend Pixie over there and I don't even care about the Queen who is now rotting in an iron barred cage inside her own Throne Room. In fact, help me get what I want and I'll set all of you free," she said diplomatically. Morpheus glanced downward trying not to show the doubt etched on his face. "I would be more than happy to assist you madam if it means helping the Queen and Pixie go free," he replied with genuine concern in his voice. "Excellent," replied Morganna. "Do you have your portal device with you," she asked hopefully? Morpheus reached into his robe pocket and produced his small Vortex Vacuum which he palmed easily in his left hand. "Excellent," replied Morganna joyfully upon seeing it.

Before making his own portal appear, he felt the need to ask Morganna a question. "I'm just curious madam; I noticed you were using an animal portal device back inside the Throne Room or a Creature Portal as some call it. Don't you find those a bit inconvenient? I'm only asking because Creature Portals will only transport animals. It just seems so inconvenient having to transform yourself into an animal every time you use a Creature Portal only to transform back into a witch after arriving at your destination. Wouldn't you feel more comfortable using a regular Vortex Vacuum? It would help avoid a whole series of unnecessary transformations if you know what I mean," he stated thoughtfully. Morganna sighed with frustration and inhaled deeply as if trying to keep her patience in check. "If you were smart court wizard then you'd know the magic barrier surrounding this palace does not allow normal portals to pass through it." Morpheus made a mental note to magically fix the palace barrier if he ever escaped from his current predicament alive.

Morganna stepped backward. "You will use my Creature Portal to get to Nectarville Morpheus. From there, you will use your own portal to return back to the Throne Room. Since you are a wizard, I assume you can transform yourself back into human form once you've arrived at

Nectarville. Is that correct or am I making too big of an assumption?" Morpheus folded his arms across his chest. "Yes mam, I can handle things from there. What sort of animal are you going to turn me into," he asked curiously? "Please don't let it be anything that can get stepped on," he pleaded seriously. Morganna laughed. "No, it will be something that runs quickly. You will need as much speed as possible to find Drake as quickly as possible. But if it happens to be a different animal entirely then I assume the great court wizard can transform himself into whatever he wishes," she said mockingly. Morpheus tried ignoring her cloak and dagger stab to his ego. "Great, shall we get moving then," he asked anxiously? Morganna pointed her serpent staff in front of them and stomped it three times on the hard packed dirt below. A black stream of smoke shot from her cobra staff; swirling in front of them and creating a vortex deeper than the night sky. She turned towards Morpheus. "Creature Portals are highly inconvenient to use but we must abide by their rules in order to use them." Pointing her long cobra staff directly at Morpheus, she zapped him with a glowing red beam of light shooting from her bronze serpent's mouth. Instantly, it transformed him into a small green turtle and he fell to the ground immediately! Retracting her right leg backward, Morganna kicked the small green shelled turtle through the open portal in front of her! Quickly transforming back into her familiar eagle form, she flew through the open portal behind him. Immediately the dark portal closed off behind her and disappeared completely.

The other end of the portal opened up into a well-lit Throne Room where the Queen continued to remain trapped inside her iron barred cage. Seeing the dark portal appear in front of her, she screamed out in terror! A small green shelled turtle shot through the opening and soared through the air in front of her cage. It flew a good ten feet before smashing up against the hard granite wall next to her and slid across the smooth marble floor before finally coming to a halt. A bald eagle came soaring through the portal's opening as well before the vortex closed off behind it.

The bald eagle landed and quickly transformed back into

Morganna. She walked over to where the small turtle was stuck lying upside-down on its back. "Okay little wizard, let's see you transform back into your normal sized self. If you can't do that then I'll have to lock you up here with the Queen because you'll be of no use to me in finding Drake."

The little turtle struggled to flip over onto its feet. Gently nudging him with her right foot, Morganna flipped him over onto his tiny turtle legs. He slid his head into his shell not wanting to be a part of her scheme anymore. "Oh, don't be shy," Morganna said playfully. Before she could say anything else, a cloud of smoke streamed from the turtle's shell. It grew taller and wider as it quickly swirled upwards around the small turtle. A hand soon protruded from the thick smoke cloud as it began to clear away. Morganna smiled. "Well done Morpheus. I knew you had enough intelligence to perform such a simple task." Morpheus coughed as he cleared the swirling smoke away from his body. "I have more power than you can imagine Morganna," he replied seriously. Morganna waved a hand in the air dismissively. "No time for that now Morpheus. We must get to our separate destinations on the double! Your final test begins now. Turn yourself into a cheetah and jump back through the portal," she commanded sternly. "A cheetah madam," Morpheus repeated curiously? Morganna walked towards him. "Like I said earlier, you will need to be a fast animal to find Drake quickly in Nectarville. I know now that you can change yourself back into a wizard when needed. It was necessary I know this or I wouldn't consider you qualified for this task Morpheus."

The Queen had been listening in on their conversation the entire time from her iron barred cage sitting directly behind them. "Please be safe out there Morpheus. Remember, Drake can be a dangerous person." Morpheus turned to face the Queen. "Of course your majesty; I should also tell you that if our quest goes well then Morganna has promised to release you from your torturous prison." Morganna pointed her snake staff towards Morpheus as an invisible force began pushing him towards the open portal in front of them. "That's enough wizard; no need to blab away our plans. Let's get a move on," she commanded authoritatively!

Morpheus quickly pointed his wand above his head and shouted the word "CHEATTELLO" which instantly transformed him into a cheetah. A black cloud quickly covered his body. Upon clearing, it was obvious to everyone in the room he had quickly taken on the form of a slender black spotted cheetah. Growling at Morganna, he took a swipe at one of her legs. Stepping back to avoid his sharp claws, she yelled at him. "Bad kitty," she screamed as she pointed her cobra staff in his direction. Growling even louder this time, the cheetah moved towards the open vortex in front of him. It didn't take long for him to vanish completely from sight.

Turning towards the trapped Queen, Morganna addressed her directly. "You better hope Drake has the Pixie Guild List like you claim he does or I will return with a vengeance," she exclaimed angrily! Pointing her open-mouthed cobra staff directly at herself; a stream of red light shot into her soul. Instantly, her body transformed back into its familiar eagle form. She flew through the open portal and vanished from sight; leaving the Queen completely caged and alone once again.

32. AVALANCHE MOUNTAIN

A gust of freezing wind woke Misty from her sleep. Opening her eyes, she found herself still on top of Claw's neck with Mojo's arms wrapped tightly around her waist. She felt relaxed and at peace with herself. Gazing ahead and beyond the clouds, she spotted a tall snow covered mountain directly in front of them. Nudging Mojo with her elbow, she woke him from his slumber. "What…what's going on," he asked tiredly? Misty pointed towards the tall snow covered mountain in front of them. "I think we've arrived at Avalanche Mountain," she replied thoughtfully. Mojo's grip around her waist grew tighter. "Misty, we need to land immediately," he said with desperation in his voice. Misty turned her head slightly to make communication between them easier. "Why Mojo? What's the hurr…."

Before she could finish her sentence, it felt as though Claw had slammed directly into an invisible force-field because the impact sent them flying over Claw's neck and into the freezing night air! Misty screamed as she soared over the dragon's head! She quickly realized how vulnerable she was without her broomstick. Mojo jetted underneath her to catch her fall. He caught her in his arms as he gently descended towards the snow packed earth below. Never had she been so grateful to have him around then at that particular moment. Wrapping an arm around his neck, she leaned in to kiss his cheek. "Oh Mojo…you saved me," she exclaimed lovingly! Mojo continued to hover downwards towards the base of the mountain below. "Oh Misty, I think I've grown quite fond of you my dear," he replied lovingly. Looking upward to see if Claw was still around, they spotted him flying towards the base of the mountain on their left. "I'm glad Claw seems to be okay," she said joyfully. "I wonder what happened up there. What did we crash into anyways?"

Reaching the base of the mountain, Mojo gently landed his feet on the snow packed surface below. "Looks like we're gonna need some warmer shoes," he exclaimed while jumping around on the freezing snow beneath his feet! Snapping his fingers, a warm pair of snow boots instantly appeared on his and Misty's feet. Misty felt their instant warmth on her feet as Mojo helped her into a standing position. She gently stole another kiss before releasing her arms from around his neck. "That's very kind of you Mojo." Almost as quickly as the words escaped her mouth, she heard them echo back at her from the snow covered mountain. Mojo rushed towards her and quickly covered her mouth with one of his hands. "Quiet Misty," he whispered gently. "They don't call this Avalanche Mountain for nothing," he said quietly. Misty removed his hand from her mouth. "Okay, but I'm talking about the invisible force-field that knocked us off Claw's neck," she replied quietly. Suddenly they heard the large dragon stomping its way towards them as the mountain echoed his footsteps back at them. Misty retrieved the miniature lamp from her robe pocket and rubbed it immediately. Claw quickly transformed into a dark shade of mist which vacuumed itself back into the lamp she was holding. "That should keep things quiet for a while," she said with a smile.

"To bad you still don't have your anti-gravity amulet Misty," Mojo said regrettably. "Don't get me wrong, I enjoy flying you around but it would probably be safer if you had it with you. Your broomstick would really come in handy too if we happened to get separated for whatever reason." Misty moved closer to him and wrapped her arms around his neck. "Oh Mojo, I'm not worried. I'm sure you'll take good care of me won't you," she replied lovingly. Mojo returned her embrace. "Of course Misty; I would never let anything bad happen to you on purpose."

Suddenly, a loud screeching sound pierced the frozen sky around them. Shifting their gaze upward, they found a beautiful bald eagle soaring high over their heads. "Oh what a gorgeous looking bird," Misty exclaimed with amazement! "Yes it is," Mojo replied letting go of their tightly held embrace. The eagle gradually descended towards them until it landed within a stone's throw away of where they were standing. "I think it's trying to tell us something Misty. It's kind of like the time when that group of bees was trying to tell me something," he reminded her softly. Misty smiled. "I'm glad they gave you the message or you would probably still be lost in the woods right now," she replied jokingly.

Mojo slid an arm around her back and another behind her legs for support as he lifted her up into the air. He flew towards the bald eagle hovering in the air just in front of them. Suddenly the eagle turned to fly in a westward direction. Mojo continued trailing it through the air until they moved around the tall side of the mountain ridge. On the other side of the ridge, they found a dark swirling portal hovering in the air about twenty feet in front of them. Misty spotted it and began shouting. "Oh Mojo, maybe the eagle is trying to tell us that the only way around this mountain is to go through this portal," she exclaimed confidently. Mojo continued watching the eagle as it began flying in circles around the dark swirling portal in front of them. "I think you're right Misty. Perhaps this is the way we should go to get to the other side of this mountain," he replied agreeably.

Mojo continued holding Misty in his arms as he flew towards the dark swirling vortex in front of them. As they entered through the portal, Mojo couldn't help but wonder why the eagle seemed so interested in helping them in the first place. The other end of the portal quickly opened up into the Queen's Throne Room. Mojo flew into it carrying

Misty in his arms. Morganna's eagle form body trailed close behind them as the vortex closed off into nothing. Misty and Mojo instantly recognized where they were but it was too late. Morganna had already transformed back into her ugly witch self and was pointing her long bronze staff directly at them. "Alright, into the cage with the Queen," she commanded authoritatively. Morganna reached into her pocket to retrieve the small golden key which she inserted into the lock on the iron cage door and twisted. The door unlocked easily as she opened it with her other hand. "Come on, get in there," she commanded sternly. They both considered fighting her for a brief moment but decided to find out what she was up to first. Mojo and Misty slid into the small iron barred cage in front of them as Morganna closed the door behind them and locked it. "Don't worry," she said cheerfully. "You'll all be out as soon as I find Drake and grab the Pixie Guild List from him. I just don't want any of you to interfere with my plans," she said coldly. Misty spoke up. "Um Morganna, we want to stop Drake as well. We were only after him to get back the stolen honeycomb he has taken from the many townsfolk and cities in the area. The fairies can't make Pixie Dust without it and there have been massive shortages of it lately." Morganna laughed. "Oh, you think Drake is the sole cause of the honeycomb shortage? Keep thinking that way girl and we might end up becoming friends someday," she replied with a twisted chuckle.

"Since you're all trapped in this cage, I might as well tell you my true intentions," she said sincerely. "I'm fed up with you fairies and have no desire for any of you to ever fly again," she exclaimed vengefully! The Queen spoke up. "Morganna, I am truly sorry if we have ever done anything to offend you. If there is any way we can pay for our wrong doings please tell us and it'll be done. As Queen of the fairies I give you my word," she replied truthfully. Morganna pointed her cobra staff towards the dream catcher still lying on the floor next to the cage. "Unfortunately, there are certain things that even magic can't undo," she said with a hint of sadness in her voice. A bright stream of red light flashed between the dream catcher and her staff. Instantly the dark portal reappeared in front of the dream catcher again. Before entering through it again, she paused for a brief moment as if contemplating something on a deeper level. "What am I thinking? I can't have you all sitting together while I'm gone. That would just give you a better chance to collaborate a better escape plan. Guards! Get in here immediately," she yelled! Bill and Phil quickly entered as if they were still under some sort of trance that they couldn't seem to break. "Take this witch and the genie down to the dungeons and keep them in separate cells. I don't want them forming a well devised escape plan while I'm gone," she commanded authoritatively.

Morganna quickly opened the cage just enough to allow Misty and Mojo to step out of it. "Go ahead, take them away," Morganna commanded the guards again. Phil and Bill pointed their spears at Misty and Mojo. "Come on, let's get a move on you two," Phil said authoritatively. Morganna decided to follow them down to the dungeon just to make sure neither of them would make a foolish attempt at escaping. They considered the possibility of making a break for it while marching down the cellar steps but decided against it since Morganna had her all powerful staff pointed directly at their backsides every step of the way. Misty knew she could probably defeat her especially with Mojo backing her up but knew it would most likely cost them some serious injuries that neither of them were willing to risk at the moment.

Reaching the dungeon, they began walking between the long row of iron barred cells. They spotted Pixie as they walked past her cell. She waved at them. They waved back sympathetically as they passed by her. Morganna locked each of them inside their own separate cells before carefully walking back upstairs to the Throne Room. She transformed herself into a cat on her way up just to avoid any suspicion. She felt lucky no one seemed to notice her on their way down to the dungeon but felt powerful enough to deal with any conflict that may arise anyways. The over-exaggeration of her own power often led to a lack of caution in her daily life but in her own mind she never over-exaggerated anything at all. "Reality is whatever I make it to be," she thought with overconfidence in herself.

The portal she had opened before venturing down to the

dungeon continued to remain open by the time she had arrived back at the Throne Room. She turned towards the caged Queen. "I would love to stay and chat dearie but Drake isn't going to capture himself unfortunately," she said with an evil chuckle. She stepped through the swirling vortex and vanished from sight.

33. MEETING WITH FLOYD

Duncan was pushing Swifty way past her limits in a desperate attempt to catch up with Drake. After hours of riding towards Boulder Mountain, he finally spotted Drake about a hundred yards ahead of him. He could tell old Swifty was getting tired of his constant nudging to make her run faster. "Come on girl! We've almost caught up with him. Don't let those tired old horses in front of you make you look bad," he said encouragingly. Duncan realized just how close they were to the base of Boulder Mountain. Drake's small wooden cabin was only another hundred yards in front of him or so.

Drake turned his head and spotted Duncan closing in behind him. "Merlin's beard, he's right behind us," he yelled at Glue and Molasses! Whipping the reins to make them run faster, they jolted into action! All he had to do now was cross the old makeshift wooden plank bridge which crossed the small creek running past his house. He had been using that old plank bridge for years and it was barely wide enough to get his two horses and wagon across without falling into the shallow water below.

Just as he made it to the makeshift bridge in front of him, he turned his head backward to see Duncan only about fifty yards behind him now. Drake's cabin was only another hundred yards away from the bridge and he could feel how close this race was getting! He pulled his wand from his robe pocket. "I hate to do this to you my friend but sometimes a guy just needs to win," he said convincingly to himself. The spell "MOVELLO" escaped his lips as a blue orb of light shot from his wand and slammed into the small crossing plank behind him. Smashing into the wooden plank, it caused it to move sideways just enough to fall into the stream. It began floating downstream similar to a wooden raft moving away with the current.

Duncan came to the stream crossing and quickly brought Swifty to a halt. "You dirty cheater," he screamed out at Drake! "Looks like you're going to have to get wet my friend," he told Swifty confidently. "Sorry about this but you can blame Drake when we catch up with him," he said with a laugh. Duncan crossed the stream without the use of a bridge even though it took him much longer than normal to get across.

Drake arrived at his log cabin, hopped off his wagon, raised both hands in the air and turned to face the incoming Duncan. "I win; I win" Drake shouted as Duncan came to a halt in front of him. Duncan stared down at him from atop his stallion. "Only cause you're a dirty cheater," he retorted. "Hey, we never agreed not to use magic," Drake replied with a laugh.

They tied their horses to the tall wooden stakes in front of Drake's wooden cabin before walking inside. Walking up the three small steps to the doorway, Drake paused. "Hey wait a second," he said to Duncan. "Floyd said he would be here this evening and the sun is going down right now. It'll be sunset soon so we should probably go check our stock supply before he gets here. I know we're both exhausted from the long ride here but we need to be ready for Floyd when he arrives. After all, that's what any good salesman would do right," he said playfully punching Duncan on the shoulder. Duncan smiled. "I suppose we could do some legitimate business every now and then," he replied jokingly.

"But Drake, there's something I really have to tell you." Drake put a hand in the air dismissively. "Sorry, it'll have to wait until later Duncan. We really must focus on our inventory right now so let's go check it out."

Instead of going directly into his cabin, Drake jumped off the porch and walked towards the northeastern side of it. An extra-large boulder stood about ten feet high and twelve feet across nearby. It stood directly in front of a six foot tall wooden doorway which was imbedded directly into the mountainside. The large boulder in front of the doorway gave onlookers the impression that it was just part of the mountainside and kept the entryway hidden quite well. A padlock on the side of the door secured it from any possible intruders that might come lurking about. To their absolute horror, they found it wide open!

"Oh no," said Drake with panic in his voice! "This isn't good," Duncan responded with an equal amount of worry in his voice. Removing the open padlock from its position next to the doorway, Drake dropped it to the dirt below. Reaching for the long metal door handle, he pulled it open. They quickly retrieved their wands and held them at the ready as they ducked inside and slowly headed into the dark cavern in front of them. Drake shot a fire-bolt from his wand which encircled the walls of the room and lit up every torch surrounding the perimeter. With the room now illuminated in front of them, they found it to be completely empty! "It's gone Drake," Duncan screamed! "The thousand stacks of honeycomb and all the honey jars are gone too!" Duncan pointed his wand at Drake. "I bet your friend Floyd stole them! This is all your fault Drake for telling Floyd where to find us! He probably got here ahead of us and stole everything!" Drake looked at Duncan sharply. "Now, calm down Duncan. We don't know that for sure. Let's keep searching and see if we can find any evidence of anything else."

They continued searching the perimeter of the cold circular dirt floor cavern for any evidence of what may have happened to their loot. Suddenly, Duncan shouted excitedly. "I found something Drake!" Drake sprinted over to where Duncan was standing at the back of the cavern next to an open and empty chest lying next to his feet. Duncan held a small note sized paper in his hand. He angled it to where they could see the writing better within the dimly lit room around them. Drake began reading the note out loud.

> "Looks like I arrived a little too early for our meeting and couldn't help but find your place of inventory Drake. I'm normally an honest man who enjoys doing honest business but I get the feeling you are not the same. I found many beekeeper names on the bottom of the honey jars and know that most beekeepers transfer honey into the buyer's jars upon purchase so they can keep their own jars for further use. Consider this to be bad karma for stealing other people's stuff in the first place. I will return the labeled jars to their rightful owners and keep the unlabeled ones as a finder's fee for returning them. I wouldn't feel right about trading the Transformation Box in exchange for stolen goods. I sincerely hope you try to make an honest living in the future."
>
> Your Humble Karma,
>
> Floyd Rusher

Duncan stared at Drake dumbfounded. "Do you realize what this means Drake!" Before Drake had a chance to answer, Duncan continued. "It means our many years of robbing and collecting goods have been for nothing! Nothing Drake! With the honeycomb shortage going on, we could have cashed in our inventory to become rich as kings! But now we'll be poor as poppers no thanks to you!" Drake tried to say something but Duncan interjected again. "I've had enough Drake! I can't work with you anymore. This is by far the stupidest thing you've ever done the entire time we've ever worked together and now our entire inventory is gone Drake! Gone! I quit!" Duncan began storming his way towards the entrance. Drake turned towards him and called out. "Duncan, we can still catch him! He probably hasn't gone far by now. Let's go catch that old man and get our loot back!" Duncan turned around to face him. "Oh Drake that old man could be miles away by now. We'll never catch him. If you want to run after him then be my guest but I think we need to go our separate ways now." Duncan walked towards the exit as Drake shouted back at him again. "I'm sorry this happened old friend. I hope you won't stay upset with me forever." Duncan shook his head as he stormed out through the exit and made his way towards the pole where his horse was tethered too. Mounting Swifty he quickly began riding back towards Nectarville.

Drake glanced around at the empty cavern and then down at the dirt floor. Retrieving his wand, he aimed it at the dirt. "LUMOFLOORESTO," he shouted as sparks of blue light sunk into the earth below him. Instantly, all of the imprints previously made on the cavern floor began glowing a bright blue color. Drake recognized many of the footprints as his own. Duncan's tracks were easy to spot as well due to his long pointy shoe size. He also happened to notice a much longer set of footprints scattered throughout the cavern. They were a unique shoe pattern which held a pair of wave imprints running horizontally across each shoe. He had never seen anything like it before.

He began following the glowing pair of blue wave pattern footprints around the cavern floor as he thought out loud to himself. "Looks like these footprints circle around the cavern before heading back outside again. Strangely, our mysterious thief seems to have only taken a single trip to nab our entire stash," he thought observingly. "I wonder how he managed that?" Even though Drake was devastated that Duncan had just broken off their business partnership, he couldn't help but wonder where Floyd had wondered off to. He continued following the outgoing footprints back outside the cavern and into the open air. He recognized the smaller sized footprints as Duncan's and continued following the longer wave pattern footprints towards the small creek next to his cabin.

Drake could tell Floyd must have flown away on something because his tracks stopped only a few feet away from the creek before disappearing completely. Pulling his wand from his deep sized pocket, he pointed it towards the last track Floyd had made before lifting off into the air. "LUMAIRO," he shouted. Instantly, a trail of glowing blue light became visible through the air from where Floyd had begun flying back towards Nectarville. "Looks like I'm headed back there again," he thought discouragingly.

He walked back to where old Glue and Molasses had been standing just outside his cabin. It was just about dark now and he knew his two old horses needed rest before trying to catch up with Floyd. He patted Molasses on the neck. "Good thing I'm a generous man," he said gently. "Don't worry; I'll let you both rest here tonight. Better get a good night sleep. Floyd isn't going to like us tomorrow that's for sure!" Drake headed back into his log cabin and passed out on his straw filled mattress lying in the corner next to his wood burning fireplace.

The night flew by quicker than anticipated and he somehow managed to get up and ready to leave before dawn. He lit a fire inside his wood burning stove and warmed up a fresh pot of mush on top of it. Pouring it into a bowl, he scarfed it down before heading out. Happy to see his horses had stayed where he'd left them the night before; he untied them and connected them up to the covered wagon in preparation to leave. He mounted the wooden seat of his covered wagon and gave the reigns a hardy flick to get his old horses moving again. The thought of having lost his loyal business partner disturbed him immensely especially when thinking about all they had been through throughout the years.

His thoughts turned towards Duncan as he continued to lead his horses over the small stream in front of his cabin and back towards Nectarville. He was fairly certain Floyd's trail would lead him directly back into Nectarville but didn't want to take any unnecessary chances. He retrieved his wand and muttered the spell "LUMAIRO" just like he had the night before. The results appeared just as expected. A bright blue trail of light appeared in front of him and he followed it with the sharp eye of a tracker closing in on his prey. He led his wagon through the dirt, weeds, briers and bushes as he continued onward. Jolting Glue and Molasses into a faster paced ride, he continued pushing them to their limits. Time seemed to slow down as his mind raced ever faster. His blood boiled at the thought of that rotten double-crossing old man Floyd stealing his entire collection of honeycomb right out from under his nose. The thought of Duncan deciding not to work for him anymore sparked his anger even further! Drake's fury continued to rise with every second that passed as he continued to ride towards Nectarville.

After what felt like an eternity of riding and tracking the blue stream of light in front of him; Drake finally spotted Merchant Road. He approached it from the north. Instead of going straight in between both lines of merchant tents found on either side of the road; the blue light veered off towards the west. Drake steered his horses towards it; carefully following the mysterious trail of light in front of him. "It's almost as if Floyd was trying to avoid one of these merchants," he thought suspiciously.

The blue stream of light led him into a small grove of maple trees before veering back towards Merchant Road. It then went directly back towards Floyd's place of business. "Why would he come back to his own merchant tent if he still has all the goods he stole from me," Drake wondered curiously? Parking his wagon behind the back of Floyd's merchant tent, he tied his horses to the nearby wooden post meant for vendors. Pulling his wand from his pocket, he stealthily parted the tent flaps and stepped inside. Even though he was ready for a duel if necessary, all he found was an empty backroom where merchandise would normally be placed. He knew the rest of the merchant shop was just through the tent flap separating him from the main items of attraction. Reaching his right hand forward, he grabbed the closed tent flap and gently pushed it aside just enough to see what was happening in the front room ahead of him.

Peeking through the curtains, he could barely see the long glass counter holding the magic boxes in front of him. Suddenly, a slender white hand came into view as it sat a small box on top of the counter. It looked like an elderly gentleman's hand was opening the box before it quickly moved out of sight again. Drake assumed it to be Floyd's hand since it was his shop and the hand seemed to be ancient as far as he could tell. The hand suddenly came back into view as Drake covered up his own mouth to avoid screaming in horror at what he saw directly in front of him. To his shock and surprise, he spotted old man Floyd's hand holding a tiny miniature sized man by the shirt collar in front of him! He placed the miniature sized man into the magic box as he screamed out for help! Drake could barely even hear the little man due to his tiny size. However, upon further inspection; the little man being placed inside the magic box looked an awfully lot like....Duncan! "Oh no," Drake thought frantically as he jumped out from behind the curtain.

"Floyd wait;" Drake screamed! "What in Merlin's Beard are you doing with my friend Duncan?" Floyd turned to face Drake as he came barging towards him; his wand drawn and pointed directly at him! "Put my friend down and back away from the counter," Drake commanded promptly! Floyd smiled. "Drake, I'm sure you're still sore about me taking your inventory but let me assure you..." Drake interrupted him. "No, no, let me assure you; you will pay for what you've done Floyd!" Floyd lifted the miniature Duncan even higher above his head then before. "Try anything foolish and I'll drop your little friend here! Considering his tiny size, it will be the end of him! You can be sure of that! Either we talk this out like civilized people or your friend here dies! It's your choice Drake."

Drake stared at the miniature Duncan dangling from Floyd's hand. "Don't worry Duncan, I won't let him drop you," he said reassuringly. "Alright Floyd, say what you need to say but be quick about it. As you can see, that's my friend you're holding there," he said gesturing towards Duncan. Floyd continued. "Alright Drake, just so you don't try anything stupid, I'm going to put your friend into my Transformation Box BUT I won't shut the lid unless you decide to do something absolutely foolish. Do you understand?" Drake nodded agreeably and carefully lowered his wand. "Alright, let's start from the beginning Floyd. First off, why do you want to put my friend Duncan into your Transformation Box? Second, why did you steal our inventory?" Floyd gently placed the miniature Duncan inside the Transformation Box but didn't close the hinged lid as promised. "Those are fair questions Drake and I'll start by telling you that I never really wanted your inventory in the first place. No, I took it because I knew you and your business partner here would soon come looking for it. My messenger, Nick the gnome, told me all about you two after your meeting with him at the Black Hawk Inn the other night. Do you remember what I told you about the Transformation Box last time we met Drake?" Drake nodded. "Yes, I specifically remember you saying that it could transform any item into rubies or anything else I desired." Floyd nodded. "That's correct. Do you also remember the required price for doing such a magnificent thing?" Drake glanced downwards. "I remember you saying it takes a tiny bit of a person's youth every time they use it." Floyd nodded again. "That's correct Drake. With that knowledge, you must also know the laws of magic simply don't allow anyone to become young again…at least that is what most magical folks would have you believe. This is why I decided to embark upon a new experiment. My thoughts were such that if I could find a younger person to place inside the Transformation Box then I could exchange their youth for my elderliness. Thus, I could restore my youthfulness and become happy once again. This is why I took your inventory Drake. I knew one of you would eventually follow my trail back here and then I could try my new experiment on whoever found me first. Your friend Duncan was lucky enough to find me before you Drake. Would you believe he demanded HIS inventory back when he caught up with me?! It almost seemed like he was trying to cut you out of the deal for some reason Drake. Luckily I was able to shrink him down to size before he could do any real damage. Don't worry though. If my experiment goes according to plan, your friend won't die. He will simply become older." Drake glanced at Floyd angrily. "Oh, but he'll be a much older man that you are now? No Floyd! It's not right or fair to take someone's youth away all because you traded yours away in exchange for a large amount of rubies!"

Floyd pulled his wand from his right pocket and pointed it at Drake. "I had a feeling it would come to this Drake. Looks like I will have to shrink you down to size as well! "ABRO…" Before Floyd could finish the spell, a swirling dark vortex appeared on Drake's right and caught their attentions immediately. They turned to look at it and saw

Morpheus hovering out of the darkness onto the shop floor in front of them! "Well, well…what have we here," he asked rhetorically?

Appearing with his wand at the ready, Morpheus turned to face Floyd. "Well if it isn't our old court wizard Floyd Rusher. Looks like retirement hasn't been kind to you old man," he said keeping his wand pointed directly at him. "Drop your wand Floyd," Morpheus commanded. Floyd was still pointing his wand at Drake. "And you must be Morpheus," he replied distastefully. "I heard you had quite a bit of learning to do once you took over as court wizard. You should have become court gesture instead," he replied mockingly. Morpheus became even more serious. "Drop the wand Floyd or your retirement days will be shorter than that trick rope you used to convince the Queen fairies can still fly," he retorted.

Drake turned towards Morpheus. "Did this old man steal from you as well," he asked curiously? Morpheus glanced back at him. "Actually, you might be surprised to learn I've been tracking you for quite a while now Drake." Drake slowly stepped back towards the shop exit behind him. "Why would you be tracking me," he asked innocently? "Oh, don't play dumb with me Drake," replied Morpheus. "I think we both know how much thieving you've done around here. Word finally reached the Queen and she sent me out to find you. It wasn't an easy task but I managed. A honeycomb salesman named Achmed told me you lived at the base of Boulder Mountain. When I arrived, I discovered you had already left. I found a note that was apparently written to you by Floyd here." Morpheus reached into his pocket and produced the note he had picked up inside the empty inventory room at Boulder Mountain. Drake shook his head. "I knew I shouldn't have left that note lying around; silly me!"

Morpheus continued facing Drake while his wand continued to point at Floyd. "There is a way we can fix all of this," he said optimistically. "There is," Drake and Floyd asked in unison as if admitting to their wrong doing? "Yes, here is what we are going to do," said Morpheus authoritatively. "Drake is going to return all of the honey and honeycomb he has stolen back to me. Floyd is then going to give me one of his magic boxes here for me to take back to the palace with me." Floyd placed both of his hands behind his head. "Whoa, hold your horses there Morpheus. I haven't even done anything wrong. What makes you think I'm going to just hand over one of my highly coveted Transformation Boxes to you?" Drake interjected. "Oh, no you don't Floyd! If I'm going down then you're going down with me," he exclaimed confidently! "Drake don't…" Drake cut him short. "Take a look inside that Transformation Box Morpheus. My friend Duncan is in there and Floyd here was about to do something really horrible to him!"

Morpheus walked over to where Floyd was standing next to the glass counter and peered inside the open Transformation Box. Just like Drake said, a tiny man was jumping up and down inside the glowing white light emanating from inside the box. Morpheus reached two of his fingers inside and gently grabbed the miniature man by the back of his collar and lifted him up out of the box. Placing him on top of the glass counter, he stepped back and pointed his wand at him. Muttering an enlargement spell, a flash of white light shot from his wand and into the miniature Duncan sitting atop the counter in front of him. Nothing happened so Morpheus tried again. Still nothing happened. "I guess that's what you'd expect from a non-qualified court wizard," Floyd exclaimed mockingly. Morpheus pointed his wand at him. "I could fry your body into crispy bacon old man so don't even test me right now," he replied threateningly. "I'll tell you what," Floyd replied gently. "How about letting me try my new experiment on the little thief first and then I'll change him back to normal afterwards," he asked hopefully? Morpheus gazed back at him curiously. "What experiment are you talking about exactly?" Drake jumped in before Floyd could say anything. "He's hoping the Transformation Box will work some sort of life exchanging magic on my friend Duncan here. He thinks it will somehow give him Duncan's youth in exchange for Floyd's old age. Meaning that Duncan would turn extremely old and leave this bastard young again! Don't let him do it Morpheus. It's bad enough he already stole my inventory but this could do irreversible damage to my friend Duncan here!"

Morpheus turned towards Floyd. "Is this true; you have Drake's inventory with you," he asked curiously? Floyd nodded. "Yea, it's true but in my defense I was only trying to lure Drake and Duncan here to perform my new experiment on them. The inventory I took from Drake never really belonged to him anyways. It's not a crime to steal from a thief Morpheus. Also, who wouldn't want to be young again?"

Morpheus rubbed the underside of his chin while thinking up his next plan of action. "You're right Floyd. It's not a crime to want to be young again and technically there's no law against transferring youth from someone else to yourself. Quite frankly, most people think it's impossible and I've never seen such a thing happen to anyone before. However, I will say that this experiment of yours could be the Queen's saving grace if we play our cards right." "What do you mean," Floyd inquired curiously? "I mean Morganna has shown herself again within the kingdom and is currently holding the Queen hostage. Look Floyd, I'm not exactly sure where your loyalties lie but I do know you were once the Queen's court wizard long before I took over that position. I'm almost completely certain you would be willing to help save the Queen on a moment's notice no matter how you may feel about me. Am I correct on that point?" Floyd rubbed a hand through his old gray hair. "Oh, I suppose I could come back with you but just keep in mind I'm not doing this for you." Morpheus nodded. "Yes, I'm highly aware of that and thank you for your service to the crown. I'm sure the Queen will reward you handsomely for any efforts you make to help rescue her," he said confidently.

At that moment Drake decided to make a beeline towards the tent exit in an attempt to escape. Morpheus turned his wand towards the dashing Drake. Just as he was about to shoot a spell in his direction, a flash of green light slammed into Drake's backside knocking him to the floor. Morpheus was shocked to discover the spell had come from Floyd's outstretched wand! Somehow Floyd had managed to beat Morpheus to the draw before he could even speak the incantation at all! At first, Morpheus thought the spell had caused Drake to vanish completely because he no longer saw him in front of him. However, upon further inspection, he found the miniature Drake running around on the dirt shop floor filled with frantic energy. He turned towards Floyd. "Looks like the old court wizard is faster than I anticipated," he exclaimed flatteringly. Floyd smiled. "I'm still young at heart Morpheus. The Transformation Box has definitely sped up my aging process though that's for sure."

Morpheus nodded agreeably. "Not gonna lie; you look pretty old my friend," he replied with a laugh. "Also, I know you desperately want to try this experiment of yours but I suggest we let Morganna give it a shot first. This way, she'll be punishing highly wanted criminals and if anything goes wrong then we won't be the ones to blame. See what I'm saying? We're really just killing two birds with one stone," he said convincingly.

The miniature Drake ran towards the tent exit but didn't get very far before Morpheus picked him up off the ground and sat him on the glass counter next to the Transformation Box. Grabbing Duncan from inside the box, he placed him on the counter next to Drake. "What do you think we should do with them," Morpheus asked Floyd curiously? Floyd glanced down at the two tiny thieves jumping up and down on the glass countertop next to him. "Well, I think we should take them with us to show the Queen and Morganna. Like you mentioned earlier, this could be our bargaining chip to help rescue the Queen," he replied reassuringly. Morpheus nodded. "I have a plan Floyd and I hope you'll be willing to go along with it because as you know, rescuing someone can be a tricky business." Floyd crossed his arms and leaned his body up against the glass countertop. "What did you have in mind Morpheus?"

Morpheus continued on with the details. "I think we should take a fake magic box with us. Let's make sure it looks similar to the real Transformation Box just in case Morganna tries to double-cross us in some way." Floyd chuckled. "What's so funny," asked Morpheus? Floyd pointed towards the glass counter holding the row of magic boxes inside of them. "What do you think all of these are old boy," he asked with a laugh? "The real Transformation Box is far too valuable to display in front of everyone who walks in here so I made these non-magical duplicates for potential customers to check out." Morpheus stared through the glass cabinet at the multiple fake magic boxes lying beneath. Every one of them looked different from the other. "None of them look the same," said Morpheus observingly. Floyd nodded. "They're all fakes except for that one right there." He pointed to the small black box with glowing blue stars scattered across it. "Aw yes," said Morpheus. "That's the one you were going to use on those two idiots," he replied pointing towards the miniature Drake and Duncan hopping up and down on the glass cabinet top next to him. Floyd nodded agreeably as he moved towards the backside of the cabinet. He reached inside and retrieved one of the fake magic boxes found inside. Pointing his wand at it, he muttered the phrase "MIRRAGGO DUBELLO BOXELLO." Touching the real Transformation Box with his wand, he then touched a fake box and watched it instantly transform into an exact duplicate of the real one. "We'll keep the two thieves inside the fake one unless we need to perform our experiment in front of Morganna. In which case, we'll transfer them into the real magic box." Morpheus looked at it closer. "How can we tell the real one from the fake one," he asked curiously? A serious expression crossed Floyd's face. "Unfortunately, we can't make a mark on either of them to tell them apart. Morganna would easily spot a phony box if we're not careful. No, we'll just have to remember which one is real and which one is fake. The two thieves will be in the fake one but if there comes a time that we need to transfer them into the real Transformation Box then we'll just have to remember which one is which."

Morpheus gently grabbed the two con artists by the back of their robes and lifted them into the fake magic box simultaneously. Their tiny sized bodies made it easy to maneuver them wherever he wished. Morpheus continued staring down at them while keenly observing their situation. "We probably shouldn't close the lid completely. I mean, what are they going to do for air?" Floyd ran a hand through his long white hair as he pointed his wand at the fake magic box. "AIRLOWMICRO," he exclaimed as a stream of blue light jetted from his wand into the box in front of him. Morpheus continued staring at it. "Nothing seems to have changed," he said softly. Floyd stared at him astonishingly. "No offence but the bar must have really been lowered for court wizards by the time you showed up," he replied with a laugh. "I'm actually glad you didn't notice the difference because that would mean Morganna could spot it as well." Morpheus observed the box from multiple angles. "It still seems the same to me. What did you do exactly?" Floyd continued. "Now, there are tiny microscopic air holes inside this fake box. They are small enough to let micro bits of air particles through without being big enough to be noticed from the outside." Morpheus picked up the black box with painted blue stars on it and inspected it further. "Magnificent! It'll work perfectly," he replied with intrigue.

Morpheus closed the lid to the fake box with the two miniature thieves still trapped inside. "I should take Drake's inventory with us as well. Where did you put it Floyd?" Floyd walked towards the back of the tent where he normally kept inventory not on display out front. "Hang on a second. I'll grab it," he replied reassuringly. It only took a moment for him to walk behind the drawn tent flap separating the front of the store from the back. He quickly returned with a large bag slung over his shoulder. Morpheus observed the giant bag skeptically. "Don't tell me that's ALL of Drake's inventory? He must have stolen way more than that!" Floyd glanced back at him dumbfounded. "And you call yourself a wizard," he replied sarcastically. "No Morpheus, everything in this bag has been shrunk down significantly. Of course, I wouldn't be able to carry his entire inventory without shrinking it down to size first." Morpheus nodded. "I see. Well, I'm glad it made it more convenient for you to carry. Let's head back to the palace than shall we?" The dark portal Morpheus had originally come through was still swirling inside the room nearby. "After you Floyd," he said gesturing towards the swirling vortex nearby. "I don't want this vortex disappearing on you so I'll follow after you just to make sure that doesn't happen," he said confidently.

As Floyd entered the vortex, Morpheus placed a hand on top of it to make sure it wouldn't vanish before he could enter through himself. Floyd made sure to pocket the real magic box inside his large robe pocket before leaving just to ensure Morpheus wouldn't run off with it. He also carried the large inventory sack over his shoulder as he disappeared from sight. Morpheus followed his footsteps and made sure to grab the fake magic box with the two shrunken thieves still inside it before entering. The portal vanished behind him as it quickly transported them towards the palace.

Within seconds the portal opened up just outside the palace walls. Both wizards stepped out onto the hard packed dirt below as the portal quickly vanished behind them. They glanced upward at the tall palace wall towering high over their heads. "Why couldn't we just portal into the palace," Floyd asked curiously? Morpheus stared at him with a false sense of amusement. "Oh, does this court wizard know something you don't," he replied mockingly. Floyd shook his head trying to ignore Morpheus's jabbing comment as he continued. "The palace has a magic barrier surrounding it which protects its occupants from any unexpected intruders that may arise. I'm surprised you didn't know this already former court wizard," he finished mockingly.

Floyd was about to reply with a snappy comeback when the clatter of hooves suddenly came clopping from the north and distracted them completely. A skinny young man with wild red hair was steering a team of horses attached to a covered wagon along the dirt road they were standing next to. Bright red letters stretched across the wagon's covering which read: "WAVE RIDERS," with the phrase, "BECAUSE FUN IS WORTH IT," written underneath it. They figured him to be a salesman most likely heading towards his merchant tent located somewhere nearby. Floyd stepped out into the middle of the dirt road as the four horses and wagon continued heading his way. "Excuse me," he called out to the team leader! The young man steering the horses quickly brought them to an abrupt halt and called back to him. "What can I do ya fer good sir," he called back curiously?

Floyd walked around to the driver's side of the wagon; gazing up at the young man. "You wouldn't happen to sell surf boards," he asked seriously? The red headed salesman glanced down at him. "Why as a matter of fact I do," he replied excitedly! "You've come to the right place mister," he said enthusiastically jumping down to the ground! "Just follow me to the back of the wagon here and I'll show you the merchandise." Morpheus didn't have a clue what sort of madness Floyd was getting himself into but he didn't want anything to do with it so he patiently waited within the shadows of the palace wall for him to finish doing his business.

The young salesman and Floyd were now in the back of the covered wagon rummaging through various items that were for sale. Floyd found a few colorful surfboards lining the sides of the wagon along with a few other trinkets a person might wear to the beach. Floyd pointed at a light blue surfboard lying next to his feet. "This looks perfect," he said excitedly. The salesman couldn't help but notice Floyd's age and tried picturing him out surfing the waves somewhere. The mental image made him smile and almost laugh a little. "Are you much of a surfer," he asked curiously? Floyd was staring at another particular surfboard lying next to his feet. "I used to surf all the time back in my younger days and thought perhaps I'd try picking it up again," he replied energetically. "Also, I was hoping to get one for my friend as well. It would be a fun activity we could do occasionally," he replied with a smile. The red headed salesman smiled back at him. "Sounds like a plan man! Let's get these bodacious boards off my wagon! Also, perhaps I could interest you in a seashell necklace for your significant other or perhaps some cologne that smells like the ocean?" Floyd shook his head. "I think this will be enough my good man. If you could just help me get these boards off the back of your wagon that would be awesome!" "Of course," replied the salesman as he picked up the light blue surfboard and jumped off the back of the wagon with it.

Stepping down from the back of the wagon, Floyd turned and paid the salesman his asking price for both boards. The young man seemed surprised he didn't even have to haggle with him. He was so used to haggling over prices that he didn't even consider the possibility that Floyd might simply agree to his first offer. This obviously meant he had just made far more than expected from the transaction. The young man accepted the handful of rubies from Floyd with a slight hesitation. "Um, I actually didn't expect you to agree to my first asking price so I'll give 30 of these rubies back to you." Floyd slid a surfboard under each arm. "No worries my good man. I was actually expecting to pay a much higher price in the first place," he replied joyfully walking away from the salesman. The young salesman waved goodbye. "Pleasure doing business with you good sir; I hope you and your friend enjoy the boards."

The salesman climbed back up into the driver's seat of his covered wagon and flicked the reigns just enough to get his horses moving again. He rode off into the distance as Floyd handed Morpheus his new bright yellow surfboard. "Merlin's beard! What are these for Floyd? Are you having a mental breakdown or something? We're on our way to save the Queen and you want to go surfing," he asked with a laugh? Floyd stared at him strangely. "That mind of yours doesn't work very hard does it," he replied mockingly. "These will help us get into the Queen's Throne Room without having to go through the main entrance," he explained tactfully.

The puzzle pieces quickly came together in Morpheus's mind. "Oh, I get it," he replied excitedly! "You're smarter than you look Floyd. I really should give you more credit in the future," he said with a chuckle. He observed the bright yellow surfboard he now held under his right arm. "I have to admit Floyd, I don't really know the spell to make a surfboard fly. Believe me, I've already gone through this whole ordeal with Misty and we couldn't make it work." Floyd shook his head and exhaled with disappointment. Pulling his wand from his inner robe pocket, he pointed it at his own light blue surfboard. "FLYDAIROPROTERRO" he shouted as a blue stream of light flew from his wand and into it. Instantly, the light blue surfboard began to hover up into the air! Floyd held onto it carefully to keep it from flying away on him.

Morpheus tried using the same spell on his own surfboard without any results whatsoever. "You must pronounce the incantation correctly. Make sure to emphasize all syllables with complete diction,"

Floyd suggested helpfully. Morpheus tried pronouncing the incantation more clearly and then again and again. His fourth attempt was finally a success as he watched his board slowly rise from the ground. Holding onto it with an outstretched arm, he managed to keep it from flying away on him. "How good are you at keeping your balance," Floyd asked? "I guess we'll find out," replied Morpheus with a laugh as he mounted his hovering surfboard. Floyd stepped onto his as well. "Alright, let's ride," he exclaimed energetically! Both wizards flew a couple of loops through the air just to make sure they had the hang of things before scaling the palace walls. Finally, they made their way upwards towards the large arched stain glass windows protruding from the Queen's Throne Room high above their heads. They prepared to make an entrance that even the Queen wouldn't forget!

34. DUELING MORGANNA

The iron barred cells inside the dungeon were absolutely impenetrable to magic. Misty, Mojo and Pixie tried every spell and enchantment they could think of to escape their tight confinements. Nothing worked at all. The iron bars didn't budge a single inch! "I have no idea how we're going to get out of here," Misty shouted to Pixie and Mojo who were standing in cells on either side of her. The cells sat close enough to each-other that they could easily reach through the bars and touch hands if they wanted too. "It's kind of funny Morganna put us in cells this close to each-other when her whole plan was for us not to collaborate with each-other in the first place," Pixie replied with a laugh. "I think her whole plan was to make it harder for all three of us to escape at the same time," Misty responded downheartedly. "I'm starting to think my old lamp was made from a metal similar to these cell bars. That's probably why it held me so well," Mojo exclaimed discouragingly.

Misty snapped her fingers as if a light just clicked on inside her brain. "That's it," she exclaimed excitedly! Reaching deep inside her silk robe pocket, she produced the miniature lamp she had been carrying around the entire time. She was about to rub it when suddenly she thought better of it. "Oh never mind, I can't bring Claw out now. He would be far too big for this cage and would probably crush me to death against the bars the moment he leaves the lamp," she said discouragingly. "Besides, I've used up all my wishes anyways," she continued downheartedly. Walking over to the left side of her cell, she called out to Pixie in the adjoining cell next to hers. "Hey Pixie, I can't use this lamp anymore. All of my wishes have been used up already. However, I can give it to you in case you ever need to use it. I would highly advise not rubbing it now though. Claw would be far too big for your cell and would most likely crush you against the bars the moment he emerged from the lamp," she said seriously.

Misty gripped the miniature golden lamp by its handle and gently passed it in between the bars into Pixie's cell. "Please take it. There is a small chain wrapped around the handle from when I last let Blackbeak wear it around his neck. You should do the same if you wish." Pixie accepted the lamp gratefully and carefully slipped the silver chain around her neck letting the lamp dangle up against her chest. "Don't worry. I'll take good care of it Misty. You have my word," she replied seriously. Misty returned her smile. "I hope you can use it sometime soon Pixie but just try and do so after you've left this cell. Remember, the genie dragon is far too big for this cell; so please don't let him loose in here. He's not your typical genie either. Nope, he was once a ferocious dragon named Claw. I'm the one who turned him into a genie Pixie." Mojo added his two cents to the conversation as well. "Well, I'm actually the one who turned him into a genie but that was only because of our deal Misty," he replied seriously. Misty nodded agreeably. "That's true. I was down to my last wish and made a deal with Mojo here. We agreed I would wish him free in exchange for transforming Claw into a genie for me. How clever was that," she asked winking at Pixie? Pixie laughed. "That was quite clever Misty. What did you use your other wishes on," she asked curiously? Misty continued. "My other two wishes were spent getting this gorgeous young body of mine and a mirror to see it with," she replied with a blush. "Well, you look quite ravishing Misty," Pixie replied flatteringly. Misty tried not to blush again. "Aw, thanks Pixie. I'm not used to getting such wonderful compliments just yet. I've been quite ugly most of my life up until recently. Of course, many people manage to find their inner beauty and are completely satisfied with it. Not me though, I wanted something more and am quite happy now that I've found it," she exclaimed joyfully!

Pixie continued the conversation thoughtfully. "I'm happy for you too Misty. Just curious though; what three wishes did you wish for from Claw? I'm kind of jealous you got so many to be honest. Most people only get three from a genie and you managed to get six from two genies," she said flatteringly! Misty smiled happily. "That's true. From Claw, I wished that he would never harm me or Mojo ever again. I also wished he would take us wherever we wanted to go. I forgot what my last wish was from him. Perhaps I haven't used it yet. I can't remember for sure. Either way, I don't mind if you take the lamp Pixie. After all, Mojo here volunteered to be my wonderful travelling companion ever since I wished him free from his lamp. Isn't that right Mojo," she asked delightfully turning in his direction? He smiled. "Absolutely Misty; I'm happy to be your travelling companion and enjoy your company very much. I'm also quite happy to be a free genie now," he replied joyfully.

Misty was about to say something else when suddenly a dark portal appeared in front of her cell door. A bald eagle soared through the dark vortex and landed directly in front of her cell door. The eagle quickly transformed into the dark witch they had all been expecting. For no apparent reason, they had all expected her to return at some point.

Morganna's tall witch form towered over Misty from outside her cell door. She quickly unlocked the iron barred door and grabbed her by the arm. "I've decided to take you and Mojo back up to the Throne Room with me. You both might possess some valuable information that could be useful." She forcefully pulled Misty by the arm outside her cell and pushed her towards Mojo's cell door. Using her cobra staff, she quickly zapped the lock on his cell door causing it to open up quickly. "You're coming with me as well genie. I'm actually surprised you haven't escaped by now. You're a poor excuse for a genie," she mocked discouragingly! Mojo was about to respond but she continued insistently.

"We'll chat more up in the Throne Room. Let's get moving," she commanded!

The three of them walked passed Pixie's cell on their way towards the dungeon steps leading up to the main floor of the palace. Pixie screamed out to them. "What about me," she pleaded? "What about you," Morganna screamed back as they continued forward towards the exit. Marching up the steps towards the main floor, Morganna gave them direct orders. "If anyone asks; we are simply going to visit the Queen up in the Throne Room. Say a word to anyone about what we're really doing and I'll zap you into oblivion," she threatened pushing Misty forward with her cobra staff! Morganna continued walking behind them all the way up into the palace Throne Room. A few of the palace workers passed by them but never stopped to question anything that was happening. They just went about their business as usual. Misty knew Morganna's face was not recognizable to most fairies since most of them hadn't ever seen her in person before. She thought about screaming out for help but knew most of the palace workers probably wouldn't be able to help them anyways. "We're probably the three most powerful people in here," she thought silently to herself as they continued marching up towards the Throne Room entrance. Morganna walked behind them with her cobra staff pointed directly at the back of their heads just in case they decided to try anything foolish.

The Queen sat alone behind her iron barred cage inside the Throne Room desperately hoping for a valiant rescuer to barge in and save her. Suddenly, the Throne Room doors burst open followed by Bill, Phil, Misty, Mojo and Morganna all marching towards the cage she was now trapped in. Morganna quickly ordered the two guards back to their posts just outside the Throne Room entrance. They closed the large double-doors on their way out. Morganna quickly produced a small golden key from her pocket and opened the Queen's iron cage door. "Alright, everyone inside! Come on now, I haven't got all day," she commanded sternly! Misty and Mojo hesitantly stepped inside. Morganna swung the hinged door forward to close it when suddenly an unexpected resistance came from the other side of it. Mojo held his hand against the cage door pushing it forward again. Morganna turned to face the genie. His eyes flashed a bright red color and his pupils transformed into tall black slits. Morganna recognized those eyes immediately and jumped back with fright! "Don't tell me you've been around cobra Con lately," she gasped pointing her snake staff at the genie. Mojo's voice suddenly resembled Con's hissing cobra voice. "Yesss, I know Con. I am Con! I've come back for revenge Morganna," Mojo hissed as he slowly began walking towards her.

Morganna continued stepping backwards in fright. "I had to leave you Con. It was the only way out of those confounded catacombs and you know it! It's not my fault those nasty Sand Trappers kept you down there as long as they did!" Mojo's genie body suddenly transformed into Con's 20 foot cobra body! He slowly slithered towards her; his fangs dripping with poisonous venom. "You could have come back for me you conniving witch! You could have rescued me from those catacombs but decided to save yourself instead!" Con raised his large cobra head leveling his eyes with hers. Morganna threw her cobra staff in front of herself protectively. "I didn't trap you inside that cobra body Con! The gnomes did that! They thought you were a bad genie who wouldn't play by their rules so they trapped you inside that cobra body instead of a lamp like a normal genie. They did it so no one would be hurt by you. On top of that, they let the Sand Trappers suck you down into their catacomb abyss! Since you couldn't fly, you couldn't leave without help. I wasn't part of their plan Con. Honest; we met in those catacombs because I was searching for the Stone of Sanity. It wasn't down there so I left immediately. I had no intention of helping you Con. We were never friends. I had no reason to help a bad genie like you leave that underground abyss the gnome's left you in."

Misty and the Queen stood far behind the long 20 foot cobra and heard every word perfectly. Misty couldn't help but wonder what had happened to her best friend Mojo. She thought it was him the entire time. She started reconnecting the dots in her mind trying to figure out what had happened down inside the catacombs underneath the Dessert of Doom. She definitely remembered Mojo helping her escape from that awful place but she was under the impression that it had been him the entire time! "Unless...unless, Con happened to switch bodies with Mojo somehow," she wondered silently? The Queen whispered into Misty's ear quietly. "Sounds like Con is a genie too. Perhaps he switched bodies with Mojo at some point. It might have been Con's only way of escaping those devastating dessert catacombs the gnome's left him in." Misty whispered back in response. "If that's true then Mojo must be trapped inside Con's dead cobra body right now! The dead snakeskin must be acting like a lamp for him. So he's not really drowning inside the Well of Life. Instead, he's living inside the dead carcass as if it were merely a genie lamp!" Both women shuttered at the disgusting thought as they continued watching the sight in front of them.

The discussion between Con and Morganna had become quite intense. Con arched his head back and opened his narrow jawline posing for an attack! Morganna drew her wand defensively as Con jutted forward attempting to bite her neck. Quickly ducking, she let the venomous fangs pass over her. Sidestepping to the right, she spoke the spell "MIRRAGGO DUBELLO," while pointing her wand directly at herself. She rapidly repeated the spell 20 more times in a row! Duplicate mirages of herself quickly appeared next to her. The room quickly filled with exact duplicates of herself. Eventually, it became difficult to tell who the real Morganna was and who was the fake! Misty clearly remembered using this exact spell to help trick Claw into getting the lamp from him and knew something must be done to stop Morganna from fighting so unfairly or she'd win this battle for sure.

Misty and the Queen knew they had to join the fight now that Con was completely outnumbered. They were aware that a loss for Con would end up being a loss for them as well. Misty observed the small army of Morganna mirages and laughed out loud. "Ha! Two can play at that game," she stated hysterically. She repeated the exact same spell Morganna had just used. She repeated it multiple times in the same way Morganna had done and watched carefully as multiple clones of herself began to appear! Misty thought about how she had used this exact same spell back at Jewel Cave in order to search the caverns found within. It had been quite difficult for her to concentrate on moving one clone and herself as well. "Drat! There's no way I can move all these mirages at once," she thought discouragingly.

All of Misty's mirages stood completely still while Morganna's mirages moved about the room freely! "She truly is a better witch then I am," Misty observed downheartedly. Morganna's mirages quickly zapped fire bolts and lightening spells at Misty's mirages. Each mirage quickly vanished in smoke with every hit they took. The Queen had her wand drawn as well. She fired wind and lightening spells at the oncoming Morganna clones. Many of them quickly went up in smoke as well. Con struck his venom into every Morganna clone he slithered next too. It felt like a battle of the mirages! Although, they knew that hitting the real Morganna with a spell wouldn't cause her to go up in smoke. So they attacked every Morganna they could reach in hopes of finally hitting the real one.

Con thought he sunk his fangs into another clone when a scream of agony suddenly shot from the real Morganna's lungs! "You stupid snake; let go of my leg!" Her pain merely encouraged the cobra to bite down even harder in hopes of pumping even more venom into the conniving witch! All of her clones quickly vanished from sight as she managed to shoot off another spell from her wand. She aimed it directly at herself and quickly transformed back into her familiar eagle form. The bald eagle hovered over the giant cobra; flapping its wings tantalizingly. She began flying towards the open cage near the center of the room. Con quickly chased after her; slithering as fast as he could to catch her! She managed to stay just out of striking range as he continued to move forward. Misty and the Queen quickly chased after the flying eagle as well. They were all so focused on catching the eagle that they didn't even notice where they were running. All three of them ended up inside open cage while chasing the eagle just as the Queen reached out and latched onto eagle's wings. "I got you now," she exclaimed angrily! Suddenly, they saw another eagle swoop down out of the corner of the room and land directly in front of the open cage. It quickly transformed into Morganna as the eagle being held by the Queen instantly vanished from sight! Morganna slammed the cage door shut; quickly locking it before they could escape her grasp again. "Ha! Bet you didn't see that coming! That took some sneaky cloning to make that happen but they don't call me the worst witch in the world for nothing," she exclaimed in a bragging sort of way! "Good thing this is an iron cage or I might worry about you escaping again Con. The rest of you aren't as tough as you might think so don't get overly cocky on me." The Queen pointed to Morganna's injured leg. "You might not be as tough as you think either Morganna. Looks like Con got you pretty good there," she said almost triumphantly. Morganna glared at her three caged prisoners clutching her injured leg painfully. "You'd better hope Morpheus returns with some good news or you'll all wish you'd never been born," she replied threateningly!

Before Morganna could say anything else, the large stain glass window located about ten feet behind them suddenly shattered into thousands of tiny pieces! Two figures jetted through the air flying on surfboards! Looking at them closer, Morganna recognized Morpheus but only the Queen recognized her former court wizard Floyd. Morpheus veered left. Floyd soared to the right. They surrounded Morganna from opposite sides of the room; each holding their wand at the ready. They shot a steady stream of fire bolts down on her one right after the other. Morganna quickly casted an invisible absorption shield around her body and stuck her wand up in the air. The absorption shield instantly channeled the incoming fire bolt directly into her wand as if it were merely charging it with more power! A small lightning ball grew just above her upheld wand as the incoming attacks seemed to make it grow even larger with every fire and lightning bolt shot at her!

Swirling her wand in the air, she split the ever growing lightning ball in half and shot each half back at her attackers! Morpheus dodged the incoming lightening ball while keeping his balance on the flying surfboard. The second lightening ball knocked Floyd's flying surfboard out from underneath him! He slammed against the palace wall to his right and fell towards the marble floor below. Morgannna shot a stream of green glowing light in his direction. Encircling his body, it caused his fall to gradually slow down until he gently landed on the Throne Room floor without being hurt at all. The green light surrounding his body also held him in place so he couldn't move a muscle! He felt like a prisoner inside his own body since he couldn't move even a little bit.

Morpheus attempted to rescue the frozen Floyd before Morganna could catch up with him. He shot a few more fire bolts in her direction. She absorbed them easily with her wand as if simply playing a game of catch with him. Morpheus aimed the point of his flying surfboard directly at the witch's face and made a down-sweep nosedive towards it! Instead of slamming into her like he had planned; she managed to snatch the surfboard out from under his feet with her outstretched hands. He fell forward holding both arms in front of his face to cushion the blow as he slammed into the hard marble floor below!

Morganna shot a stream of green light towards Morpheus as well which stunned him in the same way it had stunned Floyd. Neither wizard could move a muscle and felt completely frozen to the palace floor. Morganna walked in front of the stunned Morpheus; holding his surfboard out for him to see. "You're a foolish old wizard," she exclaimed angrily! Grabbing the surfboard with both hands, she slammed it hard over her right knee! Morpheus was shocked to see the old witch physically break his flying surfboard in half over her knee! "Where does she get the strength," he wondered curiously? His frustration continued to build as he couldn't move a muscle from where he was stunned to the palace floor. Morganna cackled. "Alright Morpheus, it's obvious I can't trust you or your friend over there since you both attacked me. I also assume you weren't able to find Drake with the guild list as I specifically ordered. However, before I completely obliterate you and your friend over there; I will give you both one more chance to speak. I suggest you both choose your words carefully as they may be your last." Bending down towards him, she yanked the wand from his stunned outstretched hand.

Quickly pocketing his wand, she aimed her own wand at his

stunned body lying on the floor. "MOVELLOREPELLO," she shouted as a blue stream of light slammed into his frozen body. Morpheus began to move. Standing up, he turned to face her. Knowing he was overpowered, he didn't want to make any dumb moves especially with his wand now in Morganna's possession. "You're absolutely right madam," he replied with a bow. "Floyd and I wanted to overpower you and save the Queen but you are obviously more powerful than either of us ever imagined," he said flatteringly. Morpheus slowly stepped towards her. "Although, I must tell you; we actually did find Drake. Not only did we find him but we got the guild list for you as well. We didn't want to just hand the list over to you but it would seem that you've beaten us at our own game," he exclaimed flatteringly. He continued walking towards her at a gentle pace.

Morganna continued pointing her wand at him. "Not another step Morpheus! Come any closer and I'll turn you into a pile of ash," she said threateningly. Morpheus stopped in his tracks. "Alright Morganna, you win. How about I simply hand you the guild list and you set everyone free. Sound fair?" Morganna shook her head. "I've only wanted the list from to begin with but now that you and your friend tried to harm me…I'd say you both owe me a little more than that," she replied angrily! "Give me the list and we'll go from there Morpheus," she exclaimed diplomatically.

It was Morpheus's turn to shake his head. "First release my friend Floyd over there," he said pointing in Floyd's direction. Morganna glanced over at the stunned old man and then back at Morpheus. "First the list Morpheus and then we'll talk," she replied authoritatively. Morpheus slowly reached into his robe pocket to retrieve the imitation magic box from it. Holding it out in front of him, he cracked open the hinged lid just enough to see the two miniature thieves sitting inside the box. Morganna gazed at the imitation magic box from the backside but couldn't see the two men sitting inside from where she was standing. Morpheus was highly aware of this fact.

Carefully grabbing Drake by the back of his robe, he gently

pulled him up and out of the box. Morganna placed her hand over her mouth in surprise as she watched the tiny man being held up by Morpheus. "What madness is this Morpheus," she asked curiously? Her gaze shifted towards the small box he was holding onto. "Is that what I think it is," she asked curiously? Morpheus quickly put the imitation magic box back into his deep robe pocket with his left hand while his right continued holding onto the miniature sized Drake. "What do you mean," he asked curiously? Morganna stepped closer to him. "Is that an actual Transformation Box you have there wizard," she asked pointing towards Morpheus's robe pocket where his left hand continued to remain.

Flipping the box over inside his large robe pocket, Duncan dropped out. Morpheus didn't want Morganna spotting him since his involvement really wasn't necessary at the moment. After dumping him out of the box and deeper into his pocket, Morpheus pulled the imitation magic box from his pocket for her closer inspection. She grabbed it immediately; holding it closer to the light for better inspection. "You can't fool me with this dubious imitation," she said confidently. "Where is the real Transformation Box Morpheus and who is this little man you have with you," she asked insistently?

Morpheus glanced downward. "This little guy in my right hand is the one and only Drake the thief!" Morganna gasped. "If he has my guild list then let's unshrink him immediately," she commanded. Morpheus glanced up at her. "That's the problem madam. We would need my friend Floyd over there to help resize him. He is the one who shrunk him in the first place and he seems to be the only one who can bring him back to size as well," he replied simply. Morganna shook her head disagreeably. "I seriously doubt that. Put him on the floor Morpheus and I'll do it myself." Morpheus sat the shrunken Drake on the hard marble floor and took a few steps backward. "With all due respect madam, I've already tried unshrinking him but perhaps you will have more success than I." Morganna glared back at him. "Quiet Morpheus; I must concentrate." Pointing her wand at the miniature Drake, she muttered the spell, "BENLARGO." A stream of red light shot from her wand and slammed into the miniature Drake below her. Morpheus was surprised at the accuracy of her aim. "I probably couldn't even hit a target that small from here," he thought silently.

The miniature Drake instantly transformed back into his normal and much larger sized self. Finding himself sitting on the hard Throne Room floor, he stared up at the ugly witch glaring back at him. "Who are you and what do you want with me," he asked masking the fear in his voice? Morganna continued pointing her wand at him. "I think you know what I want boy. I want the Pixie Guild List that everyone claims you have in your possession." Drake stood up on both feet. "What good is it to you," he asked curiously? Morganna glared at him. "That's none of your concern. Although, I am wondering what use it would be to you." Drake folded his arms defensively. "I keep it as a list of high paying honeycomb dealers I can sell to. Guild list members pay much higher prices than your average dealer." Morganna held one of her hands out towards him. "Give it to me now or face the consequences! It's your choice." Drake threw his hands in the air carelessly. "Unfortunately, I didn't bring it with me. I'll have to go back to my secret lair and get it for you," he replied deceivingly. Morganna moved closer to him. "Don't lie to me boy! Give it to me now or suffer my wrath and believe me you won't enjoy the exquisite amount of pain I have in store for you!"

The Queen interrupted the intensity between them. For a moment, the caged prisoners had been completely forgotten about until she spoke up. "Let me deal with this thief Morganna. If you remember, I was trying to track him down long before you showed up." Morganna's gaze shifted from the Queen back over to Drake. "Well, well…it would seem that you've made quite a few enemies Drake. I would suggest you learn how to make friends in the future. In the meantime, hand over that list! My patience is wearing thin young man!"

With Morganna pointing her wand directly at him, Drake felt his chances of escape quite limited at the moment. Reaching into his robe pocket, he felt his wand leaning up against the folded piece of parchment Morganna was wanting so desperately. "Don't even think about grabbing your wand boy," she hissed warningly. "Believe me, it'll be the last thing you do!" Pulling the folded guild list from his pocket, he reluctantly handed it over to Morganna. Snatching it from his outstretched hand, she scanned it over. A smile crossed her wrinkled old face as her gaze fell upon the long list of names, addresses and shops where each guild member could be reached.

She wasn't surprised to see Pixie's name at the top of the list as she was the original founder and teacher of the guild. Making a mental note to deal with her as soon as possible, Morganna placed the list inside her robe pocket and turned to face Drake. "I'm sure the Queen has already guessed what I'm planning to do with it so I might as well tell you too. When I'm done with each of these guild members there won't be a single fairy left alive who will remember how to make Pixie Dust," she exclaimed triumphantly. As an afterthought, she added; "your honeycomb selling days will soon be over Drake. I suggest you find a new line of business soon," she said seriously. Drake frowned and lowered his head. He felt a strong sense of anger, sadness and defeat all rolled into one. Somehow he managed to reply. "It doesn't matter anyways. Floyd over there came along and stole my entire inventory. It would seem that bad karma has finally caught up with me," he replied sadly.

Morganna had almost forgotten about Floyd by now. She turned to face the stunned old man still lying on the floor. He was still frozen from the spell she had cast on him. Walking over to him, she snatched the wand from his stunned outstretched hand and placed it inside her deep robe pocket next to Morpheus's wand. Pointing her own wand at Floyd, she spoke the spell "FREEBELLO" while watching it set him free from his magical bonds. Floyd began moving his arms and legs again and was about to place a hand inside his pocket when Morganna stopped him. "You're wand isn't there old man," she stated blatantly. Floyd lifted both hands from his pockets and turned his head to face her. "Who ya calling old? You're probably a hundred times older than me," he replied seriously. A green lightning bolt shot from Morganna's wand; slamming directly into his stomach! Screaming out in pain, he buckled over.

"Perhaps you need a lesson in manners old man and the first one is to never insult the person pointing a wand at you," she said seriously.

With Morganna's back turned away from Drake and Morpheus, they both quietly made their way towards the exit. Having anticipated this already, Morganna called out to them. "Don't leave yet boys! Come over here and stand next to Floyd," she commanded promptly. They both made their way back towards Floyd and stood next to him. "You've got the list Morganna. What more do you want," Morpheus asked agitatedly? Morganna stared at him seriously. "Nothing on earth could give me what I really want but this will have to do for now I suppose," she replied irritably.

Misty had been silently listening from her iron barred cage the entire time. Being a witch herself, she felt as though she could relate to Morganna's statement in many ways. "Hey, Morganna…." Morganna turned to face the caged Misty on her left. "None of this concerns you girly," she replied agitatedly. Misty spoke up again. "Actually, I know I may not look like a witch but I actually am and I know exactly what you want Morganna. You want to be young again!"

Floyd quickly anticipated where this conversation was heading and decided to interject a few thoughts on the matter. "You're right Misty. Remember that Transformation Box you saw earlier Morganna?" Morganna looked confused. "What about it? It couldn't possibly make me young again so don't even suggest it old man!" Floyd shook his head. "Take it from a former court wizard. I'm certain we both know what a Transformation Box can do." Morganna scowled. "Transformation Boxes can turn objects into other objects. Age is not an object old man," she replied agitatedly. Floyd held up his pointer finger as if he was about to deal out some serious knowledge. "Ancient magic is far different from modern magic Morganna. Many of the old ways have been lost and forgotten about. This is why I've devised a new experiment. I was going to try it myself before Morpheus showed up and stopped me." This statement peaked Morganna's interest even further. "What kind of experiment," she asked coldly? Floyd pointed towards the miniature

Drake still running around on the ground. "Put two and two together Morganna. You just saw Morpheus take Drake out of the Transformation Box. What do you think he was planning to do with him?" Morganna placed a hand to her chin thoughtfully. "Aww..I see where you're going with this old man but like I said before age is not an object. On the other hand, I have half a mind to try your suggestion just to see if it works." "That's the spirit," Floyd replied encouragingly!

Floyd wasted no time retrieving the real Transformation Box from his robe pocket. He quickly thrust it towards the old witch. "Well, go on madam. Give it a try. All you need to do is place the miniature Drake inside the box, close the lid and relish in the mental imagery of looking young again," he said encouragingly. Just the thought of becoming young again gave Morganna a renewed sense of energy as a suspicious expression crossed her face. "Wait a second; this all seems far too easy. You try it first old man!" Floyd shook his head. "I was going to Morganna but you have to remember I was going to make the life exchange with a major criminal who most likely deserves what's coming to him. The Queen over there would most likely not approve of my actions. On the other hand, she probably couldn't stop you if you decided to try the experiment yourself," he replied with a wink. The Queen's voice shouted from the barred cage on their left. "Drake should be tried in our courts Morganna! What if this little experiment kills him? Even criminals deserve a fair trial!" This statement somehow gave Morganna an extra boost of encouragement. She snatched the Transformation Box from Floyd's outstretched hands. "Alright, I'll do it." She bent down and snatched Drake up into her right hand as she popped the lid open with her left. With one quick motion, she dumped the miniature Drake into the real Transformation Box and slammed the lid shut. Holding the box out in front of her, she closed her eyes and imagined what her body would look like if she were in her twenty's again. Suddenly, a black cloud of smoke began to emanate from the box. At first, she thought it was on fire even though she never felt any kind of a burning sensation. The expanding cloud of thick smoke almost caused her to drop the box out of fear of possibly being burnt by it. Despite her fears, she continued holding onto it as the smoke surrounded her entire body.

The rising smoke continued expanding; becoming thicker and thicker until her entire body was covered in it completely. Nobody could see a single part of her until the smoke slowly began to clear away. The ugly green skinned, mole filled body she had once possessed quickly transformed into a slender, tall and radiant young woman who looked to be in her mid-twenties just as she had imagined. She glanced down at her slender youthful arms and felt a very different pair of legs beneath her robe. Everyone in the room seemed mesmerized by her incredible new found beauty! Even though Morganna felt different; she also had a burning desire to see her own reflection. "Someone get me a mirror," she commanded. She quickly covered her mouth upon hearing the sound of her own voice. It had completely changed from an old crackly sound to a much more gentle and soothing tone. It astonished everyone in the room including herself to hear it.

Floyd was the first to speak. "You look absolutely radiant madam. If you would kindly return my wand, I would be more than happy to provide a mirror for you to see yourself," he said flatteringly. Morganna shook her head. "Oh you are a sweet old conjurer but just because my body has changed doesn't mean my mind has," she replied tactfully. Cradling the Transformation Box up against her body, she opened the hinged lid and peeked inside. She found a small pile of ash where Drake's tiny body had previously been. "Looks like the little thief got what he deserved," she exclaimed carelessly as she flipped the box over to dump his ashes out onto the floor. "Although, it would be a shame to let his ashes go to waste," she said carefully pointing her wand towards the little pile on the floor. "MIRFLECTO," she chanted as a burst of red light shot from her wand into Drake's small pile of ashes. The ashes quickly grew in size as they transformed into a large circular mirror which hovered slightly above the ground in front of Morganna. She gazed into her marvelous reflection staring back at her. At first, it was difficult for her to believe the beautiful woman staring back at her was actually her! She had been an ugly old witch far longer than she ever cared to admit and her glorious newly transformed body was the most spectacular thing she had ever seen! She continued staring at herself in the mirror; admiring the curves of her own body and the softness of her own skin. "At least my skin's not green and saggy anymore and my warts are completely gone," she exclaimed gratefully!

Out of the corner of her eye, she saw something run across the floor just off to her left. Turning her head for a closer inspection, she spotted another miniature man dashing across the floor! "Was Drake still alive," she wondered curiously? "No it's impossible." She ran after the miniature figure running away from her. Morpheus placed a hand into his robe pocket in hopes of touching the top of Duncan's head. He desperately hoped it wasn't him running across the floor but soon found a small hole inside his right pocket where Duncan had managed to escape!

Morganna quickly caught up with Duncan and snatched him up off the floor with a swoop of her hand. Holding him next to her face, she stared at him closer. "Well, well…what do we have here? Another little thief I suppose! This must be my lucky day," she exclaimed excitedly! She glanced back at Floyd. "Just imagine how much younger and better looking I could be with another little man inside the Transformation Box," she said energetically! Floyd threw a hand in the air with frustration. "Morganna, with all due respect; I am an old man and would greatly appreciate a chance at using the Transformation Box as well. After all, it was the Transformation Box that took away my youth and ironically it can restore it back to me as well," he exclaimed hopefully. Morganna frowned. "Oh boo hoo," she replied sarcastically. "I've waited for this my entire life old man and I'm not about to let you take it away from me!" Just then, the Queen chimed into the conversation from her iron barred cage on their left. "I hate to interrupt you both but here at the Lake of Lost Souls we have courts, lawyers and judges to prosecute these criminals for their crimes! Not that you care Morganna but Drake's blood is on your hands now! I would hate for Duncan's life to be added to your record as well."

Morganna turned to face the caged Queen as she slipped the

struggling Duncan deep into her robe pocket. "You're not in a position to tell me what to do your majesty. In case you haven't noticed, you and your two friends here are currently stuck in this highly impenetrable cage. Looks like Con has transformed back into his genie form and even he can't seem to escape this prison despite all the ancient power he possesses. Speaking of which…you haven't said much after our little duel Con. Did I beat you that bad," she asked mockingly? Con's backside faced Morganna as she moved closer to their iron barred prison. "Turn around and face me genie! Don't be shy." Misty still felt confused since Con still looked very much like her friend Mojo. Con finally turned around to face Morganna. Seeing his red slit eyes glaring back at her caused her to gasp in horror! She felt another battle coming on and her energy had almost been completely drained after the last one she had just been through. "Oh, here we go again," she thought despairingly! "Can't you just hold off for a day or so Con," she asked hopefully? "I'm not sure I can take another battle right now," she said clutching her previously injured leg again. The pain had gotten worse and all her magic could do was slow the venom down at this point. The genie's face quickly transformed back into Con's cobra head again as he began speaking with Con's subtle hissing voice. "It's not over yet Morganna! You must suffer my wrath!"

Mojo quickly transformed back into Con's long slick slithering body once again as he carefully slid between the iron bars in front of him. Since Morpheus and Floyd were without wands, they quickly ran to the far corners of the Throne Room to avoid any stray spells that might come flying their way. Con slithered towards Morganna with a fast paced vengeance! Morganna backed away from the attacking cobra; holding her wand out in front of her. "I don't want to fight you Con but you are giving me no choice!" Morganna swirled her wand in a counter-clockwise motion above her head while shouting "MONGOFFO!" A long red lightning bolt shot from the tip of her wand straight up into the air. It soared back down onto her head; instantly transforming her into a large slender mongoose! Standing up on her hind legs, she flashed her pearly white teeth at the oncoming snake. Con raised his venomous cobra head and opened his mouth to reveal a pair of razor sharp fangs inside. His long forked tongue slipped from his mouth and darted towards the mongoose in an attempt to wrap around her neck! The mongoose sidestepped the attack and jumped up to bite the cobra's outstretched neck! Her teeth sunk deep into the smooth flesh of the attacking cobra. Shaking his neck back and forth, he tried throwing the mongoose off himself but couldn't quite manage it.

The large cobra quickly transformed into a wild looking bobcat. With the mongoose still latched onto his neck, he swiped at her backside with his new found claws. Stabbing the mongoose in the back, he managed to knock her off him. Pouncing towards the wounded mongoose with his claws outstretched, he barely missed his target. The mongoose dodged right at the last possible second barely avoiding a fatal head injury. The bobcat swiped left and drew blood from the mongoose's right arm just before she transformed into a large angry elephant! The massive size of her body towered high above him. The angry elephant stepped towards the bobcat with the intent of crushing him under the weight of her massive feet. Rolling to the right, he barely avoided a crushing blow to the head.

The bobcat quickly transformed into a tiny brown mouse with two large front teeth jutting out from his mouth. Even though Morganna wanted to smash the miniature rodent with her large elephant feet, her brain was naturally hardwired to avoid rodents of all types so she began running away from the little mouse now chasing her. Everyone watching the ridiculous chase couldn't help but laugh at the comical sight in front of them!

Floyd, Morpheus and the caged Misty continued watching the magical duel with the highest amount of interest. Floyd and Morpheus couldn't help because Morganna had confiscated their wands and Misty was obviously trapped behind her iron barred prison. Eventually the large elephant transformed herself into a house cat with fiercely sharp claws. She chased the mouse around Misty's iron cage until the mouse finally transformed into a normal sized dog and quickly began chasing the cat around the cage in the opposite direction! The cat quickly transformed into a ferocious looking tiger and quickly reversed directions to chase the dog around the cage in the opposite direction. The dog transformed into a circle of fire that quickly surrounded the cage holding Misty and the Queen hostage. The fire frightened the tiger enough to transform into a small rain cloud. She hovered above the circle of fire threateningly. Before any rain could fall onto the fire, Con quickly transformed back into Mojo and turned to face Floyd. "Toss me the box," he shouted! Floyd picked up the Transformation Box lying on the floor and threw it towards Mojo. Just as Mojo caught it, the rain cloud hovering above his head quickly transformed into a gigantic bumblebee and made a direct beeline towards his face in an attempt to sting him! Mojo quickly opened the Transformation Box and held it in front of his face. The large bee flew directly into Mojo's trap as he slammed the lid shut! He tossed the closed box back at Floyd. "Now's your chance to get what you've always wanted Floyd." The Queen tried interrupting him but Floyd knew Mojo was absolutely correct. If he waited until they freed the Queen, she would obviously object to what he was about to do so he took advantage of the situation while he had the chance.

Floyd imagined what he would look like as a much younger and better looking man. Just then, a heavy black smoke emitted from the Transformation Box in the same way it had done earlier when Morganna had used it on Drake. Smoke leaked from the box; growing thicker and thicker until it covered Floyd's entire body. It slowly cleared away leaving everyone in absolute confusion! No one recognized him at all! Morpheus observed him carefully. "And who might you be good sir," he asked playfully? Floyd smiled and wished he had a mirror to see his own reflection at the moment. Misty yelled out at him. "Hey handsome, come get me out of this cage," she called out seductively. Floyd smiled as he walked over to the iron barred cage holding Misty and the Queen.

The Queen frowned. "Mojo, we should have given Morganna and Drake a fair trial but I don't blame you for what you did. Thank you for saving us," she said gratefully. Mojo bowed gracefully. "You're quite welcome your majesty. Although, I can't help but wonder what happened to Duncan? Last I checked, Morganna put him in her pocket just before turning into a Mongoose." The Queen glanced at him thoughtfully. "Well, either Duncan became part of her when she transformed into a mongoose and he was destroyed along with her or perhaps he fell out of her pocket at some point when none of us were watching. If that is the case then Duncan is probably running around here somewhere. Perhaps he became part of Morganna and was destroyed along with her. Either way, we should be cautious and keep a sharp eye out for him just in case he managed to survive."

Misty observed Mojo carefully. "Um, Mojo I can't help but notice your glowing red snake eyes. I want to believe the curse was just broken when Floyd destroyed Morganna inside the Transformation Box but I can't help but wonder…." Suddenly, Mojo heard a subtle hissing sound inside his head. "We are one Mojo. You can't get rid of me." Mojo slapped his forehead. "I just heard Con's voice inside my head." Morpheus chimed in from the right side of him. "I'm sure we can find a cure for that," he responded confidently. "I hope so," replied Mojo optimistically.

Mojo hovered over to the iron cage and grabbed onto the bars from the outside. "My magic doesn't work on these bars," he said discouragingly. "Unfortunately, Morganna held the key to it and she is nothing more than a pile of ash now." The much younger Floyd walked over to the cage still holding onto the Transformation Box within the palms of his hands. "That's the beauty of this magic box Mojo. It can transform ANY ordinary object into whatever you desire." Misty reached one of her closed hands through the iron bars in an attempt to hand something to him. "Here, use this Floyd." Floyd reached out to accept a small hair clip from Misty's outstretched hand. Placing it into the magic box, he closed the lid and imagined it transforming into a key that would fit the cage door perfectly. Opening the lid again, he pulled small key from inside the box which fit the lock perfectly! He also felt a tiny bit of his youth slip away in the process but decided it was worth the price to help rescue the Queen and Misty.

They were soon free from their devastating prison. "I can't thank you enough Floyd," said the Queen gratefully. Floyd bowed respectfully. "I'm happy to help your majesty." Misty gasped anxiously as if she had just remembered something quite important. "We must go free Pixie from the dungeon," she exclaimed desperately! The Queen agreed and called out to her guards; hoping they were at their usual posts just outside the Throne Room. Instead of opening the double-doors as expected, two slender cobras slithered underneath them. Everyone stepped back as they moved in closer. Morpheus, Floyd and Misty still didn't have their wands as they had been confiscated and destroyed along with Morganna. Mojo stepped in front of the group in an attempt to defend them from the oncoming snakes. As if against his own will, his body quickly transformed back into Con's extra-large cobra body! He turned to face the two small snakes slithering towards him! They hissed at each-other for a brief moment as if challenging each-other to a fight! The Queen assumed the two small cobras would be no match for the gigantic Con but she also assumed that Con was on their side as well. A devastating thought suddenly occurred to her. "Mmm…just because Con and Morganna were old enemies doesn't mean he's on our side. We should probably…."

Her thoughts were quickly interrupted as all three cobras suddenly turned to face her, Misty, Morpheus and Floyd! Floyd continued holding onto the Transformation Box as he reached into his pocket. He couldn't find what he was searching for but Morpheus was two steps ahead of him already as he pulled a small vile of glowing red liquid from within his pocket. Morpheus quickly popped the small wooden quark off the top and began pouring the dark red liquid onto the marble floor in front of him. Like a magnet, all three snakes were instantly drawn towards it as if wanting it more than anything else in the world. After lapping it up into their narrow jawed mouths, all three cobras instantly passed out into an incredibly deep sleep. "Excellent! We don't have much time," Morpheus shouted. Which one is the genie again," he asked hesitantly? The rest of the group pointed towards the cobra that was supposed to be Mojo lying on the floor in what looked like a complete coma. Floyd anticipated Morpheus's next move and walked up next to him with the Transformation Box in hand. "Don't worry Morpheus. I've got this," he exclaimed confidently. He carefully reached a hand downwards as he cautiously picked up one of the sleeping cobras by the neck and gently laid him inside the Transformation Box. He carefully repeated the process with the other sleeping cobra lying next to Con. With both comatose cobras now lying inside; he carefully closed the lid and imagined what he wanted before opening it back up again. Each cobra had magically transformed into a wand! He pulled both wands from inside the box. They were longer than the box itself but no one questioned it because magic was never really meant to be logical in the first place. Floyd tossed a wand to Morpheus and kept the other for himself. He thought about transforming Con's cobra body into a wand as well but didn't want any harm to come to him in case he really was a possessed Mojo. He wasn't completely certain if it was Mojo or Con he was dealing with but he didn't like the idea of harming Mojo if it was really him inside Con's body. He formulated a quick plan in an attempt to get Mojo back to his normal self again. Picking up the sleeping cobra by the neck, he laid him inside the open magic box. Misty was still under the impression that Mojo was being possessed by Con and she screamed out after him. "No Floyd; stop!" Floyd turned towards her. "Relax Misty. I don't plan on destroying your genie friend here. I'm merely trying to get him back to his normal old self. That's all."

Just before Floyd could place the sleeping Con into the Transformation Box, his red cobra eyes popped wide open! Even though Floyd was holding him by the neck, the long snake lunged towards his face. Floyd's grip tightened just enough to keep the snake's fangs from reaching his face. With one quick motion, he hurled the cobra into the Transformation Box and slammed the lid shut before he could slip out. Floyd quickly imagined Mojo and Con switching bodies again in order to return back to their natural forms of belonging. Floyd held the lid shut with all of his might as he could feel Con desperately struggling to escape from within! Smoke seeped from underneath the lid as the box suddenly stopped moving from Con's desperate struggle to escape! Floyd inhaled deeply and opened the box in hopes of finding Mojo back to his normal genie self. Instead, he found a solid gold lamp sitting where Con had just been. Grabbing and rubbing the lamp with his other hand, a long stream of gray mist shot from its tip. Just as expected, Mojo came soaring out of the lamp with a newly restored vigor! He floated into the air and hovered there with ease. He didn't have any legs like he previously had. Instead, it was merely a stream of blue mist that connected with the rest of his body. He wore two shiny brass wrist cuffs like many other genies did. Mojo hovered next to Floyd. "What can I do for you master," he asked seriously? Misty screamed out at him. "Mojo, you're alive! I'm so happy to see you back to your normal self again! He quickly hovered over to the caged Misty. "You need to get you out of here Misty. Unfortunately, I can no longer assist you. I belong to Master Floyd now," he replied seriously. Misty thought silently about what had just happened to Mojo. "The Transformation Box must have switched Con and Mojo's genie bodies back to normal but it doesn't make sense that Mojo is no longer a free genie. She distinctly remembered using one of her wishes to set him free. What a complete waste of a wish," she thought disappointedly.

She called out to Floyd. "Hey Floyd, how about using that little key you pulled from the magic box to set me and the Queen free from this ridiculous cage," she shouted demandingly. Floyd reached back into his pocket to retrieve the little golden key and quickly inserted it into the lock of the iron cage. An audible click indicated its opening as he pulled the door open for Misty and the Queen to easily make their escapes. They thanked Floyd for his help and the Queen even made a comment about "wishing he was still her court wizard." Morpheus glanced away pretending not to hear this statement as Misty rushed over to Mojo and threw her arms around him in a loving embrace. Her arms fell straight through his body as if he were merely a ghost. "Mojo, I used one of my wishes to set you free and now you're a normal genie again. Does this mean I get another wish," she asked hopefully? He smiled back at her. "Unfortunately Misty, you've used all your wishes already and you're no longer my master. I'm also sad to say I can no longer be your traveling companion either." A tear came to Misty's eye. "Oh Mojo, you mean the world to me! I wish there was some way I could set you free again!" Mojo thought for a moment. "Unfortunately, you can't since you're out of wishes but Master Floyd would be able to grant such a request if he so desired," he replied gesturing a hand towards him. Floyd glanced over at the teary eyed Misty then back at Mojo and then back at Misty. "Oh, this is just too much fun Misty! I must have my first two wishes first and then I'll set Mojo free. How does that sound," he asked diplomatically? Misty tried to maintain her composure. "Sounds like a deal Floyd. I would be deeply grateful," she replied brushing aside another tear from her right cheek.

Floyd knew this was an emotional moment for her and didn't want to prolong Mojo's freedom any longer than he had to. Glancing up at Mojo, he made his first wish. "Genie, I wish to never grow old again." Mojo gazed down at him seriously. "I would be happy to grant your request Master Floyd but what if you meet a beautiful woman someday? You would live longer than any woman you ever fell in love with and it just might break your heart in the end. Trust me. I've seen it happen countless times before." Floyd stared up at the genie floating in the air above him. "I've considered that as well Mojo and that is why I want to make a deal with you." Mojo glanced down at him curiously. "Oh, what kind of deal did you have in mind Master Floyd?" Floyd continued. "I will set you free Mojo if you promise me that once I find the love of my life you will grant her the gift of eternal life as well. Otherwise, the deal is off and I won't set you free. Do you understand?" Mojo nodded. "I understand Master Floyd and I give you my word as a genie. Your wish will be granted as soon as you find a significant other worthy of receiving such a magnificent gift." Floyd nodded agreeably. "Alright genie, in that case…I wish for you to be free!" A whirlpool of green light quickly spun from the tip of the lamp around Mojo's ever changing body. The green light transformed into a large gray cloud that surrounded him.

An expression of shock and horror came over Misty, Morpheus, Floyd and the Queen as they watched a 20 foot long cobra begin to appear from the cloudy depths in front of them. There was no doubt about it. Con had reappeared in front of them! Con's large cobra head towered above them as Misty called out to him. "Con! We thought you were dead! What have you done with Mojo," she called out angrily?! The large cobra hissed loudly at them as Morpheus and Floyd drew their wands in front of them. "You fools! The Transformation Box is no match for my power! Mojo is trapped inside my old snakeskin below the Dessert of Doom. Just like him, I am also a genie. Morganna set me free and then cursed me to wear this cobra skin forever! She was looking for a pet to replace some raven named Blackbeak but now that she's dead the curse has been lifted and Floyd has set me free!" Without warning, a pair of eagle wings suddenly sprouted from Con's 20 foot long body! Taking to the air, he began flying circles around Floyd and Morpheus. "You fools! You think a simple magic box is more powerful than me?!"

Misty and the Queen still didn't have wands to use but Floyd and Morpheus had already begun shooting fire bolts at the large flying serpent making circles in the air around them. Their fire bolts didn't affect the flying snake in the way they had hoped. Instead, his large cobra body simply absorbed them as if they were nothing but rain drops falling on his thick reptilian skin. Con laughed menacingly. "Think you can hurt a genie? Better think again!" Floyd tried changing his spells from fire to lightening in an attempt to harm the flying snake. Morpheus tried shooting metal spikes from his wand! The lightening did nothing whatsoever and the metal spikes simply bounced off the snake's body as if bouncing a rubber ball off a brick wall. Con smirked as he basked in his moment of power. He circled around them in the air one more time just to prove their desperate attempts to bring him down would have no effect on him whatsoever.

After making a couple of failed attempts at freezing Con, Floyd quickly realized that genie magic was far superior to anything they could conjure up. Raising his wand in the air, he called out to flying serpent. "Alright Con, you win! There's no way we can beat you! Morpheus, stop your tornado of death. It's no use. Con will most likely overpower us soon. We should surrender immediately." Con called back to them. "That would be wise old man! Now that you've both had your fun; I'm going to have mine," he replied cunningly. Inhaling deeply, the flying cobra blew a venomous green cloud of mist straight towards them. The green cloud filled the room quickly; causing Floyd, Morpheus, Misty and the Queen to fall asleep immediately. They each hit the palace floor in a deep slumber. "I'll finish them off nice and slow," Con thought slyly. He quickly wrapped his 20 foot cobra body around everyone in the room and closed in tight! Forcing all four of them into the center of his coiled body, he debated which one he would eat first. "Perhaps Floyd should go first," he thought energetically. "He has been the worst troublemaker of them all so far."

Con's mouth opened wide enough to fit Floyd's entire head inside. Before biting down on it, the sound of glass shattering quickly caught everyone's attention. Turning his head towards one of the stain glass windows nearby, he couldn't believe what he was seeing! A fierce looking fire breathing dragon stood directly in front of him. A small raven flew beside him and began to squawk. "Alright Claw, show this no good wanna be genie what you're made of," Blackbeak commanded! "As for my last wish…I wish for Con and Mojo to switch bodies for the rest of eternity!"

Claw spread his wings and flew high into the air. Floyd and Morpheus were excited to see a genie battle take place right in front of their eyes which is why Floyd was caught completely off guard when the dragon began flying directly towards him! Even Con seemed a little perplexed by this move. Just as the dragon flew close enough to touch Floyd, Claw made a U-turn in mid-air! As his long pointed tail swirled around in the air, Claw positioned it just underneath the Transformation Box Floyd was holding onto with both hands. With one quick swipe upwards, he knocked it high into the air and out of Floyd's hands. Using his tail again, Claw hammered the box even higher into the air. Turning his head back towards it, he blew a long jet of green mist into the airborne magic box. It quickly became a thousand times larger than its original size! The box continued dropping towards the ground heading straight towards the coiled up cobra sitting on the floor beneath it. Claw swiped his airborne tail up against the flying box one more time to give it just enough lift and direction to cover its target. Floyd could see the box needed just a little more tilt and push to get it exactly over the coiled snake's body. He was surprised to see Misty and the Queen using their anti-gravity amulets to escape Con's coiled up body and fly alongside the box. With the Queen on one side and Misty on the other, they managed to steer and push the large airborne box directly over Con's coiled up body. Just before dropping it, a stream of green mist shot from Con's venomous mouth covering Claw in its thick cloud. Instantly losing consciousness, the dragon fell to the ground as the giant Transformation Box fell over Con's body; trapping him inside it. The large cobra struggled to escape but the box was simply too large and too heavy to budge. The magic began working on the trapped cobra as smoke emanated from the bottom of the box.

It wasn't long before the entire group heard the sound of a struggling Mojo. "Hey, what's going on? Let me out of here," he said sharply. Misty and the Queen quickly used their anti-gravity amulets to hover back over to the giant box and lift it up just enough for him to slide out from underneath it. Misty hovered back down to the ground in front of Mojo and threw her outstretched arms around his neck. "Oh Mojo, I'm so glad you're alive," she said with relief and excitement in her voice! Mojo returned her embrace. "Oh Misty, I'm just glad you guys didn't leave me stuck down there in that old dead snakeskin. It really worried me being trapped in that rotten old thing! Apparently, Con switched bodies with me when we all thought he died." The Queen interjected her thoughts. "Con was also a genie trapped inside a cobra's body because Morganna cursed him long ago for it to be so. It looks like he did some sort of genie body switch between the two of you. Also, it seems to have taken the power of another genie to make the switch happen. We all thought the Transformation Box had enough power to handle it on its own but apparently another genie was needed for the switch to work properly. I'm just glad Morganna, Drake, Duncan and Con are no longer around to bother us. Sure, it would have been proper to have a fair trial for them but I'm fairly certain we can all attest to their crimes." She glanced over at Floyd and Morpheus. "Thank you both for your dedicated service. If I can ever repay either of you just say the word and it will be done." The much younger and handsomer looking Floyd stared back at her. "Your Highness, I finally have what I was seeking. I have attained my youth again and can assure you I won't be using the Transformation Box anymore. I want to keep my good looks as long as possible," he said with a wink. The Queen smiled back at him. "Perhaps I can provide a better home within the castle walls for you to reside or even a small fortune if you so desire? I would like to repay your dedicated service if possible." Floyd smiled. "Any amount of rubies would be greatly appreciated your grace. Up until now, I've been using the Transformation Box to change regular objects into rubies but we both know youth is not a fair price to pay for such things."

The Queen turned towards Misty. "Misty, please bring forth the ruby case." Misty reached into her deep robe pocket and produced the small briefcase. She handed it over to the Queen. "You'll have to resize it first your majesty." Since neither of them currently carried a wand, the Queen turned towards Morpheus. "Would you do the honor Morpheus?" Morpheus already had his wand at the ready. "It would be a pleasure your highness." He touched the miniature briefcase with his outstretched wand while muttering the spell "BENLARGO." Instantly the briefcase enlarged itself and quickly grew into its normal size. "Now for the six digits," the Queen exclaimed thoughtfully. Misty twisted the dial combination to reveal the first two numbers of 1 and 8 followed by Pixie's two numbers of 2 and 4. Andrew had the final two digits. Misty brought her Jargon Band up to her face and spoke the passcode into it. "If wishes were fishes we'd all have a fry." The Jargon Band lit up green immediately as she attempted to speak with Andrew. "Andrew…Are you there?" Instantly, one of Morpheus's many Jargon Bands lit up as the entire group heard Misty's voice emanate from it. The Queen stared at him questionably. "Why in blazes do you have Andrew's Jargon Band Morpheus?" Morpheus glanced downward shamefully. "Well, it's a long story your highness. I didn't want to tell all of you this but Andrew recently had a fatal accident and gave me his Jargon Band to keep in touch with Misty and Pixie in case they ever decided to call in. It has been a slow recovery for him but he should be back to normal soon enough. Unfortunately, he never actually gave me the last two digits of the passcode but I will ask him about it as soon as possible." The Queen shook her head disapprovingly. "That's ok Morpheus. I can ask him about it right now. I have a direct connection with him as well."

The Queen rolled up the long sleeve on her left arm only to

reveal a long line of Jargon Bands similar to what Morpheus had beneath his sleeve as well. She spoke the passcode into all of them without really knowing which one would connect with Andrew since they all looked the same. "Andrew, you are the greatest accountant in the world." Everyone in the room tried to avoid snickering at the funny sounding passcode. "He set up the passcode," she replied with a laugh. "I really need to make a law about making these bands look different from each-other. It's so difficult to tell which one is which," she noted silently. Andrew's voice soon rang through the air. "Yes my Queen; how may I assist you today?" The Queen leaned in closer to her glowing Jargon Band. "Morpheus claims you've recently been in a fatal accident. Is that true?" A short silence followed before the reply came. "Yes my Queen. It was pretty bad. I almost lost my life but hopefully I'll be okay." Morpheus quickly wiped away a trickle of sweat beading down his forehead. The Queen continued. "I'm sorry Andrew. That is unfortunate. What exactly happened to you?" Another brief silence followed before Andrew continued. "Well, did Morpheus tell you anything about it already," he asked curiously? The Queen shook her head. "No, I was hoping to hear about it from you directly." Morpheus loosened the collar around his neck as Andrew continued speaking. "Well, I was hiking around Turban Waterfall hoping to find a rare type of glow-in-the-dark frog when suddenly I slipped and fell! I was completely out of Pixie Dust and didn't have the means to fly away so my fall ended up being quite terrible like Morpheus was saying. I broke one of my legs, an arm and even some ribs. Thankfully, Morpheus happened to see my fall from a long distance away and came over to rescue me. He took me to the Circle of healing where Luna helped me recover. Thank goodness for healers!" The Queen nodded agreeably. "I'm glad you're okay Andrew. I'm also glad Morpheus's story can be verified by you. Morpheus has the Jargon Band I gave you; connecting him with Misty and Pixie. I was just wondering if you gave that to him after your accident?" Another brief silence filled the air before Andrew's voice came back on the line again. "Absolutely, I gave that to him just in case he might have to communicate with the ladies on my behalf. After all, serious injuries are no laughing matter," he replied seriously. The Queen continued. "I couldn't agree more and I'm glad you're recovering well Andrew. That being said, we are currently trying to open the case of rubies and need the last two digits of the combination. Can you please provide us with those last two numbers?" Andrew continued. "It sounds like the case of rubies is right there with you in the palace. Is that correct?" "Yes, that's correct," the Queen replied promptly. Andrew continued. "In that case, it sounds like the rubies were never used for their intended purpose which was to bribe Drake into giving up his current location. Is that correct?" The Queen replied again. "That's also correct Andrew. Drake, Duncan and Morganna are dead now. We don't need to worry about them anymore thankfully." "I'm thrilled to hear that," Andrew replied enthusiastically. "In that case, simply have Morpheus return the case of rubies to the Accounting House and I will deposit them back into your account my Queen."

The Queen nodded. "That is quite thoughtful of you Andrew but I would like to pay my heroes handsomely for rescuing me," she replied gratefully. Andrew continued. "I would love to hear more of how that all happened my Queen. Tell you what, how about we all meet up at the Throne Room tomorrow morning and we'll open the case together? I would feel much better about that as opposed to simply giving you the passcode over the airwaves. It would also give me a chance to catch up with your heroes and the adventures they've recently been on." The Queen nodded agreeably. "Alright Andrew, I'm assuming you're trying to give yourself more recovery time by waiting until tomorrow to show up. Is that correct," she asked curiously? Andrew replied promptly. "That's correct my Queen. I'm in pretty bad shape at the moment but hopefully I'll have enough strength to make it over to the palace tomorrow morning if all goes well."

The Queen decided to suggest a different approach. "On second thought, I could just have everyone come visit you at the Circle of Healing tomorrow if that would be more convenient for you Andrew?" Andrew replied promptly. "It's okay my Queen. I'll try my best to make it to the Throne Room tomorrow morning. It'll give me some motivation to get moving again," he said hopefully. "Alright Andrew, we'll all plan on seeing you here tomorrow morning. Take care of yourself and please get better soon," she stated hopefully. "Thank you my Queen. I look forward to seeing you all tomorrow. Goodbye for now." The Queen said her goodbyes and quickly used the shutdown passcode to close off the communication lines between them.

She turned to face the small group standing next to her. "Looks like we'll have to wait until tomorrow morning to open up the case of rubies; Andrew is recovering at the Circle of Healing and will try his absolute best to make it here for tomorrow's meeting. I expect you all to do the same." Everyone nodded agreeably. The Queen continued. "In the meantime, take good care of that ruby case Misty. Don't lose it or let anyone try to steal it from you. Do you understand?" Misty nodded. "I understand completely my Queen."

The Queen continued speaking to the entire group. "Originally, we were going to trade these rubies with Drake in an effort to find the location of his stolen stash of bees and honeycomb. Speaking of which…did any of you ever figure out where Drake was keeping his stolen goods before he passed on?"

Floyd reached into his robe pocket and felt the shrunken bag of inventory sitting there comfortably. He debated on whether or not to tell the Queen about it because he did in fact have quite a large fortune literally sitting inside his pocket at the moment. He decided to speak up in an effort to reassure the Queen of his loyalty to the crown. "I managed to repossess the goods before Duncan could escape with them your Majesty," he said loyally. The Queen glanced at him proudly. "Well done Floyd. Where is the stolen inventory now?" Floyd debated telling the entire truth to the Queen. He wasn't ready to give up an entire fortune just yet. "I have Drake's stolen inventory back at my shop," he lied. "I can retrieve it for you and have it back here tomorrow morning when we all meet up again," he replied cunningly. "Excellent," replied the Queen. "I would like you to give Drake's old inventory to Morpheus. From there, I want Morpheus to take the guild list and divide the stolen goods evenly amongst everyone on that list. There is no way of knowing which goods belong to whom at this point so this is how we'll divvy it up. This should help the guild list members make more Pixie Dust in the future. In return for your efforts Morpheus, I will be happy to pay you substantially for everything you've done and will continue to do. Please report back to me once you have evenly redistributed the stolen goods back to all the guild list members and then we'll discuss further payment alright?" Morpheus nodded agreeably. "Thank you your Majesty. I appreciate your generosity in all its forms."

Over in the far corner of the room Misty and Mojo were smooching up a storm and the sound of their kissing had grown to an annoying decibel! "Hey, cut it out you two," Blackbeak squawked teasingly! Misty glanced back at him briefly. "I'm glad you arrived just in the nick of time Blackbeak! You saved us all when you unleashed Claw from the lamp! I imagine you were able to get that from Pixie somehow?" Blackbeak nodded. "Yes, I grabbed it from her when I helped rescue her from the dungeons. For some reason she was more worried about finding Andrew than anything else. She gave me the lamp and flew off to find her lover boy," he replied with a laugh. Blackbeak glanced over at the unconscious dragon lying on the Throne Room floor not too far away from him. "Thank goodness for Claw. He definitely saved us all," Blackbeak exclaimed while rubbing the miniature lamp attached to the small chain around his neck. A cloud of smoke streamed from the lamp's opening and enveloped the sleeping dragon. The smoke swirled around his sleeping dragon before sucking him back into the lamp.

The Queen turned towards Blackbeak. "You really did show up in the nick of time Rueland! Just curious, how did you get separated from your traveling companions anyways? You must have not been with them when Morganna found and captured them. I can't help but wonder why?" Blackbeak glanced over at Morpheus. Morpheus threw a hand in the air carelessly. "By all means, tell her! Now that you're the hero, she'll be okay with it." The Queen stared at Morpheus curiously. "Okay with what," she asked? Blackbeak continued with his explanation. "Well your majesty…the truth is that I never actually left with the group you sent me out with. Morpheus held me back in order to help me remember my former powers I once had before Morganna cursed me to forget them." The Queen placed her hands on her hips as a look of disappointment crossed her face. "Morpheus, my plan was for you to train Blackbeak AFTER he returned from his quest to find Drake…not before!" Morpheus bowed. "My apologies your highness but my worries lie with the bat army attacking us any time they wish. We simply can't afford another attack like the previous one. I speak on behalf of our entire army when I say that your majesty." The Queen nodded understandingly. "You're absolutely right Morpheus. Time is not a luxury we can afford when it comes to defending our precious city. In fact, I apologize to you. You acted wisely without my permission and I humbly acknowledge your actions to be justifiable and admirable. Thank you for your valiant efforts even though I did not approve of them in the first place." Morpheus smiled at the compliment just before giving Blackbeak a noticeable wink. "See, I told you our actions would be justifiable once you were seen as a hero." The Queen held up a finger and was about to say something before Morpheus quickly interjected. "No worries your majesty. I'm just glad everything worked out well for us," he said lightheartedly.

Blackbeak turned towards the Queen. "I have some important news to tell you my Queen." The Queen looked at him seriously. "Oh, and what news would that be Rueland?" Blackbeak continued. "I happened to come across a couple of bat spies while flying around the city. They lead me to their king and we worked out a deal. The city should be safe for another year at the least." The Queen's jaw dropped open. "What in the world did you say to him Blackbeak? What kind of deal are you talking about?" Blackbeak glanced around the room suspiciously. "Oh, I'm sure it's probably not a big deal but I offered our gravity beam machines in exchange for an entire year of peace and prosperity." The Queen slapped the palm of her hand against her forehead. "Oh Blackbeak, no offense but you really messed up this time! Don't you realize our army uses those gravity beam machines to bring down huge numbers of their army when they attack?" Calling her guards into the room, she quickly ordered them to send troops to all gravity beam machines operators throughout the city and to guard them well.

"Sorry Blackbeak, but you basically agreed to give away our best weapons to our enemies in hopes that they'll actually leave us alone for a year. Sorry but that was an incredibly foolish thing to do! In fact, you better hope the bats don't attack again right after taking those machines away from us or we're all doomed! It might be the end of us if that happens!"

Blackbeak glanced downward ashamed by his own foolish actions. "My apologies my Queen; you're absolutely right. I shouldn't have made such a foolish deal on behalf of the entire city. I was too trusting that the bats would actually keep their word when in reality they probably lied to me and will most likely attack our city after removing the gravity beam machines from around it. It would be wise to check on them as soon as possible before they get carried away," he suggested seriously. The Queen nodded agreeably. "I couldn't agree more Rueland. I will give the order as soon as we disperse. Let's all plan on meeting back here tomorrow morning. Hopefully Andrew will be well enough to join us by then. Misty, make sure to bring that case of rubies with you tomorrow morning and keep it as safe as you possibly can in the meantime." Misty nodded. "I'll do my best your grace."

The group dispersed immediately and went their separate ways with the intention of meeting up again in the morning. The Queen quickly ordered a battalion of guards to guard the gravity beam machines surrounding the city walls. They were ordered to keep all bats from flying off with them no matter what they might say about Rueland's new found peace treaty. The guards instinctively knew an attack was on the way after hearing the news and quickly prepared themselves for battle. They sharpened their throwing spears, added ammo to their guns and gathered as much Pixie Dust as they could find. To their absolute surprise, one of the soldiers shouted. "I can't believe it! I can fly again! I didn't even use Pixie Dust and I can fly again! The curse is broken at last!" Every soldier in the army shouted for joy upon discovering such news to be true!

35. SECRET MEETINGS

Behind Turban Waterfall Morpheus sat on his wooden chair patiently waiting for his Jargon Band to glow green. His feet were kicked up over the top of his wooden desk as he carefully leaned back on the two back legs of his chair just enough so it wouldn't tip over completely. One of the many Jargon Bands strapped across his left wrist finally lit up. He sat up and brought his chair to an upright position immediately.

A scratchy high pitched voice came across the airwaves. "Morpheus, I did what you asked. Don't forget to cut me in on the deal or it'll be the end of you!" Morpheus laughed dismissively. "Don't worry Nick. You'll get what's coming to you. By the way, you did an excellent job imitating Andrew's voice. The Queen would have thrown me in the dungeon for sure if it wasn't for you my friend!" Nick's voice came back on the line again. "If the Queen decides to visit Andrew at the Circle of Healing anytime soon she'll quickly discover he was never actually there. You should probably skip town soon Morpheus." Morpheus nodded agreeably. "You're right Nick but remember we can't leave until we've snatched that ruby case from Misty. Meet me tonight at the palace gates and we'll have that briefcase faster than you can say Cobra Con!" Nick laughed. "I like your plan Morpheus but why are we meeting at the palace gates? Do you plan on strutting straight through the front entrance without any confrontation at all," he asked almost jokingly? Morpheus smiled to himself. "Being the palace court wizard has its perks Nick. Believe it or not we won't even have to sneak into Misty's chambers. Hold onto your chair Nick because I've actually arranged for two loyal guards to escort us directly into her chambers in the dead of night! Yep, their names are Bill and Phil." Nick burst into laughter. "No way Morpheus; I don't believe it! So, if you have two loyal guards escorting you than why even have me come along?" Morpheus cleared his throat. "That's a good question Nick. You see, the guards will only escort us to the room door. From there, I will knock on the door and speak with Misty directly. No offence but your small size will really come in handy at this point. From here, you will use your incredible speed and dexterity to sneak past Misty and into the open room behind her. I will carefully keep her distracted while you search her entire room for the case of rubies. Once you've found it; simply sneak back out of the room and we'll call it a "done deal" my friend!"

A short silence followed that statement before Nick's voice was heard again. "I like your plan Morpheus. I'll meet you tonight just outside the palace gate then. I'll also bring my extra quiet pair of shoes just to be safe," he said with a chuckle. Morpheus laughed a little as well. "Sounds good Nick; I'll see you then." Morpheus quickly spoke the shutdown passcode to end communication between them.

"There's just one more person I need to speak with now," Morpheus thought to himself. Moving his face towards the long line of Jargon Bands strung across his left wrist, he flinched as he spoke the passcode. "ANDREW, ANDREW, ANDREW….I WILL LOVE YOU TO THE END OF TIME!" He absolutely hated the thought of having to speak in Pixie's high pitched voice again but knew he had too in order to get the last two digits of the passcode. A devastating thought suddenly occurred to him…"Oh no, if he's with Pixie right now then I'm sunk!" He kept his fingers crossed desperately hoping Andrew wasn't sitting next to Pixie at that exact moment.

Andrew's voice quickly came on the line. "Hello Pixie? Is that you?" Morpheus took a deep breath and began speaking in Pixie's high pitched voice again. "Yes Andrew; it's me." Andrew sighed deeply. "Oh, that's a relief! I know you just left but there was one more thing I wanted to tell you." Morpheus sighed as well and wiped the sweat off his forehead. He felt incredibly lucky at the moment as he continued on with his charade. "Well I'm glad I caught you silly. What was it you wanted to tell me? I can never seem to get enough of you Andrew," he replied flatteringly. Andrew continued. "I just wanted to say that you should come back tomorrow as soon as possible. I have a special gift I wanted to give you." Morpheus smiled. "A gift? How exciting Andrew! I can't wait to find out what it is for sure!" Andrew continued. "You're gonna love it Pixie! I put a lot of thought and effort into it!" Morpheus picked up from there. "I really can't wait to see it Andrew. More importantly, I can't wait to see you! You truly are a treasure my love," he replied flatteringly. He tried desperately not to gag on his own saliva as the disgusting words exited his mouth.

He decided to change the subject before he got too disgusted with himself. "Um, Morpheus darling…I was just wondering if you could possibly give me your two digits to the ruby case? I mean, you know everyone is back from their quests now and we all just want to take a quick peek at those dazzling rubies before returning them to the Accounting House tomorrow." A brief silence followed the pleading. "Oh Pixie, I do trust you but I just don't want them falling in the wrong hands is all." Morpheus continued. "Don't worry Andrew. Mojo, Misty and I will all help keep them safe. Besides it's only until we return them tomorrow. None of us has ever seen three and a half million credits worth of rubies before and it would really give us an exciting story to tell during our future travels. Oh please Andrew! We'll have them back to you at the Accounting House tomorrow for sure." Another brief silence followed before Andrew responded again. "Oh, alright Pixie; I do trust you and I suppose there's no harm in letting your little group look at the rubies just one time before returning them. Apparently, the Queen trusts you all quite well or she never would have given your little group so many credits to take care of in the first place. Alright you've convinced me my little cupcake! My two digits are 7 and 0. Remember, that'll have to be our little secret Pixie." A delightful grin crossed Morpheus's face as he barely maintained his composure. "Absolutely Andrew! No worries; your secret is safe with me as well as the rest of our little group here." Andrew picked up on the conversation again. "That reminds me…is Misty or Mojo with you at the moment? I wanted to speak with them about something." Morpheus continued. "Unfortunately, I'm all alone at the moment Andrew; just sitting here on my bed inside my little palace room. Although, I am getting quite tired at the moment; I'll chat with you tomorrow Andrew. I can't wait to see you again," Morpheus continued on reassuringly. "You as well Pixie; oh you are so delightful to speak with! I can't wait to see your beautiful face again tomorrow as well!" Morpheus held in the vomit creeping up the back of his throat. "You too Andrew. Bye for now darling." He quickly spoke the shutdown passcode to close off communication between them. "I'll be home soon," he said as his Jargon Band quickly stopped glowing green. He breathed a sigh of relief from finally obtaining all six digits of the ruby case combination! "The only thing left to do is snatch it away from Misty," he said to himself quietly. He was emotionally exhausted but knew the night was just beginning for him. He quickly made preparations to meet Nick the gnome at the front of the palace like they had planned.

36. MISTY'S CHAMBERS

Morpheus showed up at the palace entrance under the cover of darkness. He didn't rely too heavily on it though since his plan was to appear as if he were on official palace business anyways. Being the Queen's court wizard caused most of the palace servants not to question his comings and goings in the first place and he didn't plan on anyone stopping him tonight either.

He waited around for Nick to show up. He didn't want to look as if he were simply doing nothing so he began pacing along the cobblestones of the palace grounds. A few guards and palace workers passed by him with nothing more than a glance. They all knew who he was and he didn't bother disguising himself to avoid any possible suspicion.

Suddenly, he felt a tap on his left shoulder. He turned to see who it was only to find nobody standing there at all. He felt another tap on his right shoulder this time. He turned to face his mysterious prankster on his right only to find nobody there again. He glanced downward and made a 360 degree turnabout in hopes of finding Nick the gnome somewhere nearby. To his disappointment he couldn't seem to catch the mysterious intruder invading his space.

Morpheus called out. "Alright Nick, I know you're here! You can show yourself now." Suddenly, a scratchy voice sounded from behind him. "That was fun!" Morpheus laughed out loud. "Come on Nick…We don't have time for games right now. I'll head towards Misty's room and you tag along behind me. By the way, I'm quite glad you're as fast and sneaky as you are! You're going to need that speed and dexterity when we arrive at Misty's chambers shortly."

Morpheus casually walked to the palace entrance where the two guards Bill and Phil stood on either side waiting for him. Phil was the first to speak. "Glad you made it Morpheus. Where is your friend you said you were bringing?" Morpheus glanced around hoping to catch a quick glimpse of Nick. "He's practicing being stealthy for when we arrive at Misty's quarters. Don't worry though. I'm sure he'll be following us all the way up there." They both nodded understandably.

Bill and Phil escorted Morpheus through the palace and up to Misty's quarters. They found themselves inside a darkly lit hallway with the full moon shining through a row of narrow glass windows on their right. To their left stood a row of doorways; each leading into a separate bedroom chamber. "I'm pretty sure Misty's door is the eighth one on the left," Bill said confidently. They began counting the doors as they passed by each one until they finally arrived at the eighth one on their left. "Here we are," said Bill reassuringly.

Morpheus quickly scanned the perimeter and began to whisper. "Nick, are you there? I need to know that you're here before I knock on her door or this plan is going to be a complete failure," he exclaimed seriously. Suddenly, he felt a slight tug on his robe. Glancing downward, he found the small gnome waiving up at him with a smile. "I'm pretty good hu," he whispered proudly? Morpheus smiled back at him. "That's why I hired you my friend. You're the best! I couldn't do this without you. I'm about to knock on the door so I hope you're ready," he stated quietly. Morpheus glanced up at the wooden arched doorway and then back down at Nick. He had disappeared completely! "That little guy is faster than a roadrunner on the fairway," Phil said observingly. Morpheus glanced at the two guards standing behind him. "Perhaps one of you should knock on the door and introduce me. Tell Misty I'm here to give her some important information about Andrew and that you both escorted me here for security purposes since it's so late at night." Phil nodded understandingly before rapping his fist on the door a few times.

Morpheus observed the two guards carefully. "Remember not to crowd the doorway too much. Nick needs to slide past us without being seen." Bill moved to the right a bit and stood next to Phil. Morpheus took a few steps backward and stood next to Bill; leaving a more open pathway leading to the doorway. Even Phil made sure not to crowd the doorway too much. He didn't want to ruin the plan either.

The door opened suddenly and a sleepy eyed Misty stepped outside. She was dressed in a nightgown and a soft pair of slippers. She yawned widely as she leaned up against the doorframe. "Morpheus, what are you doing here this time of night?" Phil was the first to speak. "Morpheus has some important news about Andrew that he wants to share with you. Bill and I escorted him here due to the lateness of the hour and for security reasons as well. After all, we wouldn't want any unexpected attacks on our court wizard," he continued reassuringly. Misty yawned again. "No, of course not. I just don't see what could be so important that it can't wait until morning? Unless…Oh no! Andrew didn't die from his fatal accident did he," she asked with worry in her voice? Morpheus suddenly had to recall the lie he had told everyone back at the Throne Room earlier that day. "No, he hasn't passed away thankfully but his condition is far worse than we ever imagined. Do you mind if I come in and tell you more about it," he asked stepping towards the doorway? Misty moved her left arm across the doorway and leaned it up against the metal doorframe. "Actually, I'd prefer you didn't. I don't want to make this an all-night visit Morpheus and I truly am tired." Morpheus stepped back again desperately hoping Nick had somehow managed to make it passed them and into her chambers by now. "Of course, we can discuss it out here," he replied coolly. "I mean, Bill and

Phil don't know about the devastating news yet but I suppose it doesn't matter if they know too. What I wanted to tell you is that Andrew won't be able to attend our little meeting tomorrow morning due to the fatal injury he sustained while climbing Turban Waterfall. It truly is unfortunate but I think his healing process is going to take much more time than we ever anticipated." Misty put a hand to her mouth. "I'm truly sorry to hear that. I hope he recovers soon. I'm sure Pixie will be even more devastated to hear the news since she is the one who seems to be madly in love with him," Misty said seriously.

Morpheus still wasn't sure if Nick had managed to sneak into Misty's room yet and wanted to give him ample time and opportunity to do so. He quickly devised a devious plan to get inside her chambers again. "Unfortunately, I won't be able to attend the meeting either. The Queen is sending me off on some urgent business that can't be ignored unfortunately. That being said, Andrew told me to give you his two digit portion of the passcode to open the ruby case when the time comes. Of course, it is highly sensitive information and I would prefer to give it to you inside your chambers if you don't mind?" Misty glanced over at Bill and Phil standing next to her doorway. "Oh alright Morpheus but let's not take too long. I've got a lot of sleep to catch up on you know."

Morpheus followed Misty into her chambers and held the door open just long enough for Nick to sneak in or out; assuming he hadn't snuck in already. Carefully closing the door behind him, he immediately found himself covered in absolute darkness. "Is there a candle around here we can light," he asked hopefully? "Yea, there are a few candles around here. Just keep stepping Morpheus. I'll light them for you," she replied reassuringly. Morpheus continued walking until he bumped his knee up against something hard. "Ouch," he exclaimed painfully! He couldn't tell what the object was exactly due to the complete darkness surrounding him. "Oh, that's probably my chair you just bumped into. Go ahead and have a seat Morpheus. I'll get the lights," she said reassuringly.

Morpheus carefully felt the form of the chair where his knee had bumped against and slowly sat down. "I really hope Nick can find the ruby case in this darkness," he thought silently to himself. Misty shot a lighting spell from her wand which instantly lit every candle in the room simultaneously. Morpheus suddenly felt a giant net cover his entire body the second the room lit up. A chorus of voices shouted "SURPRISE" immediately following his capture. He glanced up at the mysterious group only to find the Queen, Andrew, Pixie and Misty all standing next to where he now sat on a wooden chair tangled up inside their net. Andrew held the net gun and glared at him angrily! "You didn't think you would get away with this did you," he asked mockingly? Pixie hovered in the air next to Andrew. "I came back to tell Andrew something not long after you called him on your little Jargon Band Morpheus. He told me about the conversation you had with him in my voice!" The Queen pointed her wand at Morpheus threateningly. "Your little game is over Morpheus. We figured you'd come back and steal the ruby case from Misty the moment we found you had been lying to Andrew this entire time!" Misty added her two cents into the conversation. "Not to mention how you wanted me and Pixie to reveal our combinations to you just before taking Pixie back to the Lake of Lost Souls through your portal. That was sneaky Morpheus but we never thought you'd get the last two digits from Andrew. That was a shock to all of us! Good thing we stopped you before you could steal the ruby case right out from under my nose," she said agitatedly!

Morpheus took a moment to inhale deeply before replying. He wasn't sure if Nick the gnome had managed to make it in and out with the ruby case or not but decided to try and find out. "How do you know your precious ruby case isn't missing already Misty? Perhaps you should check on it before getting too cocky with yourself," he said confidently. "Perhaps Floyd came looking for it before I did. You never know who might be looking for a case full of three and a half million credits worth of rubies," he said quickly casting doubt on Floyd's loyalty. The Queen shook her head disapprovingly. "I seriously doubt my old court wizard would betray me like that Morpheus. Besides, I already told both of you I would reward you handsomely for saving my life. Why would you go and do something like this? Don't I pay you enough?" Morpheus glanced downward shamefully. "Your highness, we both know magic can't transform ordinary objects into rubies unless you're using a Transformation Box. In which case, it would take a nasty toll on your youth. That being said, a case of three and a half million rubies would help a poor wizard retire early…no matter how much I enjoy or don't enjoy my job," he replied seriously.

The Queen exhaled slowly. "I'm sorry Morpheus but you've really disappointed me. I thought you were far more loyal than you appear to be now. Guards! Get in here now," she called out to the two guards standing just outside Misty's chamber door. Phil and Bill rushed inside wondering what was wrong. "Your majesty, I didn't know you were here," Phil replied shockingly. "Neither did I;" said Bill tactfully. "Is everything okay," he asked hopefully? The Queen looked at both guards seriously. "I don't want to think you were in on Morpheus's little plan to steal the rubies," she continued seriously. Phil glanced at Bill and then back at the Queen. "Steal the rubies? What rubies are you talking about your grace," he asked innocently? The Queen glanced downward to avoid showing the judgmental expression etched on her face. Her expression quickly softened as she glanced back up at the guards. "Morpheus was trying to steal three and a half million credits worth of rubies from Misty's chambers tonight and you both escorted him here. You can see why I might find that a little suspicious. Don't worry; we won't talk about that right now. Right now I'd like you both to please escort our friend Morpheus down to the dungeon. He will be tried fairly by our courts in a weeks-time from now. Until then, he will remain in the dungeon to think about what he's done."

Phil bowed gracefully. "Yes, your majesty. It shall be done." He moved towards Morpheus who still sat entangled by the net and grabbed his upper left arm. "Come with me Morpheus and don't even think about trying to escape. We'll be watching you like a hawk," he said threateningly. Bill grabbed Morpheus by the other arm as they escorted him out of Misty's chambers towards the dungeon below. Suddenly, Misty screamed out in horror! "The case is gone! Where did it go?!" The Queen stepped out into the hallway and yelled at the departing guards.

"Search Morpheus immediately! Make sure the ruby case isn't anywhere on him!" The guards quickly began searching him for the miniature briefcase. They reached into his robe pockets only to find his wand and Vortex Vacuum which they confiscated immediately. "Nope, he doesn't have the ruby case your highness," Bill yelled back in reply to the Queen down the hallway. The Queen placed a hand to her chin curiously. "Perhaps Floyd might be in on this thievery after all," she said discouragingly.

37. THE MORNING MEETING

Morning finally arrived and everyone had gathered inside the Throne Room as planned. Pixie, Misty, Mojo, Blackbeak, Andrew and the Queen were all in attendance. The Queen spoke up loudly to get their attention. "Excuse me everyone…the meeting is now in session! Please pay attention. I'm sure many of you already know about the tragic events of last night. Most of you are probably already aware that Morpheus tried to sneak into Misty's quarters last night in attempts to steal the most valuable case of rubies found there. Thankfully, we were able to catch him just in the nick of time due to Pixie going back to visit Andrew last night. Apparently, Morpheus has duped us all. He tricked us into thinking he was a loyal servant when in reality he was after the case of rubies the entire time! He is currently being held inside the dungeon and will be tried for his treachery by weeks-end."

The Queen paused for a moment to let that information sink in before continuing. "Even though we caught Morpheus at the scene of the crime, we didn't actually catch him with the ruby case anywhere on him. This creates a problem because we don't actually know who stole the rubies. Perhaps someone arrived at Misty's chambers before

Morpheus did. Although, he did mention Floyd might have taken the rubies before he even showed up. Speaking of which, has anyone seen Floyd lately? I noticed he wasn't able to attend our meeting today. Unfortunately for him, his absence creates a greater suspicion for this case."

The Queen waited for a brief moment to see if anyone would say anything about Floyd's absence. Since no one volunteered any information, she continued. "Despite the missing ruby case, I'm sure we can all find a great deal of joy in finally having the curse lifted from our fair city! Fairies everywhere can rejoice and finally fly once again! We no longer need Pixie Dust to help us fly anywhere thankfully. Yes, I know that might be a hard fact for the Pixie Guild to accept because it's a devastating loss in business for them but I'm sure they will move on and find other wares to sell. Ironically, it would be a major loss in business for Drake and Duncan if they were still alive today as well. Since Pixie Dust will no longer need to be made, it also means that honeycomb won't be nearly as valuable anymore. Assuming that Floyd is off selling Drake's stolen inventory to potential buyers…it doesn't really matter since the honeycomb is no longer worth as much as it once was. We also have to remember that we couldn't return all of the stolen goods to everyone accurately since they're not labeled and the victims would most likely fudge their inventory numbers to get an unfair return anyways. That's just the nature of thievery when combined with poor people unfortunately. "

The Queen continued. "Regarding the wearing of your anti-gravity amulets; don't worry about returning them. They are yours to keep as my way of saying thank you for all of your hard work and bravery on your quests to find Drake and Duncan. Turns out that this quest of yours ended up leading to more than we ever thought it would." Misty chuckled a bit under her breath. "You can say that again your Highness. My original plan was to find the Hand of Midas. This was just a pit stop along the way in order to obtain these precious anti-gravity amulets," she replied seriously. The Queen smiled at her. "Thank you again Misty for your dedicated service. You and your company have been a tremendous help in lifting the curse from the fairies! I commend you all for your efforts and would like to reward each of you with a token of my appreciation."

Walking over to her golden throne nearby, she picked up a fancy looking red box with a golden perimeter surrounding its edges. It measured four feet wide by three feet high and was quite shallow in depth. The Queen carried it over to the small group. Holding the box from underneath with one hand, she managed to open top with the other. Inside sat five brand new gold plated Jargon Bands. They looked different from any of the other Jargon Band they had ever seen. "I had these specially designed for each of you. They will give you a direct connection with me. If you look on the back of each of them you'll notice a capital Q inscription. This will help you remember who gave them to you and who they will connect you with. Since all the Jargon Bands currently look the same, I thought I'd have them specifically designed for each of you. You'll even notice each of your names carefully engraved on the backside of the one that is made for you specifically. Go ahead and try them on," she said joyfully.

They each found their own specially engraved Jargon Band and carefully slipped it around their wrist. Misty and Pixie took off the old Jargon Bands the Queen had given them earlier and returned them back to her. They were all ecstatic at having a direct way of communicating with the Queen just in case they ever needed to speak with her in the future. A serious expression crossed her face. "I only want you to use these in case of an emergency. I will be glad to send help to any of you if you ever need it. I tried making the passcodes as normal sounding as possible just in case you don't want someone knowing you're attempting to communicate with me. To activate them, simply say DOUBLE TROUBLE BOIL AND BUBBLE." The entire group burst into laughter at the ridiculous sounding passcode. Each of their Jargon Bands began glowing green upon being activated. "The shutdown passcode is I LIKE STEW," the Queen said as each of their Jargon Bands quickly stopped glowing again. "I know they're funny sounding passcodes but if you can work them into a natural conversation somehow then you can transmit entire conversations to me without your capturer even knowing about it. I mean, let's hope you never get captured in the future but if you ever do…at least you'll have a possible way of being rescued," she said delicately. Everyone thanked the Queen for her generous gift before she continued with the conversation. "Before we part ways; I'd just like to say one final thing about Rueland here," she said looking directly at Misty. "I know you really love having your raven friend by your side Misty but I would really like to have Rueland stay behind with me to protect our city. He has powers beyond anything even he can imagine and despite the fact that our army can fly once again without the use of Pixie Dust…we could still use his protection immensely!" She turned towards Blackbeak who was now wearing his new golden Jargon Band around his neck. "I hope you will stay here with me Rueland and help protect the city against the bat army. Will you," she asked hopefully? Rueland looked at the Queen and then over at Misty and then back towards the Queen. "I really would enjoy going on further adventures with my best friend in the whole world but I also understand that saving lives is far more important than any adventure I could possibly go on," he replied looking back at Misty. "So, I suppose I must stay here for the good of the fairies!"

Misty walked up to Blackbeak who was standing on his four foot high wooden perch and petted his head gently. "I shall miss you my friend. Perhaps I'll come back and visit you sometime," she said lovingly. "I'd like that very much Misty," replied Blackbeak sadly. Misty continued. "I'm sure you'll do an excellent job protecting the city once you remember how to use all of your former powers. Also, keep an eye out for a female raven flying around. I know you've been searching for quite a while now." Blackbeak laughed. "Ya never know…she might fall out of the sky someday and I'll catch her inside my giant magical arms. It'll be love at first sight," he replied jokingly. Misty laughed. "Oh Blackbeak, you always have such a great sense of humor. Of course, that's when you're not complaining about other stuff," she teased jokingly patting him on the back. Blackbeak laughed along with her. "Oh alright, we all better go our separate ways before I start crying," he replied seriously.

Misty walked over to where Mojo was now hovering slightly above the ground and wrapped her left arm around his neck in a side embrace. "You ready for some more fun adventures Mojo," she asked playfully? Mojo hugged her back. "Of course Misty, we'll have plenty of good times together for sure!" Pixie flew up next to Andrew and wrapped her left arm around his shoulders in a side embrace. "I just can't wait to get to know this guy better," she said to the entire group! Everyone laughed. The Queen could see two happy couples standing in front of her when an idea suddenly struck her. "It's just a thought but…perhaps we could have a double wedding for the four of you! Wouldn't that be exciting," she suggested joyfully! Everyone laughed as they seriously considered it.

38. MORPHEUS ESCAPES

Morpheus sat behind his cell bars inside the dungeon beneath the palace. He couldn't believe his horrible luck! Since his wand and Vortex Vacuum had been confiscated, he wasn't sure how he was going to escape. He leaned up against the stone wall behind him and placed a hand against his forehead thinking deeply. He knew Bill and Phil would probably help him escape but he also knew the Queen already suspected them of helping him so maybe they would avoid helping him for the time being just to avoid suspicion. He had heard Misty scream out that the case was missing back when the guards we're escorting him down the hallway and towards the dungeon. "Nick must have gotten away with it," he thought gratefully. "The only trouble is that Nick's out there and I'm in here," he thought depressively.

He moved his legs up towards his head and wrapped his arms around them in a fetal position. It suddenly occurred to him that he still had his long line of Jargon Bands strapped across his arm! "Why didn't I didn't think of that earlier," he wondered stupidly? He lifted his left sleeve up to reveal his long line of Jargon Bands strapped across his left wrist and up his arm. He was about to speak a passcode into them when suddenly he heard a scratchy voice come out of nowhere. "Don't bother Morpheus. I know you probably weren't expecting it but I came back to help you out!" Morpheus ran to the edge of his cell. "Nick! You came back for me! That's incredible! I'm so glad to see you my friend." Nick shook his head. "Yea yea…suddenly I'm your best friend in the whole world," he replied with a laugh. Nick pulled his pointy hat from the top of his head and reached into it as if he were searching for something particular. He finally pulled out a large set of keys attached to a wide metal loop. He fingered through them carefully looking for the correct one. "Let's see…I haven't used the dungeon set for quite some time now. Mm…this might be it," he said latching onto a particular golden key. "But before I help you escape Morpheus; you should know a few things." Morpheus was desperate to leave his iron barred cell so he responded promptly. "Anything Nick; just tell me!" Nick continued. "For starters, I'm sure you're curious about whether or not I got the ruby case from Misty's chamber the other night," he stated blatantly. Morpheus nodded. "I was wondering about that. You're so quick Nick. I can never catch you coming or going," he replied flatteringly. A look of amusement crossed Nick's face. "The answer is yes. I snatched the ruby case right out from under her nose," he continued proudly. "That being said, I could have easily walked away with three and a half million credits worth of rubies without coming back for you Morpheus."

Morpheus stared at him seriously. "Well, why did you come back to rescue me then Nick? You like me too much to leave me rotting in a jail cell right," he asked charmingly? Nick spit on the floor. "Don't kid yourself Morpheus. I'm here because Floyd paid me to come break you out of here." An expression of shock crossed Morpheus's face! "But you've already got a case full of three and a half million ruby credits. What more could he possibly pay you?" Nick glanced around carefully to make sure no one was else was listening in on their conversation. "Floyd claims to have a map leading directly to the Hand of Midas! He says he'll cut me in on finding it if you promise to go with us. He also says the deal is off completely if you decide not to go so I highly suggest you take him up on the offer," Nick said almost threateningly.

Morpheus placed a hand on his chin thoughtfully. "I do like the idea of having an object that can turn anything into gold. I mean, gold isn't worth nearly as much a rubies but it's still pretty dang valuable! I just have to ask though…would you even consider giving me a portion of the rubies you took from Misty? After all, I'm the one who got you inside the palace in the first place Nick. That whole ordeal was my plan to begin with! I appreciate that you're here to bust me out of this place but I feel like I'm being swindled by my own swindler," said Morpheus angrily!

Nick held one of the keys up to the cell lock and glanced up at Morpheus seriously. "I'm keeping the ruby case for myself Morpheus. Like I said; I could just walk away and leave you here or we can walk out of here together and meet up with Floyd to go searching for the Hand of Midas. It's your choice but tell me quickly. I don't want to sit around waiting for an answer all night."

Morpheus sighed deeply. "Alright Nick, you've got yourself a deal. The only problem is that Bill and Phil confiscated my wand and Vortex Vacuum before throwing me in here so it's going to be a bit of a problem getting out of here unnoticed." Nick inserted the key into the cell door lock and twisted it open. "That won't be a problem Morpheus. I had a little chat with them earlier today and happened to snatch your wand and Vortex Vacuum back for you. I figured it would be easier for us to use your Vortex Vacuum to escape as opposed to sneaking past multiple guards standing just outside the dungeon and all throughout the palace." "Good thinking Nick," replied Morpheus as he stepped outside the cell.

Nick reached into his pointy red hat and retrieved Morpheus's wand and Vortex Vacuum that he had so conveniently stolen back for him. He handed both items to him directly. "I hope you realize just how helpful I'm being right now Morpheus. You may think I cheated you in keeping the ruby case but always remember what I'm doing for you right now. You're a free wizard again Morpheus. Don't ever take that for granted!"

Morpheus pointed his Vortex Vacuum in front of them as a dark whirlwind of mist quickly emanated from it in front of them. Suddenly he remembered something quite important. "Oh drat, this isn't going to work Nick! I just remembered the magic barrier surrounding the palace won't allow us to travel through it using a regular portal. I need an animal portal similar to what Morganna used to get past the barrier." Nick glared at him furiously. "This isn't good Morpheus! I can get myself in and out of here without being noticed but you are much slower than me." "Thanks for the reminder," Morpheus replied downheartedly. "Perhaps you could distract the guards while I sneak past them," he suggested hopefully. Nick shook his head disapprovingly. "Unfortunately, there's far too many of them out there to distract all of them. It would take a miracle for you to get past a good majority of them."

Without warning, Floyd suddenly stepped through the open portal as if it had been there for his use the entire time! Morpheus glanced at him with shock and amazement etched on his face! "How in the…What did you…" His voice trailed off in complete wonder. Floyd smirked at Morpheus. "Ha! And you call yourself a wizard," he replied mockingly! "Alright, let's get out of here before the guards show up," he said casually. They each stepped through the portal with Floyd being the last to follow. The dark vortex quickly closed off behind them.

39. PORTALS RUBIES AND STONES

The vortex quickly opened up inside Floyd's shop as the three of them stepped out onto the dirt floor below. The portal closed off immediately behind them. Morpheus wasted no time bringing up the subject on his mind. "Alright Floyd, I have to know…how in the name of Merlin's Beard did we get past that magic barrier surrounding the palace using a regular portal? Floyd laughed. "You've still got a lot to learn Morpheus. Tell you what; I'm in a generous mood so I'll go ahead tell you. Who do you think created that magical barrier around the palace in the first place? Yep, that was yours truly! The first thing you must learn is that there are three types of portals. There are animal portals, regular portals and forwarding portals." Morpheus looked confused. "Forwarding portals," he asked curiously? Floyd nodded. "Yep, no one talks about them much; mainly because even the ancients used them very little. Essentially they are used as a middle portal between two portals. Basically, I built a forwarding portal in between the magic barrier surrounding the palace so I could safely use it to connect both portals; one on the inside of the magic barrier and the other on the outside of the barrier. The trick is that I had to actually open the forwarding portal in order for it to work properly. Otherwise, it wouldn't connect the two portals together without having the middle one open. Does that make sense," he asked hopefully? Morpheus nodded. "I think so. So what you're saying is that you had a regular portal on the inside of the barrier, one on the outside of the barrier and a forwarding portal in between both of them that connected them together when you opened it properly?" Floyd slapped Morpheus on the back reassuringly. "Now you're getting it! I'll make a true wizard out of you yet," he replied jokingly! Morpheus smiled. "You never cease to amaze me Floyd. I feel like I'm learning new things from you all the time," he replied flatteringly.

Nick cleared his throat. "I should tell you Floyd that I've updated our friend here about our plans to search for the Hand of Midas and he's all in." "Excellent," Floyd replied reassuringly. "There's nothing quite like the idea of having all the gold you could possibly get your hands on," he said excitedly! "Did Nick tell you where it was located exactly?" Morpheus shook his head. "No, we were kind of in a rush to get out of there," he replied seriously. Floyd nodded. "I'm sure you were." Morpheus wasn't used to being around such a youthful and energetic Floyd. He was used to old man Floyd. It was taking him a moment to readjust his way of thinking to Floyd's much younger and energetic self.

Floyd continued. "Follow me." He led them back to his glass case filled with imitation Transformation Boxes inside. Reaching beneath the glass countertop, he retrieved a rolled up piece of parchment which he quickly unrolled on top of the glass cabinet. It looked to be an ancient map. Floyd pointed to a spot near the center. "Here's where we're located at the Lake of Lost Souls and here is where the Hand of Midas can be found," he said moving his hand to the northeast. "Here is what the dwarves call the Mines of Madness. Apparently, it is haunted by ancient dead dwarves. Legend has it that every dwarf who ever wondered into the Mines of Madness came out completely mad! The sad part is that they never recovered no matter how much magic was used on them! The dwarf king Magnarock claims to have found what he calls the Sanity Stone. Apparently, this stone has the power to shield you from the dead and will keep you safe while walking through the mine. The only catch is that he keeps it to himself and never lets it out of his sight. However, I figure he might give it up for the right price. He might just give it up for oh, I don't know…three and a half million rubies perhaps," he said casually looking at Nick. Nick shook his head. "Nope, I don't think so! I'm not giving up my newly acquired fortune for the mere CHANCE of finding an object that can turn anything into gold…Although, it would probably be a greater fortune if we did find it! Oh alright; I'll do it if I must," Nick replied with disappointment etched on his voice. Floyd nodded. "That's good Nick because you might not be the only one giving up a small fortune. I may have to trade Drake's old stash of honeycomb to help sweeten the deal," he replied seriously.

Suddenly, Morpheus caught a glimmer of one of his Jargon Bands glowing from beneath his sleeve. He quickly rolled it up and heard a sound he would never forget. "So you thought I was dead hu," the voice exclaimed angrily! Chills surged down Morpheus's spine as he registered who the voice belonged too. It was Duncan!! Morpheus exhaled slowly as the voice continued. "Yep, I cut a hole right through Morganna's pocket and slipped out just before the wizard duel took place. By the way, I was not okay with you taking mine and Drake's inventory Floyd! You might want to check your pockets for the shrunken inventory bag to see if you still have it," Duncan said mockingly before continuing. "Oh and Nick might want to check his pockets for that coveted shrunken ruby case of his. That's right; consider this payback for killing my old business partner Drake! He never would have wanted any of you to have our rightfully stolen items. Good thing those items were already shrunken down to size or I never would have gotten away with them," he said seriously.

Floyd placed his hands in his pockets only to find a giant hole inside one of them! "Blast you Duncan," he shouted! Nick checked his pockets for the miniature sized ruby case he was planning to resize later on. A giant hole was in his pocket as well! "Duncan, we'll get you for this," he shouted threateningly! "Where are you? So help me if you don't tell us we'll track you down and…" The Jargon Band suddenly cut off all communication between them as it stopped glowing green.

Floyd suddenly grew suspicious of Morpheus. "Why do you even have a Jargon Band connecting with him in the first place," he asked seriously? Morpheus glanced around the room quickly scanning it for eavesdroppers. "Originally, I was trying to track down Drake and Duncan myself back before the Queen assembled her little group to go find them. I happened to run into Duncan one day at a little merchant shop called Honey for Money. He claimed to be a wholesale distributor for the shop owner named Achmed. I told him I was a honeycomb salesman myself who worked for the palace. We exchanged Jargon Bands in hopes of doing business later on in the future. He never completely trusted me since I worked for the palace. However, I continued to try and set up meetings with him and Drake in hopes of finding out where they kept their secret stash of honeycomb. Unfortunately, they would never meet up with me and we lost contact up until now."

Floyd turned his head towards Morpheus and then over towards Nick. "I don't know Nick…perhaps Morpheus is working with Duncan. Maybe they are in cahoots and planned this entire charade to steal your three and a half million ruby credits along with my extra-large inventory!"

Morpheus slowly reached deep within his robe pocket to retrieve his wand. Floyd did the exact same thing at the exact same moment! Both wizards pointed their wands at each other at the exact same time! Nick interrupted their concentration. "There's no need to fight. How about we all go searching for the Hand of Midas together? The playing field has been leveled. We've all been reduced to nothing and Duncan has everything. That gives us even more of a reason to find the Hand of Midas. As for the Stone of Sanity…we'll just have to coordinate a better plan to find it," he suggested seriously. Morpheus glanced at Nick and then back at the fuming Floyd. "He's got a point Floyd. Let's just lower our wands and start over. I'm not working with Duncan; I promise you that." Floyd scowled. "That's easy for you to say Morpheus but how can I trust you for sure," he asked seriously? Morpheus conjured up a plan. "Tell you what, how about I give you the Jargon Band that connects me with Duncan and you can destroy it completely. Sound fair?" Floyd slowly lowered his wand. "Alright Morpheus; let's have it then," he replied impatiently.

Morpheus slowly lowered his wand. Carefully rolling his left sleeve up, he revealed the long line of Jargon Bands found underneath. He pulled one of them off his wrist and acted as if he were about to toss it to Floyd. "Here Floyd; catch," he said tossing it high into the air towards him. The Jargon Band soared high over Floyd's head. Floyd heard it land on the floor behind him and quickly turned around to pick it up. By the time he turned back around to face Morpheus; he had disappeared completely! An open portal stood where he had previously stood and it closed off quickly before Floyd could pursue him through it!

An angry expression crossed his face as he inspected the Jargon Band Morpheus had tossed to him. Suddenly, he began laughing hysterically. "Looks like I have a lot to learn as well young wizard," he said to no one in particular. Turning back towards, Nick he glanced at him seriously. "Looks like we'll be the only ones heading to the Mines of Madness Nick. We don't need a traitor like Morpheus coming with us anyways. I'm truly sorry about your ruby case. Unfortunately, we don't have the passcode to make this Jargon Band work. Otherwise, we could get back in touch with Duncan and strike up a deal with him."

An angry expression crossed Nick's face upon realizing the total loss of his fortune. "I suppose we'll just have to track Morpheus down and get the passcode. It's the only way we can get in touch with Duncan," he replied seriously. "Assist me with this Floyd and I'll split my entire ruby fortune with you 50/50; assuming we find that case again." Floyd took a moment to think about it. "Alright, sounds like a deal Nick. Although, I have no idea where Morpheus transported himself to. We can try searching his little hideout behind Turban Waterfall. He thinks that place is such a big secret but he always seems to forget I was the one who originally found it. He could learn so much more from me if he only tried."

Floyd and Nick quickly prepared to leave for Turban Waterfall. "This search shouldn't take long," Floyd said retrieving his Vortex Vacuum from his robe pocket. "Portals can really speed up the process if you know what I mean," he said winking at Nick. Nick sighed deeply. "I wouldn't know Floyd. I've had to walk and run everywhere my entire life. What are the chances I could get one of those little gadgets anyways," he asked curiously? A serious expression crossed Floyd's face. "Well, let me think…what's half of three and a half million rubies," he asked jokingly? "Oh you're a funny one," Nick replied sarcastically. Floyd quickly caused a dark swirling vortex to appear in front of them using his own Vortex Vacuum. They stepped through it quickly transporting towards Turban Waterfall in hopes of finding their traitor Morpheus!

40. RETURNING THE INVENTORY

Duncan sat inside Drake's old log cabin located at the base of Boulder Mountain holding the stolen inventory in one hand and a copy of the Pixie Guild List in the other. He had just finished visiting a few of the Pixie Guild Members before returning back to his hideout at Boulder Mountain. He started thinking about the first guild member he had gone to visit. Alex Avery told him the curse had been lifted but he wasn't going to tell his customers that because he wanted to keep selling Pixie Dust as long as he could before they figured it out as well. After all, if all the fairies could fly again then there was really no point in making Pixie Dust in the first place! Alex said his customers would eventually figure this out but he still wanted to make as much profit as possible in the meantime. Even though Duncan was thrilled about the curse being lifted, it also left him in a peculiar predicament. "If the Pixie Guild Members are going out of business soon due to the curse being lifted then my inventory isn't going to be worth much," he thought despairingly.

He quickly decided to return the stolen inventory and disperse it equally among each of the Pixie Guild Members in exchange for information about the dwarf king Magnarock. He began spreading horrible rumors that the honeycomb thieves had been caught and that the two thieves responsible for the honeycomb shortages were Morpheus and Floyd. He layered his lies by saying that the Queen herself had sent him out to disperse the inventory equally among them because there was no way of knowing who each item belonged too individually. "It's not like every piece of honeycomb had the previous owners name written on it," Duncan thought to himself. Nobody questioned his motives since he was simply handing out free goods for them to accept at their leisure. They simply accepted the lie that he continued spreading throughout Nectarville along with the surrounding lands. He told everyone to be on the lookout for two court wizards and not trust them no matter what. The guild list members simply nodded and accepted their portion of the stolen inventory without question. "It's funny how no one questions a possible lie when you hand them free stuff," Duncan thought cunningly to himself.

Along the way, Duncan picked up a few bits of interesting information regarding the dwarf king Magnarock and the Mines of Madness. He quickly discovered that the dwarf king had found a special type of stone known as the Sanity Stone which helped him navigate his way safely through the Mines of Madness without going completely insane. He thought about how he might obtain such a special stone from Magnarock and where he might find the mine as well. He wasn't exactly sure where the Mine of Madness was located but figured he could find a map leading to it somewhere if he searched long and hard enough. He considered paying the dwarf king for the Stone of Sanity but knew it would be a long journey ahead before he would even have that opportunity. "He would be complete fool to turn down three and a half million ruby credits in exchange for it," Duncan thought seriously.

He continued asking around town, hoping to find a map to the Mine of Madness. Everyone he asked didn't have a clue where it could be found. He felt incredibly discouraged at his dire situation. Evening quickly arrived and he thought it best to check into a nearby inn for the night. He parked his horse inside the stable and walked into his new favorite inn. "Black Hawk Inn is really starting to grow on me these days," he thought joyfully as he spotted a beautiful blond lady standing behind the front desk. Coreena Cordell recognized him instantly!

A joyful expression crossed her face immediately upon seeing him. "Duncan! It's so good to see you again! I was hoping you'd be back soon," she said excitedly! Duncan smiled back at her. "It's good to see you again pretty girl," he replied flatteringly. "A lot has happened since I last saw you Coreena," he said seriously. Coreena became quite curious. "Oh, I want to hear all about your adventures Duncan! Perhaps you could tell me more about them later on tonight after I get off work," she asked hopefully? Duncan smiled. "I'm sure I could and I'd be more than happy too but…" His voice trailed off. "But what Duncan," she asked discouragingly? He smiled and leaned over the tall desk to get closer to her. "Um, Coreena…I would absolutely love to take you out for a drink sometime but…" A frown crossed her face as he continued to speak faster. "…but I have two angry wizards tracking me down at the moment and staying here would really put me in harm's way assuming they were to find me." Coreena understood what he was saying perfectly. "Oh Duncan, I'm sorry to hear that! I know the perfect place you could hideout for a while if you'd like," she suggested confidently. A relieved and curious expression crossed his face. "You do? Where would that be exactly," he asked with surprise?

Coreena walked out from behind the desk and casually grabbed him by the left hand. "Follow me Duncan. I'll show you," she replied gently leading him outside the inn. She led him back out to the stables where he had parked old Swifty. "No one ever searches the stables," she exclaimed confidently. "You can sleep out here with the horses," she continued excitedly as though she had just thought up the perfect plan. Duncan smiled. "That's awfully kind of you Coreena. The two wizards chasing me are Floyd and Morpheus. They think I stole their case of rubies along with their secret stash of honeycomb. But just for the record, the honeycomb stash belonged to me and Drake before he passed away and the ruby case was something they stole from the Queen before I got to it. So they're the real thieves Coreena. I simply took back what they stole from me and suddenly I'm the thief in their eyes," he said sarcastically. "Anyways, my plan is to find the dwarf king Magnarock in hopes of trading for the Stone of Sanity. The idea is that it will help me navigate through the Mines of Madness unscathed. From there I'm going to try and find…" Coreena interrupted him. "The Hand of Midas…Oh Duncan, you're not the first to try and find such a valuable item. I've talked with many travellers passing through Black Hawk Inn in search of the exact same thing. In fact, I can point you to an old fellow who claims to have actually been there before. He goes by the name of Jimbo Jenkens. He's a travelling salesman who does quite well for himself selling various goods and services wherever he goes. He lives just on the north side of Boulder Mountain if you know where that is?" A shocked expression crossed Duncan's face. "Interesting, Drake and I used to stash our inventory on the south side of Boulder Mountain. Funny we never bothered exploring the other side of it. I suppose I'll have pay him a visit then. Perhaps he can help me find a map to the mine and tell me where the dwarf king can be located."

Coreena inched closer to him; wrapping her arms around his shoulders. "I wish you wouldn't leave so soon Duncan. I would love to come with you on your quest but unfortunately I would get fired from my job here at Black Hawk Inn if I did. This job is my only source of income sadly but I hope you will return to me soon Duncan," she pleaded gently. He returned her hug. "If I didn't have two wizards tracking me down at the moment I'd definitely stay longer pretty girl," he replied sincerely. "Tell you what, how about we take a ride on old Swifty here," he said pointing to the black stallion a couple stalls away. "It'll give us a chance to get out and see the countryside for a bit," he said convincingly. "I would like that very much," Coreena replied joyfully.

They quickly made their way over to the old black stallion. Duncan mounted the horse and lent her a hand up as she mounted directly behind him. She wrapped her arms around his waist as he flicked the reins to get old Swifty moving. Steering Swifty outside the stable and onto the open dirt road, they began riding at a slow trot in a southward direction. "So, how far do you want to go before we turn around," Coreena asked curiously? "Oh, I figure we can just ride until the sun goes down," Duncan replied jokingly. Their laugh was cut short as a blue bolt of fire flew past them! Turning their heads to look behind them, they quickly discovered their attacker to be Morpheus! He was about a hundred yards behind them and catching up fast! He flew through the air on a flying surfboard as if it were the easiest thing in the world. "I wonder where Floyd's at," Duncan thought curiously? "I thought you said two wizards were chasing after you," Coreena asked from behind him? "Yea, I'm not sure where Floyd is at the moment. Maybe he'll jump out at us at the last second. Be on the lookout Coreena. Morpheus might be chasing us right into a trap!"

More fire bolts flew past their heads as Duncan kicked Swifty into a faster paced gallop! "Hold on tight Coreena! He's gaining on us," he yelled! He snapped Swifty to run as fast as her legs would possibly carry them! He knew a few more fire bolts aimed at the correct spot would easily throw them off the horse. He glanced back again only to find Morpheus about fifty yards behind them now. He knew it was only a matter of time before Coreena or he would be injured by an incoming fire bolt. He figured Coreena would most likely take the heat since her body was currently shielding his from behind. He considered pulling Swifty over and surrendering before she actually did get hit from behind.

Just as he was about to bring Swifty to a halt, Coreena shouted into his ear from behind. "Don't stop Duncan! I'll protect us," she said reassuringly. He wondered how she was going to do that since she didn't have any powers that he was currently aware of. Despite his doubts, he continued riding forward. Two more fire bolts shot towards them and quickly bounced off some sort of invisible energy shield now surrounding them. "Let's have some fun with him," Coreena whispered in Duncan's ear. "Turn around Duncan and we'll charge him," she said authoritatively! "Are you crazy Coreena," he asked seriously? "Just do it Duncan! I promise we'll be okay."

Duncan immediately circled Swifty back around to face the oncoming Morpheus. He was only about 30 yards behind them now. Duncan inhaled deeply and charged Swifty straight towards the oncoming Morpheus. The shock of the immediate turnabout caught the old wizard by surprise. Quickly recovering from the shock, he dug deep into his bag of tricks and cast a duplicating spell on himself. Immediately, a half circle of clones suddenly appeared charging towards the oncoming Duncan and Coreena! One Morpheus had suddenly transformed into five duplicates! Duncan wanted to turn around as the five duplicate wizards continued charging towards him in a crescent moon formation! Coreena encouraged him onward. "Keep going Duncan! I promise we'll be fine. Trust me," she said confidently. She spread her arms out as if attempting to expand the invisible barrier surrounding them. The invisible barrier not only expanded in size but it also slammed into all five duplicate wizards charging at them! All five clones flew from their flying surfboards; each hitting the ground in separate directions!

"Quick, let's grab a surfboard," Coreena shouted to Duncan. "Hold my legs," she yelled! She slid head first off the side of the horse. Duncan quickly grabbed one of her legs to keep her from falling off the horse completely. He continued riding towards the surfboard lying in the dirt only a few yards away. Coreena now rode upside down with Duncan holding onto one of her legs for support. He held on tight as she reached down and snatched up the surfboard with both hands. "Okay, let go of me Duncan," she said forcefully. Duncan didn't want to let go of her but decided that maybe she had more skill with flying a surfboard than she had ever told him about. Trusting her not to fall, he let go of her leg as she fell towards the ground with the surfboard held up in front of her face. Instead of landing directly on the ground, she immediately began hovering in the air all while doing a handstand atop the flying surfboard! Duncan was highly impressed to see such incredible acrobatics! He snuck another glance backward just in time to see her front flip onto the hovering surfboard! "Wow, she is quite impressive," he thought again as he scanned the area for another other loose surfboard lying around. He spotted Morpheus running towards one on his left. Turning Swifty towards the idle surfboard, he raced towards it in hopes of grabbing it before Morpheus could. Morpheus picked up the pace as well and managed to snatch the surfboard up off the ground just as Duncan galloped right up next to him. Duncan reached his left arm out; wrapping it around the side of the surfboard. Bringing it closer to his body he quickly reached his other hand around it to grip onto it better. Just when he thought he had a firm handle on it Morpheus ripped it away from him! Quickly letting go of the surfboard, he brought his arms back in to steady himself. Swifty continued galloping forward. Duncan considered the possibility of turning around to make a second attempt at snatching the surfboard away from Morpheus when Coreena suddenly zoomed up next to him on her flying surfboard! "Forget about it Duncan. Let's head out to Boulder Mountain. We can talk more there," she said reassuringly.

Forgetting about the surfboard, they readjusted their coordinates and headed towards Boulder Mountain leaving Morpheus behind them. Morpheus's mirages had quickly vanished upon being hit by their invisible body shield a while back. Their worries about being followed by them had vanished along with them as well. Coreena flew alongside Duncan's horse on her surfboard. "Morpheus will probably keep chasing us Coreena," Duncan said as Swifty continued to gallop next to her. "That's okay Duncan. We'll outrun him. Looks like we're in this together now," she replied with a wink.

Duncan glanced over at her. "I suppose you're right Coreena. Thanks for saving us back there by the way. I didn't know you even had magic," he replied surprisingly. Her flying surfboard continued to keep pace with his galloping stallion trotting next to her. "I actually don't have magic Duncan," she replied seriously. "But I am a really great acrobat and I happened to pick up a special pendant quite a while ago that I've never told anyone about." Duncan suddenly became quite curious. "Really? I've never seen you wear it before. You must hide it quite well," he replied seriously. She glanced downward. I wear it around my neck but keep it well hidden underneath my shirt. I don't want anyone to know I have it. Turns out it has multiple protective powers which is quite a rare trait for any magical pendant," she exclaimed. Duncan's curiosity remained. "That's quite interesting. Most pendants only contain one protective power. What kind of pendant is it?" Coreena suddenly grew extremely serious. "I'll only tell you if you promise never to tell another soul Duncan." Duncan knew a pendant's protective power was a serious matter and he could see why she wanted to keep it a secret. "Don't worry Coreena, I promise I won't tell a soul about your special pendant but I am curious about it though. Is it a fire pendant that keeps you safe from fire bolts," he guessed curiously? She nodded. "It does that and more. It also keeps evil spirits from haunting or hurting us." Duncan about fell off his horse! "Merlin's beard Coreena! Don't tell me you have the…" Coreena finished his sentence for him. "…Stone of Sanity…Yep, that's the one!" Duncan suddenly had a whole lot of questions to ask her!

41. BAT ATTACK

Alvin was bored out of his mind waiting next to the Gravity Beam Machine. He had considered changing jobs multiple times but enjoyed the freedom of lying around and doing nothing. It was relaxing and boring all at the same time. "Last exciting thing that happened around here was that eagle attack on those two guards. Good thing I was here to save them," he said heroically to himself.

Suddenly two bats snuck up behind him and startled him out of his lackadaisical mind. "Yikes," he screamed out in fright! "I didn't see you two come in. What do you want and why are you here?" One of the bats moved closer to him. "I'm Matt and this is Rat. We just wanted to let you know we've got an entire battalion of bats headed your way. No pressure or anything but we'll be taking these Gravity Beam Machines from around the perimeter of the city. It was the deal we made with your diplomatic raven in exchange for a year of peace between us. I assume the Queen has already informed you of our deal?" Alvin shook his head disagreeably. "Actually, I know nothing of such a deal." Rat looked westward into the sky and spotted the entire battalion of bats headed his way just like they had warned! "You better hurry and tell the other guards what's happening or we might have another war on our hands," Rat suggested seriously.

Alvin quickly brought his Jargon Band up to his mouth and spoke the passcode into it. "BACKUP BACKUP 119…COME IN GUARD LEADER, COME IN GUARD LEADER…" His Jargon Band instantly glowed a deep green as a raspy voice came over the airwaves. "Yes, Alvin what is it this time?" Alvin cleared his throat. "Sorry to disturb you sir but I have two bats here with me who insist that their battalion is going to take all of our Gravity Beam Machines from around the city's perimeter in exchange for a year of peace between us. Do you know anything about this sir?" The guard leader cleared his throat. "I know nothing of such orders. Don't trust them Alvin! I will send a squad of soldiers your way. Hold them off the best you can!" Alvin looked nervously at the two bats listening in on his conversation and then up at the bat battalion headed their way! "Um sir, perhaps we should really double check with the Queen about this whole ordeal because I can't hold off an entire bat battalion of bats all by myself! Seriously; we are very much outnumbered here!" The Guard Leader spoke again. "You hold them off until we get there Alvin! That's an order!" He spoke the shutdown passcode to end the communication between them.

Rat glared at Alvin menacingly. "Looks like you have a bit of a problem on your hands good sir." Suddenly, each Gravity Beam Machine surrounding the city wall began firing at the incoming bat battalion. Hundreds of bats quickly became trapped inside the large gravity beams being shot at them. The beams quickly pulled large groups of them inward to where giant iron cages were waiting for them upon landing. Over half of the bat battalion quickly became prisoners while the rest of them quickly retreated. Rat glared at Alvin angrily. "You and your people will pay for this little fairy! When our glorious leader discovers what you have done; our entire army will return with a vengeance! You've seen how massive our forces are and I highly advise surrendering your Gravity Beam Machines before we take them by force!" Matt and Rat quickly flew away leaving Alvin alone with his thoughts. Alvin quickly became upset with his Guard Leader's response to such a tragedy. "I wonder why the squad hasn't arrived yet," he wondered agitatedly. "Normally they have much quicker response times during emergencies such as this."

Rueland stood atop the castle gazing at the large battalion of attacking bats headed his way. He spotted three or four more battalions only about a hundred yards behind them headed towards the city as well! He closed his eyes and reached deep into his soul. Drawing upon his innermost powers, he spread his wings outward. Time suddenly stood still as a powerful wave of green energy soared from his core out into the world around him. An invisible protective barrier shot from his inner self and surrounded the entire city! Every attacking bat quickly felt its presence as they slammed directly into it! Thousands of bloodthirsty bats quickly found themselves smashing up against the giant invisible wall now in front of them. Many tried biting and slashing at it with their claws only to be shocked and electrified by its stunning power! It didn't take long for the entire army to give up and retreat back to where they had come from.

Rueland quickly fainted from exhaustion and began to topple off the palace roof! When he finally regained consciousness he found himself lying on the Throne Room floor with the Queen staring down at him. "Oh good, you're up Rueland. I'm so glad you're awake and alive! I just wanted to personally thank you for saving our entire city! I realize your powers aren't as strong as they could be yet but thankfully the bats retreated when they did or they might have penetrated your barrier when you fainted like you did. We had a run of good fortune thankfully! Anyways, thanks again Rueland. This is exactly why I requested you to stay at the Lake of Lost Souls for this exact reason and you have proven yourself quite loyal and useful already! Is there anything I can do to repay your honorable service Rueland," the Queen asked humbly? Rueland stood up trying to get his mental bearings straight. He still felt a bit dizzy and uneasy from the fall. "Just curious, who saved me from that horrible fall off the roof? I remember blacking out before falling so who…" The Queen interrupted him. "Believe it or not, another raven named Regan came along and managed to catch you. She was wearing an anti-gravity amulet so it made the process of catching and flying you here much easier. She claims to have gotten it from an eagle who must have stolen it from one of my guards. She didn't go into much detail about how she got it from the eagle but I let her keep it as a reward for saving your life. I normally only give those anti-gravity amulets out to my loyal subjects but I'm sure she deserved it after what she did on your behalf," the Queen replied seriously.

Blackbeak flapped his wings as a wave of curiosity rushed over him. "You wouldn't happen to know where she went," he asked inquisitively? The Queen nodded. "She said she'd be hovering around Turban Waterfall sometime if you ever wanted to go find her," the Queen replied with a wink. Rueland suddenly remembered Morpheus's hideout behind Turban Waterfall and quickly figured he might be flying into a trap if he were to go searching for her. He also figured that Morpheus might have transformed into another raven just to lure him into a trap. He knew Mojo enjoyed disguising himself as a raven as well. He didn't know what or who to believe anymore but decided to take a chance in hopes that maybe…just maybe…he might find himself a girl raven like Misty had suggested just before leaving.

The Queen continued. "Well, don't let me stop you Rueland. Go find her if you wish," she suggested hopefully. Rueland bowed gracefully. "Thank you your highness. I shall speak with you later concerning this matter…assuming I find her of course." Rueland took his leave from the palace; flying straight towards Turban Waterfall. The Queen quickly retrieved her wand from deep within her dress pocket and pointed it at herself. "TRANSFORMELLA BODELLO," she exclaimed as a thick cloud of darkness quickly covered her entire body. Once the smoke cleared, a tall wizard form stood in her place. Morpheus raised a hand to his chin thoughtfully. "It's not over yet Rueland. Perhaps you can save the Queen again while you're snooping around Turban Waterfall," he said maniacally laughing to no one in particular.

ABOUT THE AUTHOR

J.R. Carlson is an upcoming fantasy author who enjoys writing fun adventurous novels for young readers. "If escaping reality was as simple as dealing with it then we'd all simply wave our magic wands and create the life we really want. Until that day happens; here's a fun book to help you forget about your troubles for a while. Please read as long as you wish and share with your friends. Hope you enjoy. Thanks again for your support!"

(J.R. Carlson)

www.ingramcontent.com/pod-product-compliance
Lightning Source LLC
Chambersburg PA
CBHW020946310726
48980CB00001B/75

* 9 7 8 0 5 7 8 9 4 3 0 2 2 *